APPLE CRUSH

Also by Lucy Knisley

French Milk

Relish

An Age of License

Displacement

Something New

Kid Gloves

Stepping Stones

Picture Books

You Are New

By Lucy Knisley
Colored by Whitney Cogar

RH
GRAPHIC

New York

Apple Crush was drawn and colored digitally.

Text, cover art, and interior illustrations copyright © 2022 by Lucy Knisley

All rights reserved. Published in the United States by RH Graphic, an imprint of Random House Children's Books, a division of Penguin Random House LLC, New York.

RH Graphic with the book design is a trademark of Penguin Random House LLC.

Visit us on the web and sign up for our newsletter! RHKidsGraphic.com • @RHKidsGraphic

Educators and librarians, for a variety of teaching tools, visit us at RHTeachersLibrarians.com

Library of Congress Cataloging-in-Publication Data is available upon request.
ISBN 978-0-593-12538-0 (hardcover) — ISBN 978-1-9848-9688-9 (lib. bdg.)
ISBN 978-1-9848-9687-2 (paperback) — ISBN 978-1-9848-9689-6 (ebook)

Designed by Patrick Crotty
Colored by Whitney Cogar

MANUFACTURED IN CHINA
10 9 8 7 6 5 4 3 2 1
First Edition

A comic on every bookshelf.

Jen McInnes

APPLE CRUSH

By Lucy Knisley

For

Marie King ♡

and all the teachers & librarians who have known "Just the book for you."

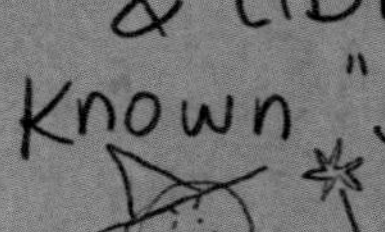

Chapter One

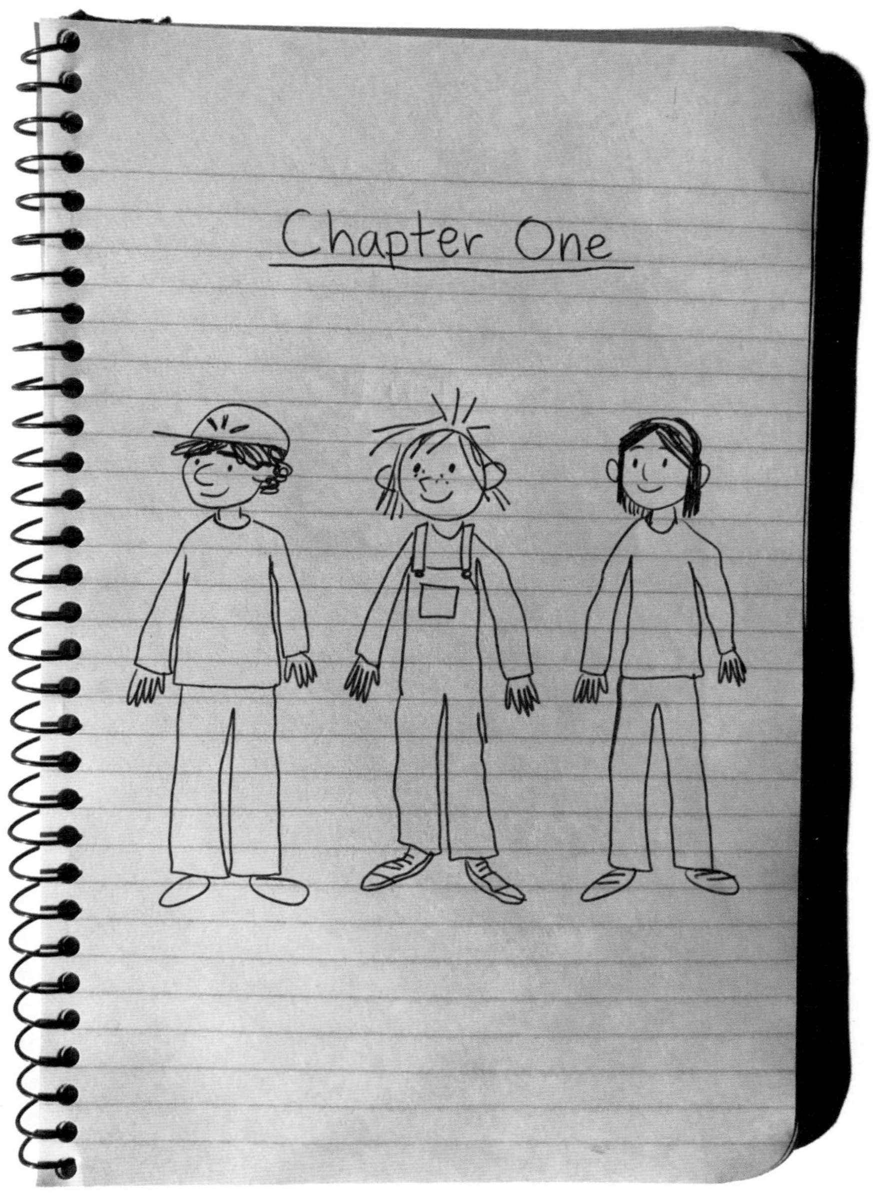

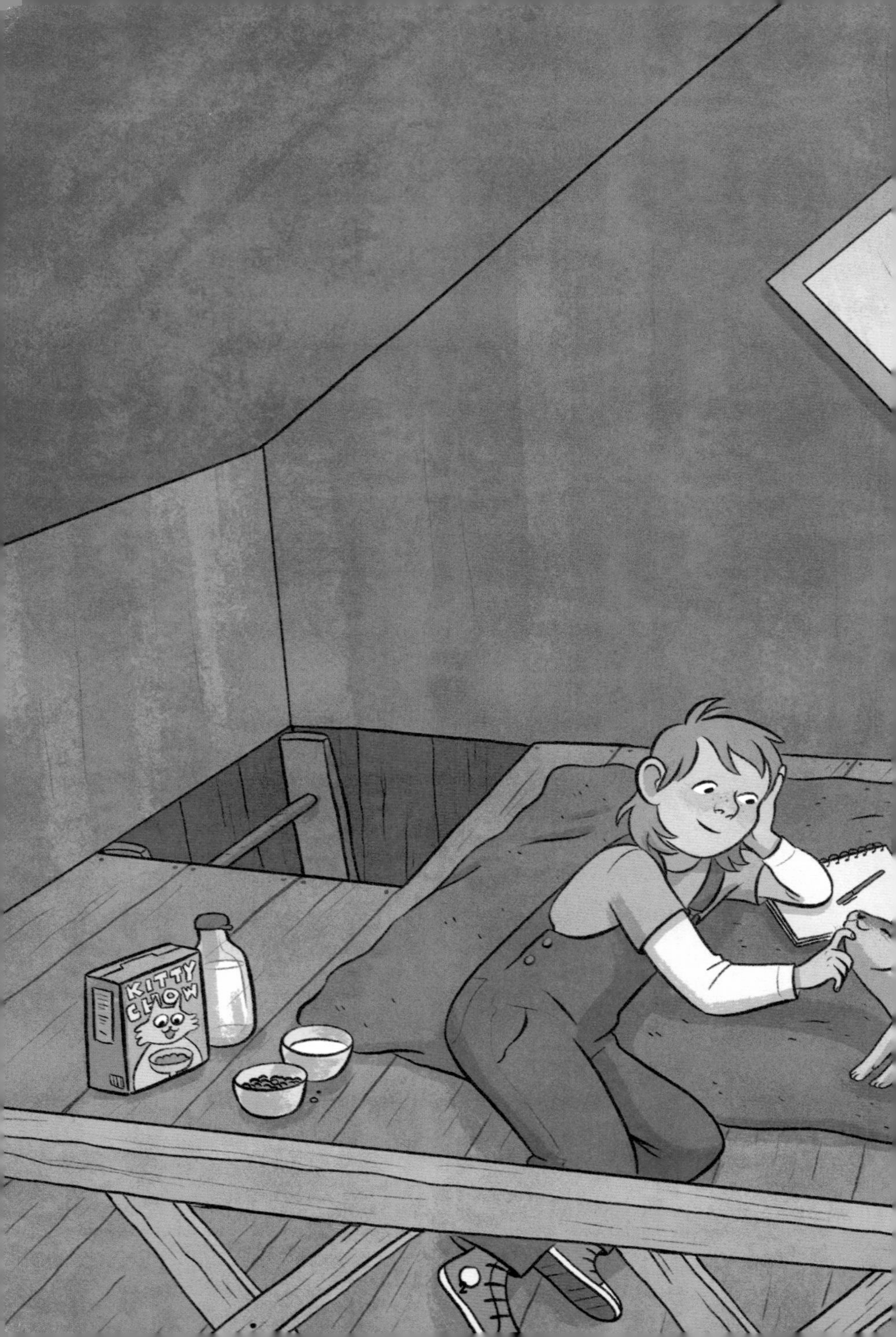
KITTY CHOW

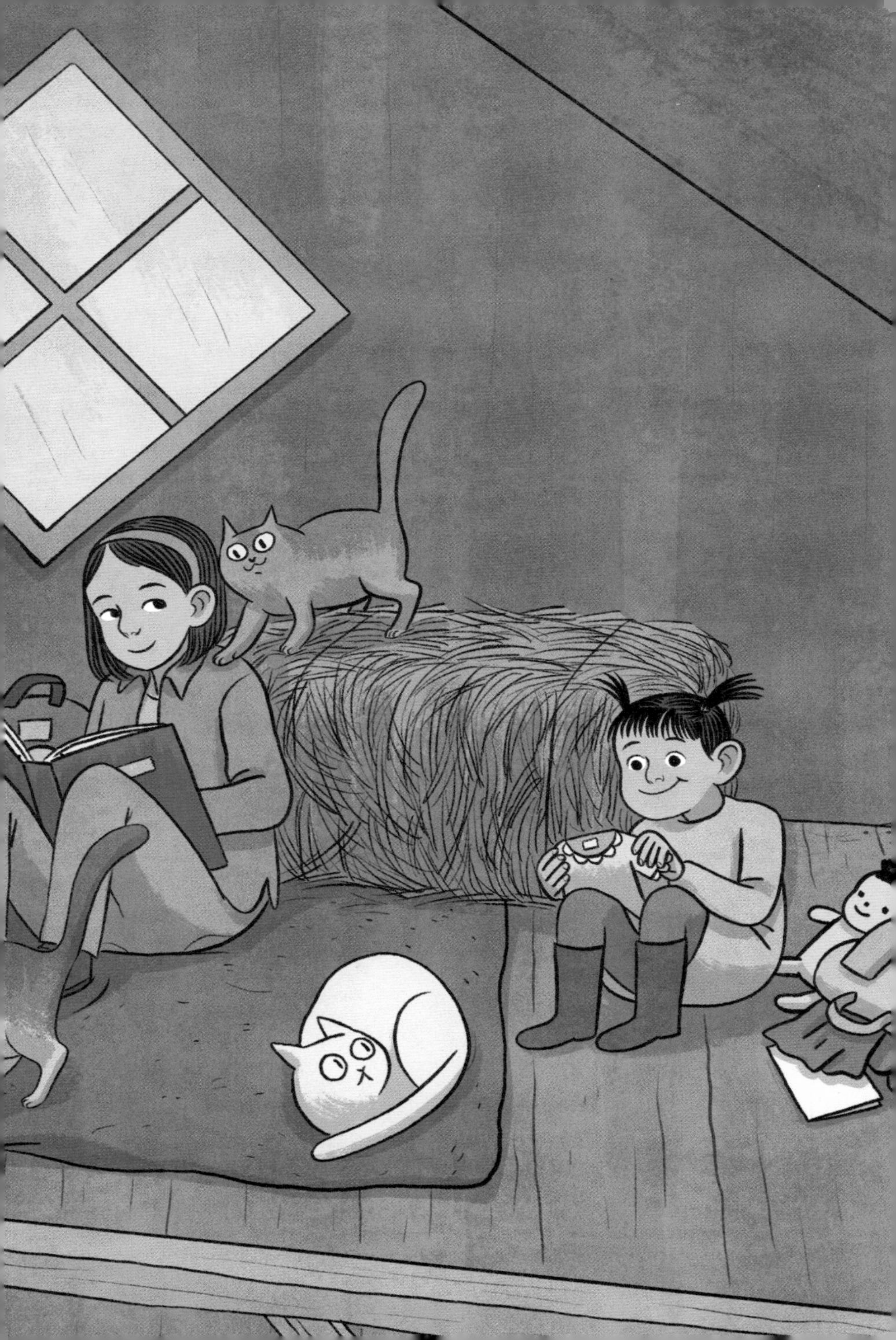

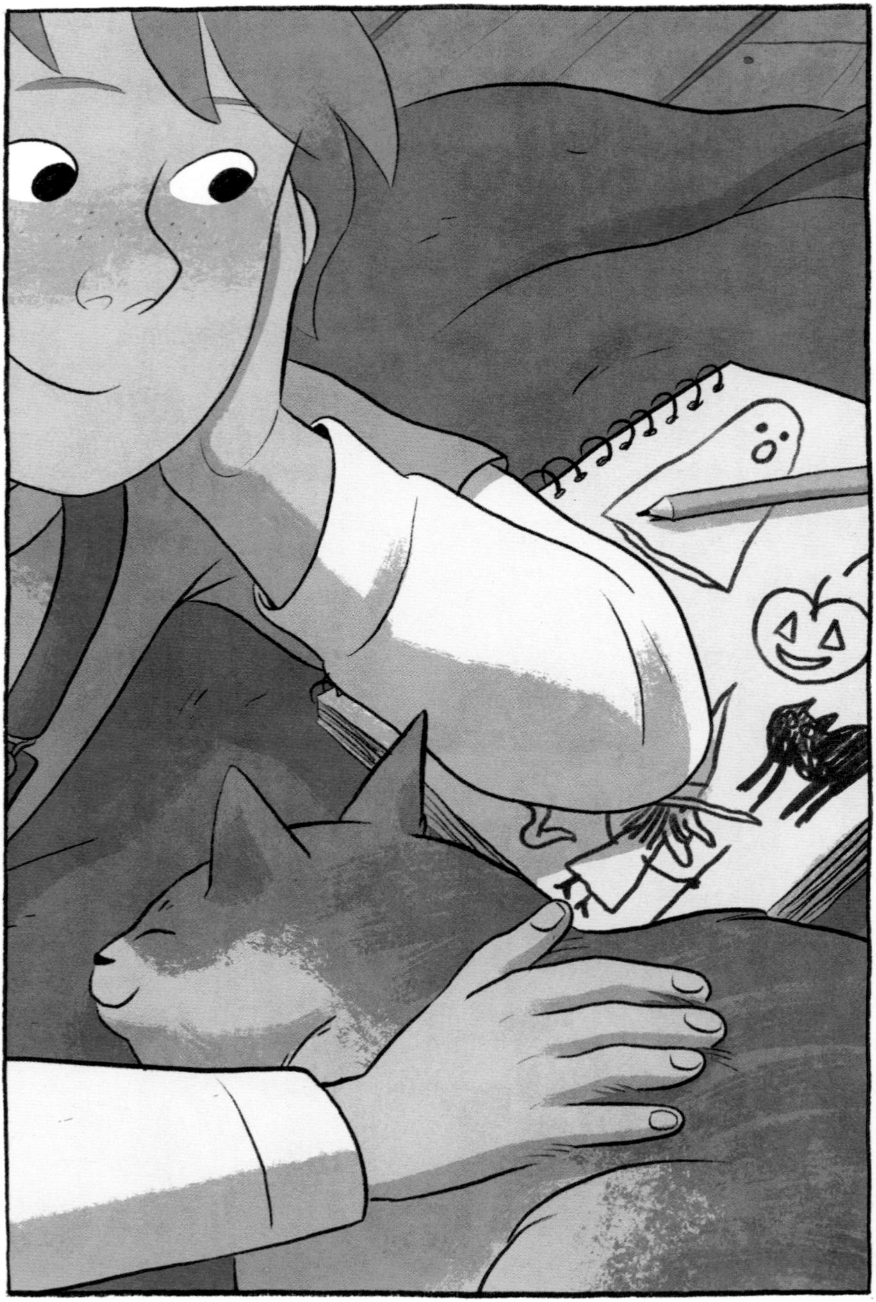

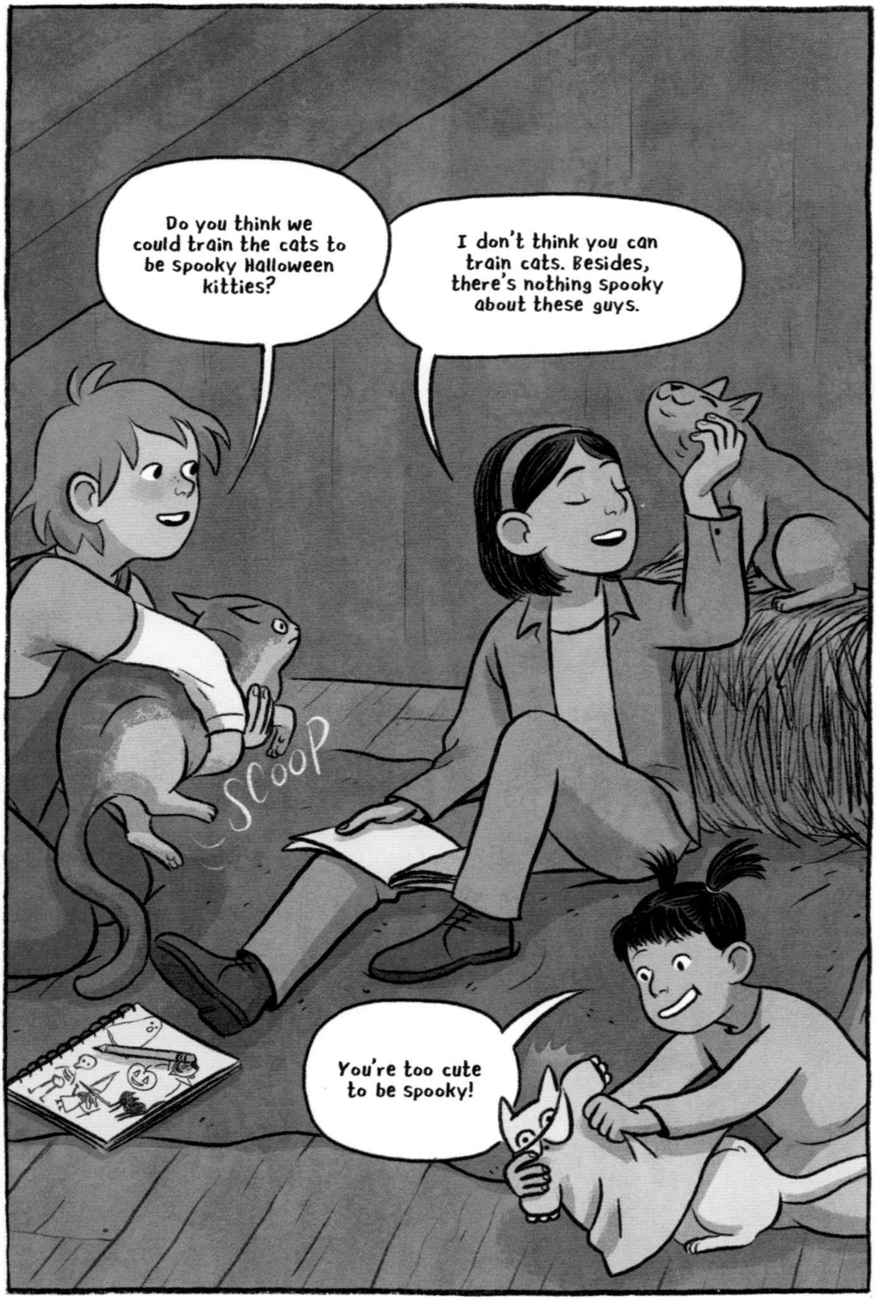
Do you think we could train the cats to be spooky Halloween kitties?
I don't think you can train cats. Besides, there's nothing spooky about these guys.
SCOOP
You're too cute to be spooky!

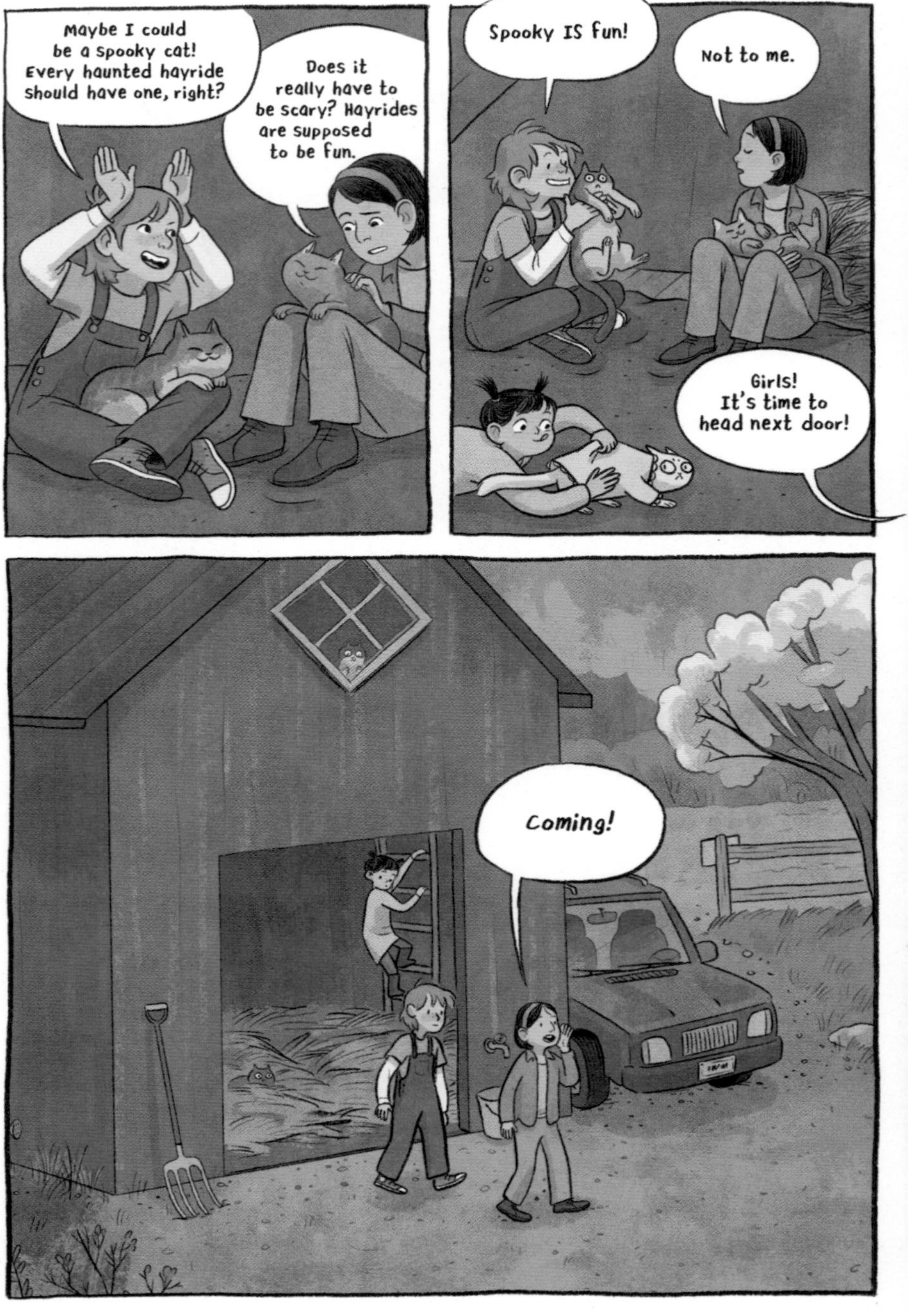
Maybe I could be a spooky cat! Every haunted hayride should have one, right?
Does it really have to be scary? Hayrides are supposed to be fun.
Spooky IS fun!
Not to me.
Girls! It's time to head next door!
Coming!

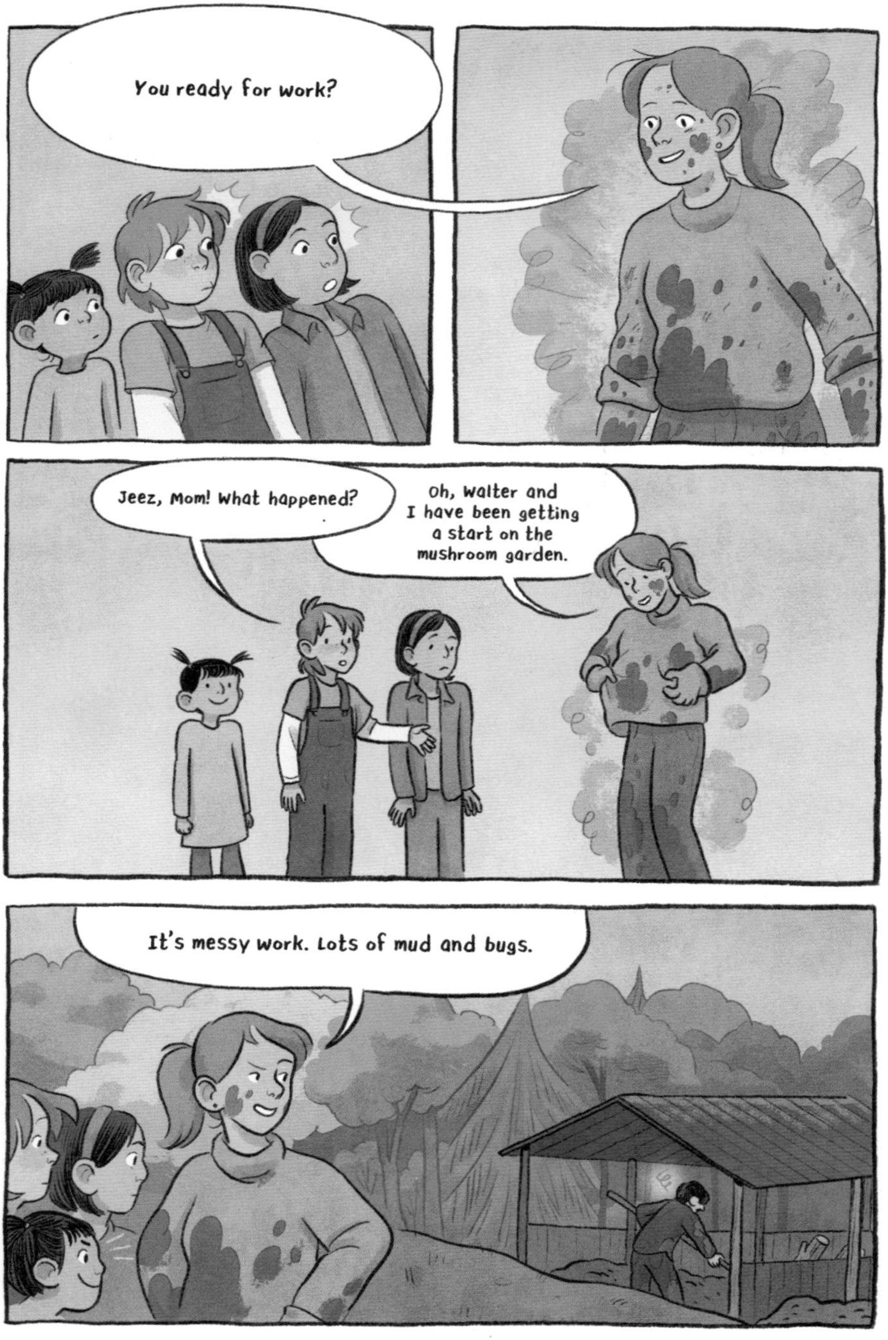
You ready for work?
Jeez, Mom! What happened?
Oh, Walter and I have been getting a start on the mushroom garden.
It's messy work. Lots of mud and bugs.

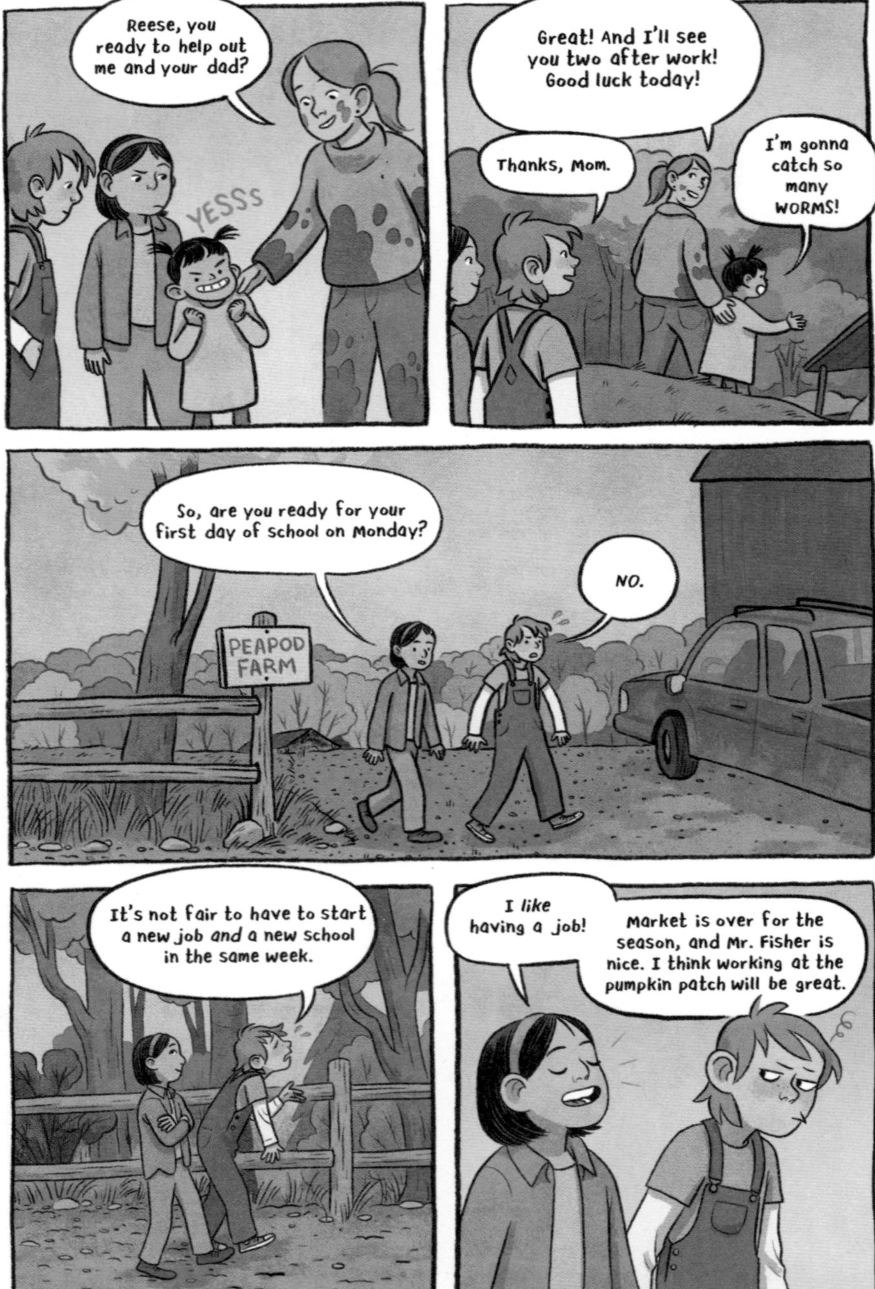
Reese, you ready to help out me and your dad?
YESSS
Great! And I'll see you two after work! Good luck today!
Thanks, Mom.
I'm gonna catch so many WORMS!
So, are you ready for your first day of school on Monday?
PEAPOD FARM
NO.
It's not fair to have to start a new job *and* a new school in the same week.
I *like* having a job!
Market is over for the season, and Mr. Fisher is nice. I think working at the pumpkin patch will be great.

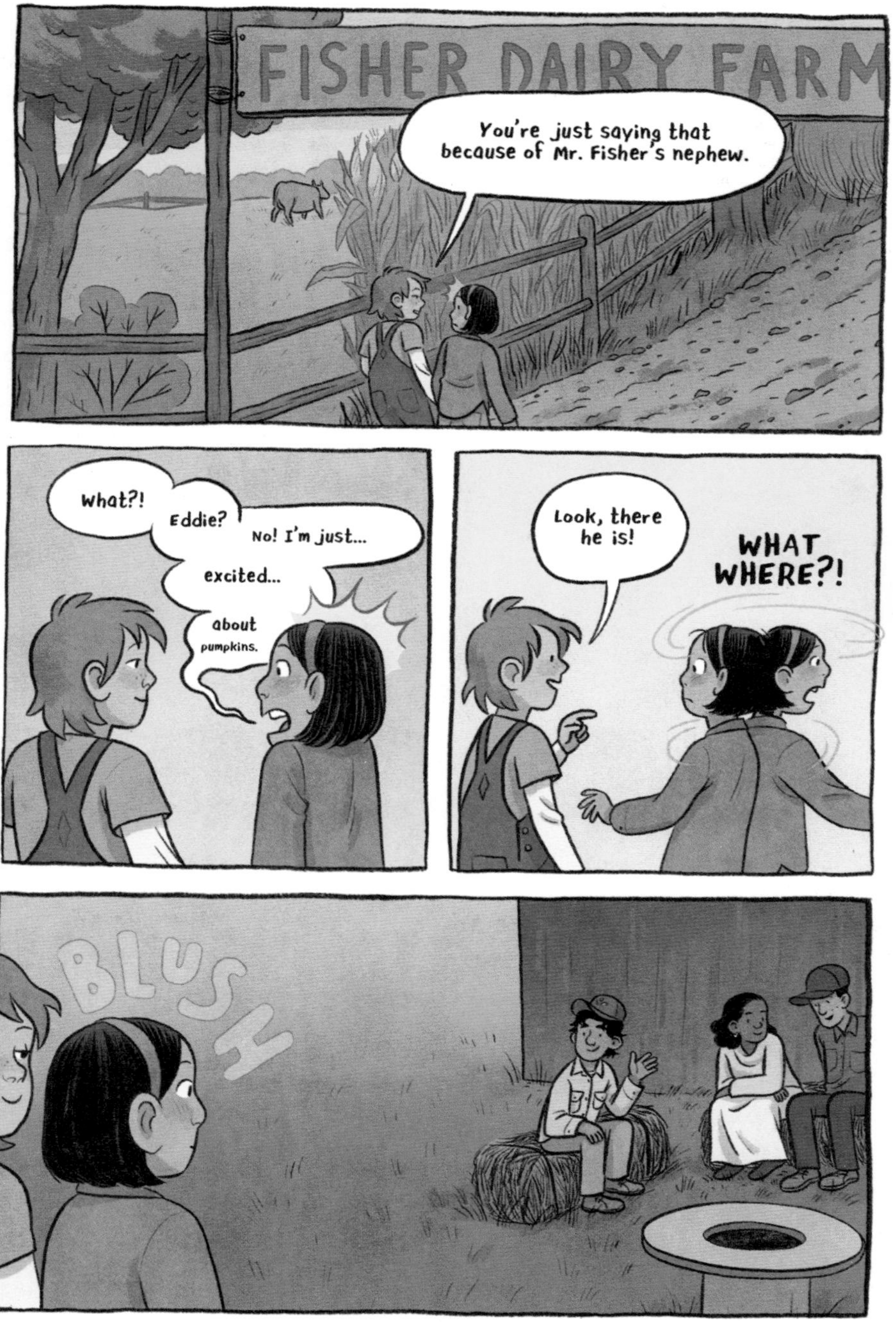
FISHER DAIRY FARM
You're just saying that because of Mr. Fisher's nephew.
What?!
Eddie?
No! I'm just...
excited...
about pumpkins.
Look, there he is!
WHAT WHERE?!
BLUSH

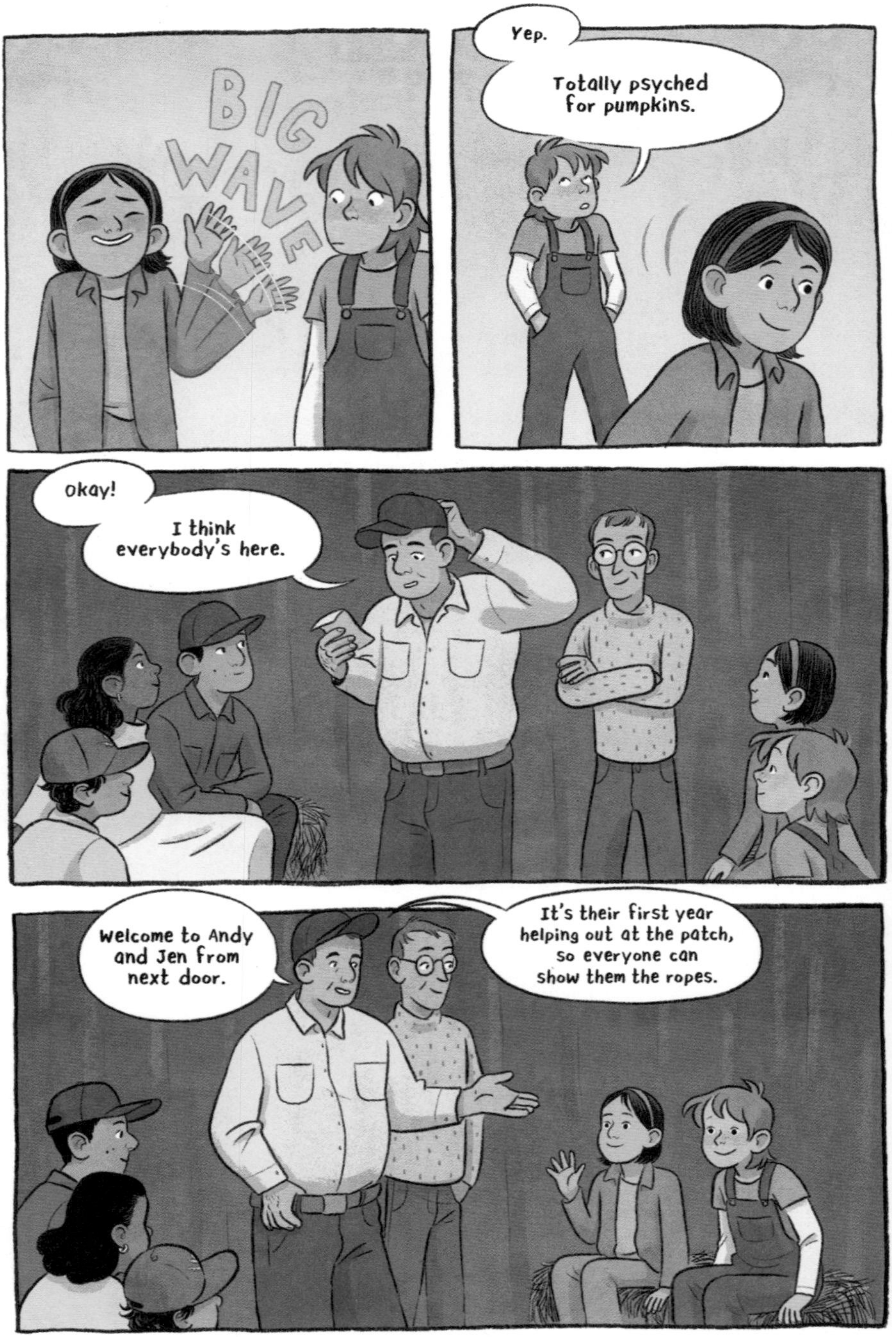
BIG WAVE
Yep.
Totally psyched for pumpkins.
Okay!
I think everybody's here.
Welcome to Andy and Jen from next door.
It's their first year helping out at the patch, so everyone can show them the ropes.

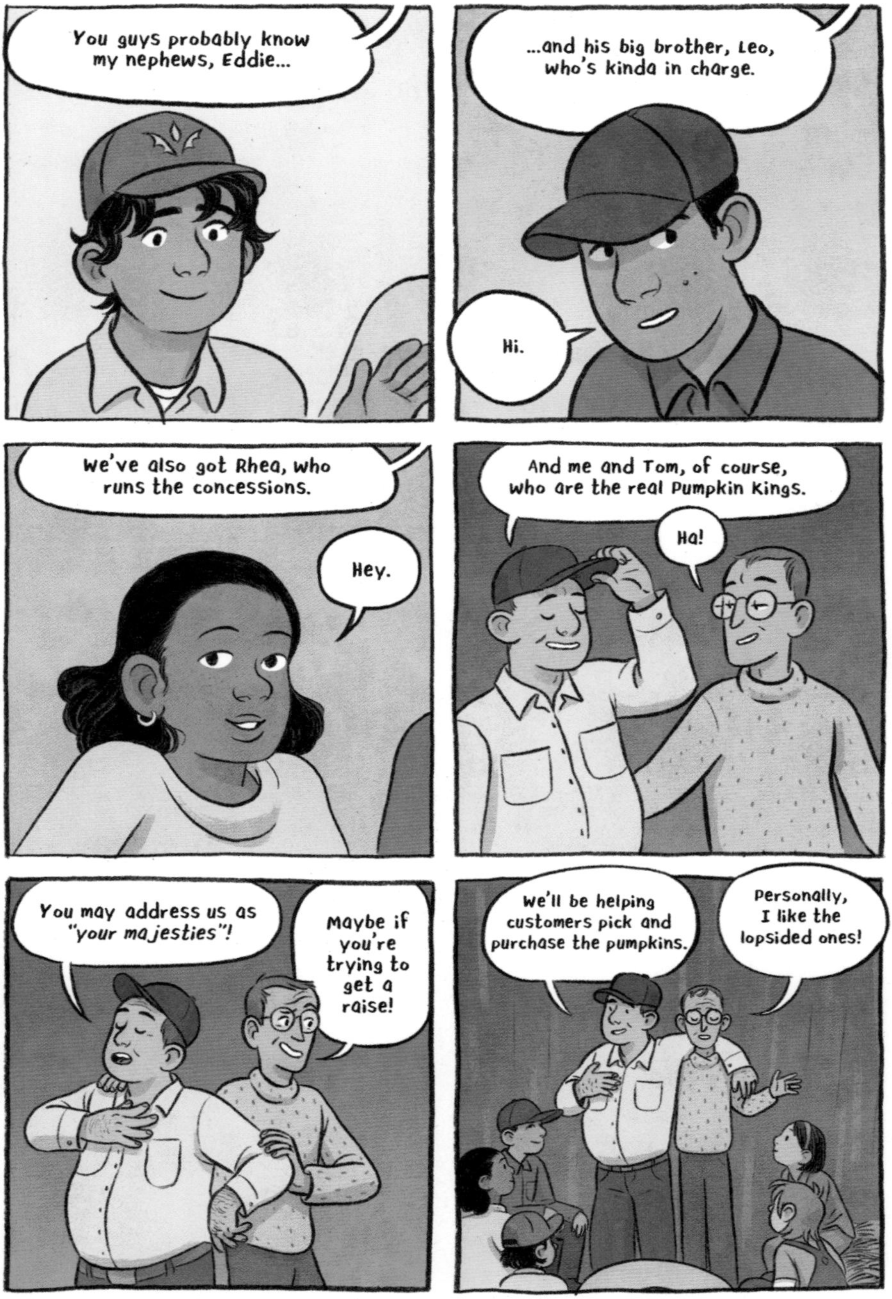
You guys probably know my nephews, Eddie...
...and his big brother, Leo, who's kinda in charge.
Hi.
We've also got Rhea, who runs the concessions.
Hey.
And me and Tom, of course, who are the real Pumpkin Kings.
Ha!
You may address us as "your majesties"!
Maybe if you're trying to get a raise!
We'll be helping customers pick and purchase the pumpkins.
Personally, I like the lopsided ones!

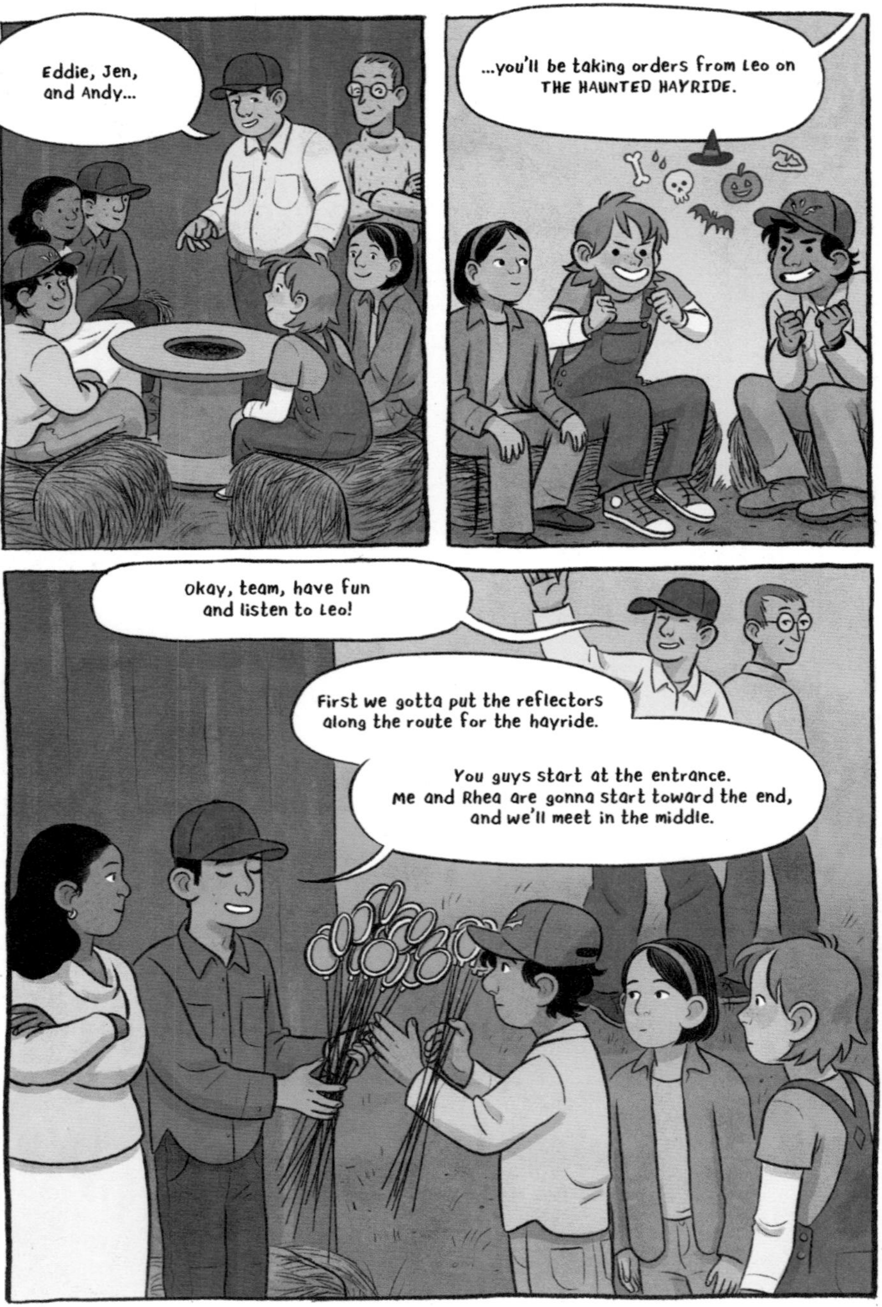
Eddie, Jen, and Andy...
...you'll be taking orders from Leo on THE HAUNTED HAYRIDE.
Okay, team, have fun and listen to Leo!
First we gotta put the reflectors along the route for the hayride.
You guys start at the entrance. Me and Rhea are gonna start toward the end, and we'll meet in the middle.

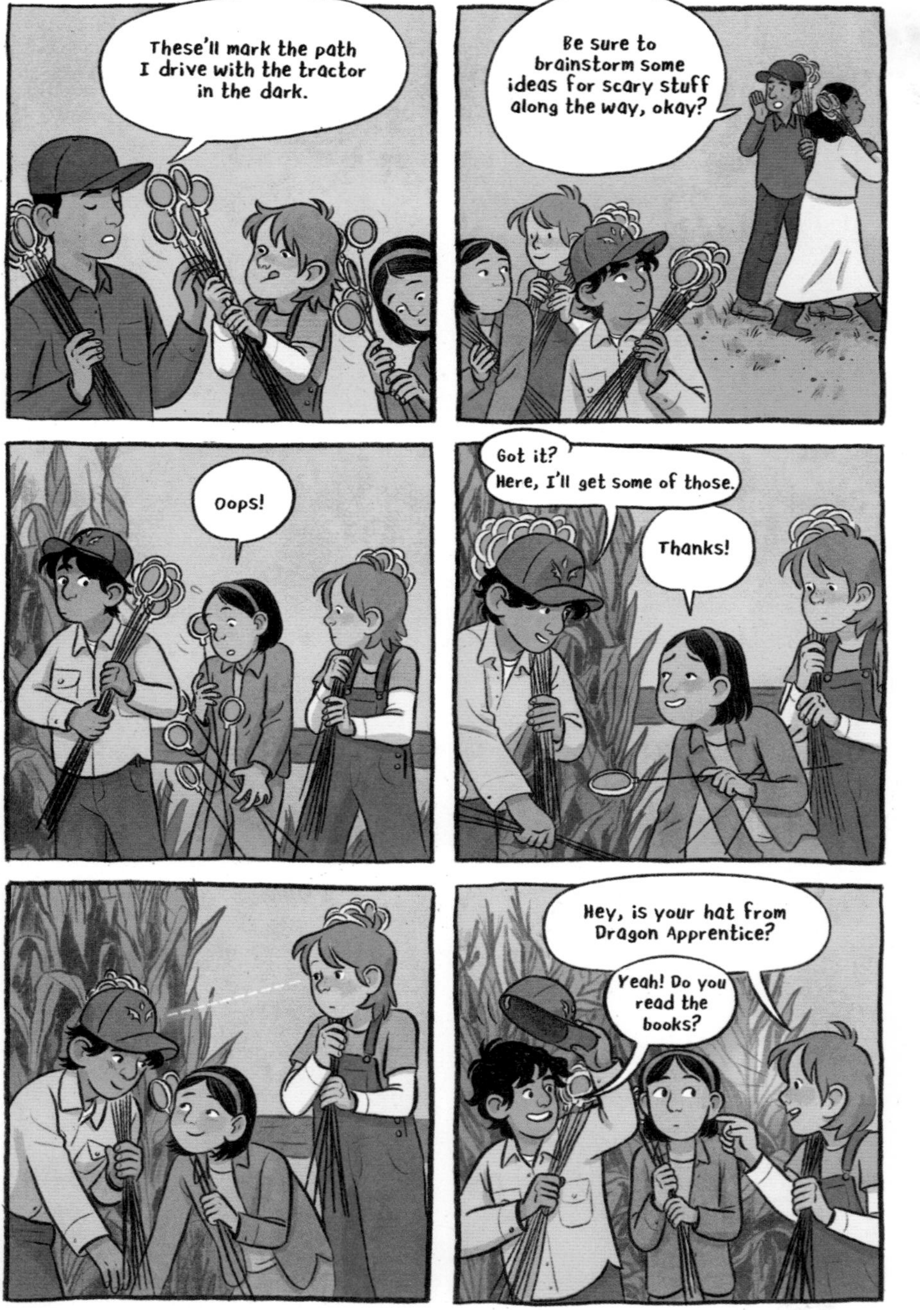
These'll mark the path I drive with the tractor in the dark.
Be sure to brainstorm some ideas for scary stuff along the way, okay?
Oops!
Got it? Here, I'll get some of those.
Thanks!
Hey, is your hat from Dragon Apprentice?
Yeah! Do you read the books?

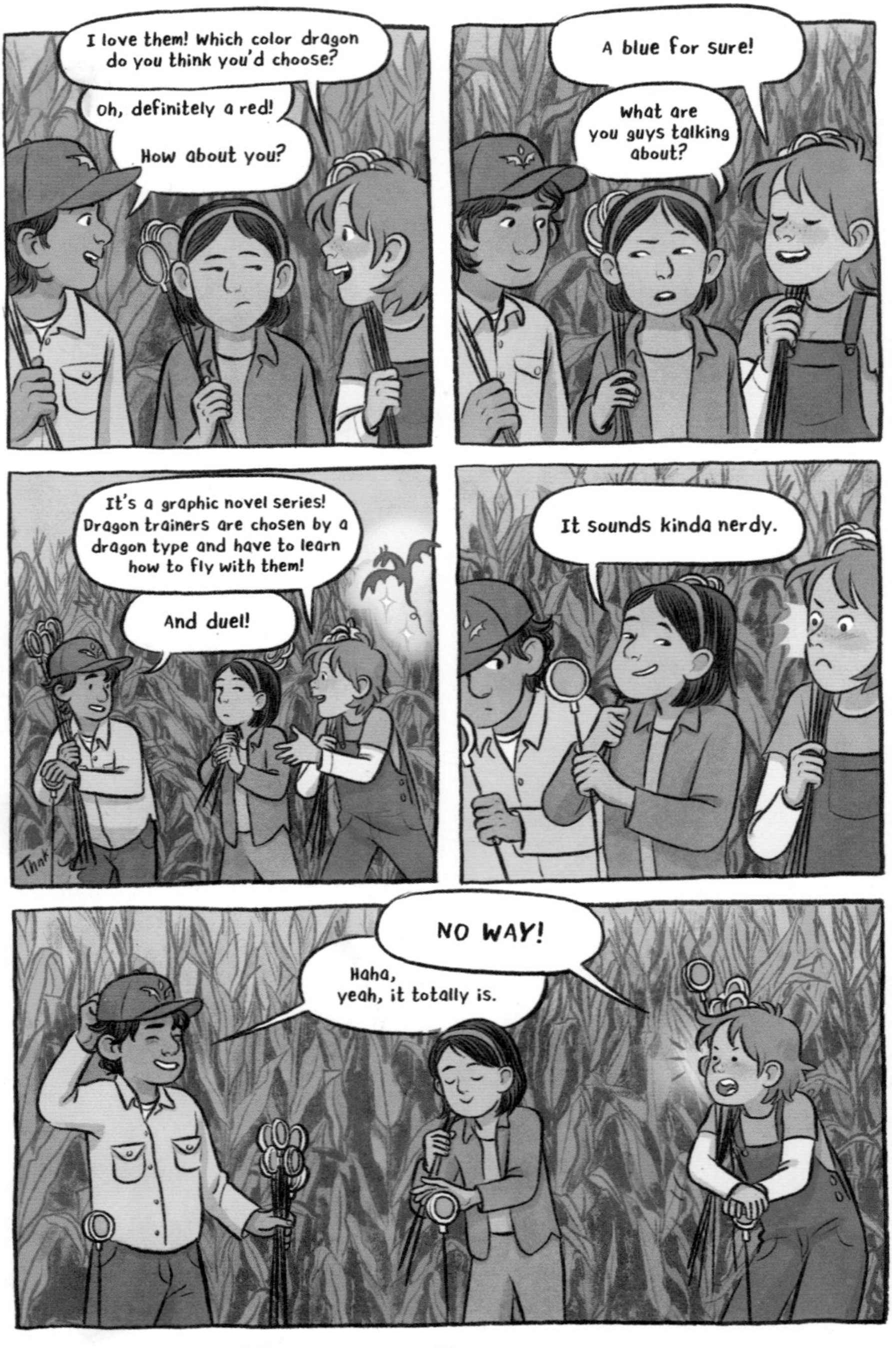

I love them! Which color dragon do you think you'd choose?
Oh, definitely a red!
How about you?
A blue for sure!
What are you guys talking about?
It's a graphic novel series! Dragon trainers are chosen by a dragon type and have to learn how to fly with them!
And duel!
Thnk
It sounds kinda nerdy.
Haha, yeah, it totally is.
NO WAY!

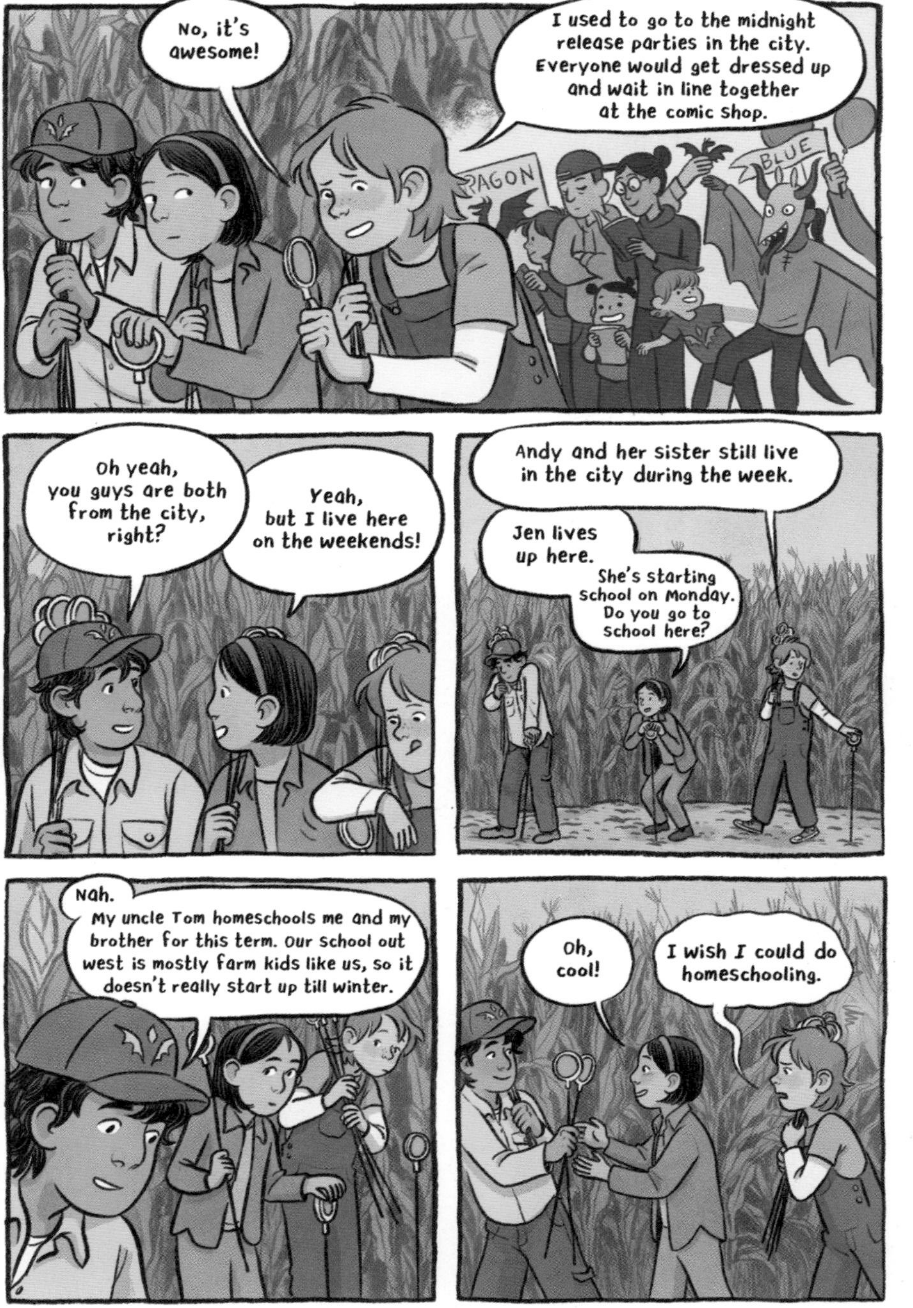
No, it's awesome!
I used to go to the midnight release parties in the city. Everyone would get dressed up and wait in line together at the comic shop.
AGON
BLUE
Oh yeah, you guys are both from the city, right?
Yeah, but I live here on the weekends!
Andy and her sister still live in the city during the week.
Jen lives up here.
She's starting school on Monday. Do you go to school here?
Nah.
My uncle Tom homeschools me and my brother for this term. Our school out west is mostly farm kids like us, so it doesn't really start up till winter.
Oh, cool!
I wish I could do homeschooling.

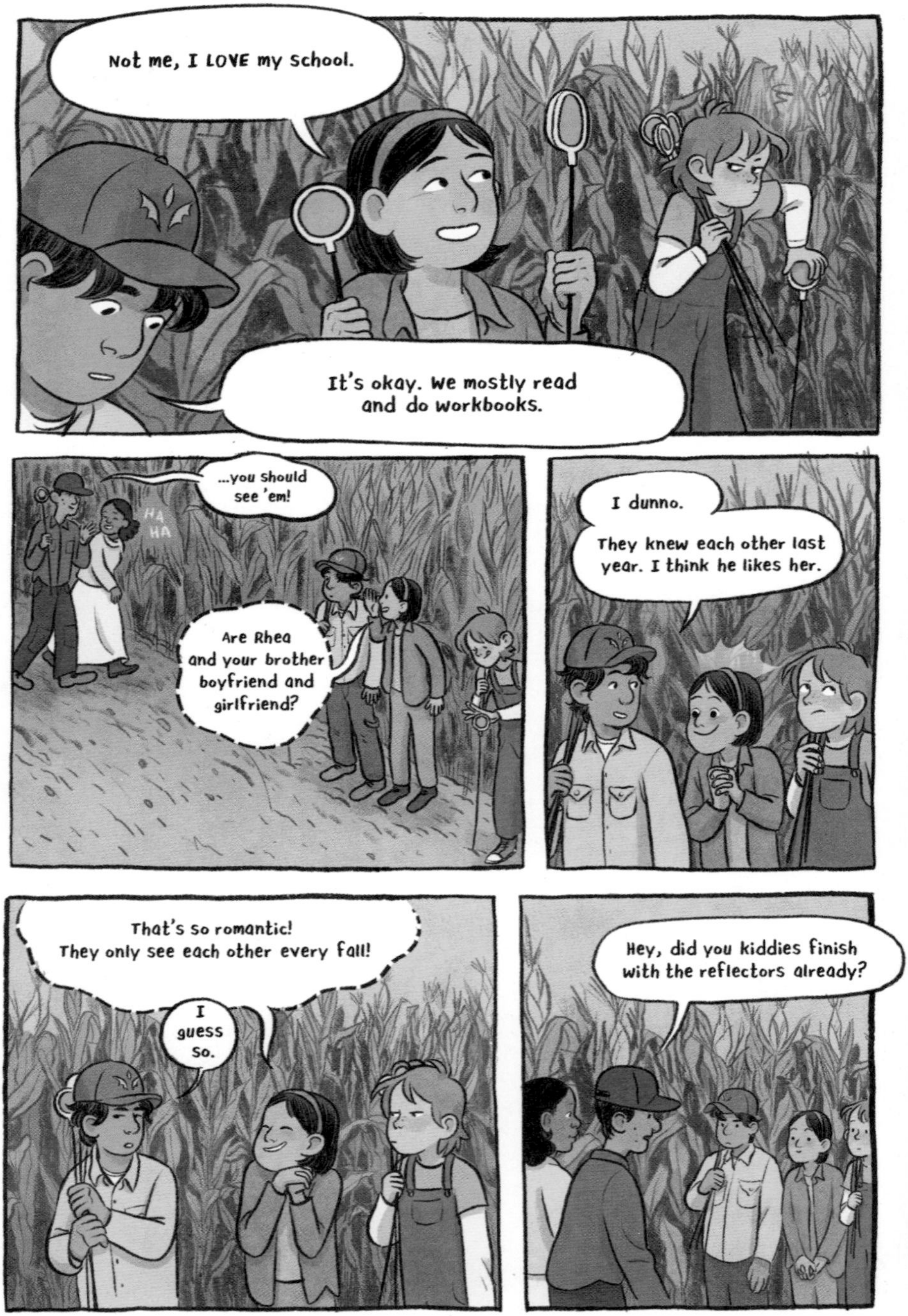
Not me, I LOVE my school.
It's okay. We mostly read and do workbooks.
...you should see 'em!
HA HA
Are Rhea and your brother boyfriend and girlfriend?
I dunno.
They knew each other last year. I think he likes her.
That's so romantic! They only see each other every fall!
I guess so.
Hey, did you kiddies finish with the reflectors already?

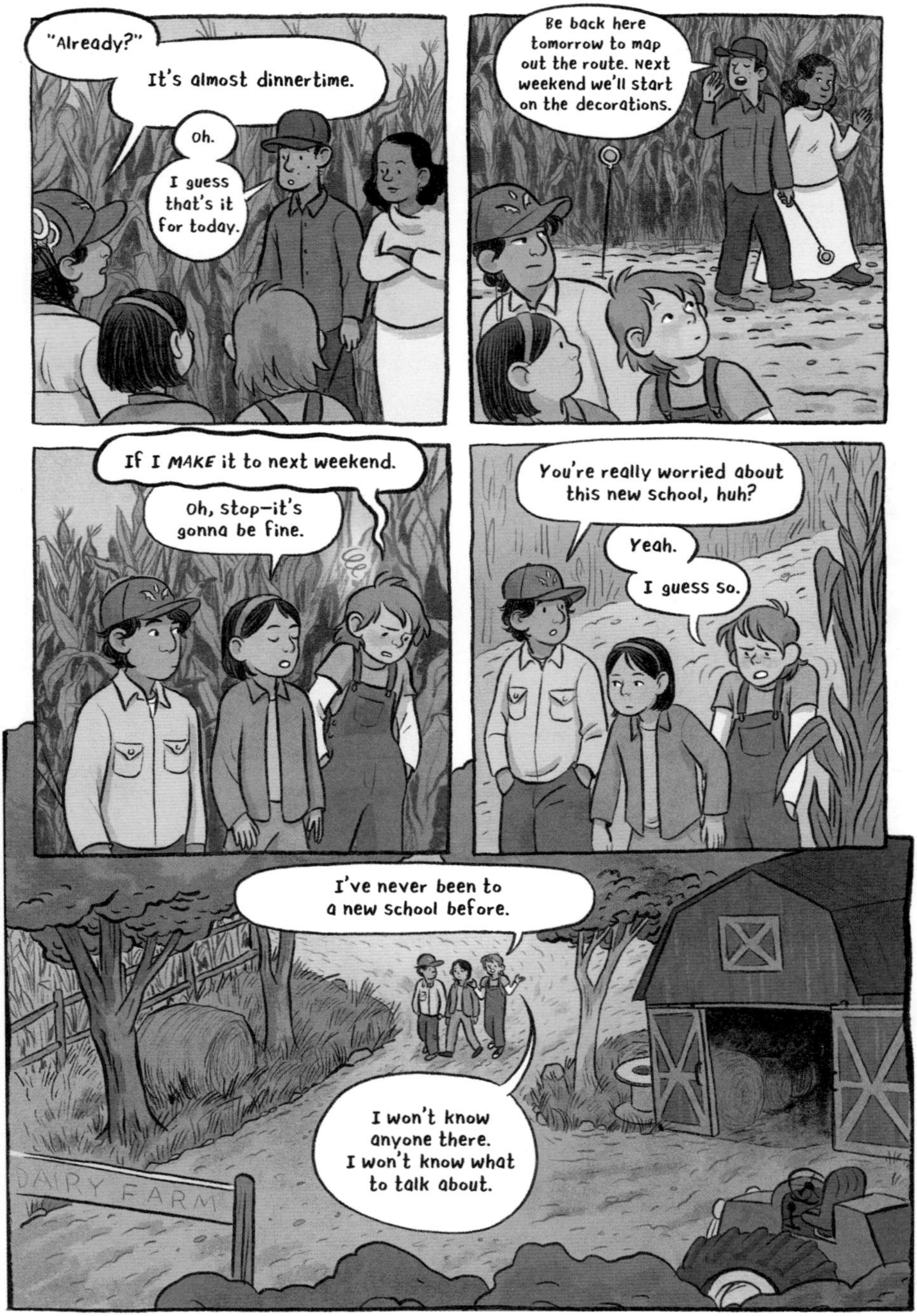
"Already?"
It's almost dinnertime.
Oh.
I guess that's it for today.
Be back here tomorrow to map out the route. Next weekend we'll start on the decorations.
If I MAKE it to next weekend.
Oh, stop—it's gonna be fine.
You're really worried about this new school, huh?
Yeah.
I guess so.
I've never been to a new school before.
I won't know anyone there. I won't know what to talk about.
DAIRY FARM

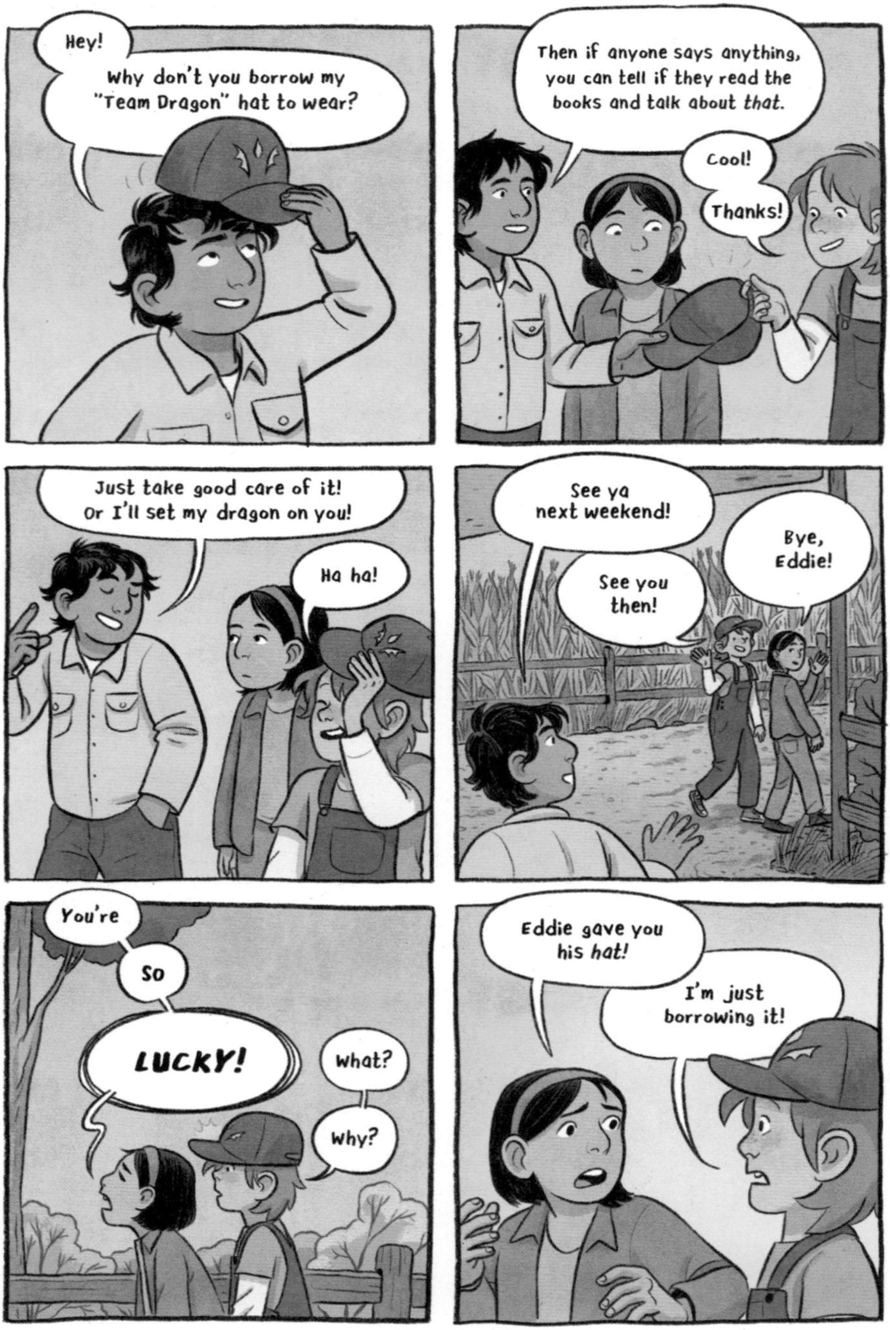

Hey!
Why don't you borrow my "Team Dragon" hat to wear?
Then if anyone says anything, you can tell if they read the books and talk about *that*.
Cool!
Thanks!
Just take good care of it! Or I'll set my dragon on you!
Ha ha!
See ya next weekend!
See you then!
Bye, Eddie!
You're
so
LUCKY!
What?
Why?
Eddie gave you his *hat!*
I'm just borrowing it!

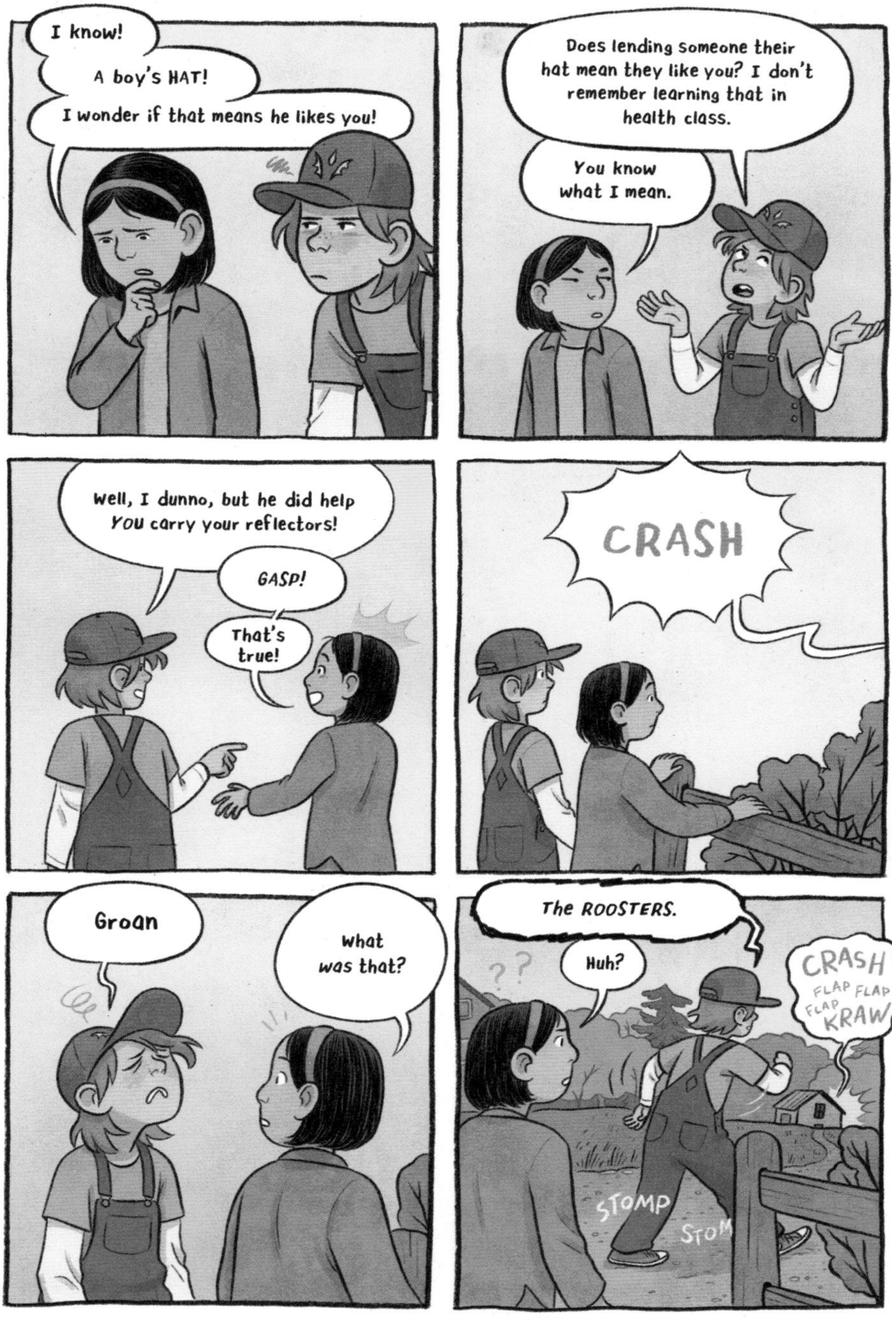
I know!
A boy's HAT!
I wonder if that means he likes you!
Does lending someone their hat mean they like you? I don't remember learning that in health class.
You know what I mean.
Well, I dunno, but he did help YOU carry your reflectors!
GASP!
That's true!
CRASH
Groan
What was that?
The ROOSTERS.
Huh?
CRASH
FLAP FLAP
FLAP
KRAW
STOMP
STOM

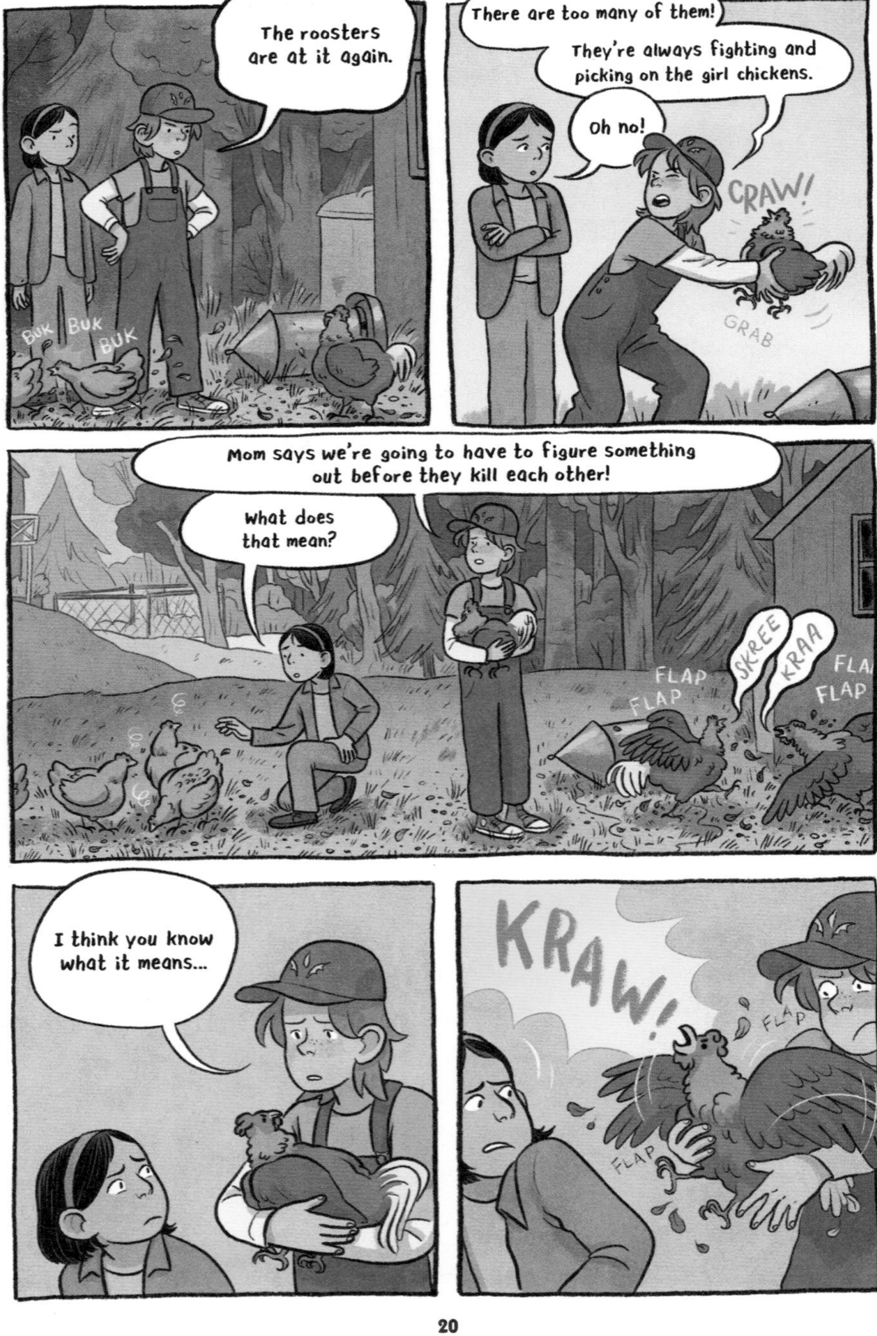

The roosters are at it again.
BUK BUK BUK
There are too many of them!
They're always fighting and picking on the girl chickens.
Oh no!
CRAW!
GRAB
Mom says we're going to have to figure something out before they kill each other!
What does that mean?
FLAP FLAP
SKREE
KRAA
FLAP FLAP
I think you know what it means...
KRAW!
FLAP
FLAP

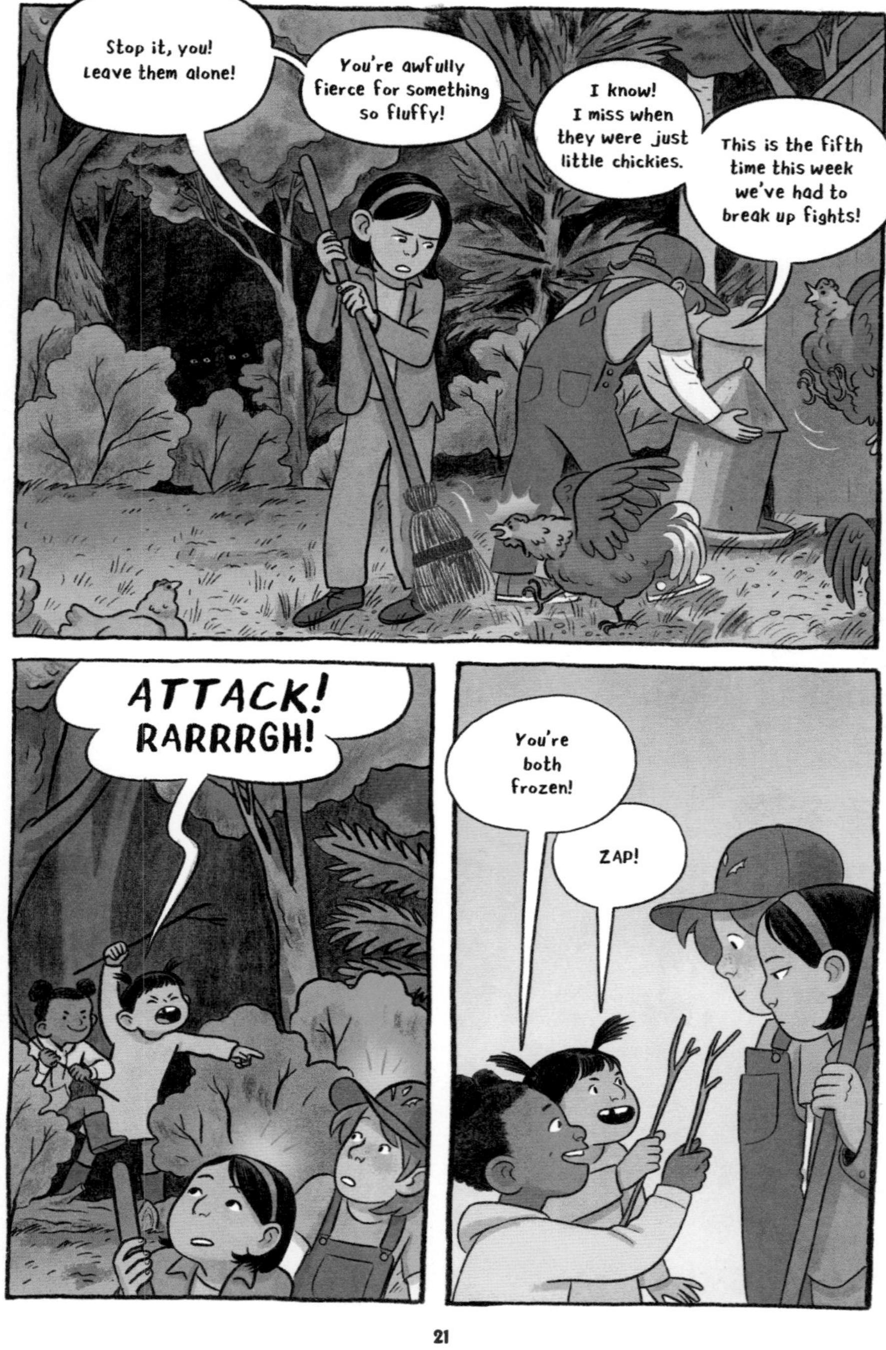
Stop it, you! Leave them alone!
You're awfully fierce for something so fluffy!
I know! I miss when they were just little chickies.
This is the fifth time this week we've had to break up fights!
ATTACK! RARRRGH!
You're both frozen!
ZAP!

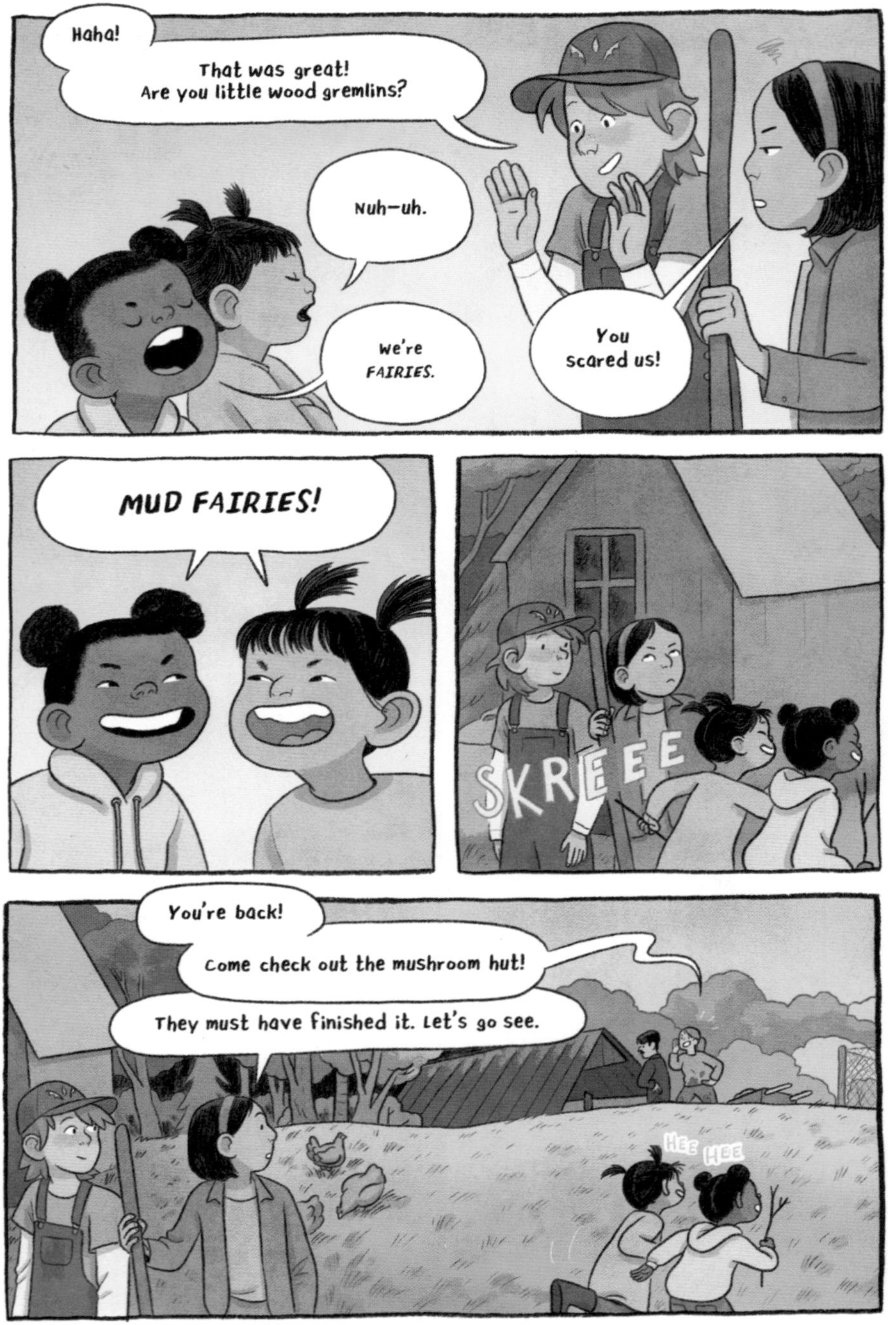

Haha!
That was great! Are you little wood gremlins?
Nuh-uh.
We're FAIRIES.
You scared us!
MUD FAIRIES!
SKREEE
You're back!
Come check out the mushroom hut!
They must have finished it. Let's go see.
HEE HEE

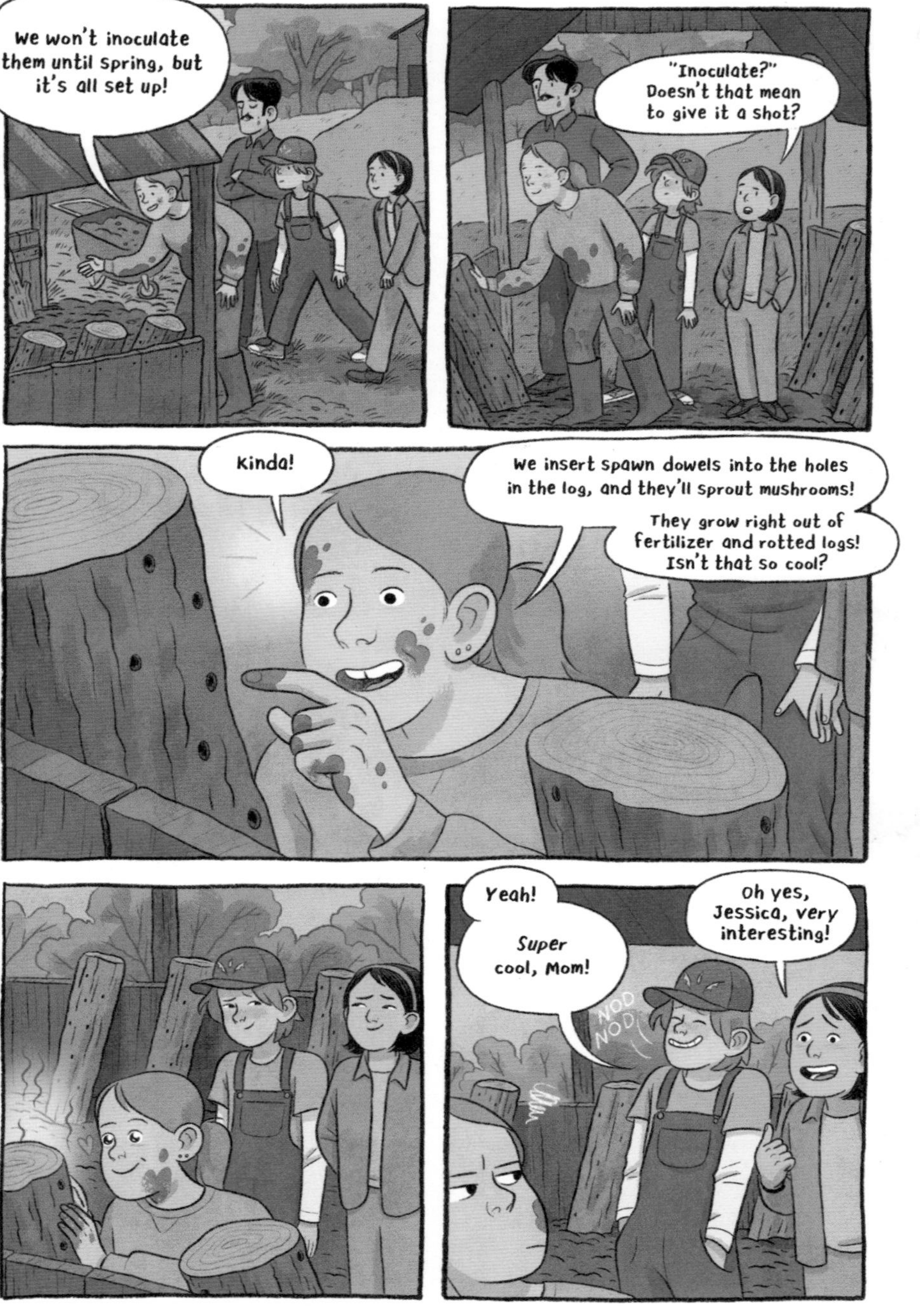
We won't inoculate them until spring, but it's all set up!
"Inoculate?" Doesn't that mean to give it a shot?
Kinda!
We insert spawn dowels into the holes in the log, and they'll sprout mushrooms!
They grow right out of fertilizer and rotted logs! Isn't that so cool?
Yeah!
Super cool, Mom!
Oh yes, Jessica, very interesting!
NOD NOD

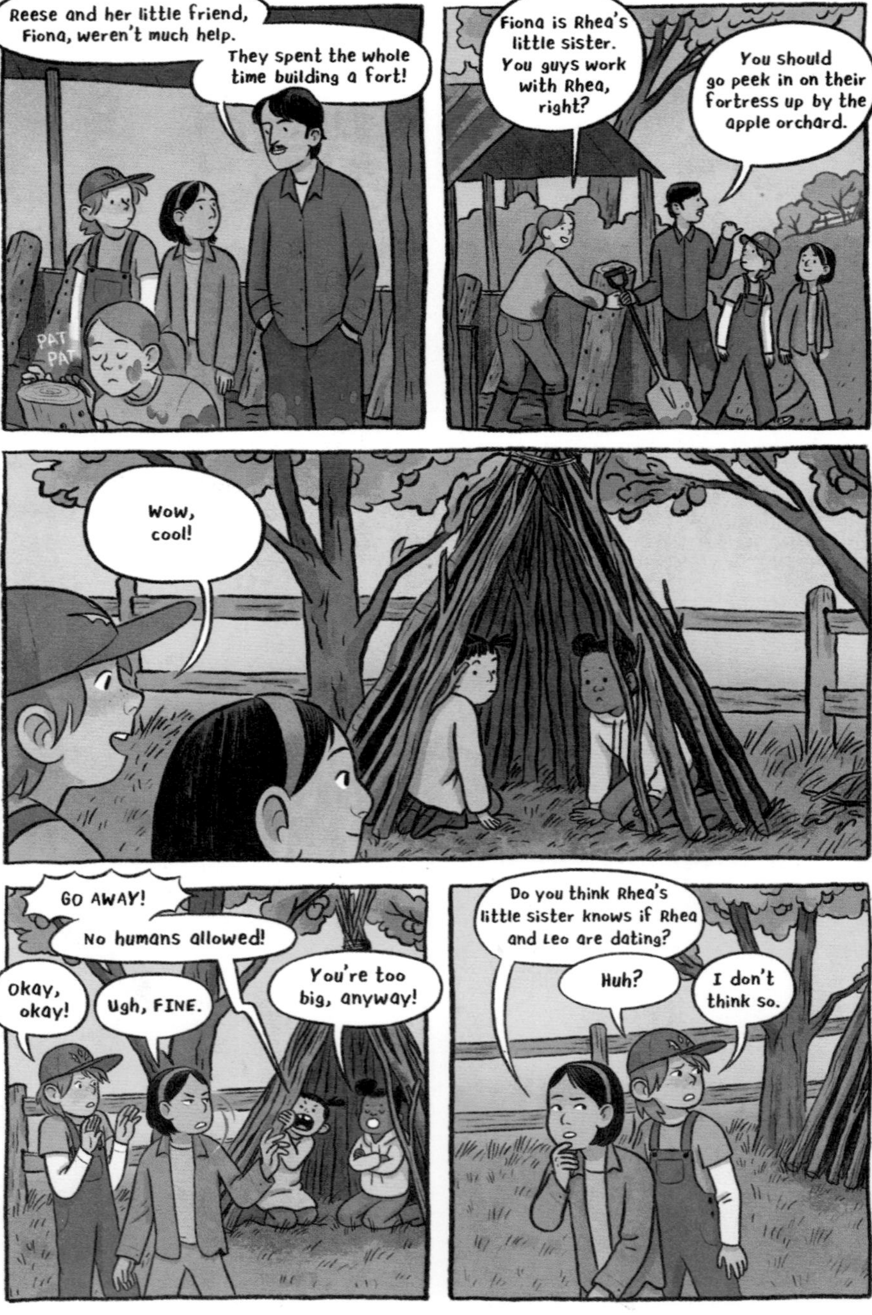
Reese and her little friend, Fiona, weren't much help.
They spent the whole time building a fort!
PAT PAT
Fiona is Rhea's little sister. You guys work with Rhea, right?
You should go peek in on their fortress up by the apple orchard.
Wow, cool!
GO AWAY!
No humans allowed!
Okay, okay!
Ugh, FINE.
You're too big, anyway!
Do you think Rhea's little sister knows if Rhea and Leo are dating?
Huh?
I don't think so.

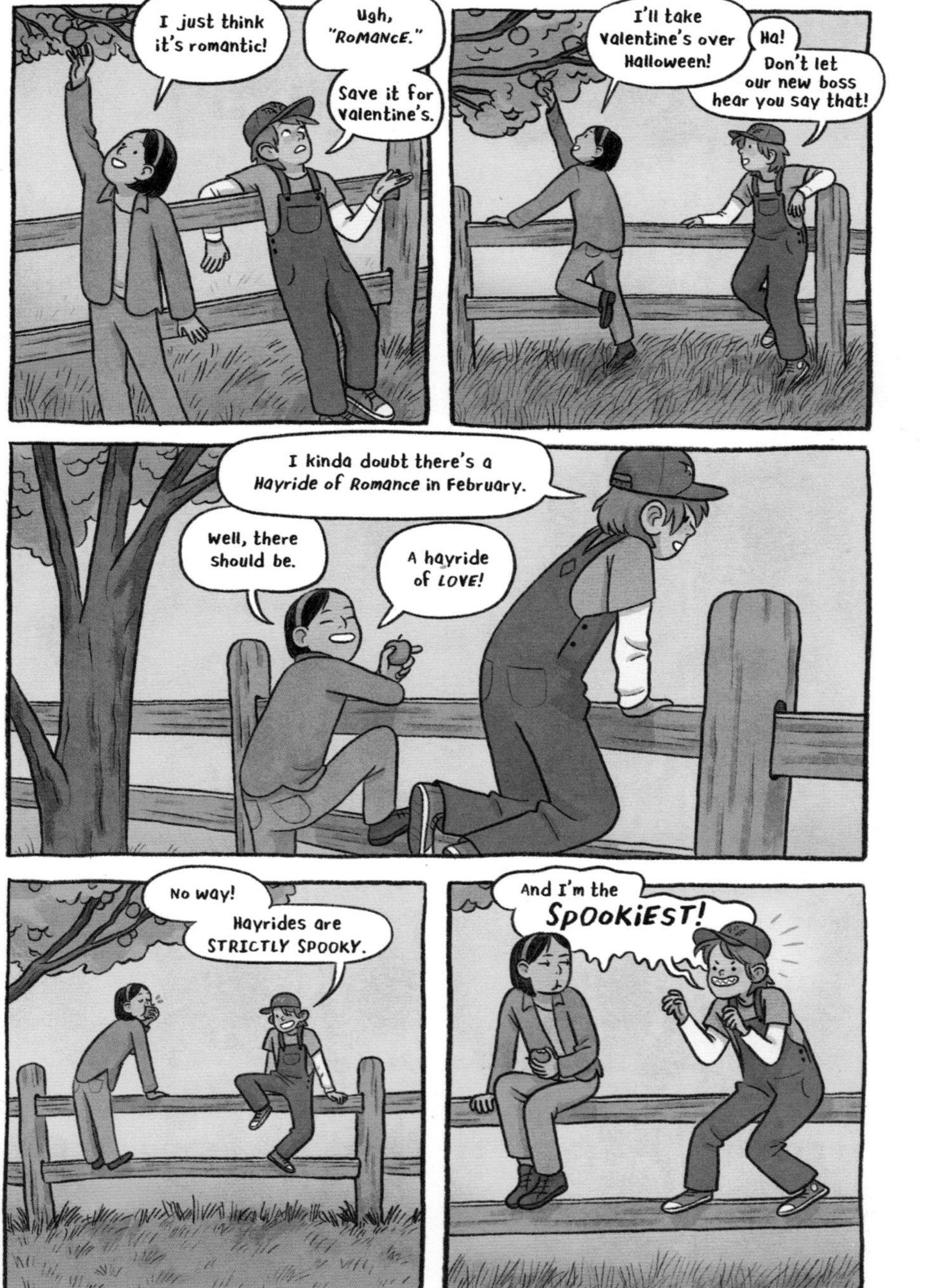
I just think it's romantic!
Ugh, "ROMANCE."
Save it for Valentine's.
I'll take Valentine's over Halloween!
Ha! Don't let our new boss hear you say that!
I kinda doubt there's a Hayride of Romance in February.
Well, there should be.
A hayride of LOVE!
No way!
Hayrides are STRICTLY SPOOKY.
And I'm the SPOOKIEST!

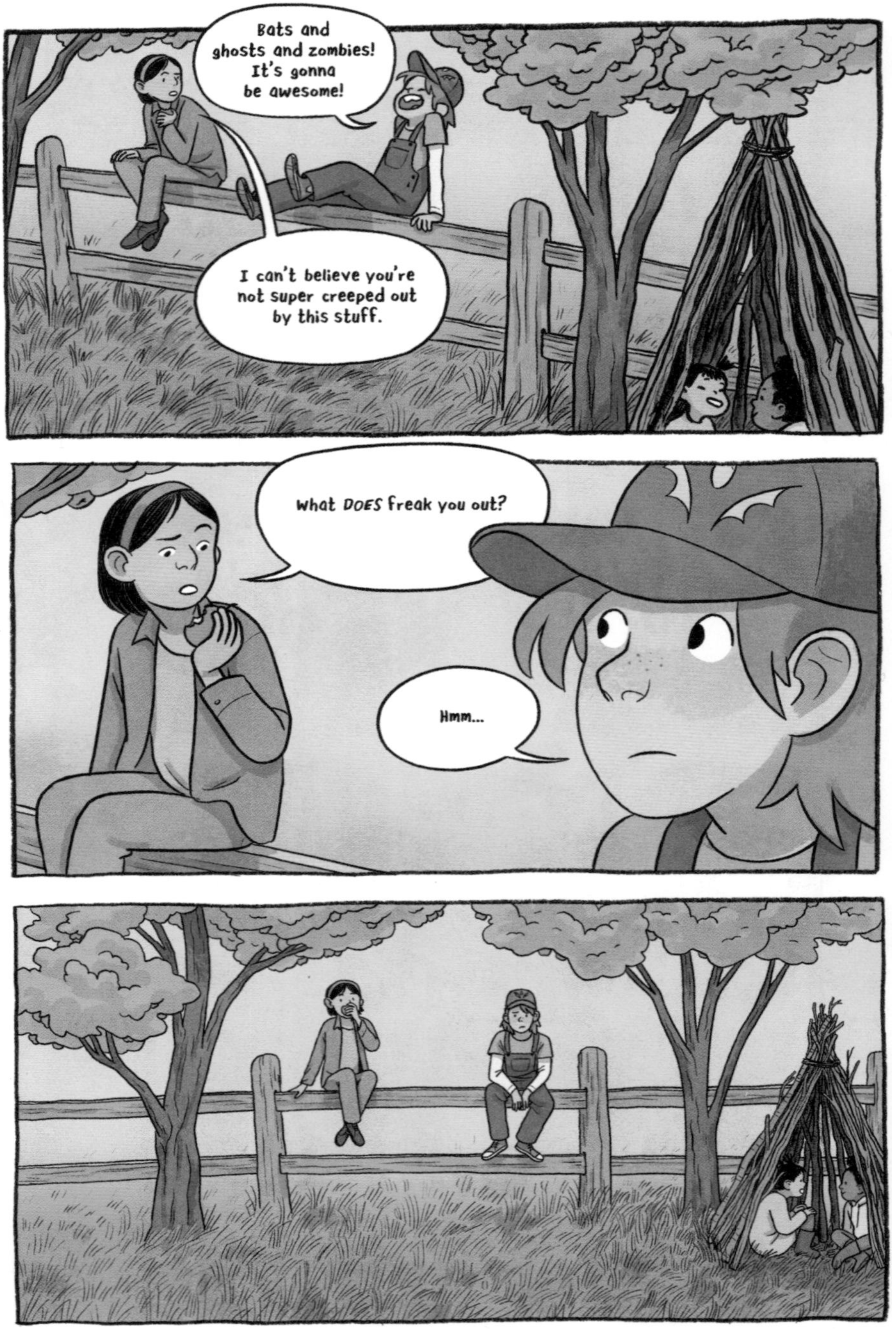
Bats and ghosts and zombies! It's gonna be awesome!
I can't believe you're not super creeped out by this stuff.
What DOES freak you out?
Hmm...

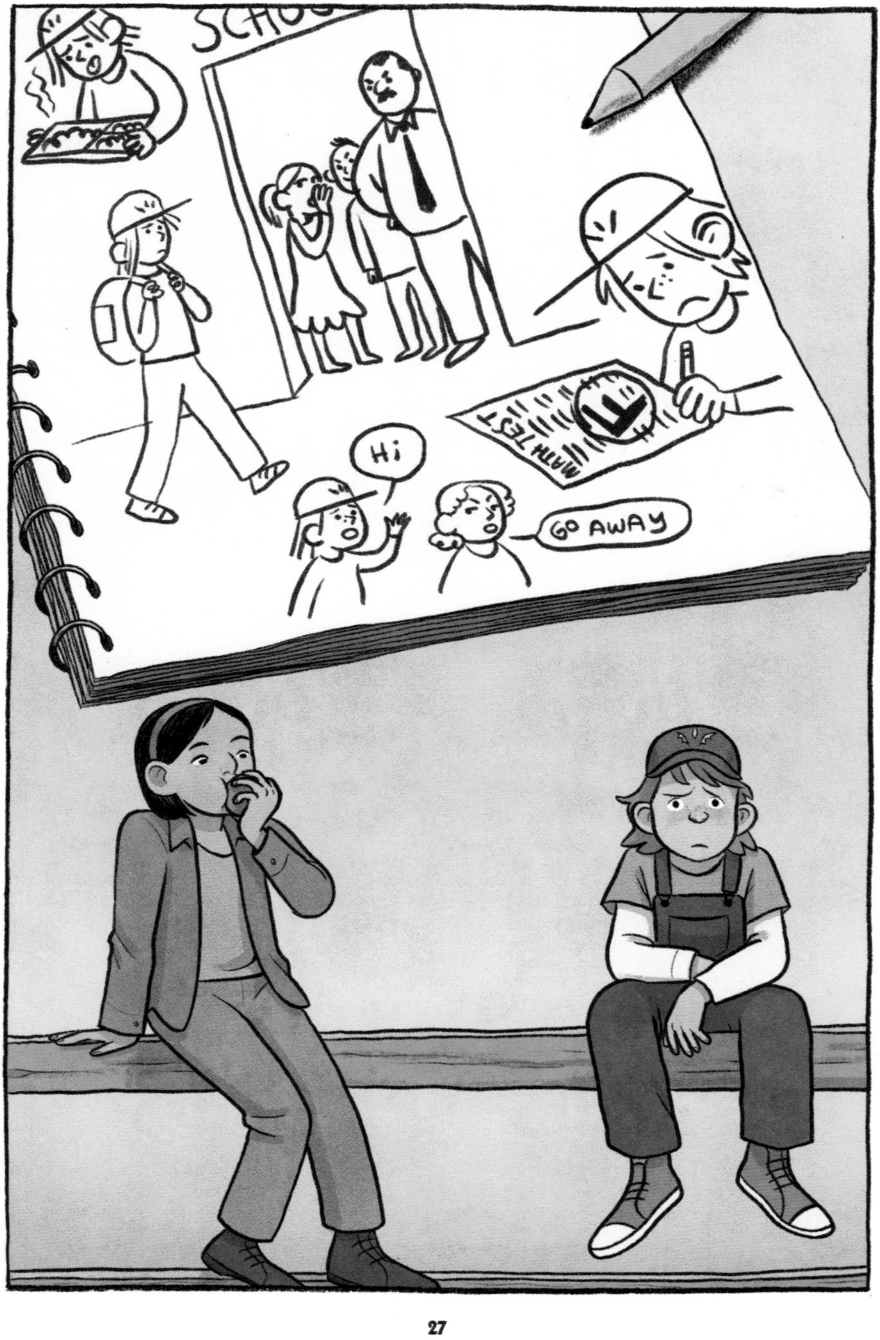
SCHOO
MATH TEST
F
Hi
GO AWAY

Chapter Two

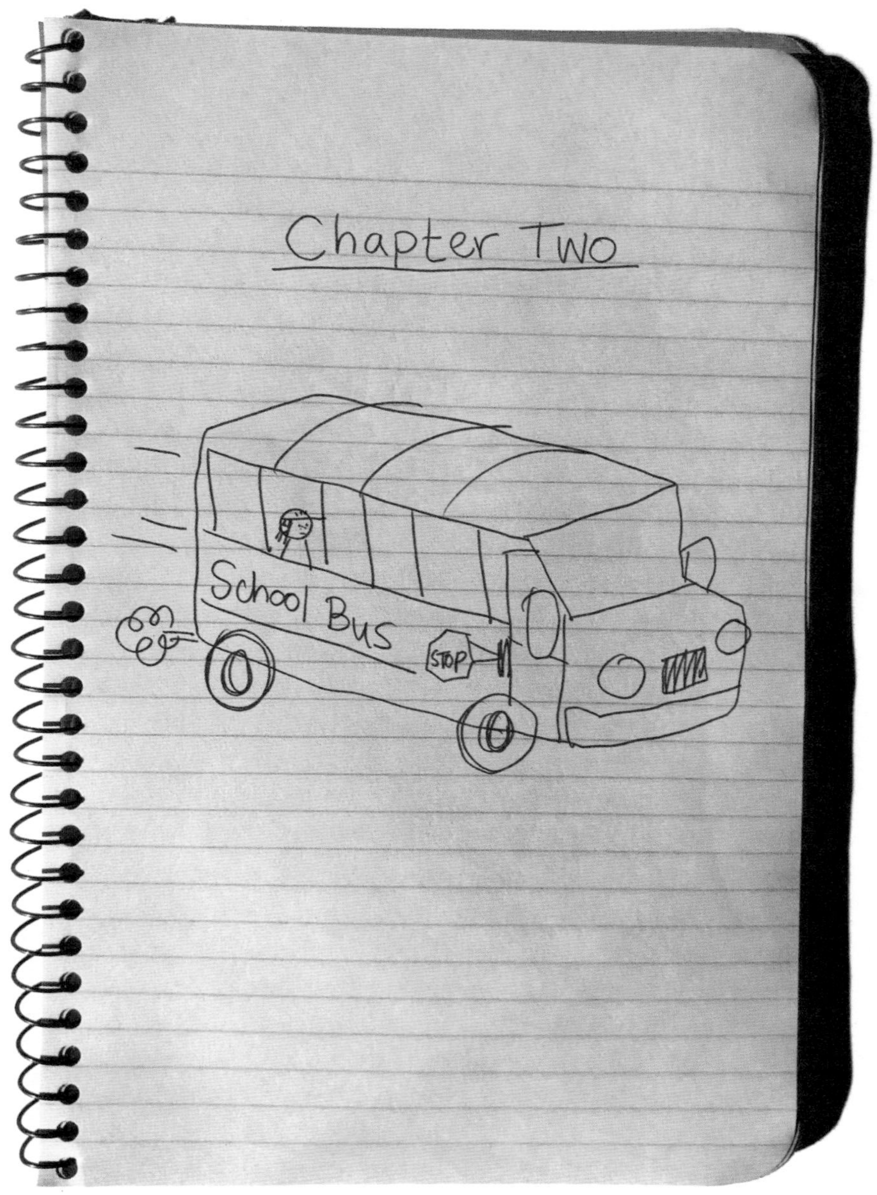
School Bus
STOP

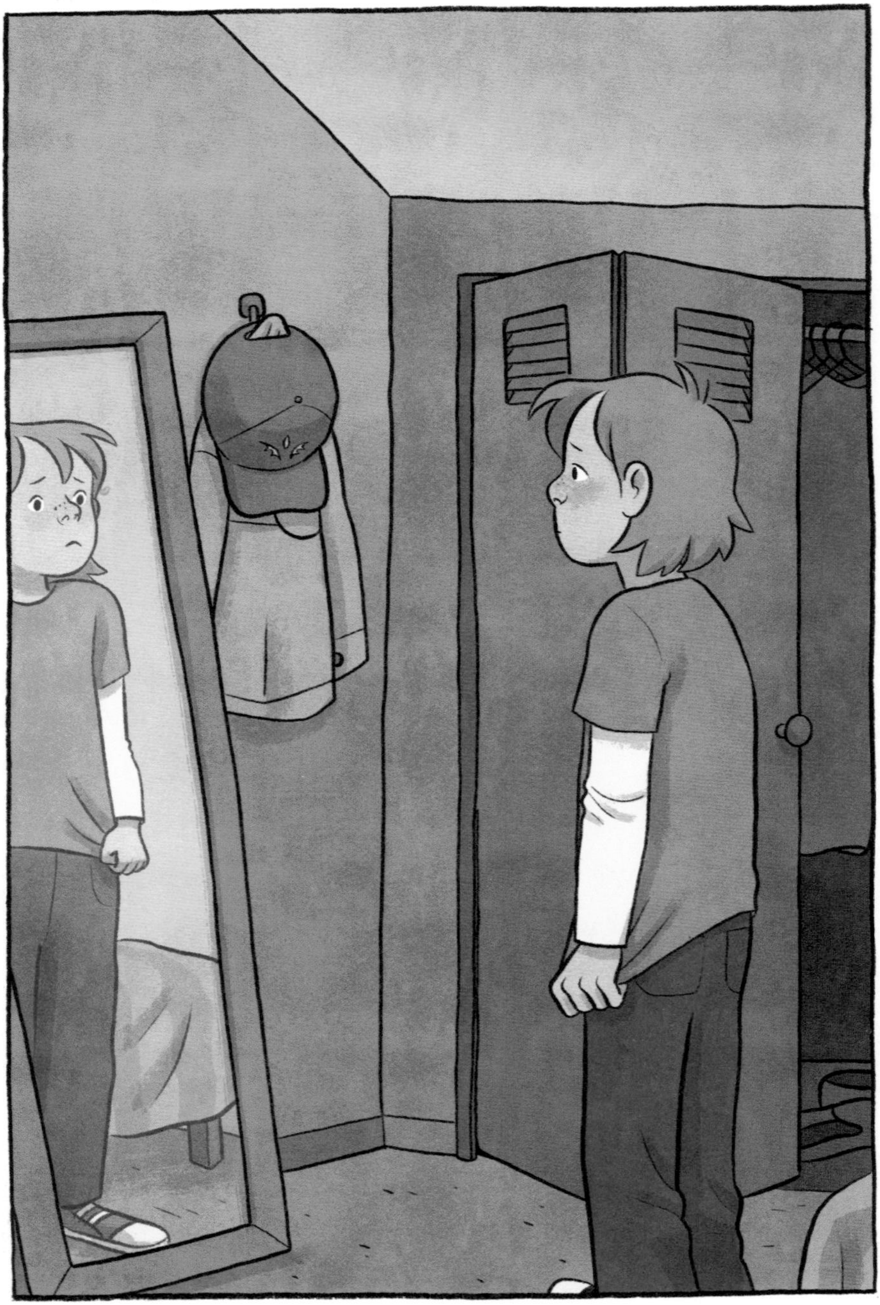

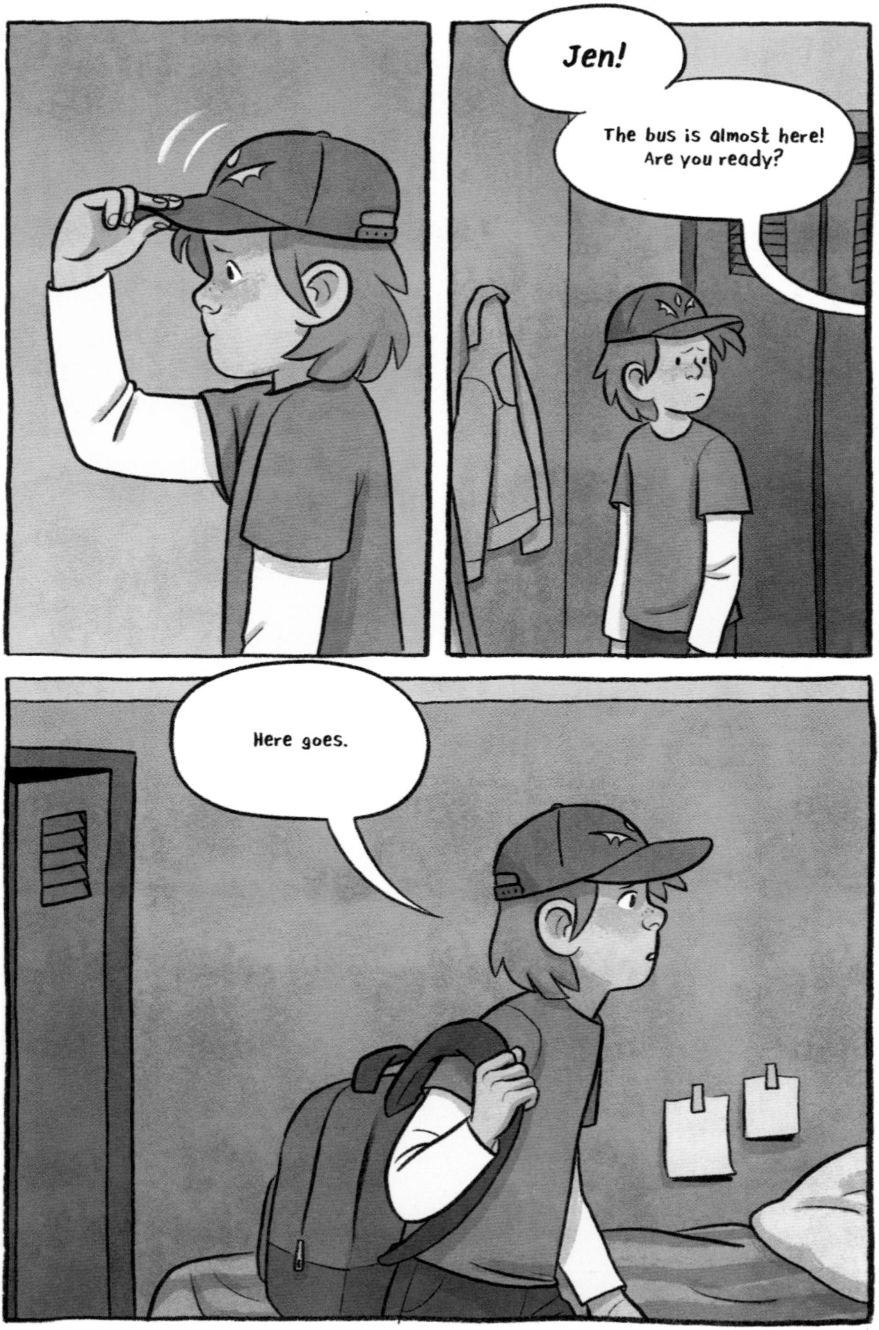
Jen!
The bus is almost here! Are you ready?
Here goes.

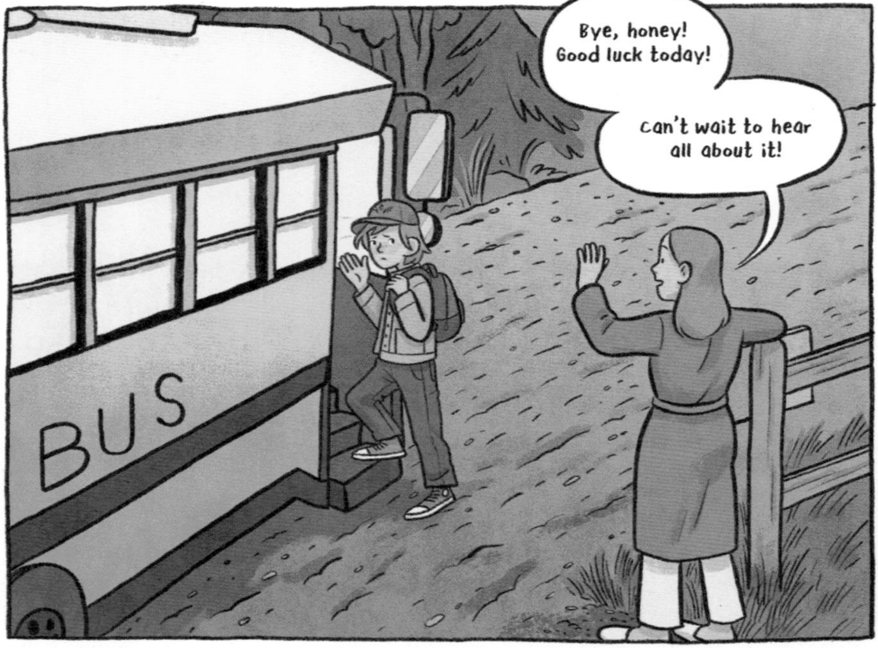
Bye, honey!
Good luck today!
can't wait to hear
all about it!
BUS

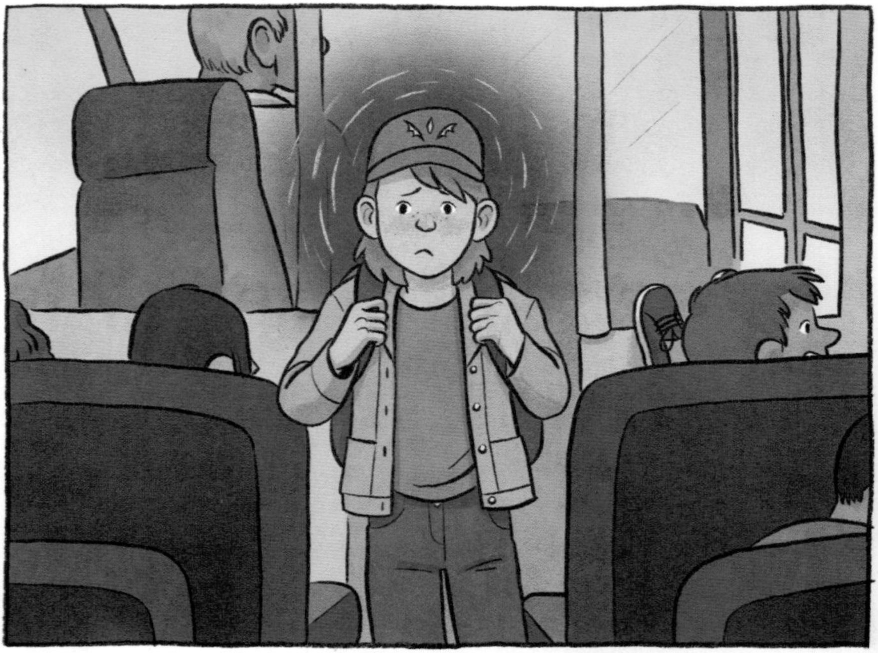

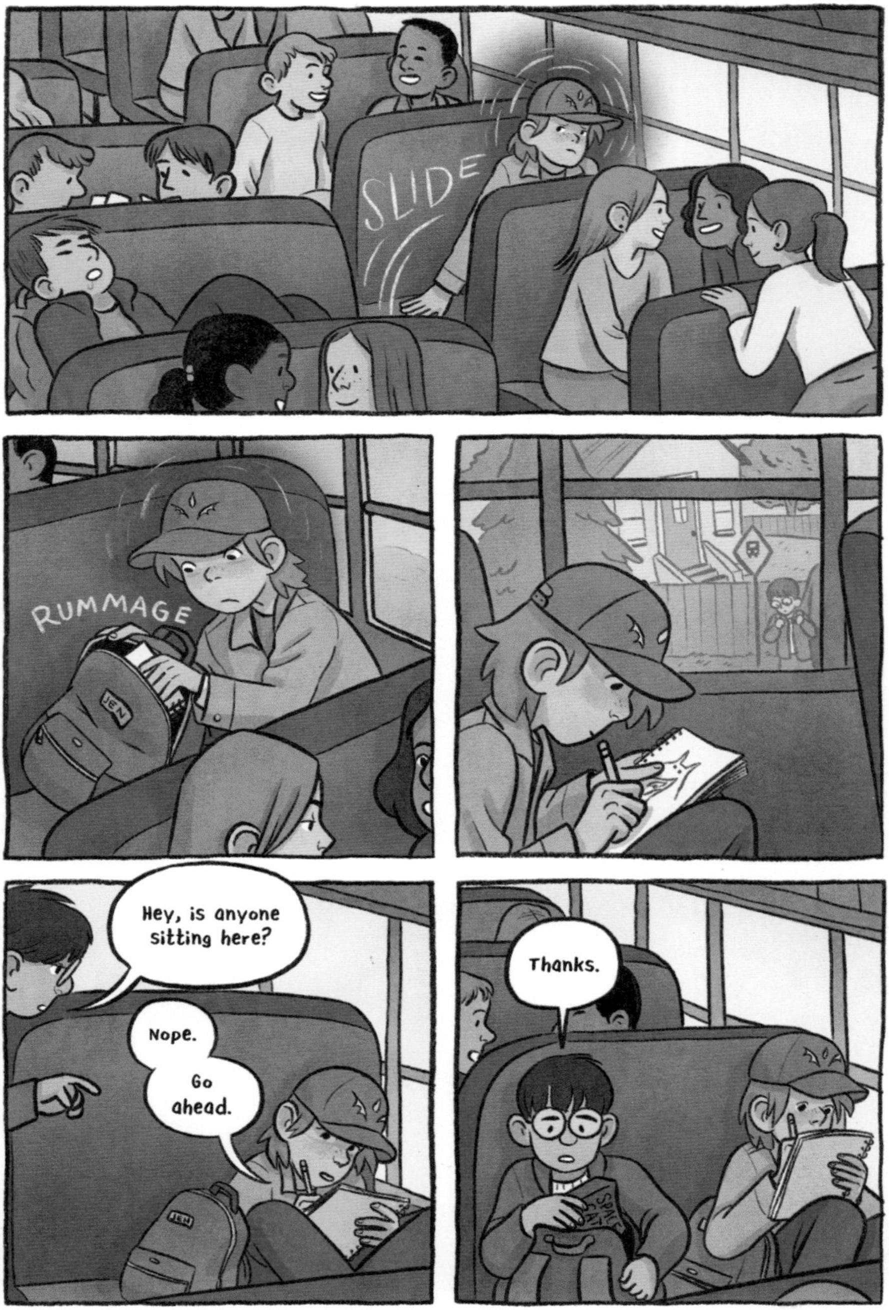
SLIDE
RUMMAGE
JEN
Hey, is anyone sitting here?
Nope.
Go ahead.
JEN
Thanks.

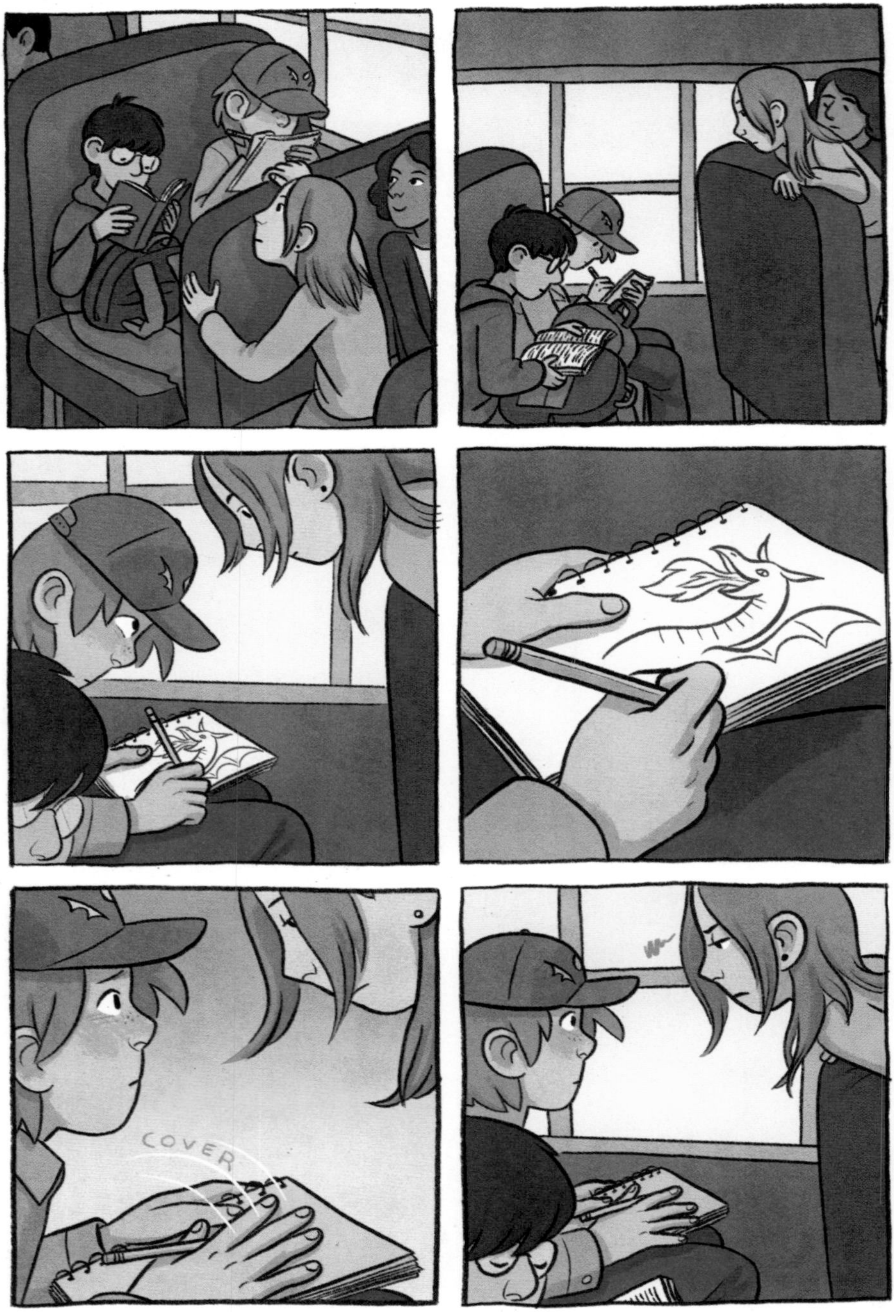
COVER

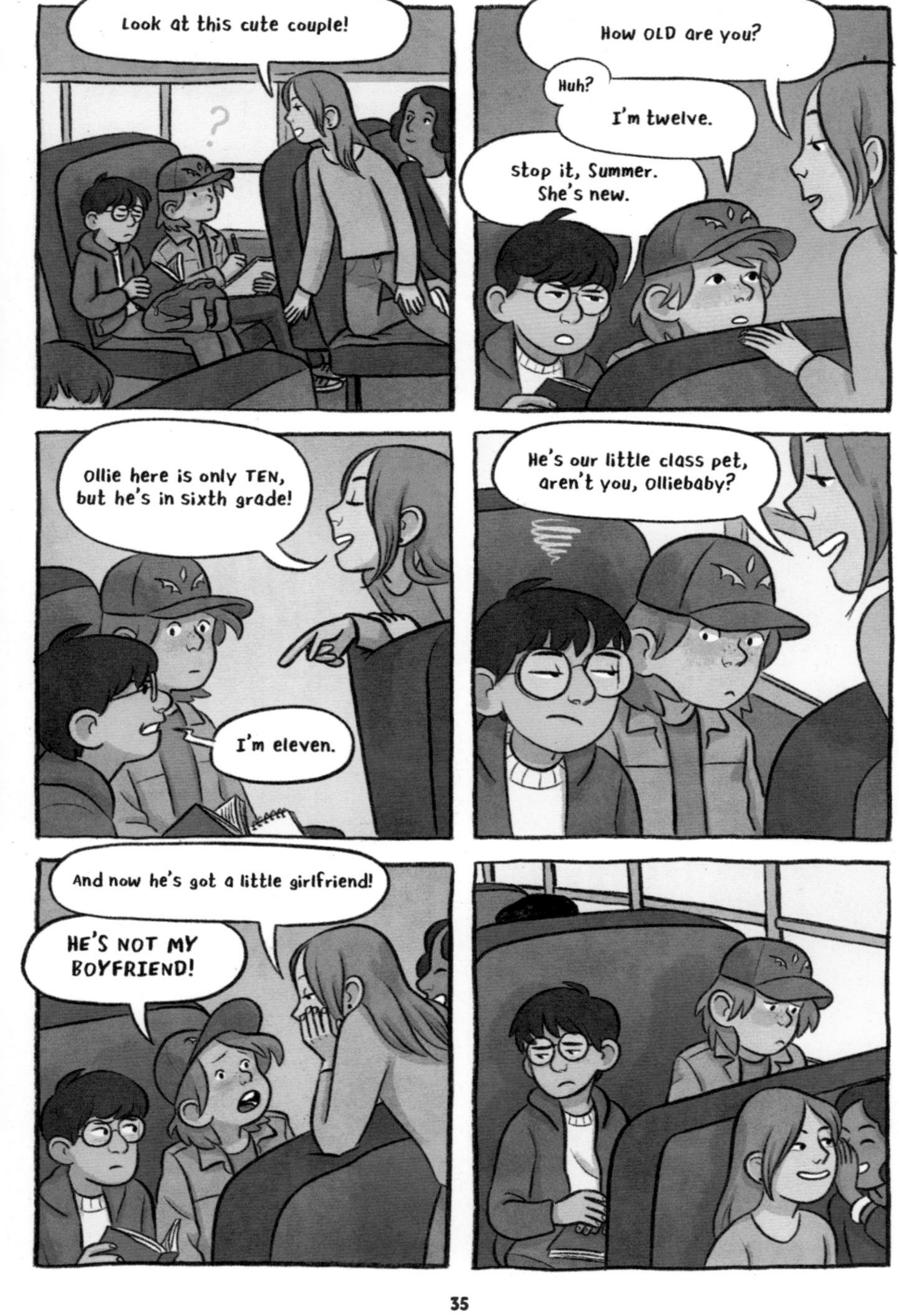

Look at this cute couple!
How OLD are you?
Huh?
I'm twelve.
Stop it, Summer. She's new.
Ollie here is only TEN, but he's in sixth grade!
I'm eleven.
He's our little class pet, aren't you, Olliebaby?
And now he's got a little girlfriend!
HE'S NOT MY BOYFRIEND!

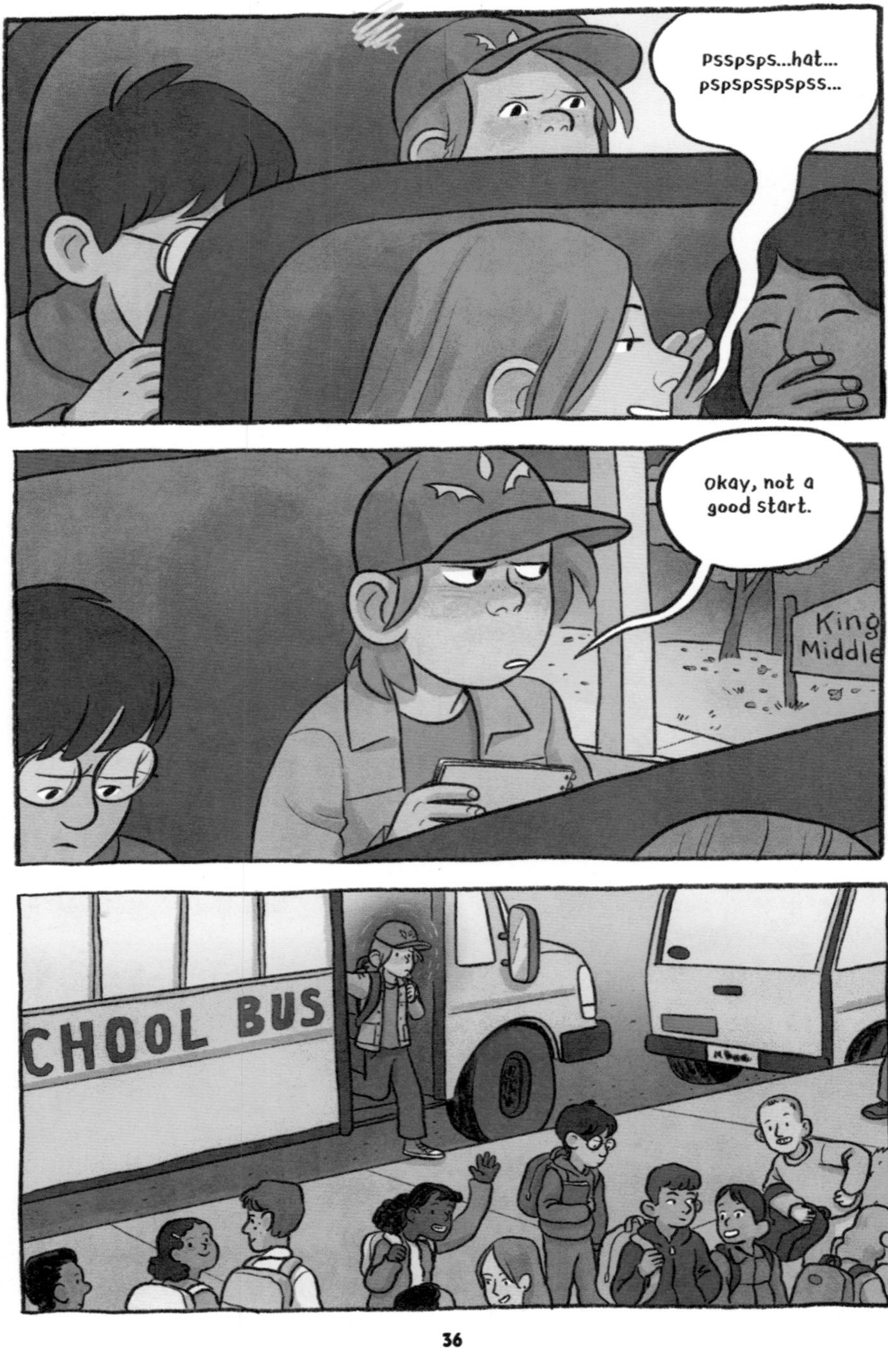
pssps ps...hat... pspspsspspss...
okay, not a good start.
King
Middle
CHOOL BUS

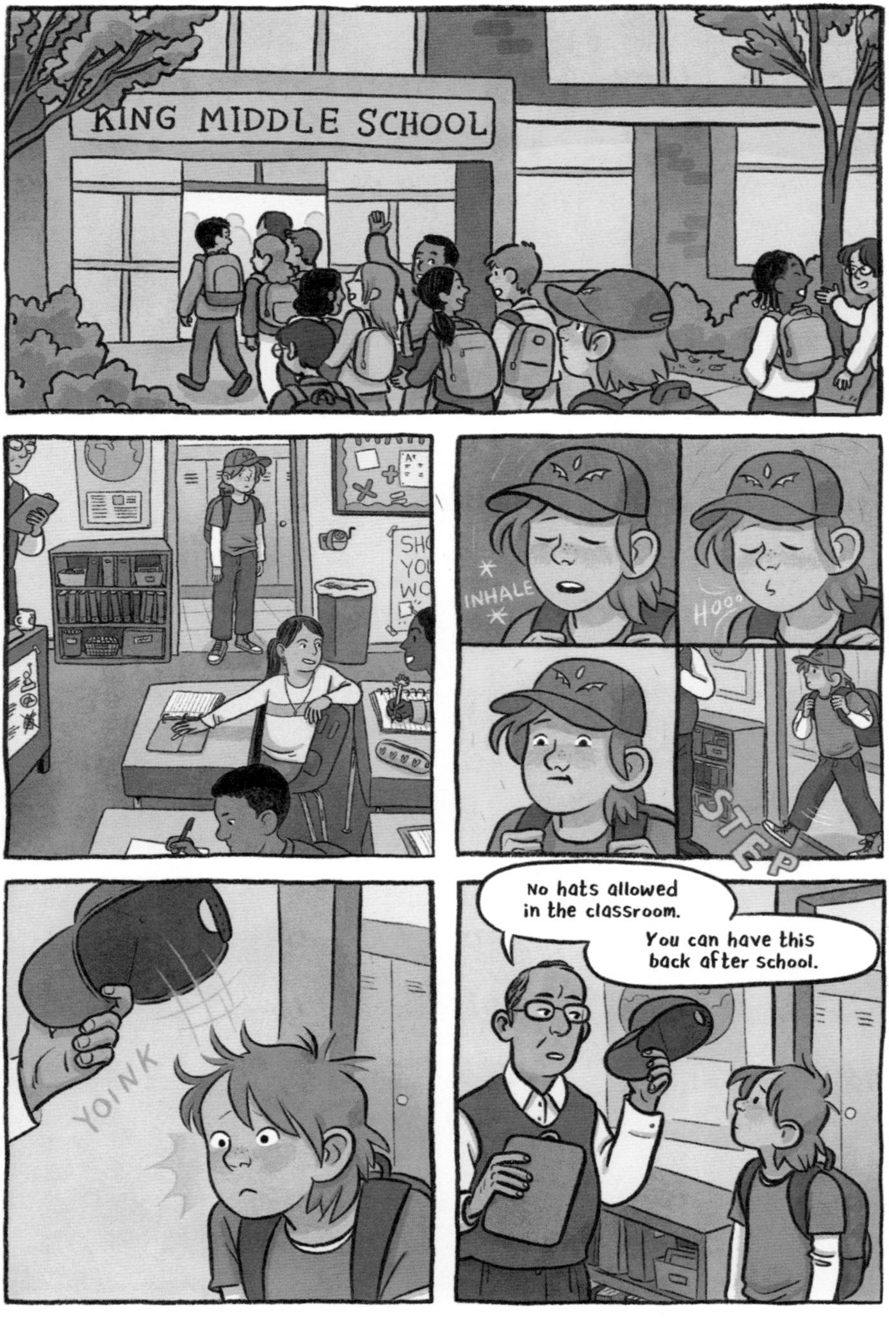
KING MIDDLE SCHOOL
INHALE
HOOO
STEP
YOINK
No hats allowed in the classroom.
You can have this back after school.

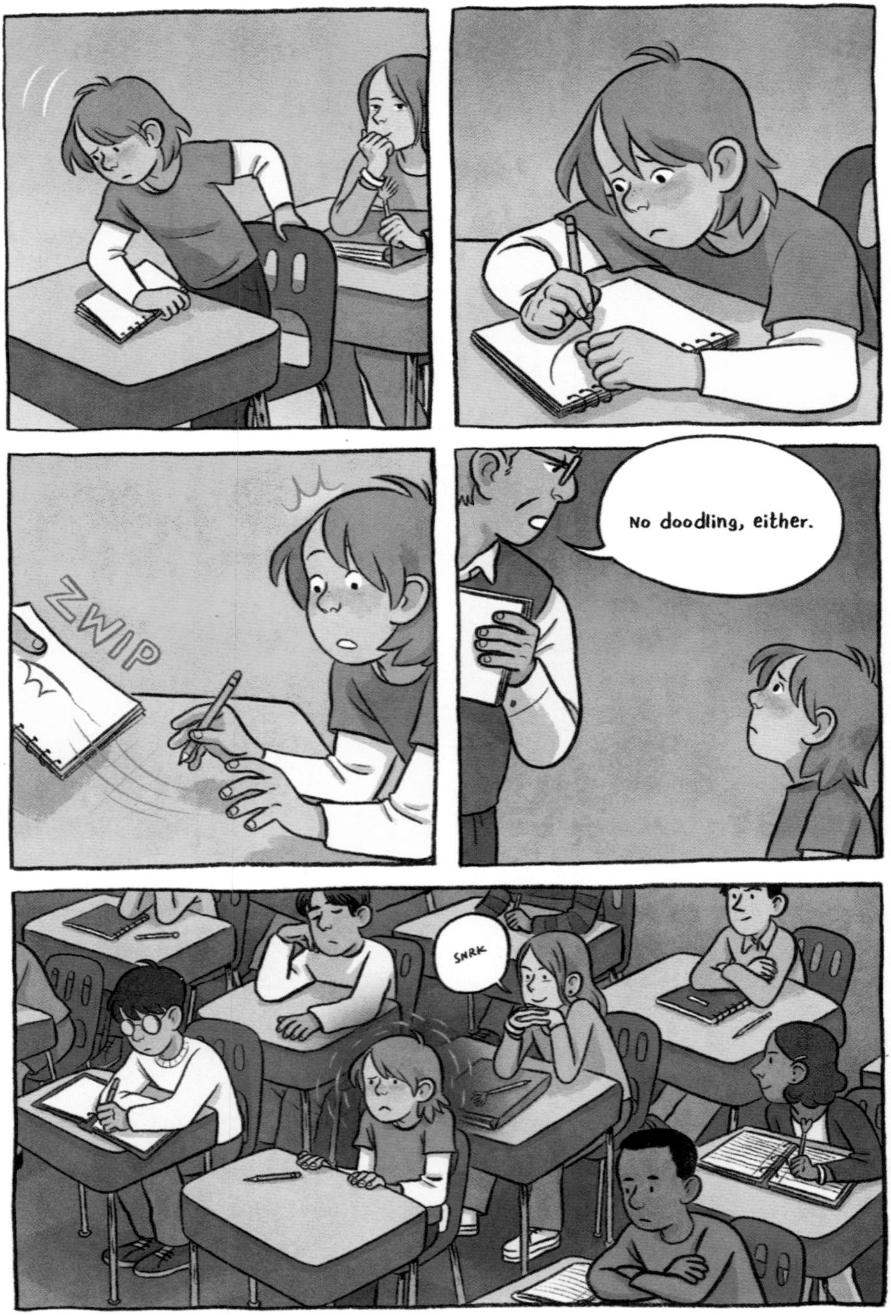
ZWIP
No doodling, either.
SNRK

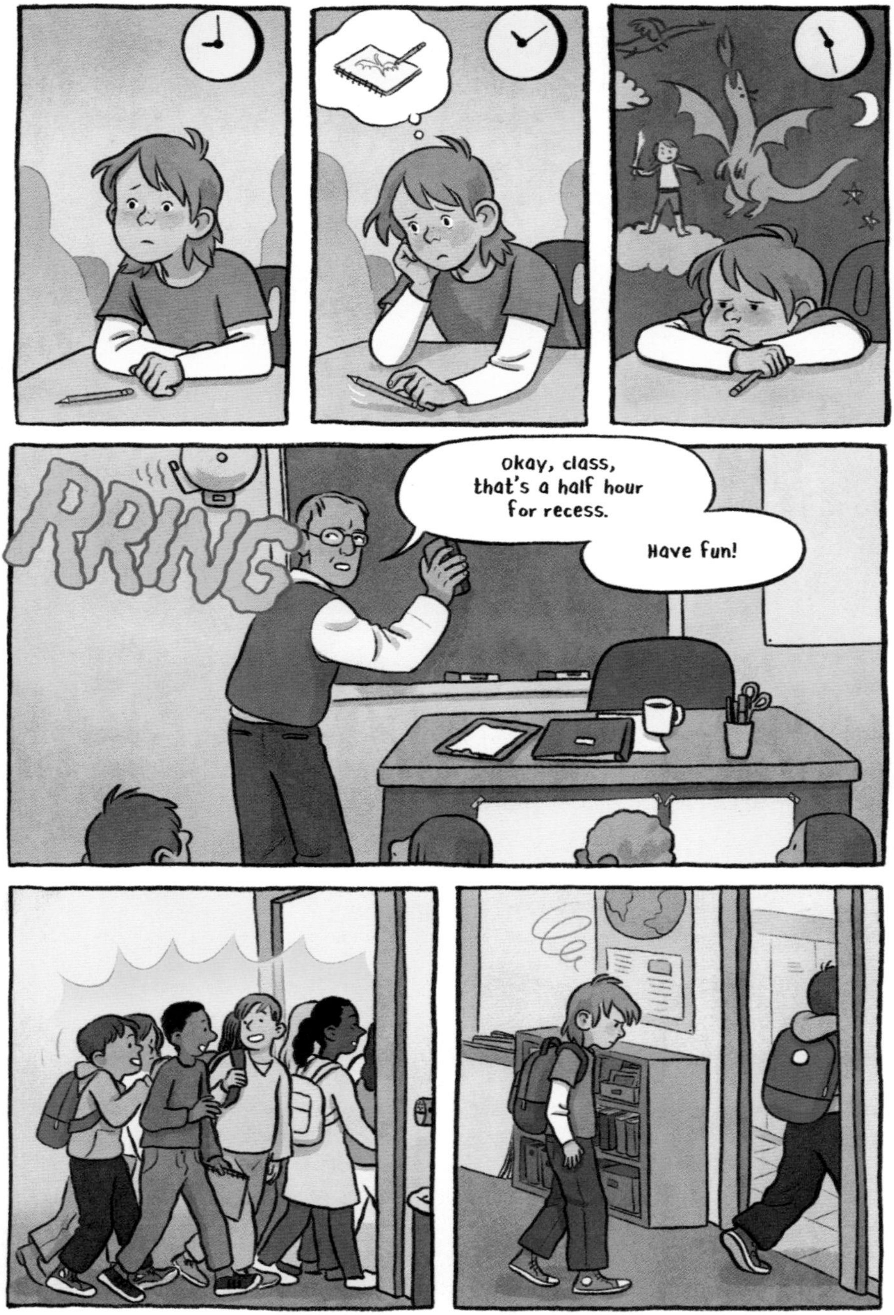
RRING
Okay, class, that's a half hour for recess.
Have fun!

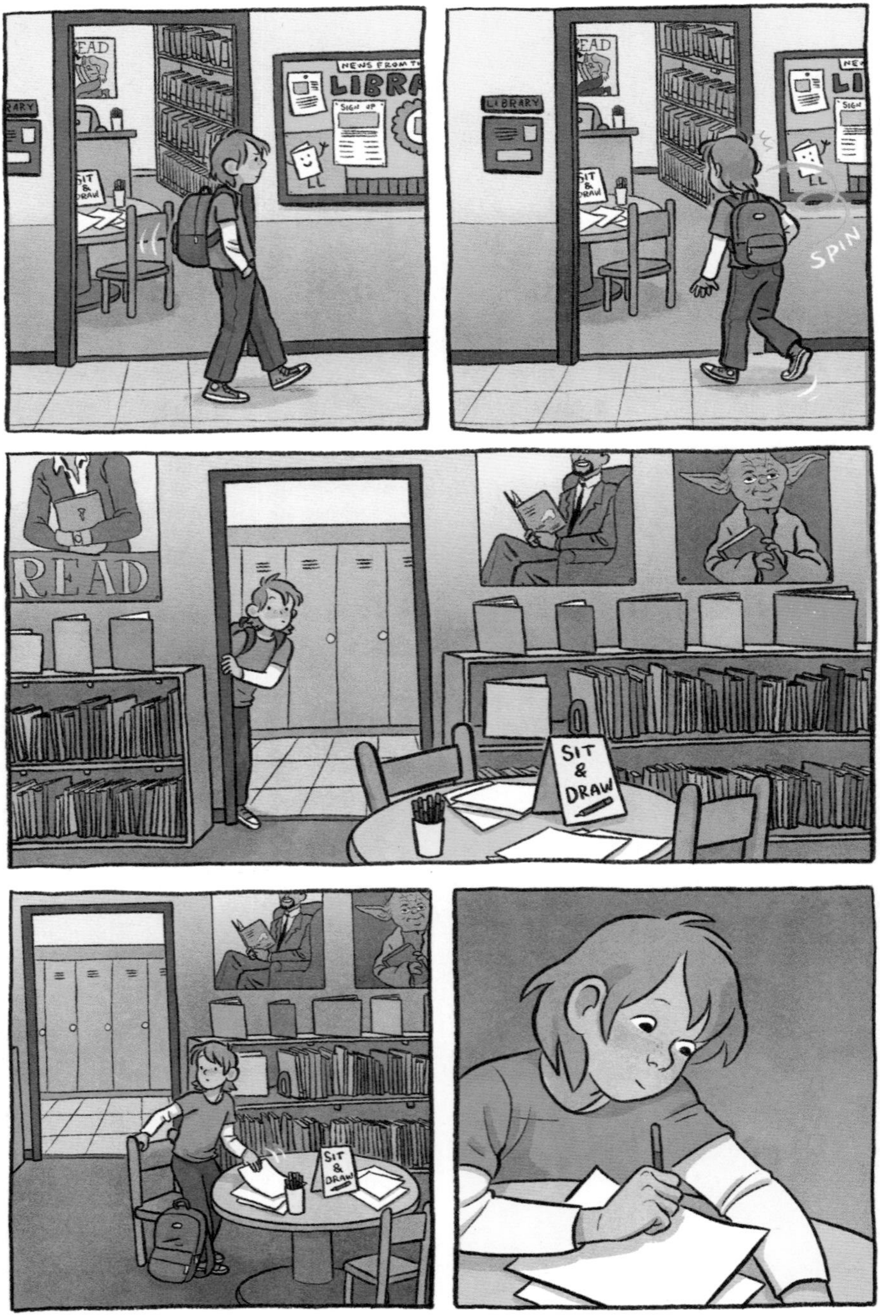
NEWS FROM TH
SIGN UP
SIT & DRAW
LIBRARY
SPIN
READ
SIT & DRAW
SIT & DRAW

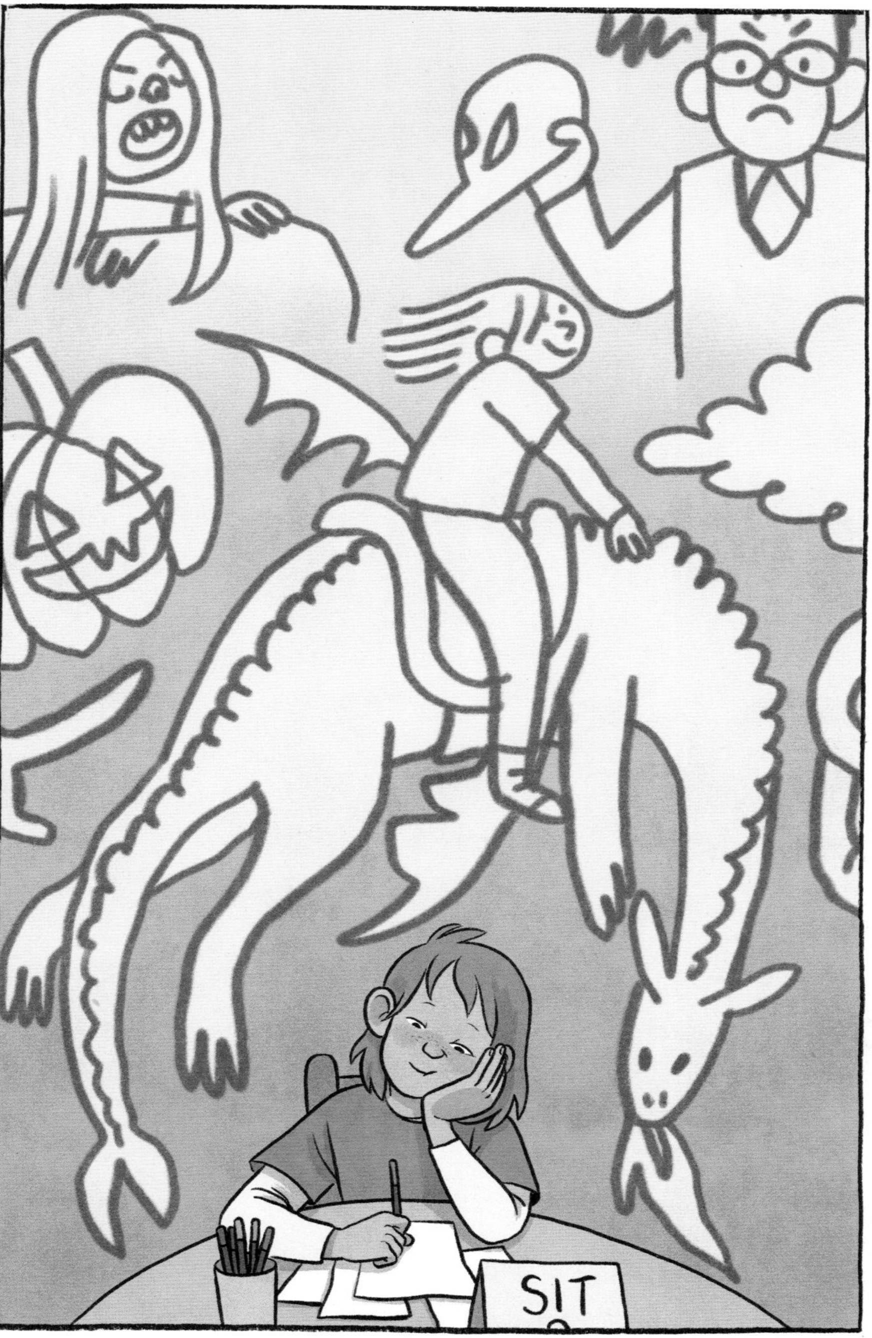
SIT

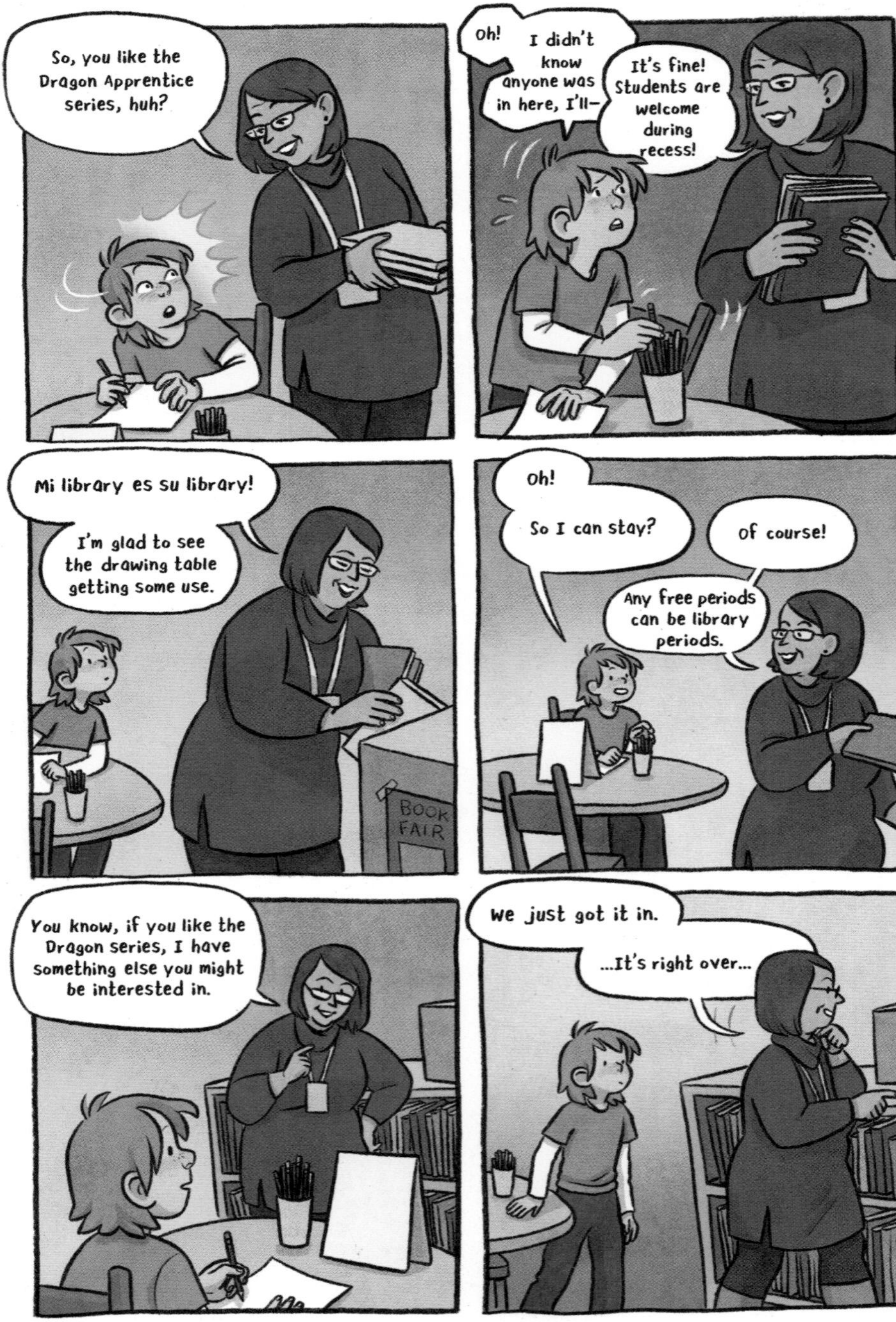
So, you like the Dragon Apprentice series, huh?
Oh!
I didn't know anyone was in here, I'll—
It's fine! Students are welcome during recess!
Mi library es su library!
I'm glad to see the drawing table getting some use.
BOOK FAIR
Oh!
So I can stay?
Of course!
Any free periods can be library periods.
You know, if you like the Dragon series, I have something else you might be interested in.
We just got it in.
...It's right over...

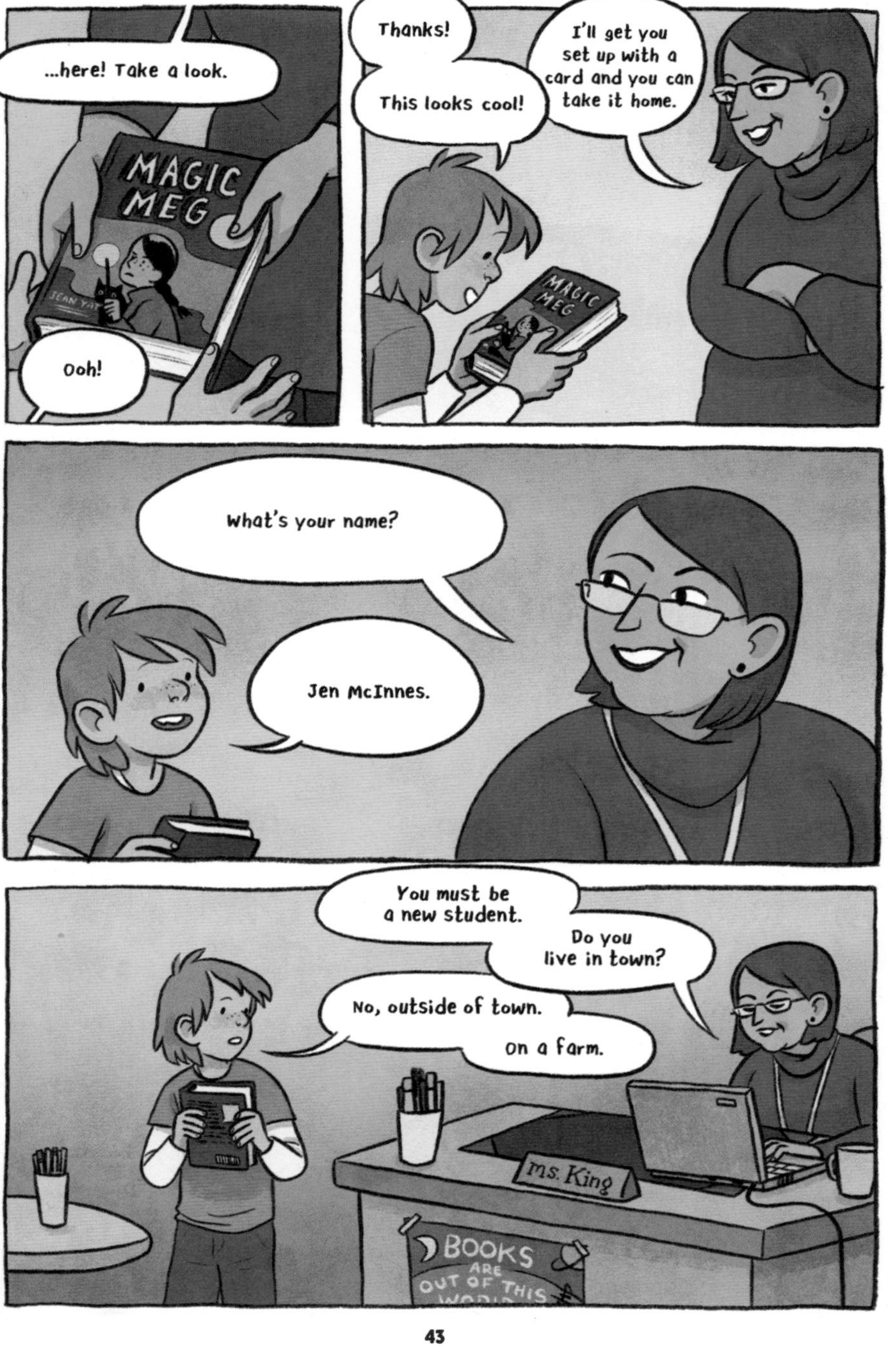
...here! Take a look.
MAGIC MEG
JEAN YAT
Ooh!
Thanks!
This looks cool!
I'll get you set up with a card and you can take it home.
MAGIC MEG
What's your name?
Jen McInnes.
You must be a new student.
Do you live in town?
No, outside of town.
On a farm.
Ms. King
BOOKS ARE OUT OF THIS

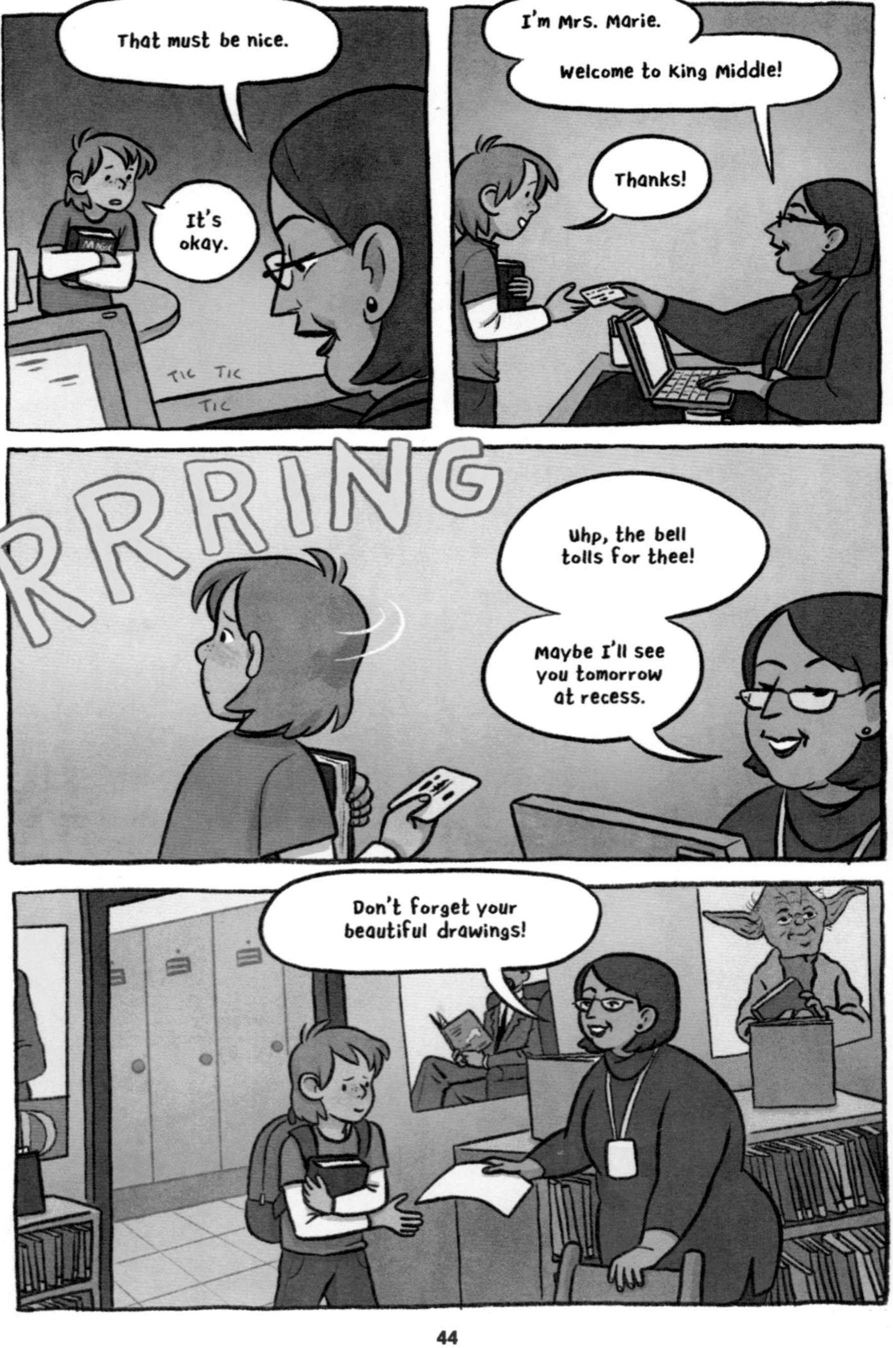
That must be nice.
It's okay.
TIC TIC
TIC
I'm Mrs. Marie.
Welcome to King Middle!
Thanks!
RRRING
Uhp, the bell tolls for thee!
Maybe I'll see you tomorrow at recess.
Don't forget your beautiful drawings!

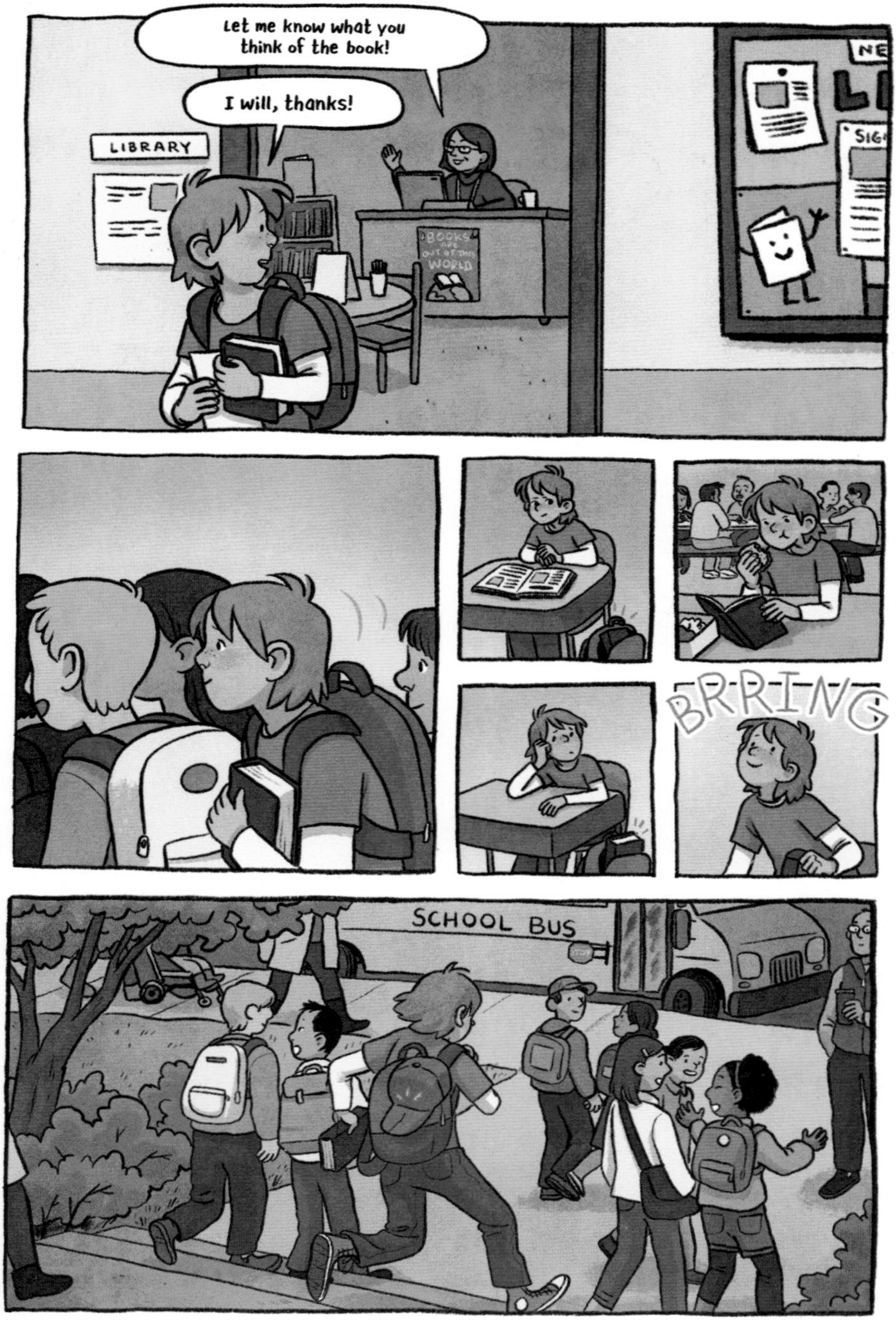
Let me know what you think of the book!
I will, thanks!
LIBRARY
BOOKS ARE OUT OF THIS WORLD
BRRING
SCHOOL BUS

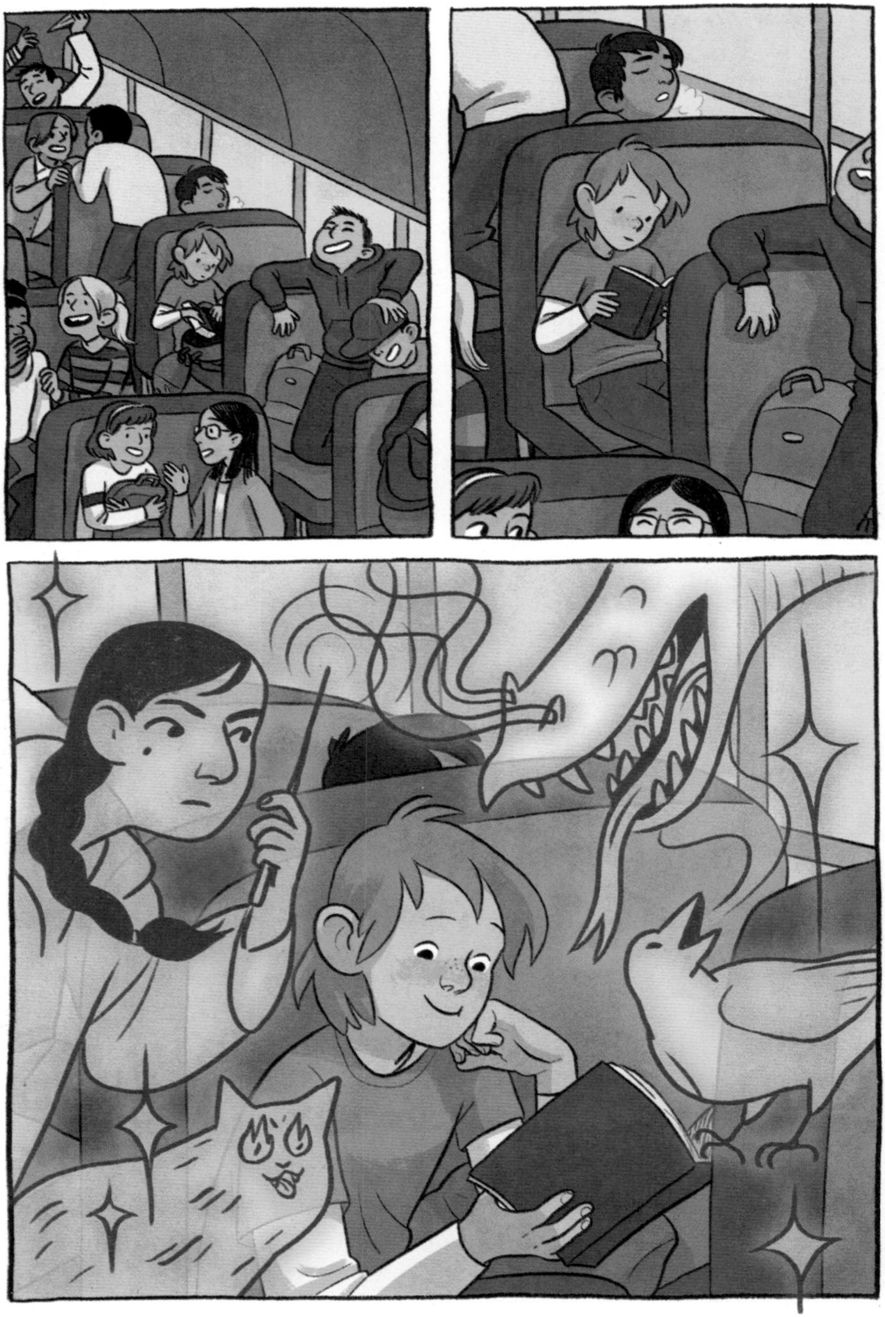

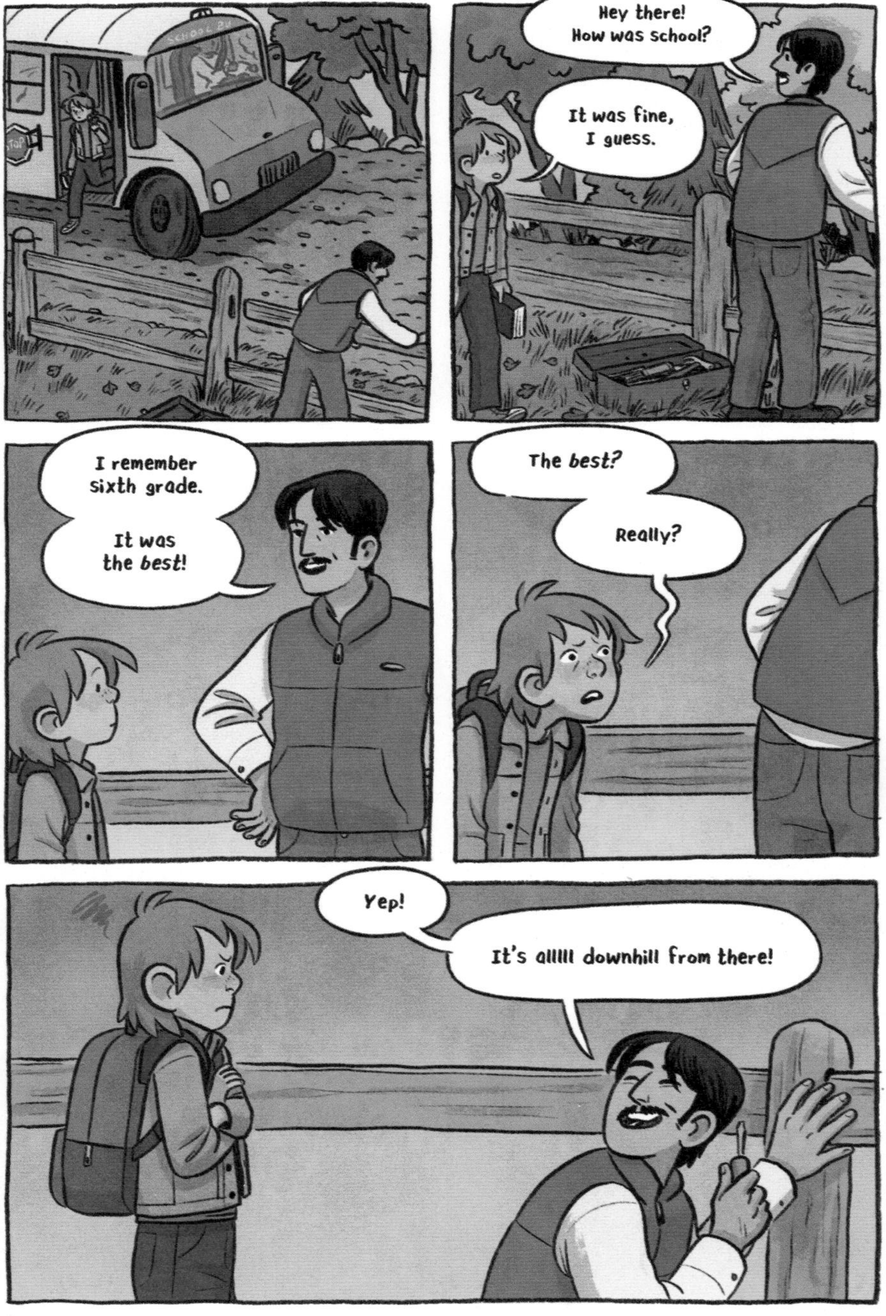

Hey there! How was school?
It was fine, I guess.
I remember sixth grade.
It was the *best*!
The *best*?
Really?
Yep!
It's alllll downhill from there!

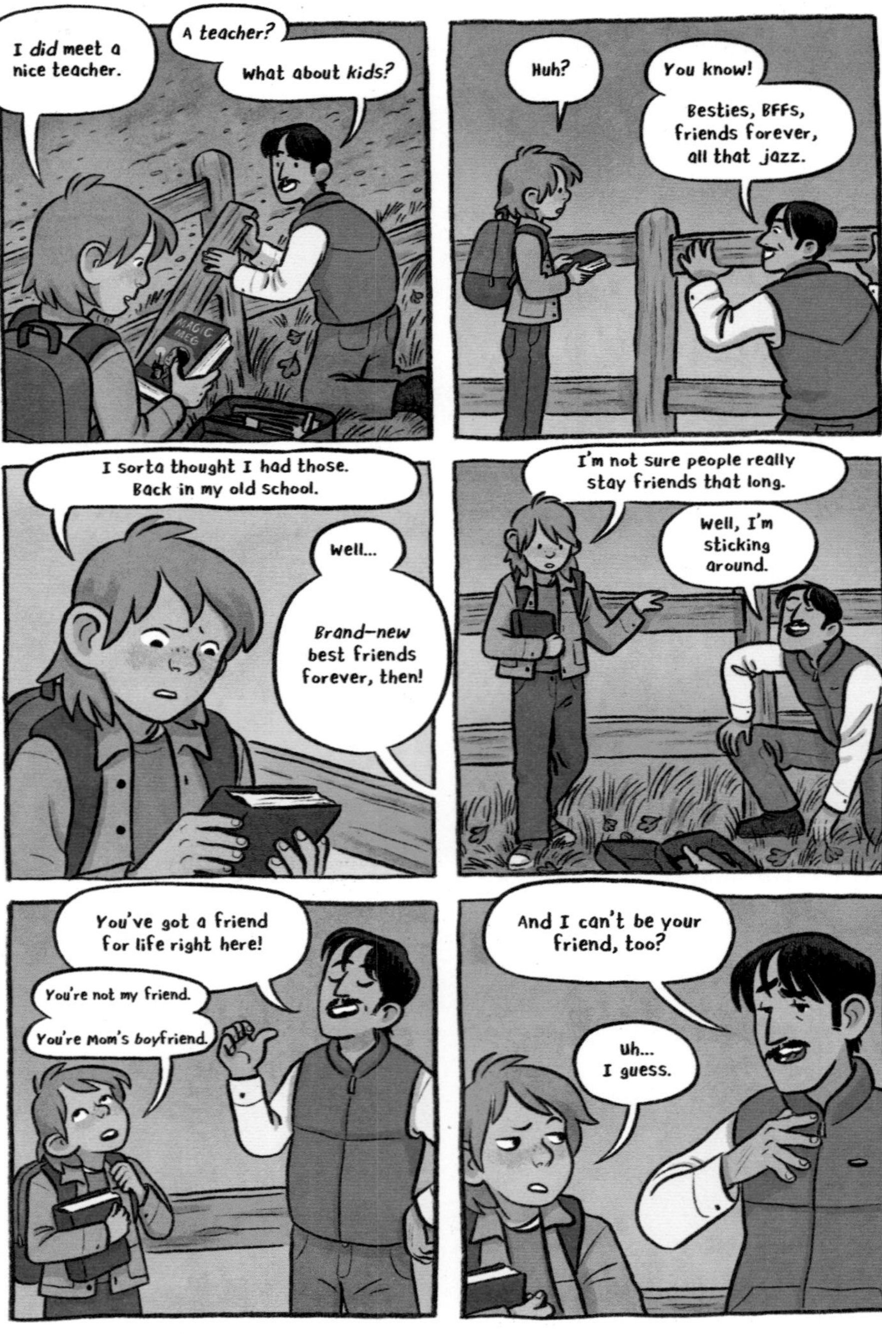
I did meet a nice teacher.
A teacher?
What about kids?
Huh?
You know!
Besties, BFFs, friends forever, all that jazz.
I sorta thought I had those. Back in my old school.
Well...
Brand-new best friends forever, then!
I'm not sure people really stay friends that long.
Well, I'm sticking around.
You've got a friend for life right here!
You're not my friend.
You're Mom's boyfriend.
And I can't be your friend, too?
Uh... I guess.

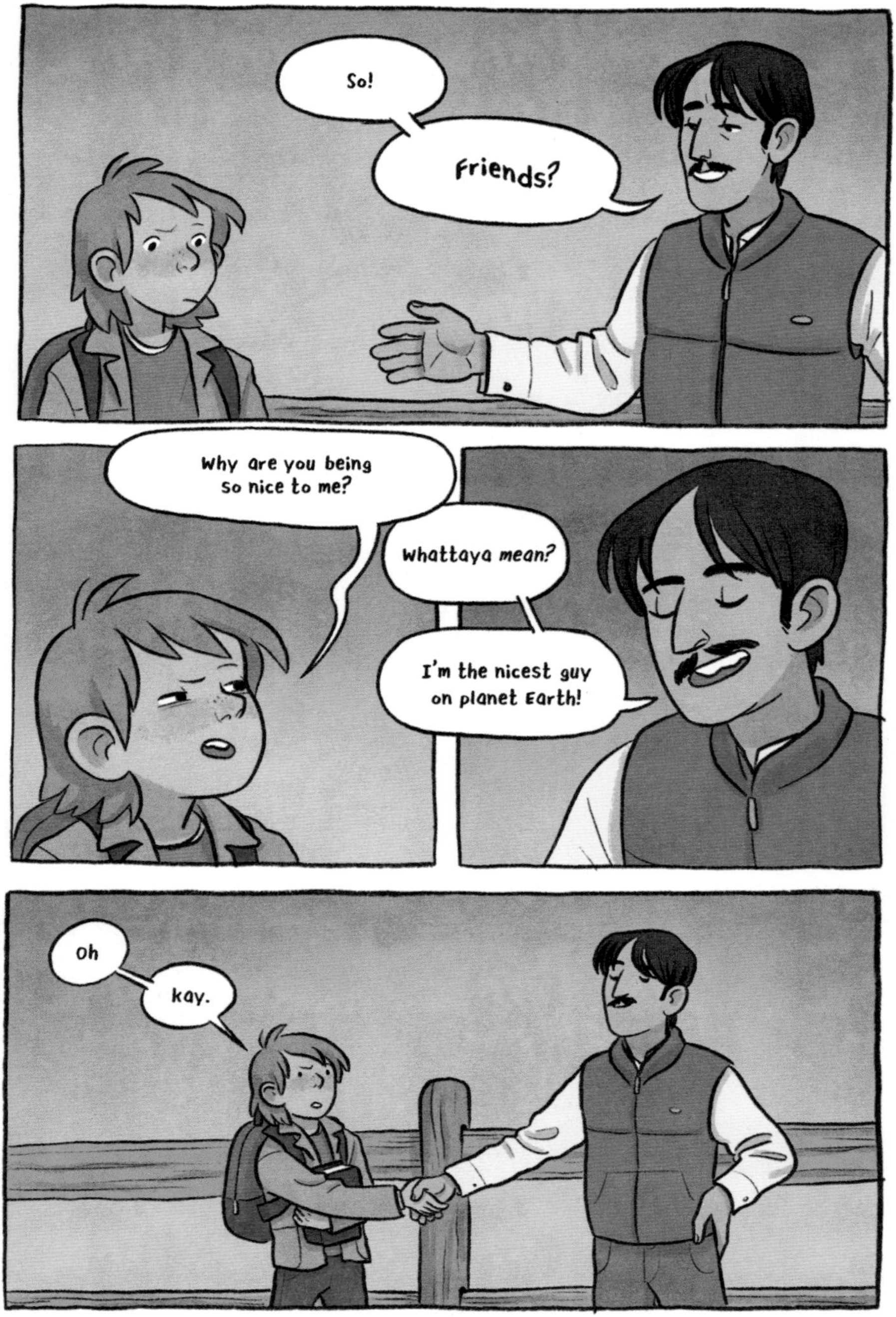
So!
Friends?
Why are you being so nice to me?
Whattaya mean?
I'm the nicest guy on planet Earth!
Oh
kay.

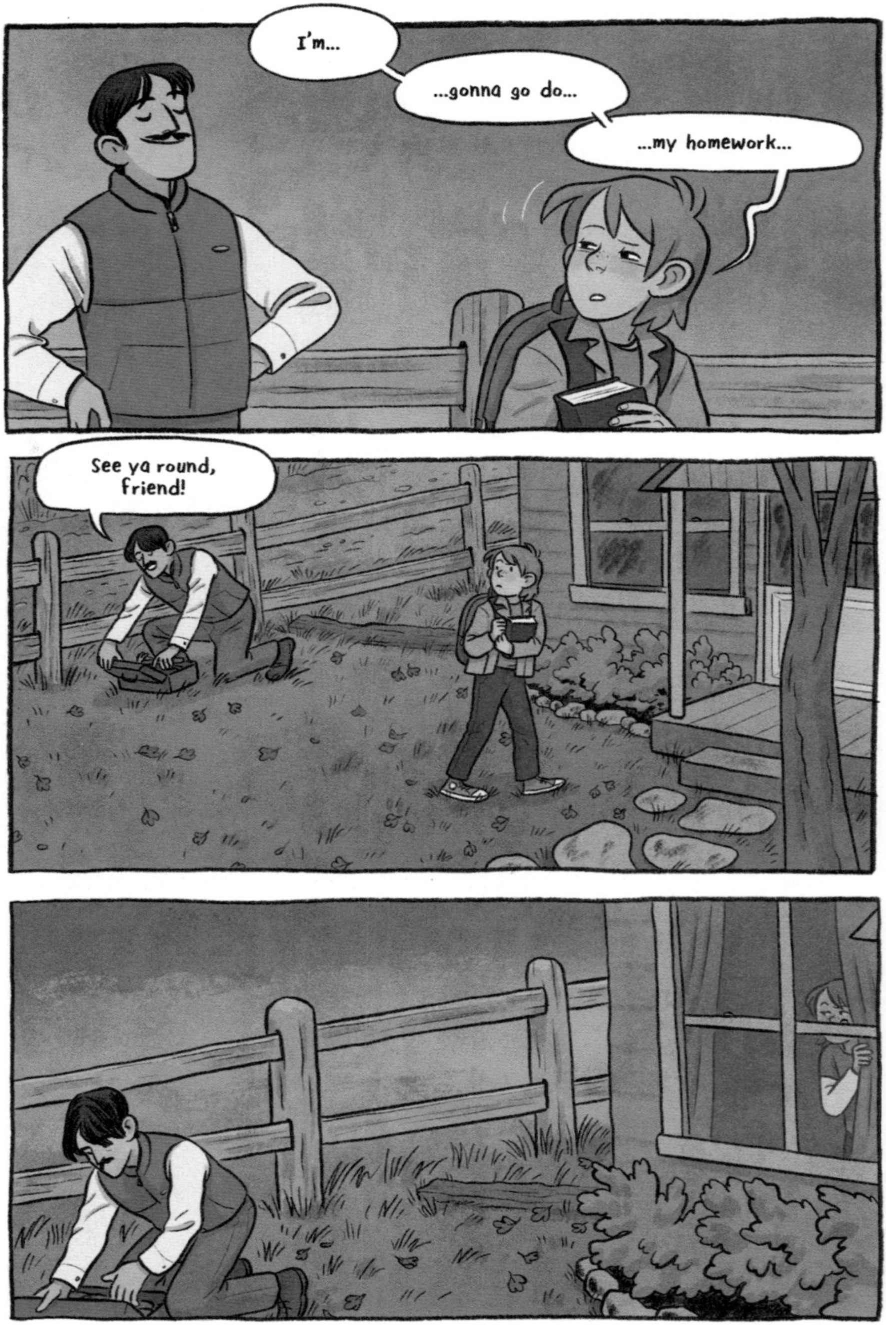
I'm...
...gonna go do...
...my homework...
See ya round, friend!

Chapter Three

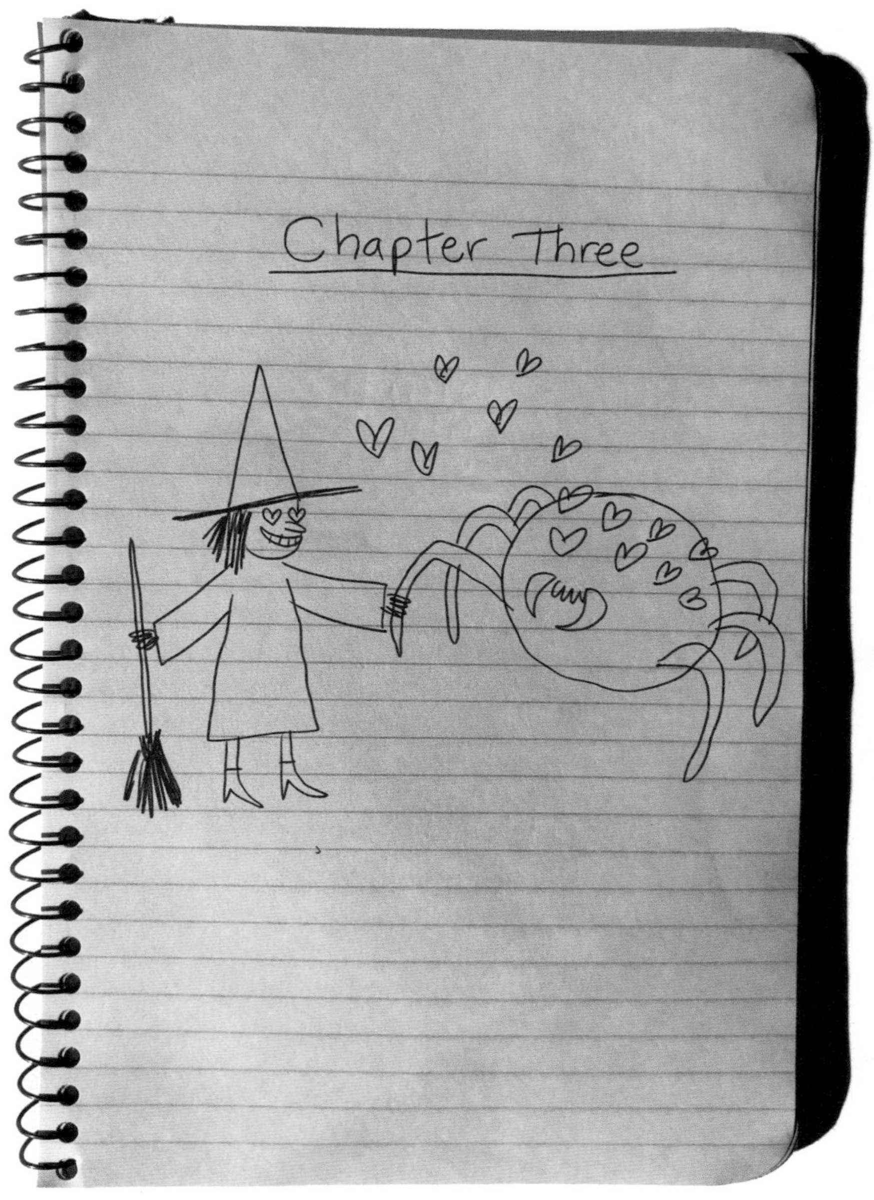

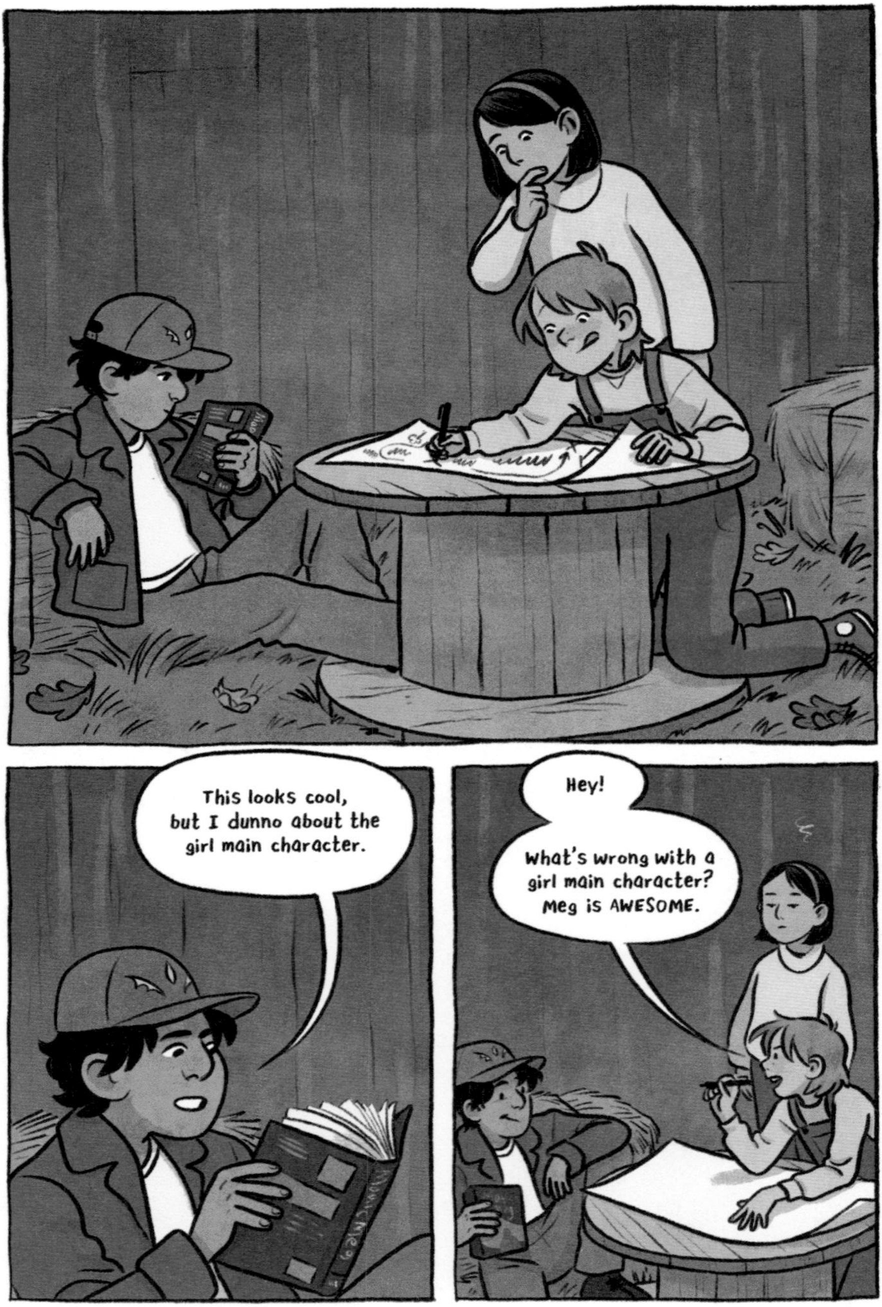
This looks cool, but I dunno about the girl main character.
Hey!
What's wrong with a girl main character? Meg is AWESOME.

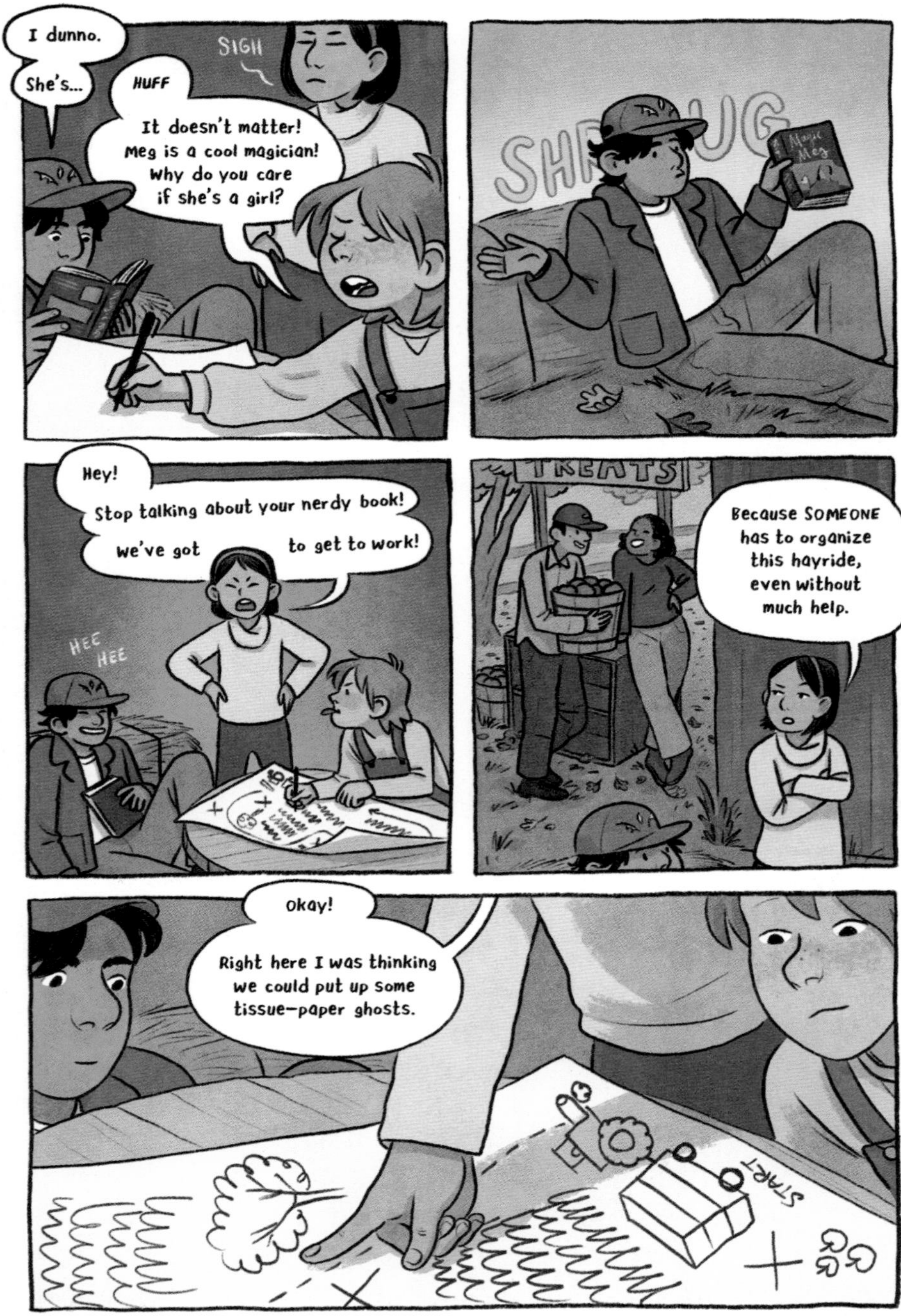
I dunno.
She's...
HUFF
It doesn't matter! Meg is a cool magician! Why do you care if she's a girl?
SIGH
SHRUG
Magic Meg
Hey!
Stop talking about your nerdy book!
We've got
to get to work!
HEE HEE
TREATS
Because SOMEONE has to organize this hayride, even without much help.
Okay!
Right here I was thinking we could put up some tissue-paper ghosts.
START

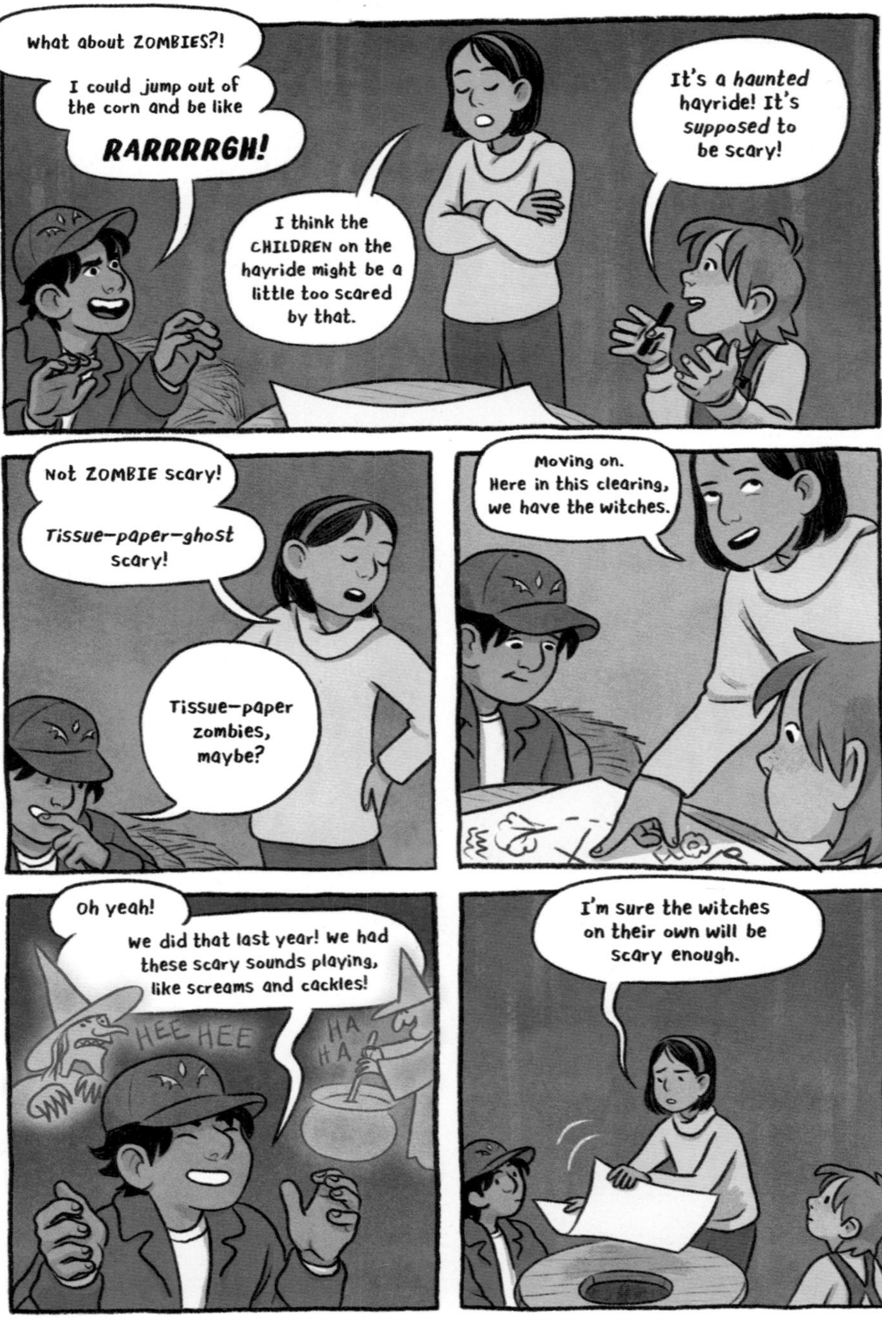
What about ZOMBIES?!
I could jump out of the corn and be like
RARRRRGH!
I think the CHILDREN on the hayride might be a little too scared by that.
It's a *haunted* hayride! It's *supposed* to be scary!
Not ZOMBIE scary!
Tissue-paper-ghost scary!
Tissue-paper zombies, maybe?
Moving on. Here in this clearing, we have the witches.
Oh yeah!
We did that last year! We had these scary sounds playing, like screams and cackles!
HEE HEE
HA HA
I'm sure the witches on their own will be scary enough.

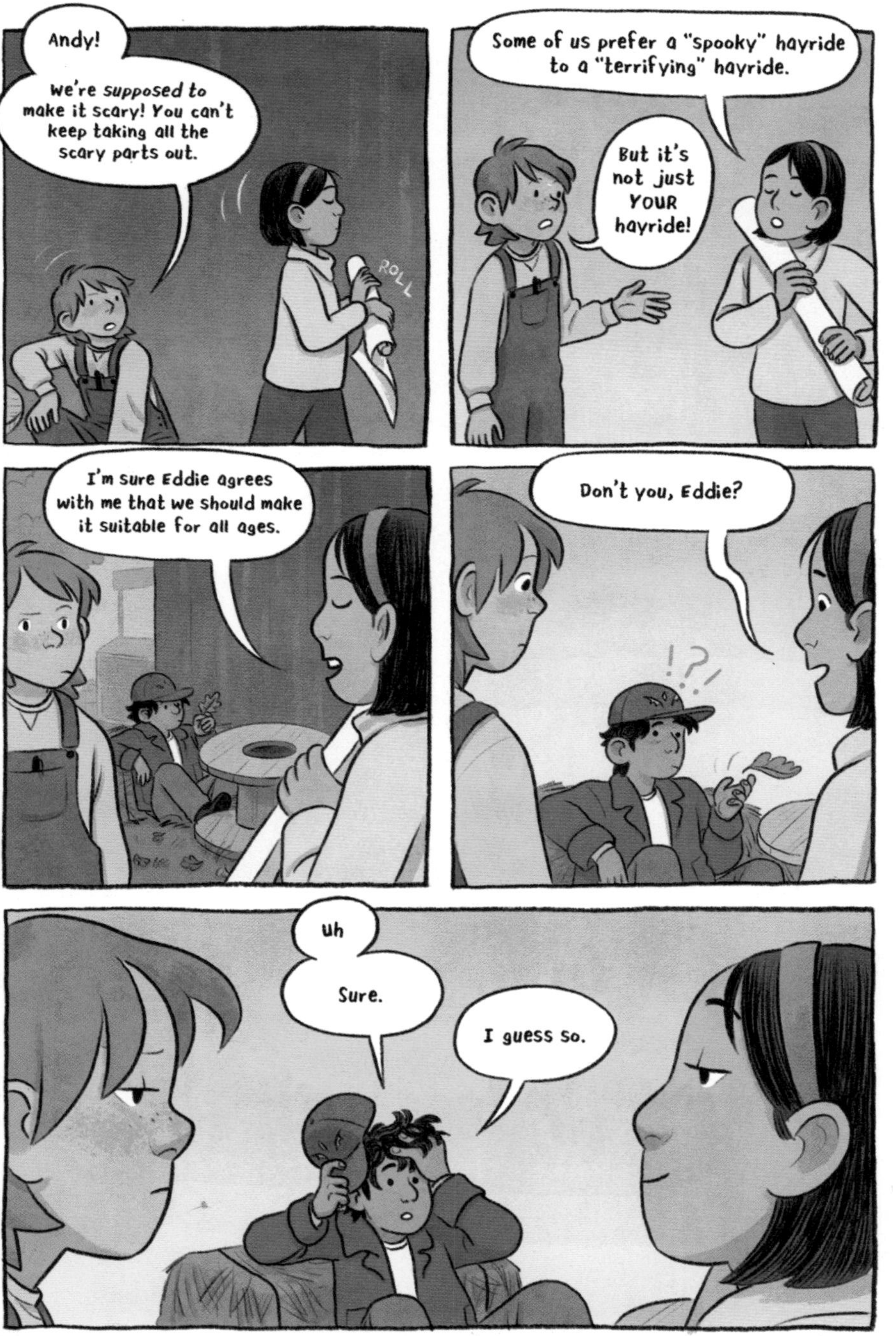
Andy!
We're *supposed* to make it scary! You can't keep taking all the scary parts out.
ROLL
Some of us prefer a "spooky" hayride to a "terrifying" hayride.
But it's not just YOUR hayride!
I'm sure Eddie agrees with me that we should make it suitable for all ages.
Don't you, Eddie?
!?!
Uh
Sure.
I guess so.

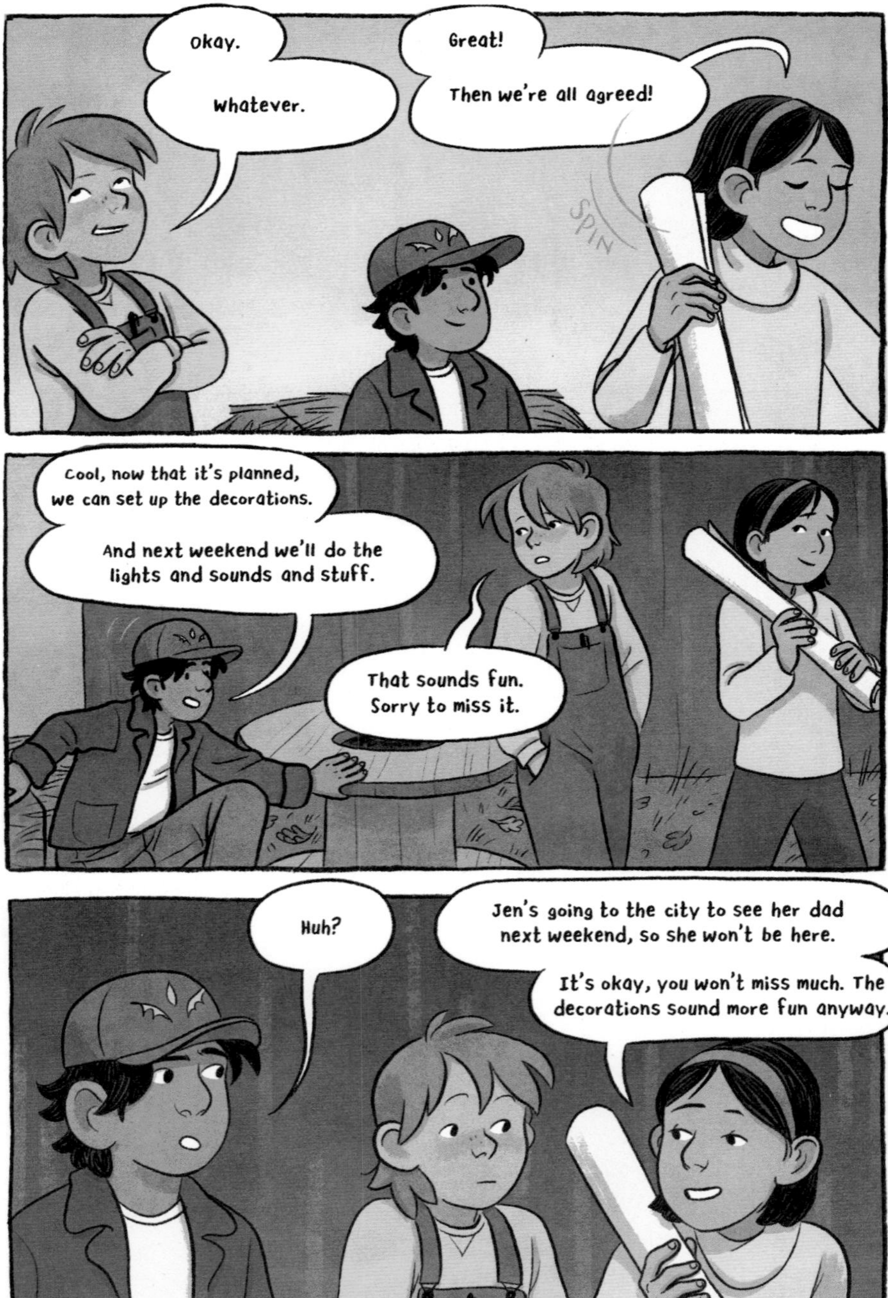
Okay.
Whatever.
Great!
Then we're all agreed!
SPIN
Cool, now that it's planned, we can set up the decorations.
And next weekend we'll do the lights and sounds and stuff.
That sounds fun. Sorry to miss it.
Huh?
Jen's going to the city to see her dad next weekend, so she won't be here.
It's okay, you won't miss much. The decorations sound more fun anyway.

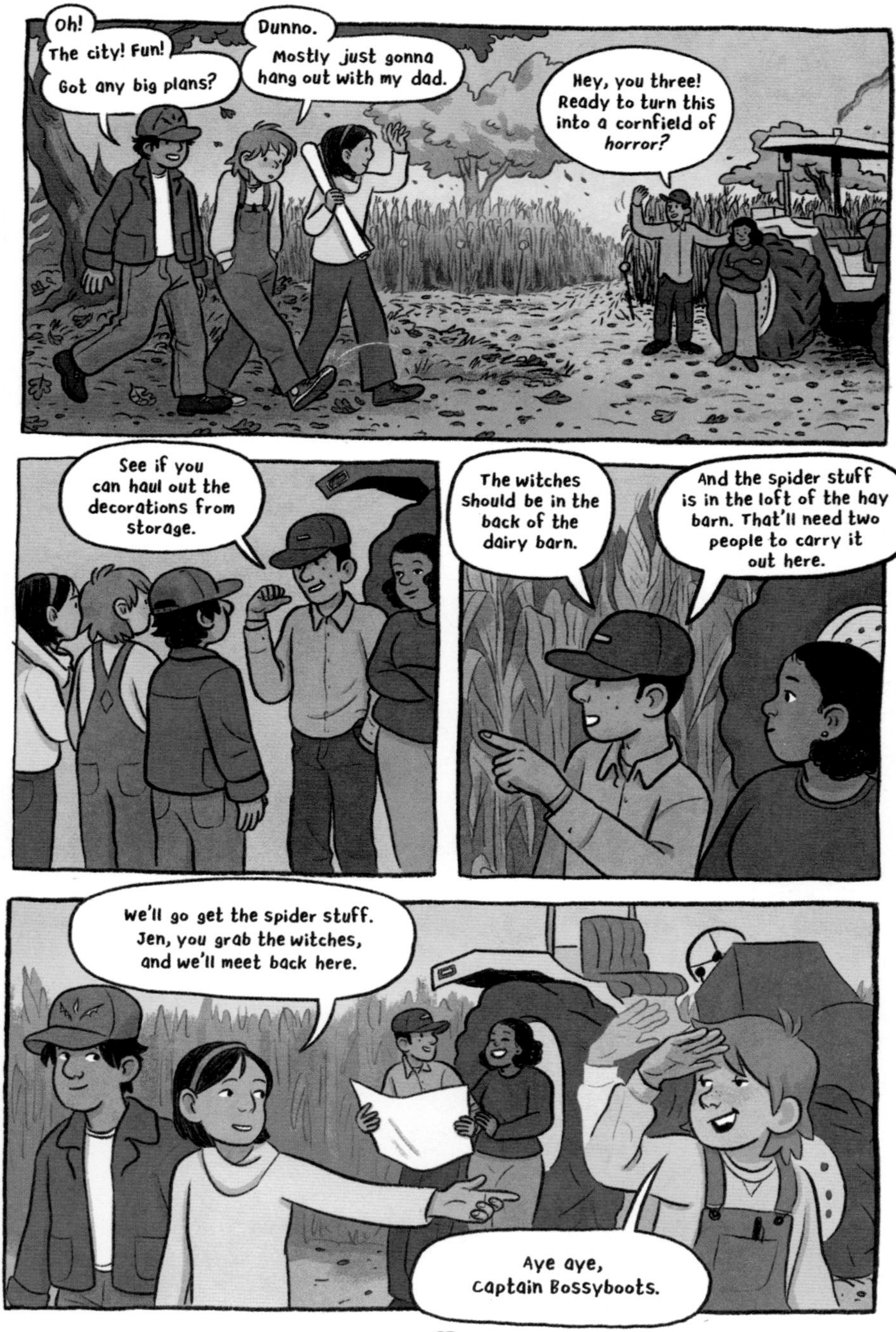

Oh!
The city! Fun!
Got any big plans?
Dunno.
Mostly just gonna hang out with my dad.
Hey, you three! Ready to turn this into a cornfield of *horror?*
See if you can haul out the decorations from storage.
The witches should be in the back of the dairy barn.
And the spider stuff is in the loft of the hay barn. That'll need two people to carry it out here.
We'll go get the spider stuff. Jen, you grab the witches, and we'll meet back here.
Aye aye, Captain Bossyboots.

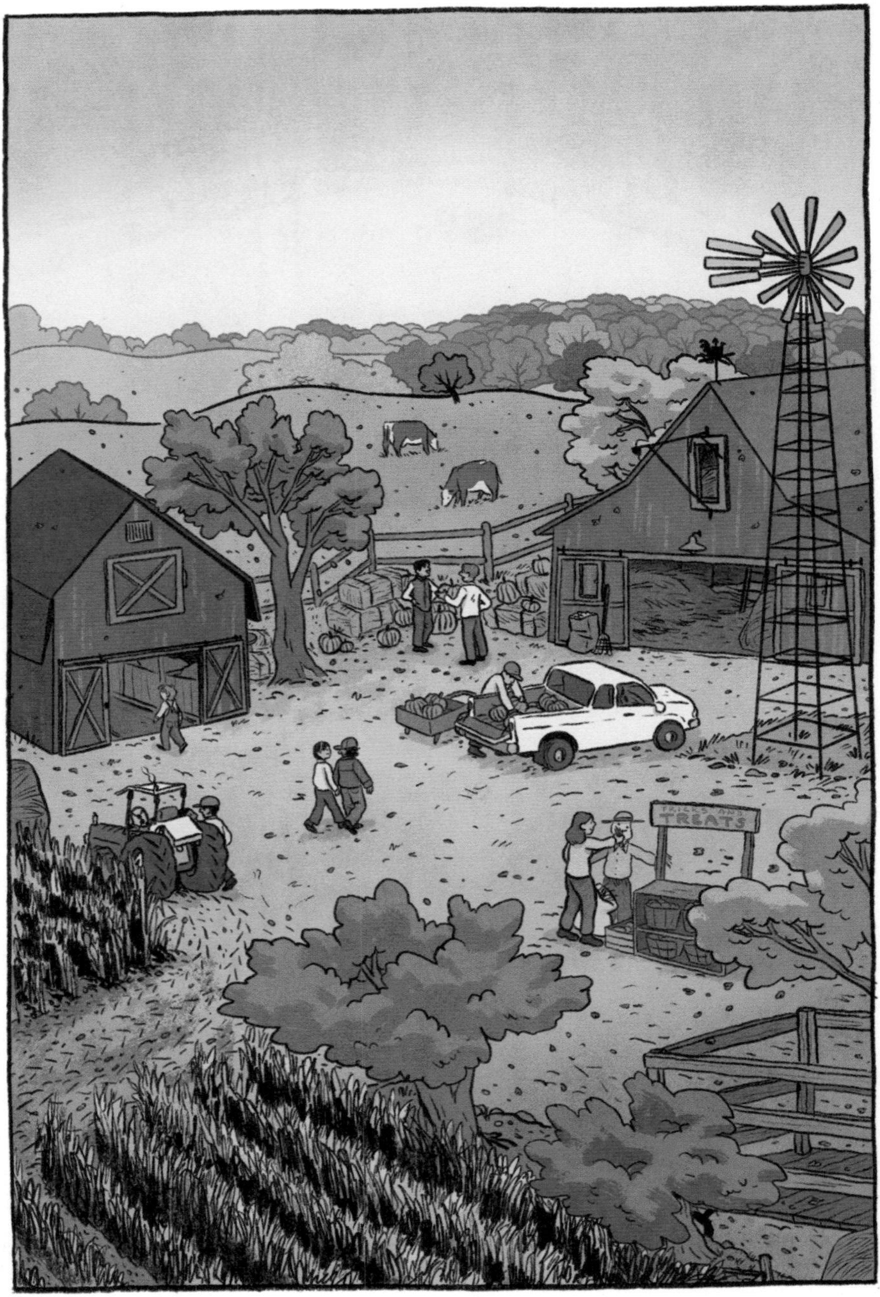
TRICKS AND
TREATS

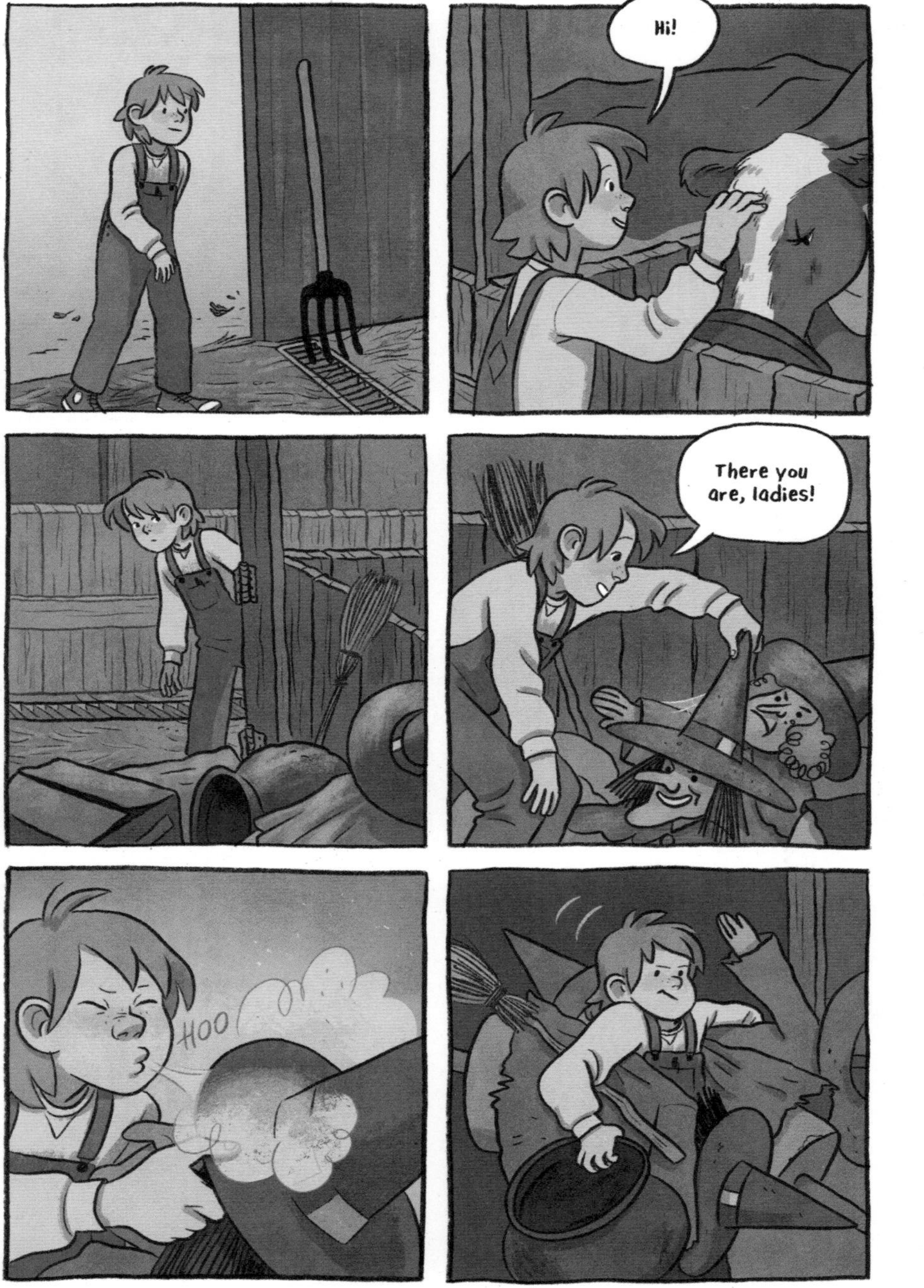
Hi!
There you are, ladies!
HOO

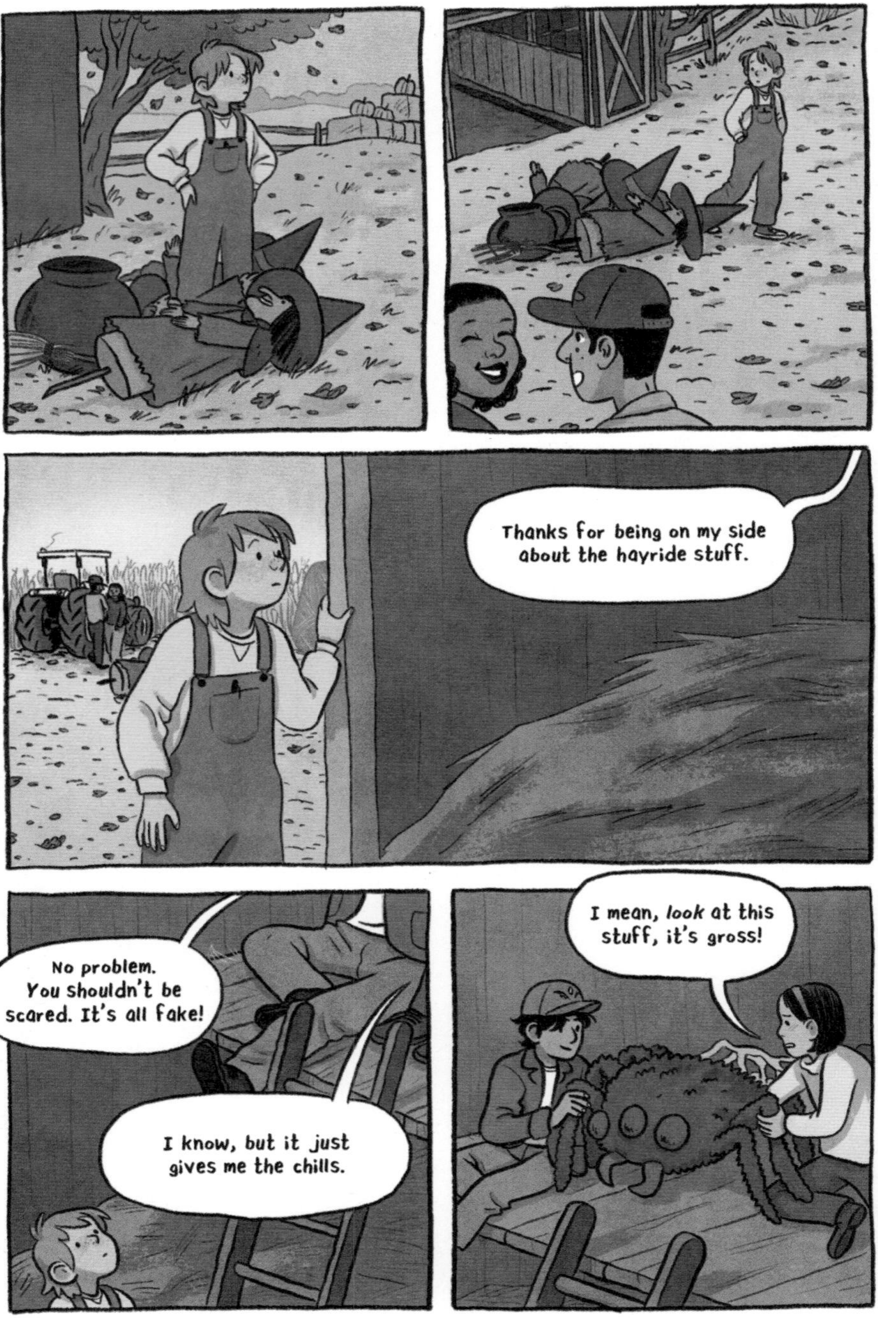

Thanks for being on my side about the hayride stuff.
No problem. You shouldn't be scared. It's all fake!
I know, but it just gives me the chills.
I mean, *look* at this stuff, it's gross!

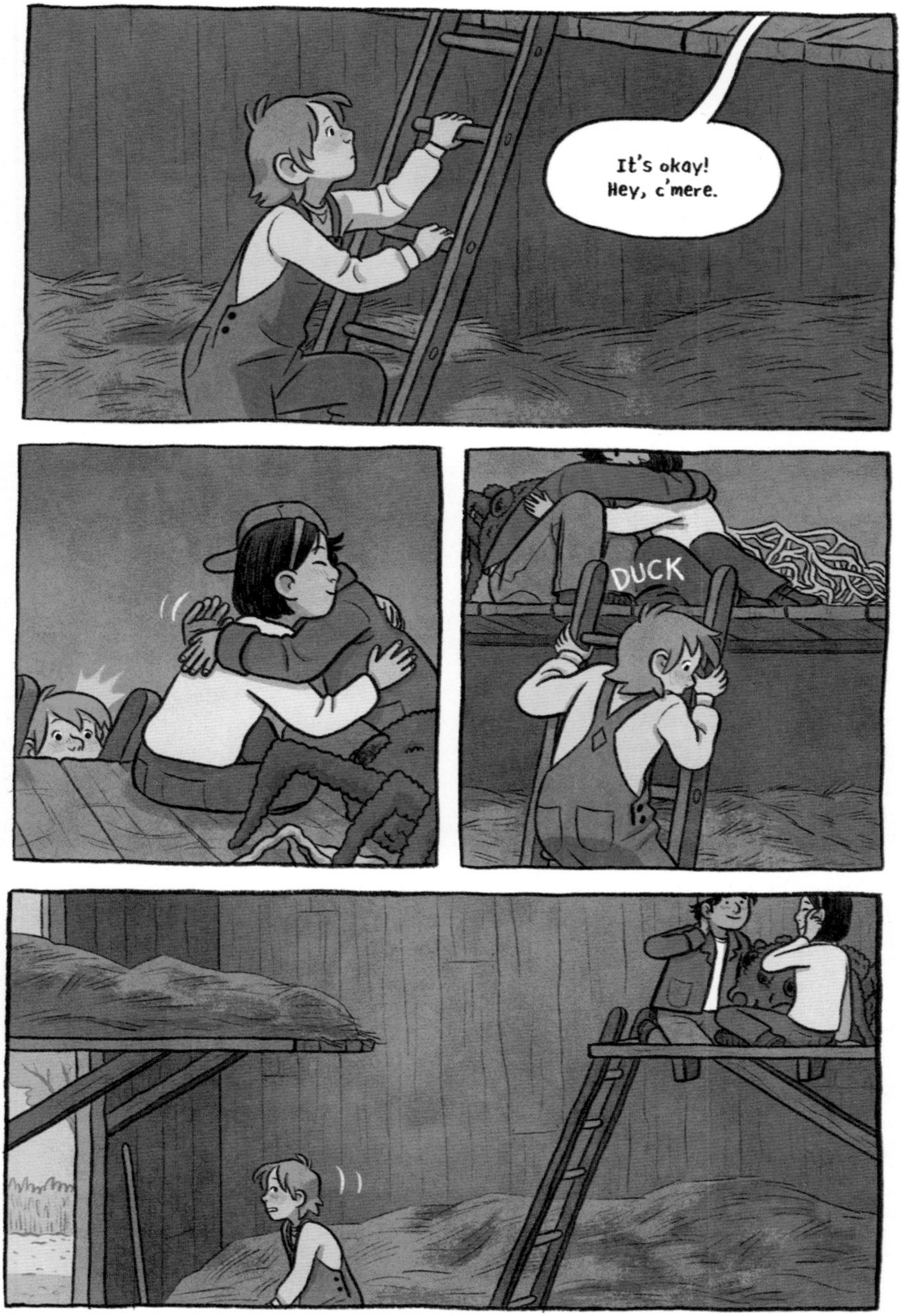
It's okay!
Hey, c'mere.
DUCK

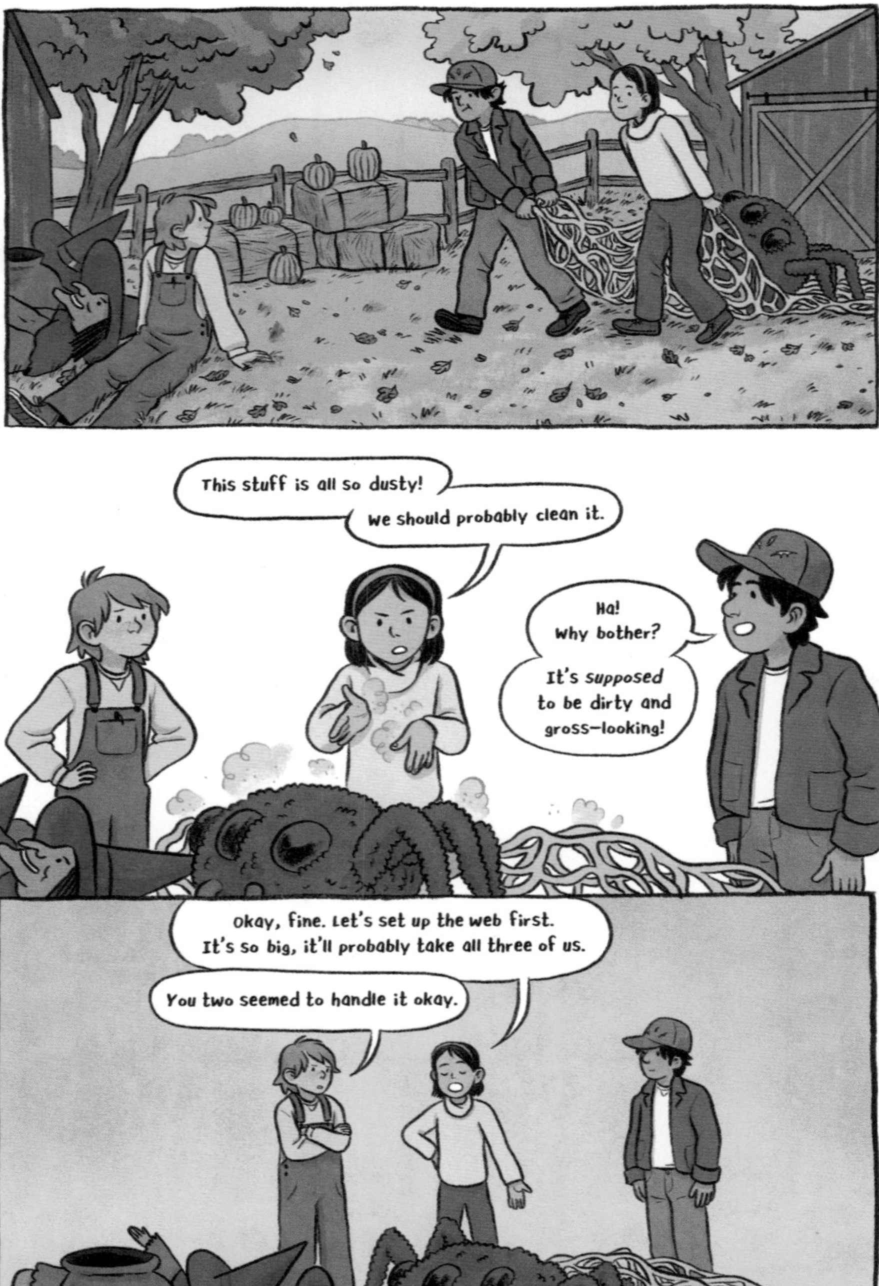
This stuff is all so dusty!
We should probably clean it.
Ha!
Why bother?
It's *supposed* to be dirty and gross-looking!
Okay, fine. Let's set up the web first.
It's so big, it'll probably take all three of us.
You two seemed to handle it okay.

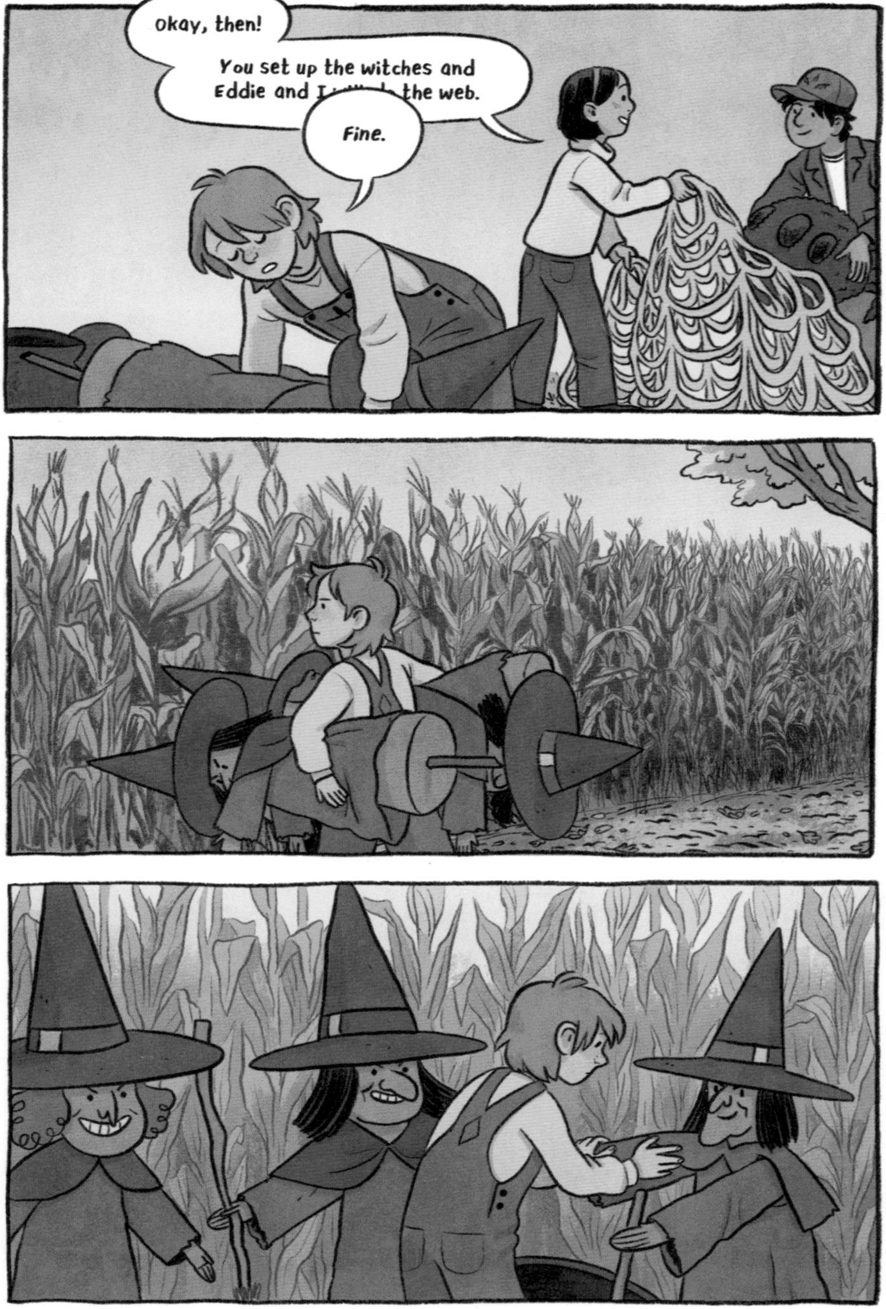
Okay, then!
You set up the witches and Eddie and I the web.
Fine.

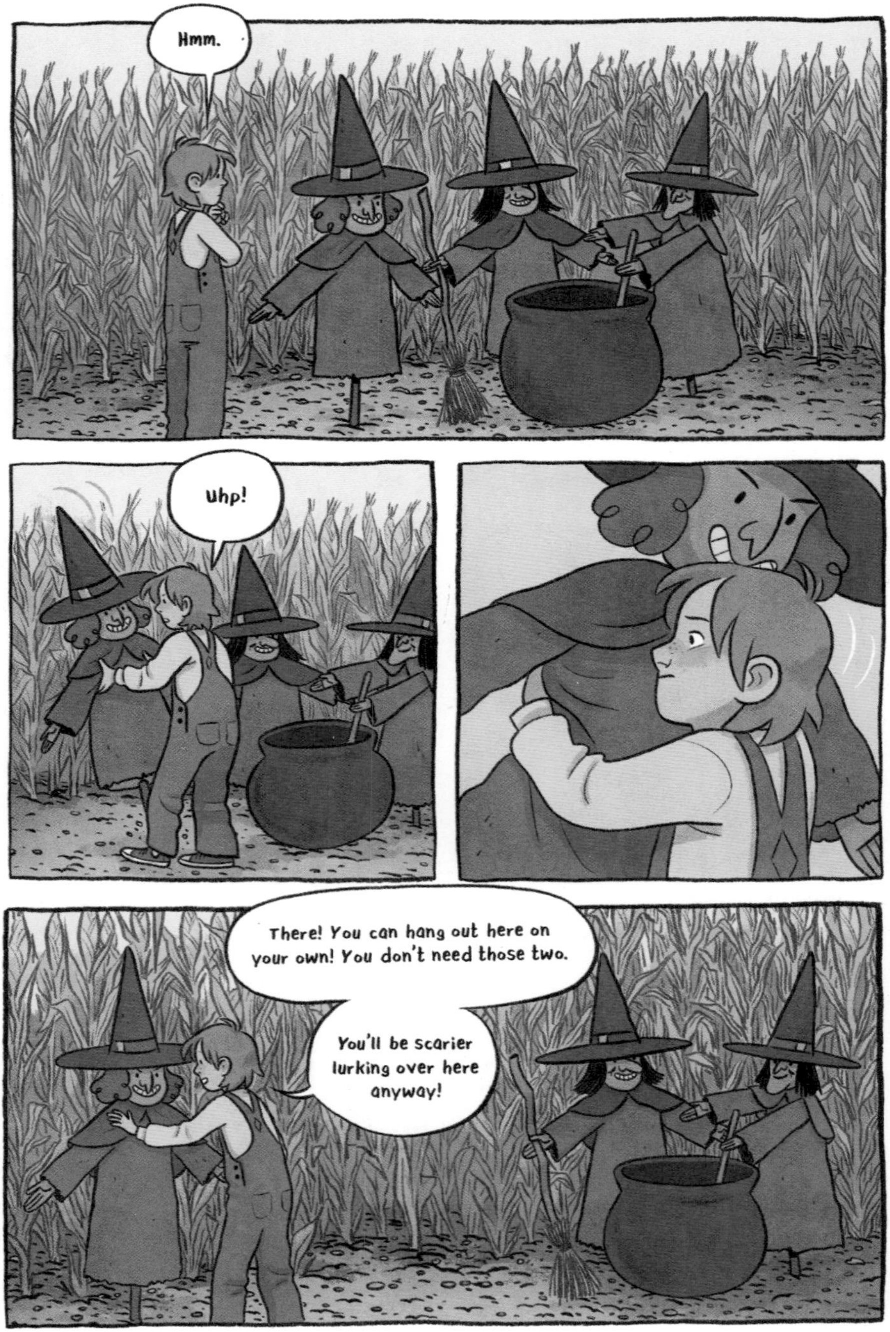
Hmm.
Uhp!
There! You can hang out here on your own! You don't need those two.
You'll be scarier lurking over here anyway!

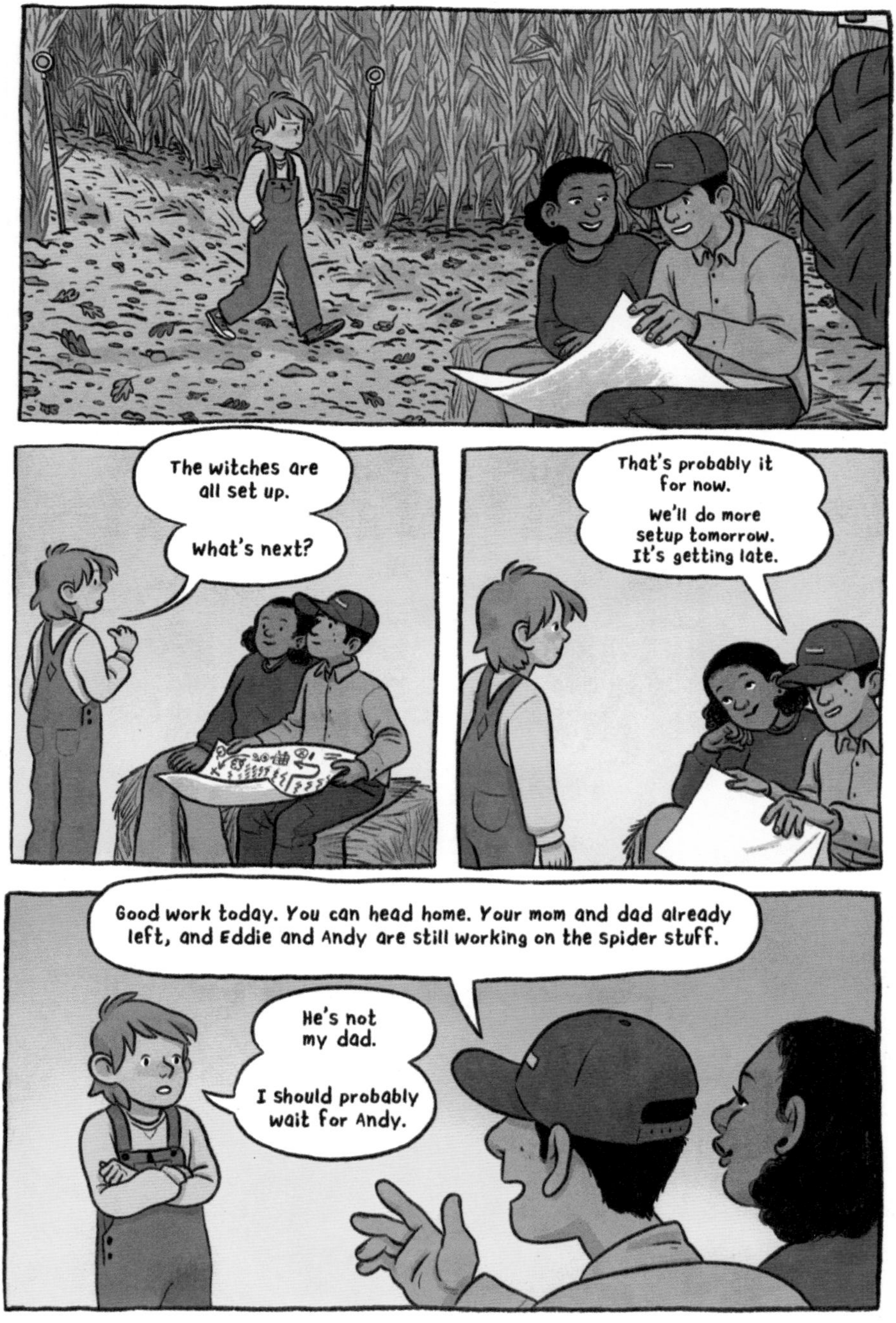
The witches are all set up.
What's next?
That's probably it for now.
We'll do more setup tomorrow. It's getting late.
Good work today. You can head home. Your mom and dad already left, and Eddie and Andy are still working on the spider stuff.
He's not my dad.
I should probably wait for Andy.

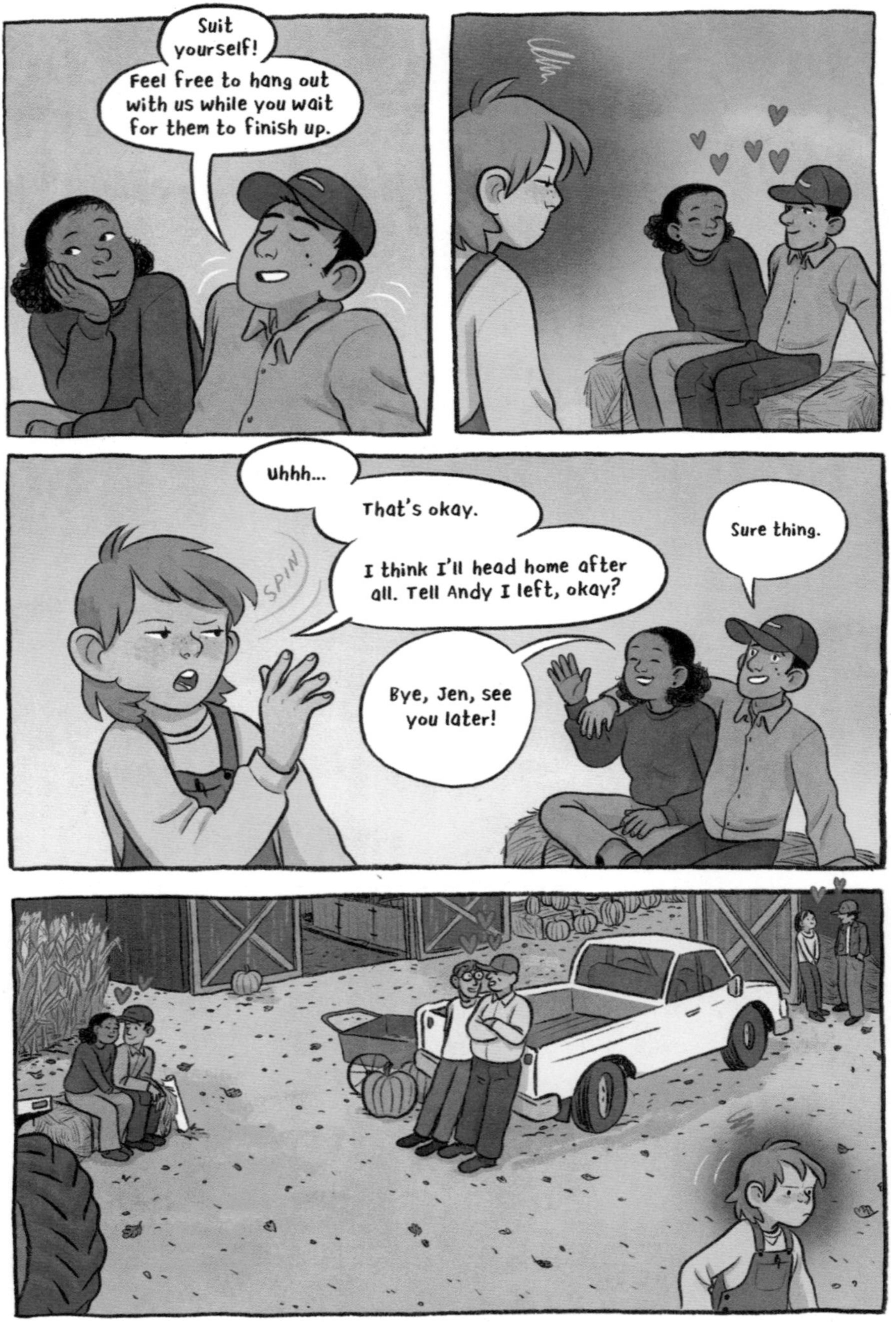

Suit yourself!
Feel free to hang out with us while you wait for them to finish up.
Uhhh...
That's okay.
I think I'll head home after all. Tell Andy I left, okay?
SPIN
Sure thing.
Bye, Jen, see you later!

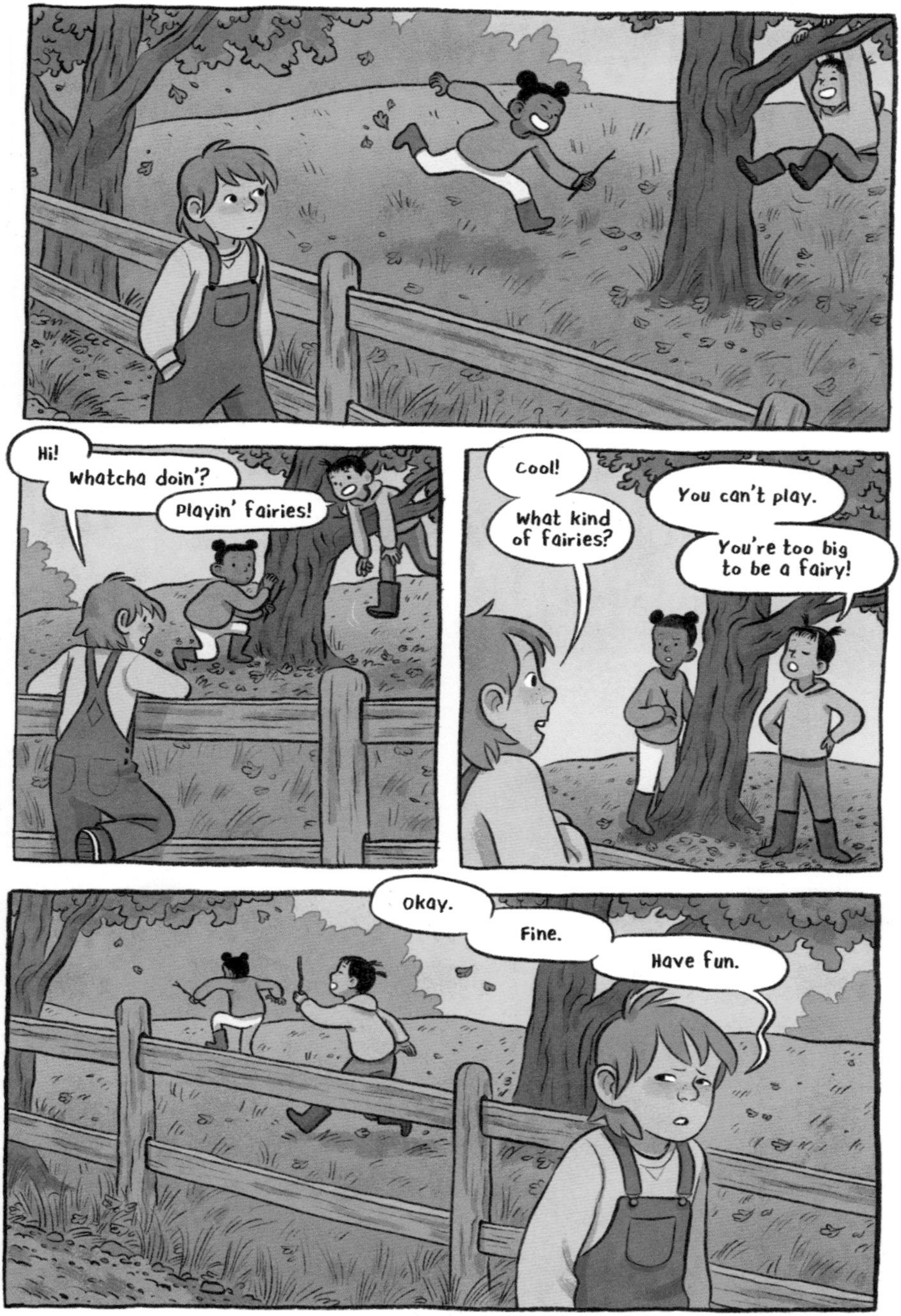
Hi!
Whatcha doin'?
Playin' fairies!
Cool!
What kind of fairies?
You can't play.
You're too big to be a fairy!
Okay.
Fine.
Have fun.

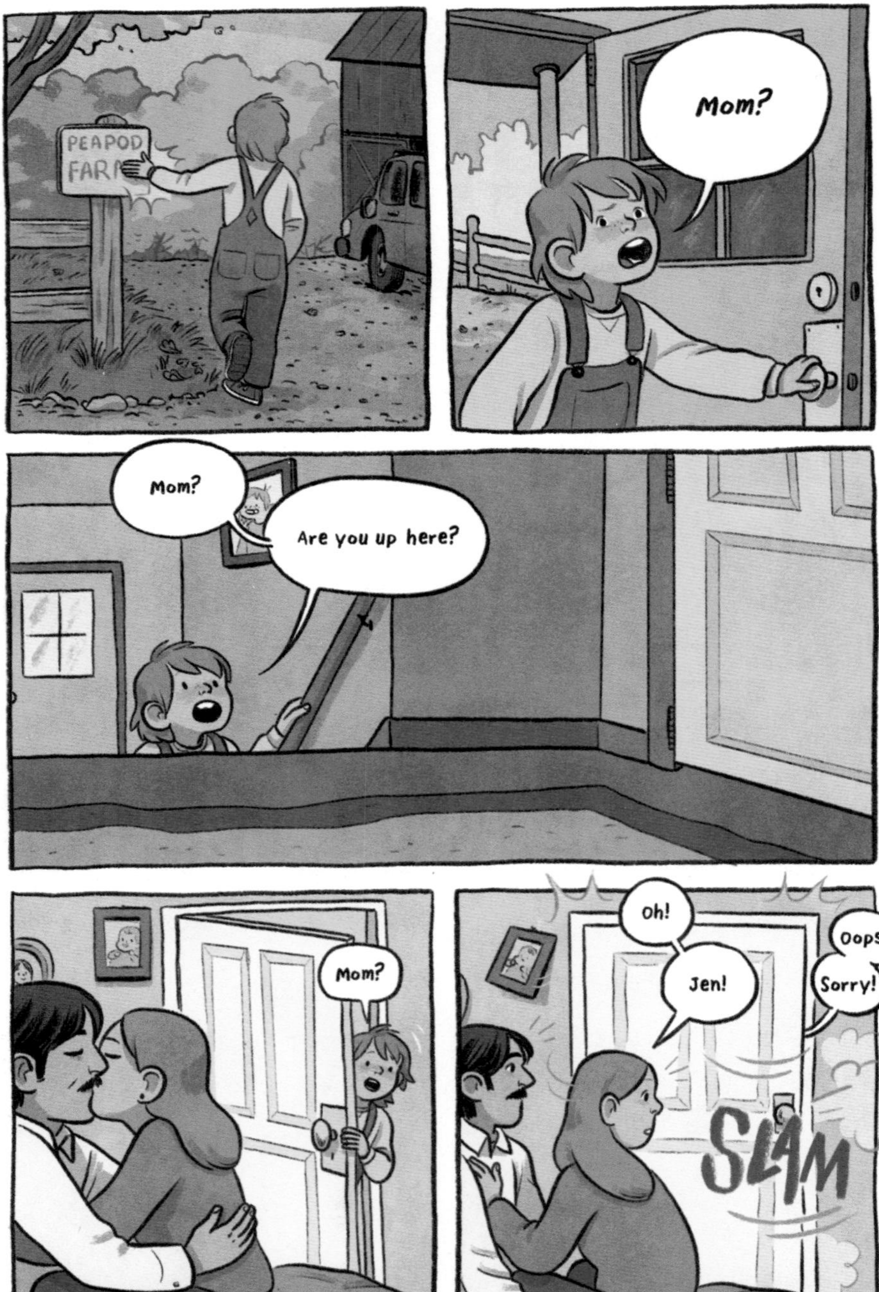
PEAPOD FAR
Mom?
Mom?
Are you up here?
Mom?
Oh!
Jen!
Oops!
Sorry!
SLAM

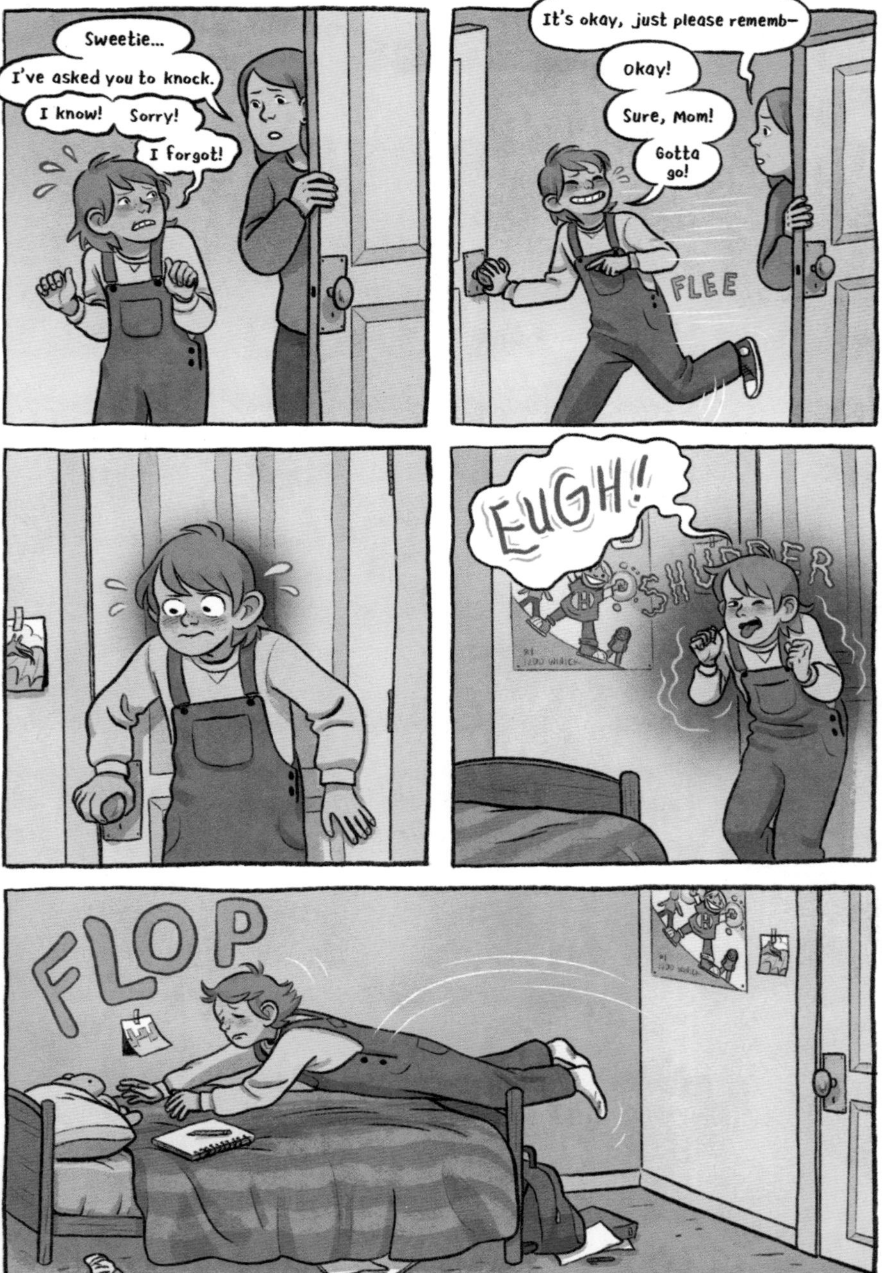
Sweetie...
I've asked you to knock.
I know!
Sorry!
I forgot!
It's okay, just please rememb—
Okay!
Sure, Mom!
Gotta go!
FLEE
EUGH!
FLOP

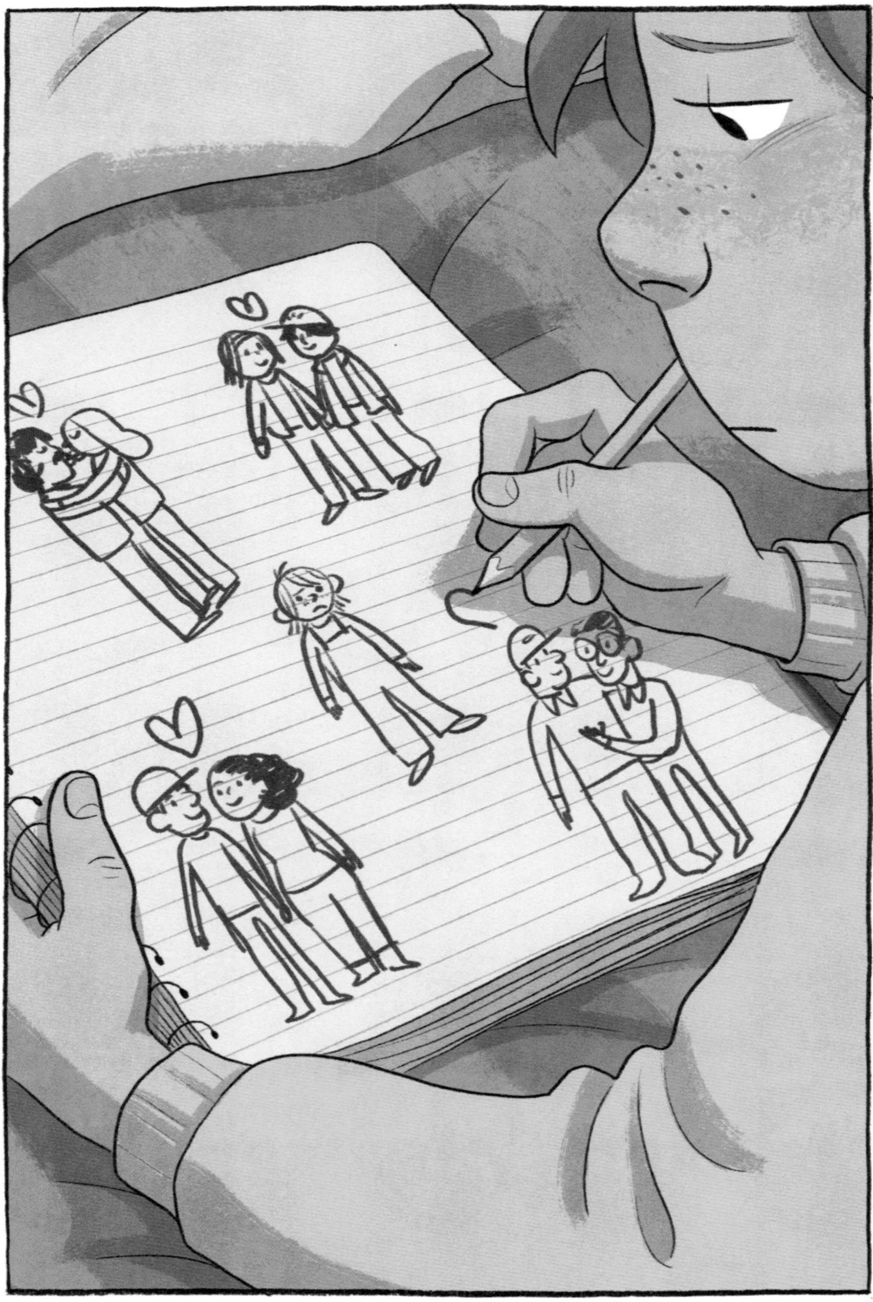

Chapter Four

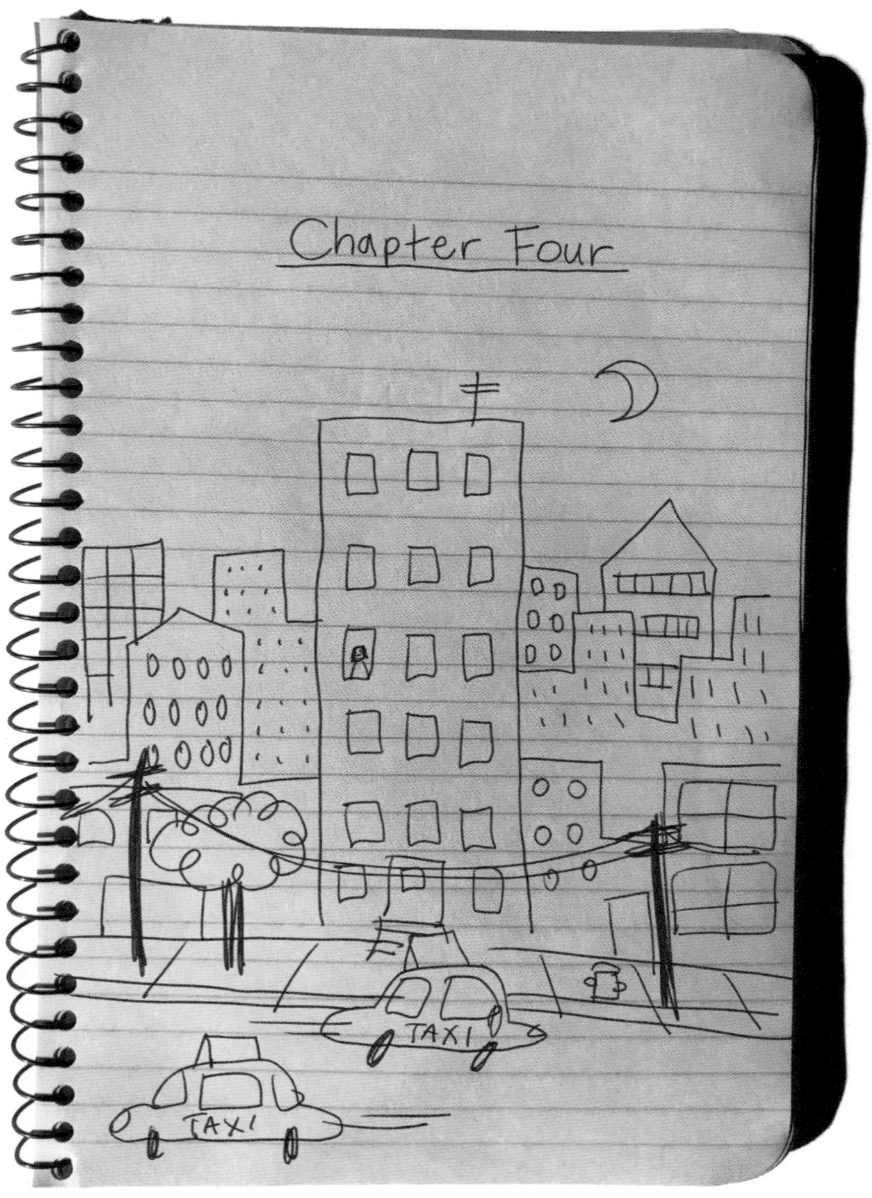

TAXI
TAXI

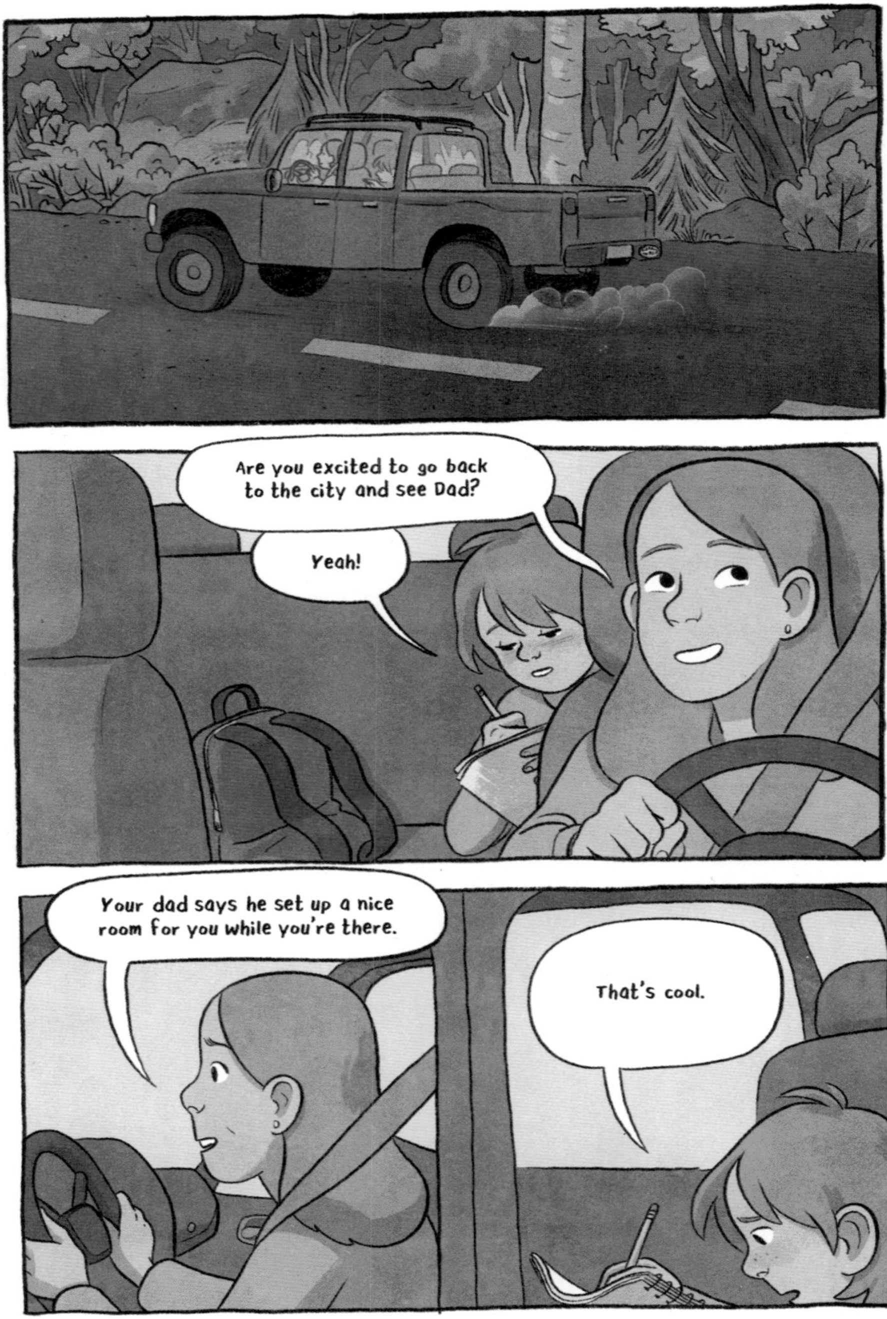

Are you excited to go back to the city and see Dad?
Yeah!
Your dad says he set up a nice room for you while you're there.
That's cool.

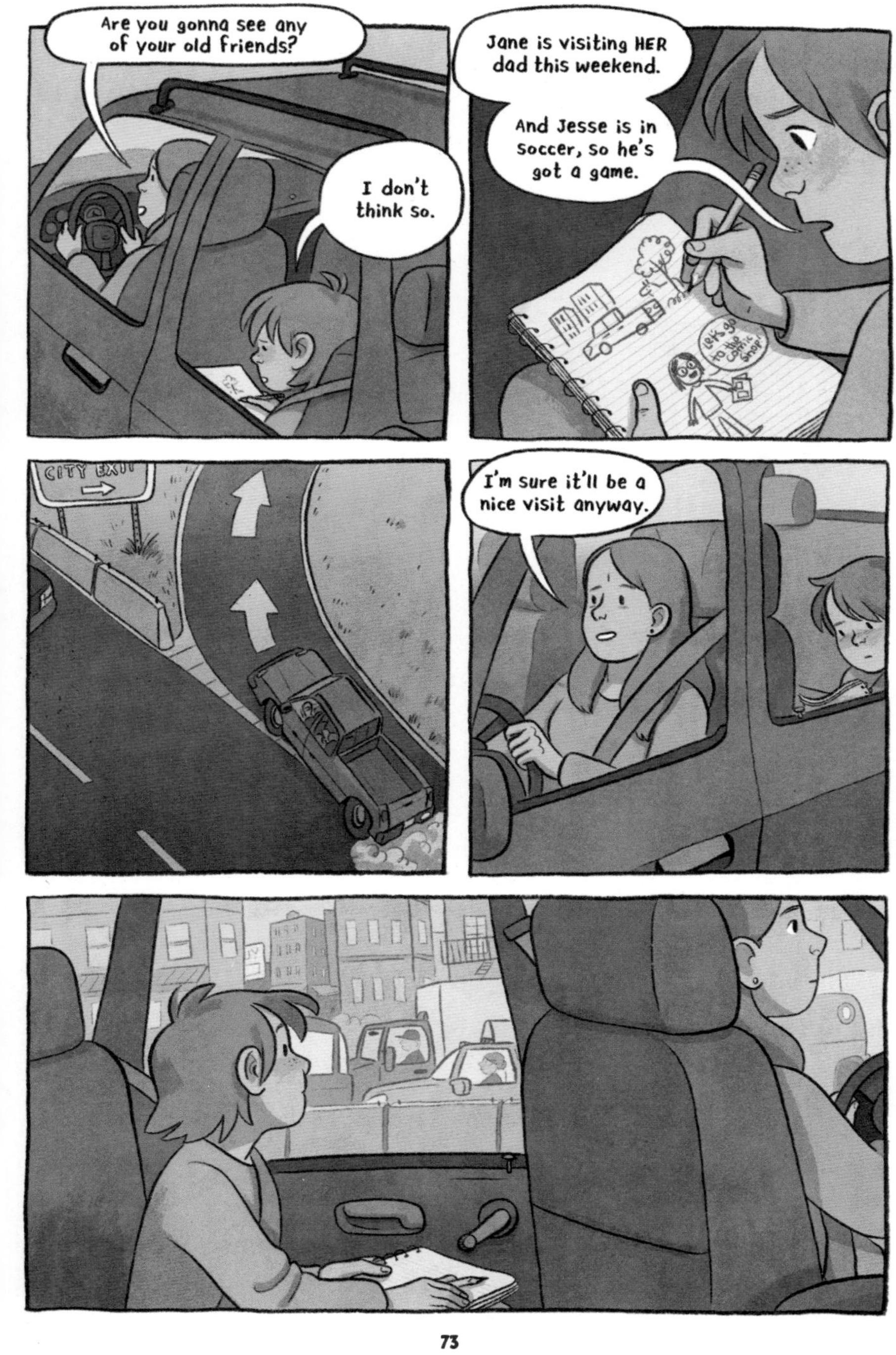
Are you gonna see any of your old friends?
I don't think so.
Jane is visiting HER dad this weekend.
And Jesse is in soccer, so he's got a game.
CITY EXIT
I'm sure it'll be a nice visit anyway.

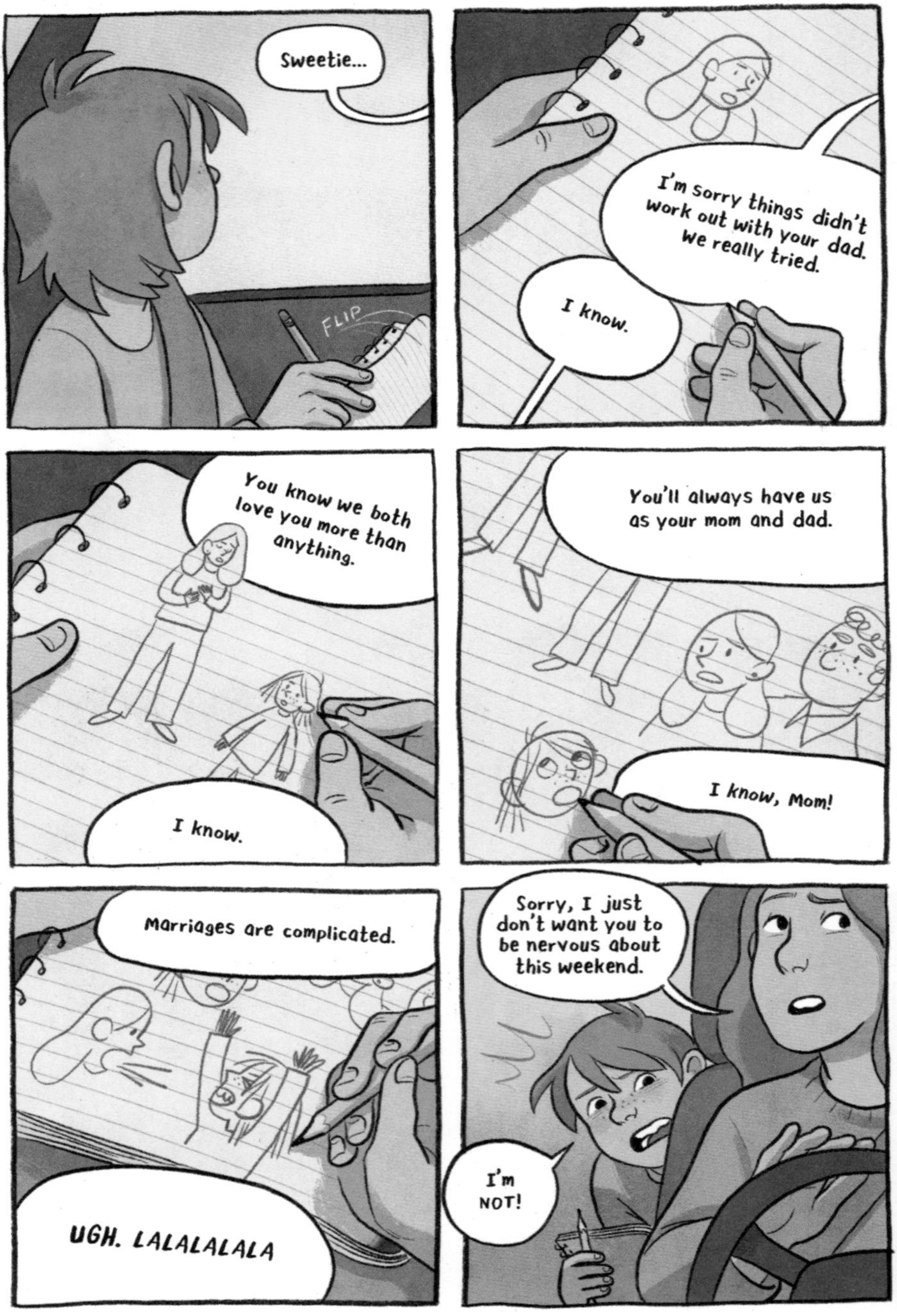
Sweetie...
FLIP
I'm sorry things didn't work out with your dad. We really tried.
I know.
You know we both love you more than anything.
I know.
You'll always have us as your mom and dad.
I know, Mom!
Marriages are complicated.
UGH. LALALALALA
Sorry, I just don't want you to be nervous about this weekend.
I'm NOT!

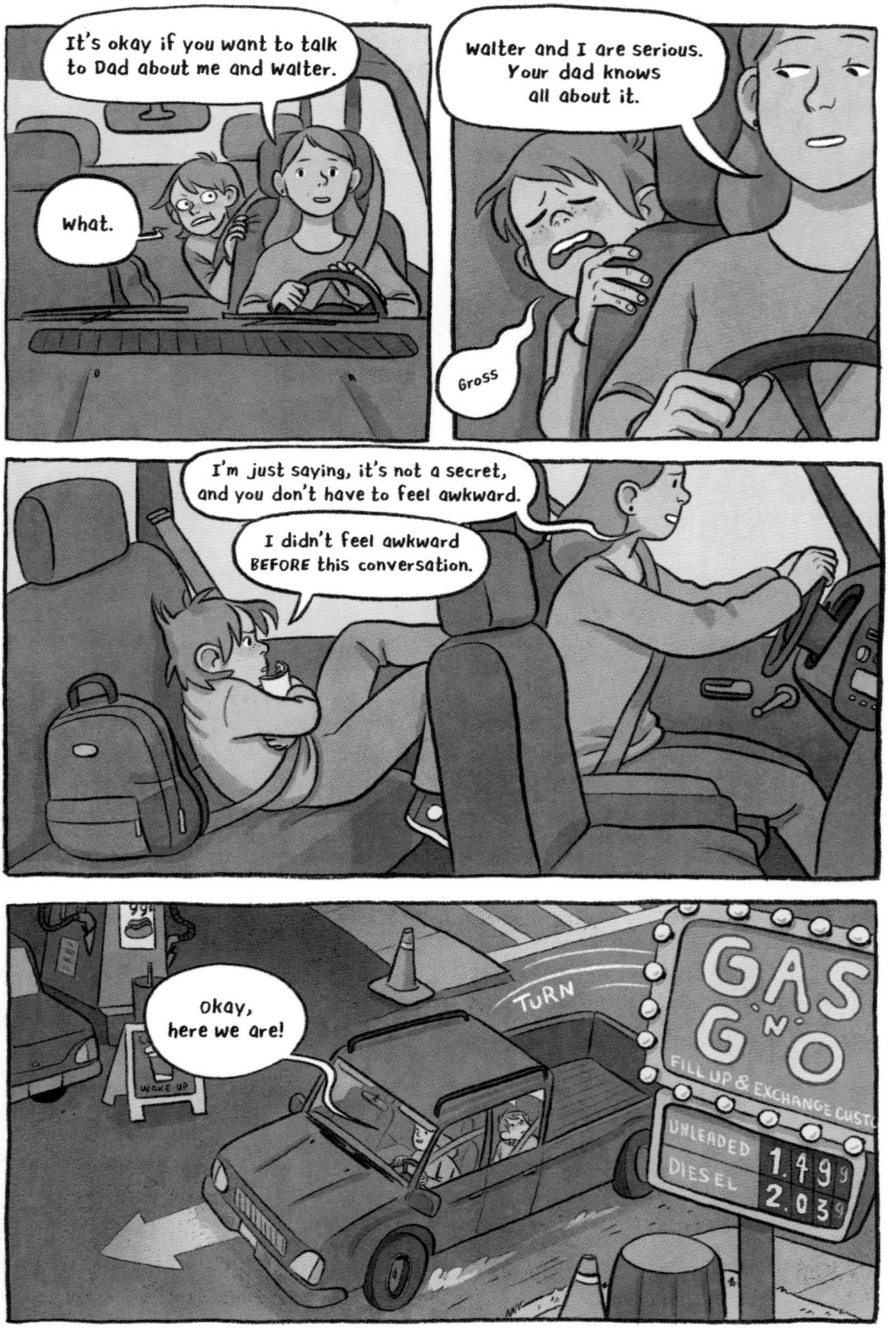
It's okay if you want to talk to Dad about me and Walter.
What.
Walter and I are serious. Your dad knows all about it.
Gross
I'm just saying, it's not a secret, and you don't have to feel awkward.
I didn't feel awkward BEFORE this conversation.
TURN
Okay, here we are!
WAKE UP
GAS 'N' GO
FILL UP & EXCHANGE CUST
UNLEADED 1.49 9
DIESEL 2.03 9

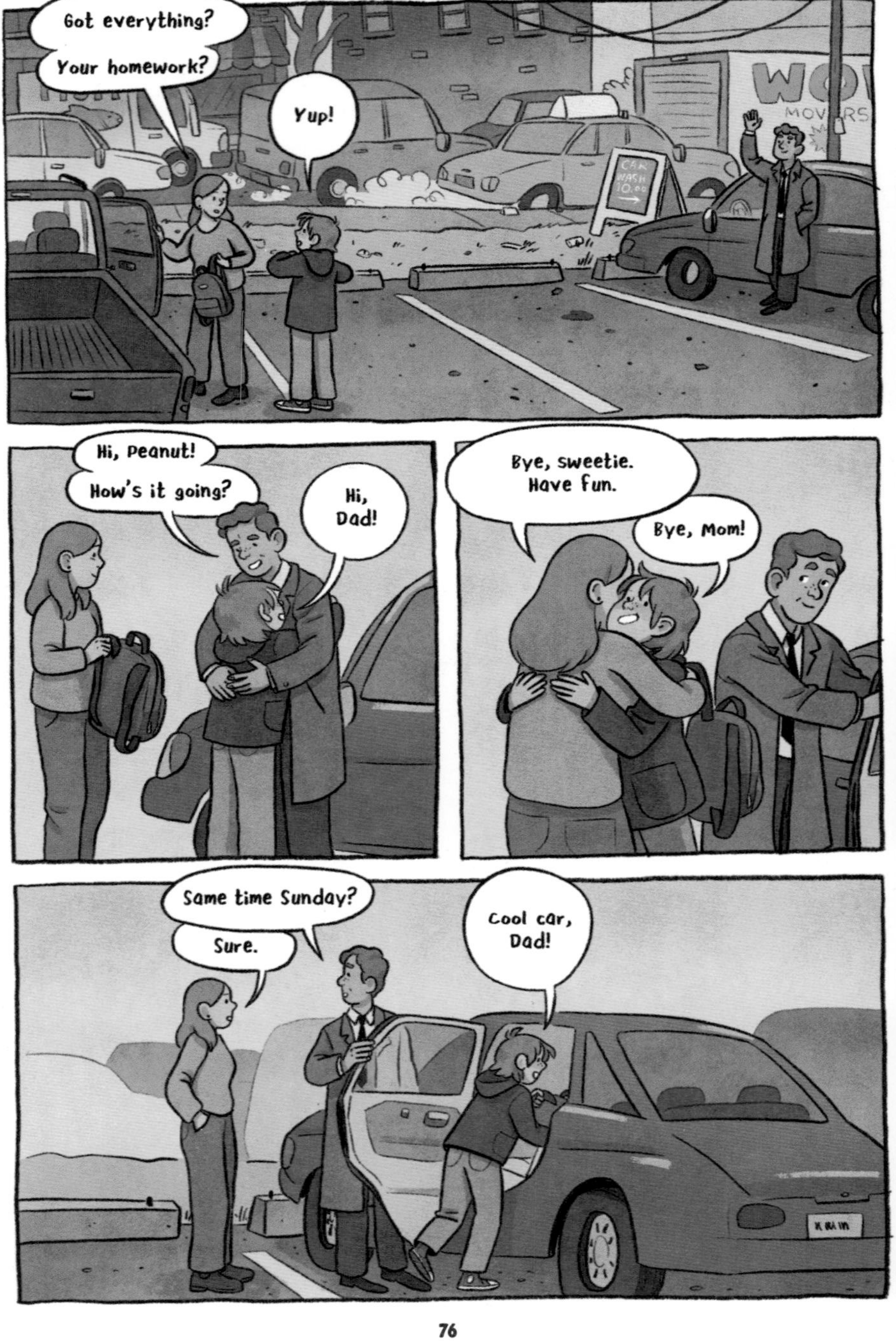
Got everything?
Your homework?
Yup!
Hi, Peanut!
How's it going?
Hi, Dad!
Bye, sweetie. Have fun.
Bye, Mom!
Same time Sunday?
Sure.
Cool car, Dad!

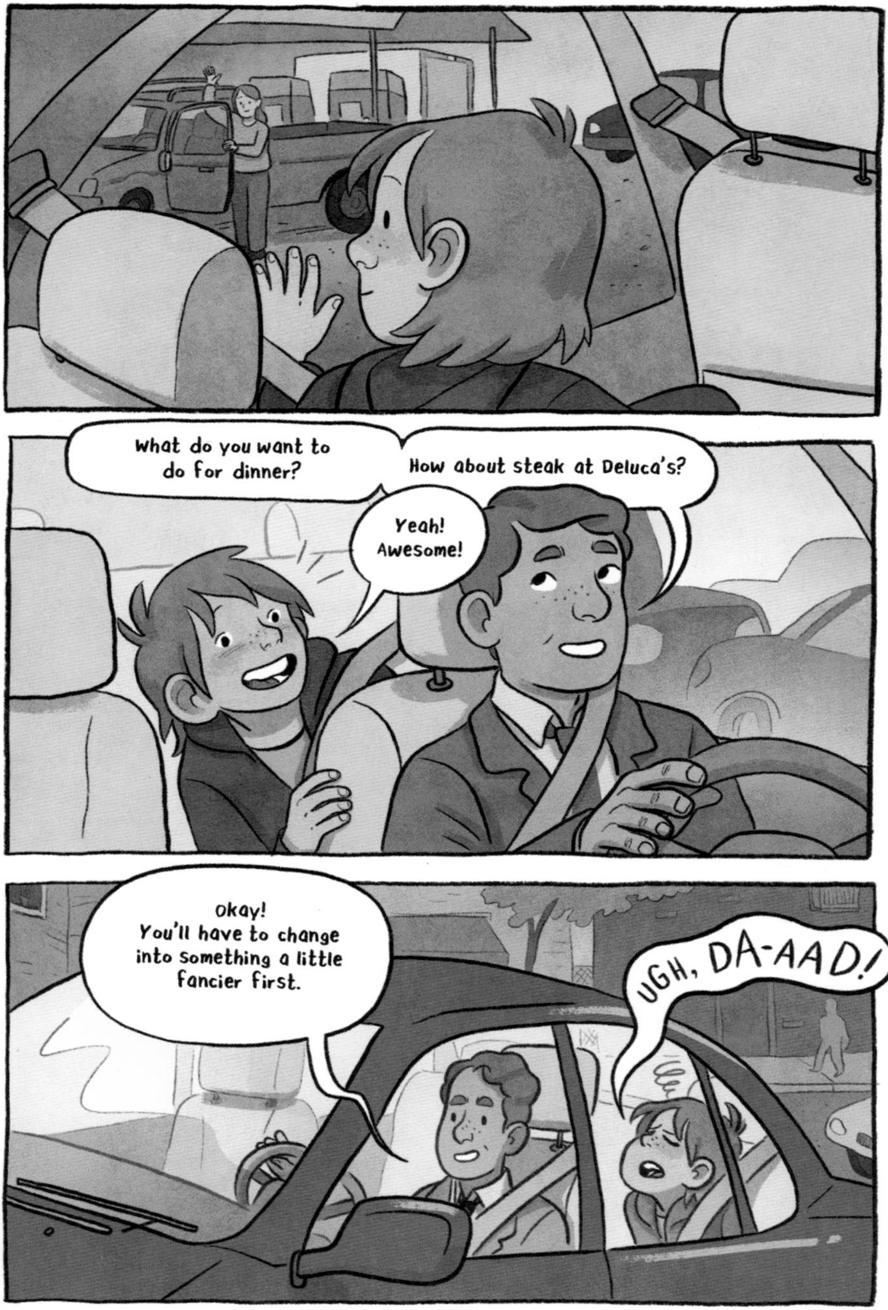
What do you want to do for dinner?
How about steak at Deluca's?
Yeah! Awesome!
Okay! You'll have to change into something a little fancier first.
UGH, DA-AAD!

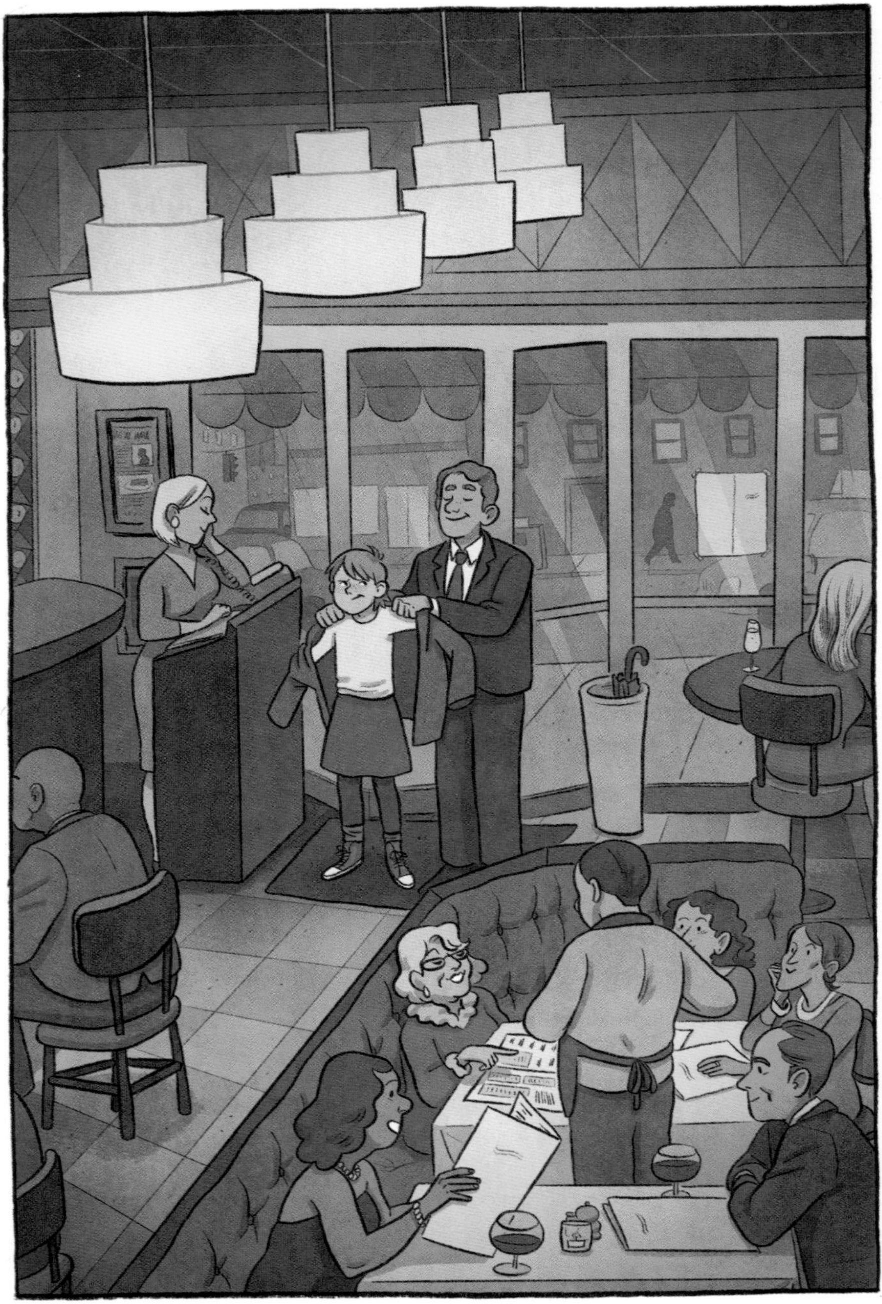

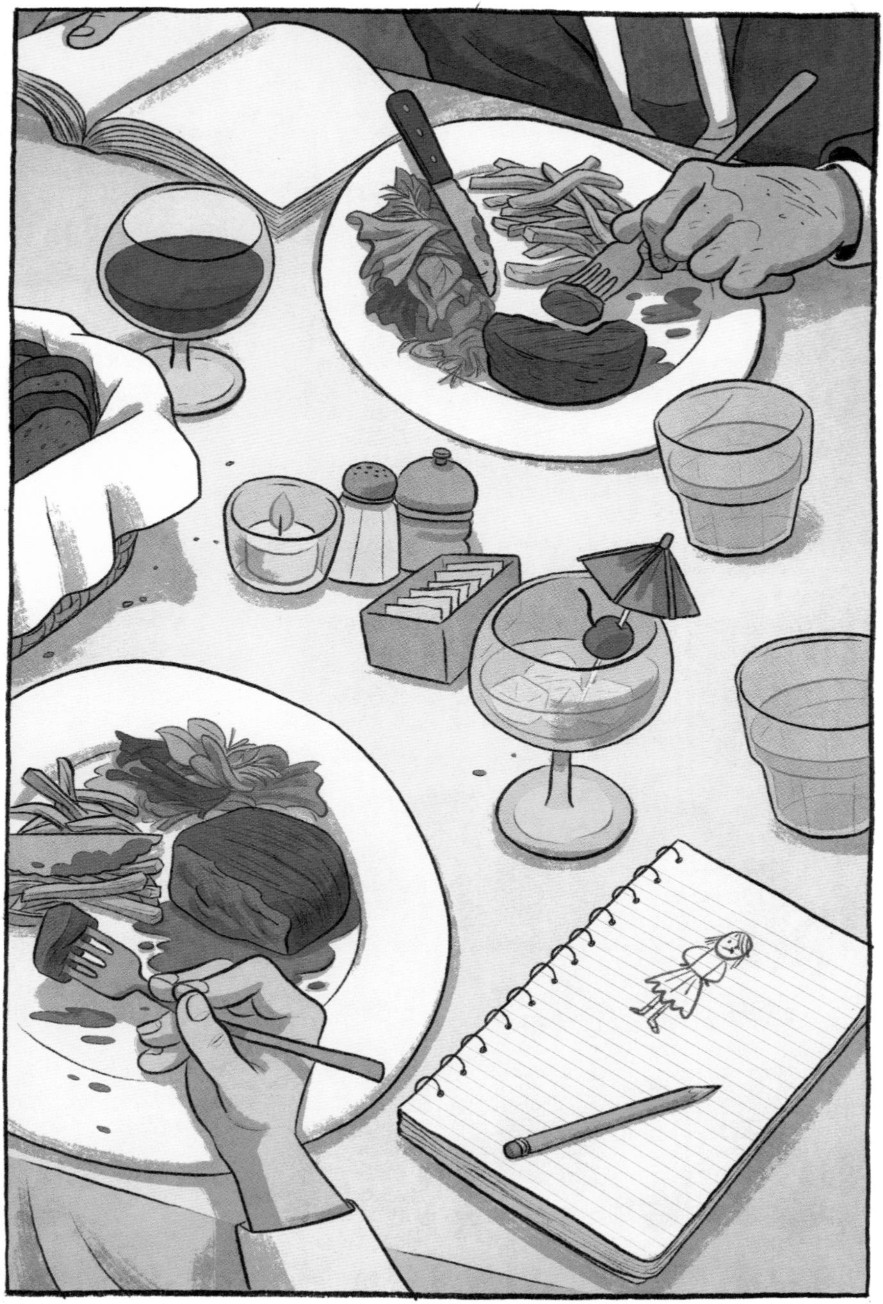

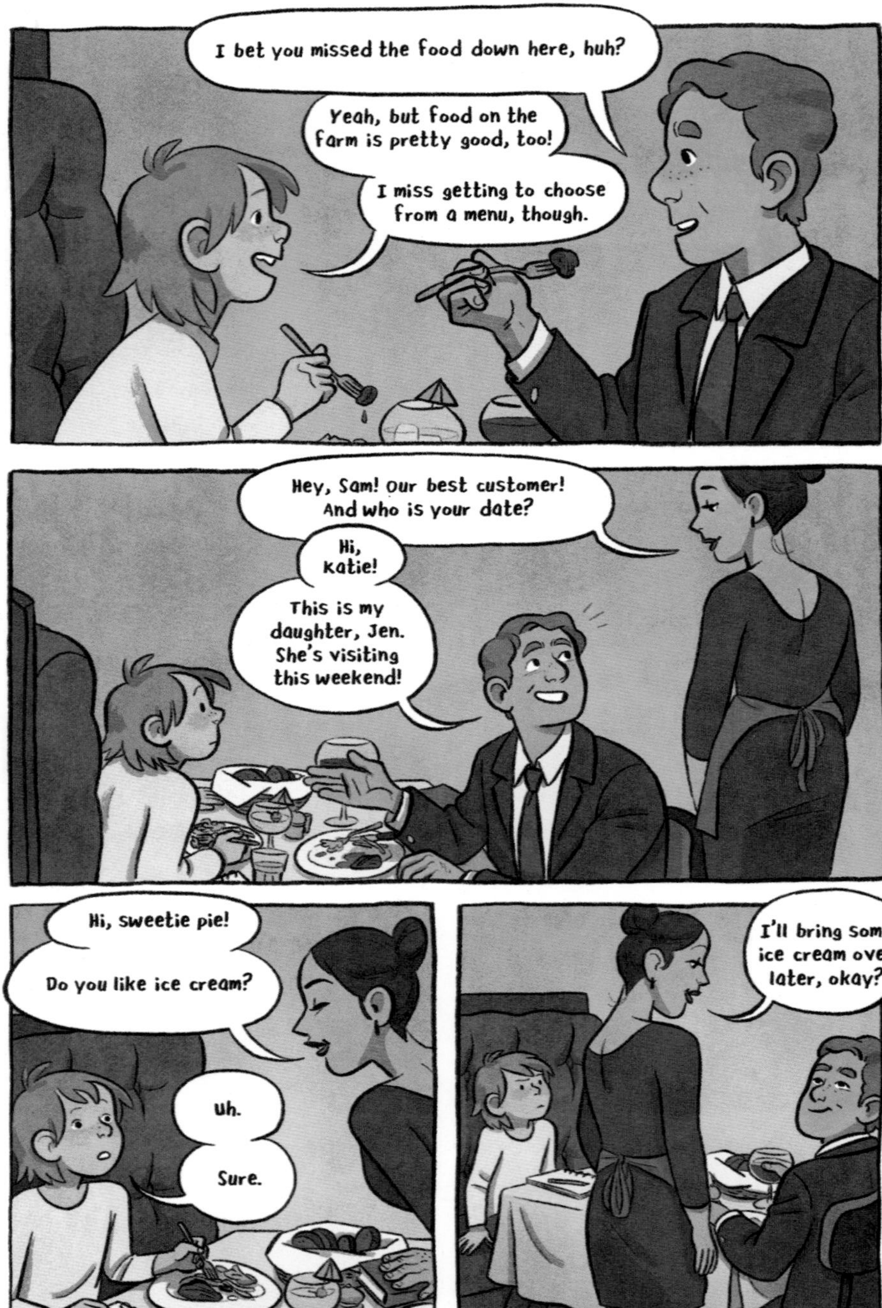
I bet you missed the food down here, huh?
Yeah, but food on the farm is pretty good, too!
I miss getting to choose from a menu, though.
Hey, Sam! Our best customer! And who is your date?
Hi, Katie!
This is my daughter, Jen. She's visiting this weekend!
Hi, sweetie pie!
Do you like ice cream?
Uh.
Sure.
I'll bring some ice cream over later, okay?

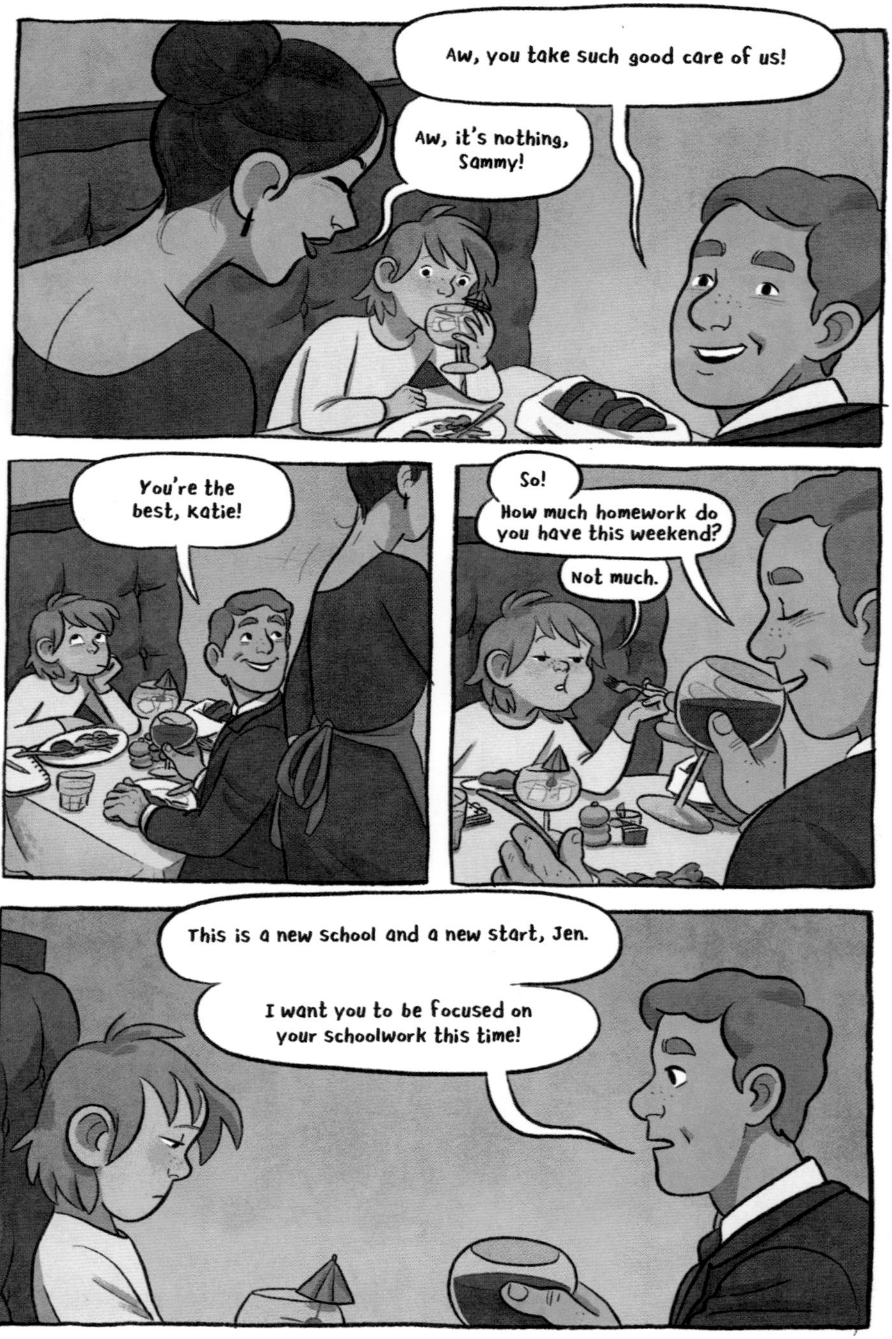

Aw, you take such good care of us!
Aw, it's nothing, Sammy!
You're the best, Katie!
So!
How much homework do you have this weekend?
Not much.
This is a new school and a new start, Jen.
I want you to be focused on your schoolwork this time!

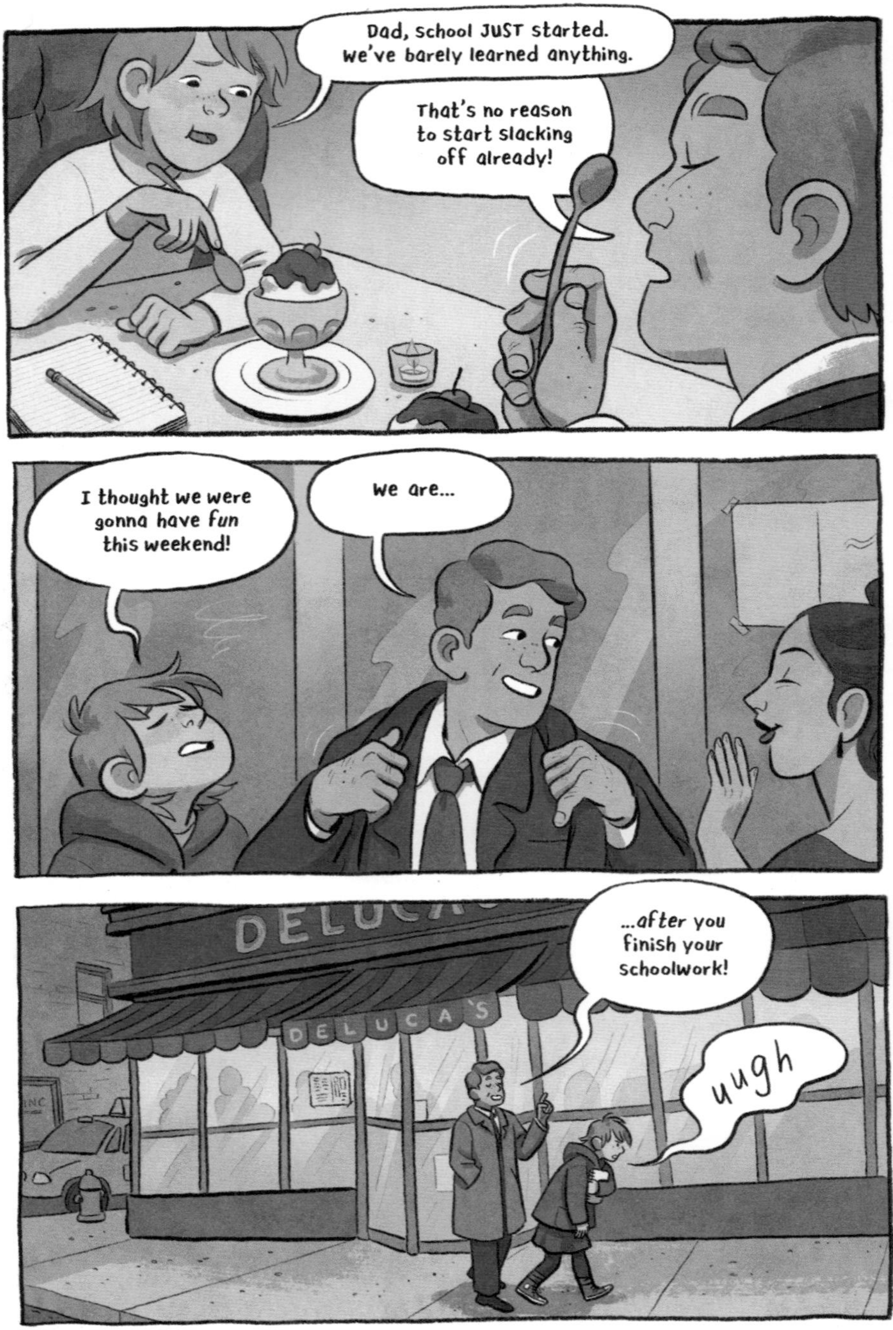
Dad, school JUST started. We've barely learned anything.
That's no reason to start slacking off already!
I thought we were gonna have fun this weekend!
We are...
DELUCA'S
...after you finish your schoolwork!
uugh

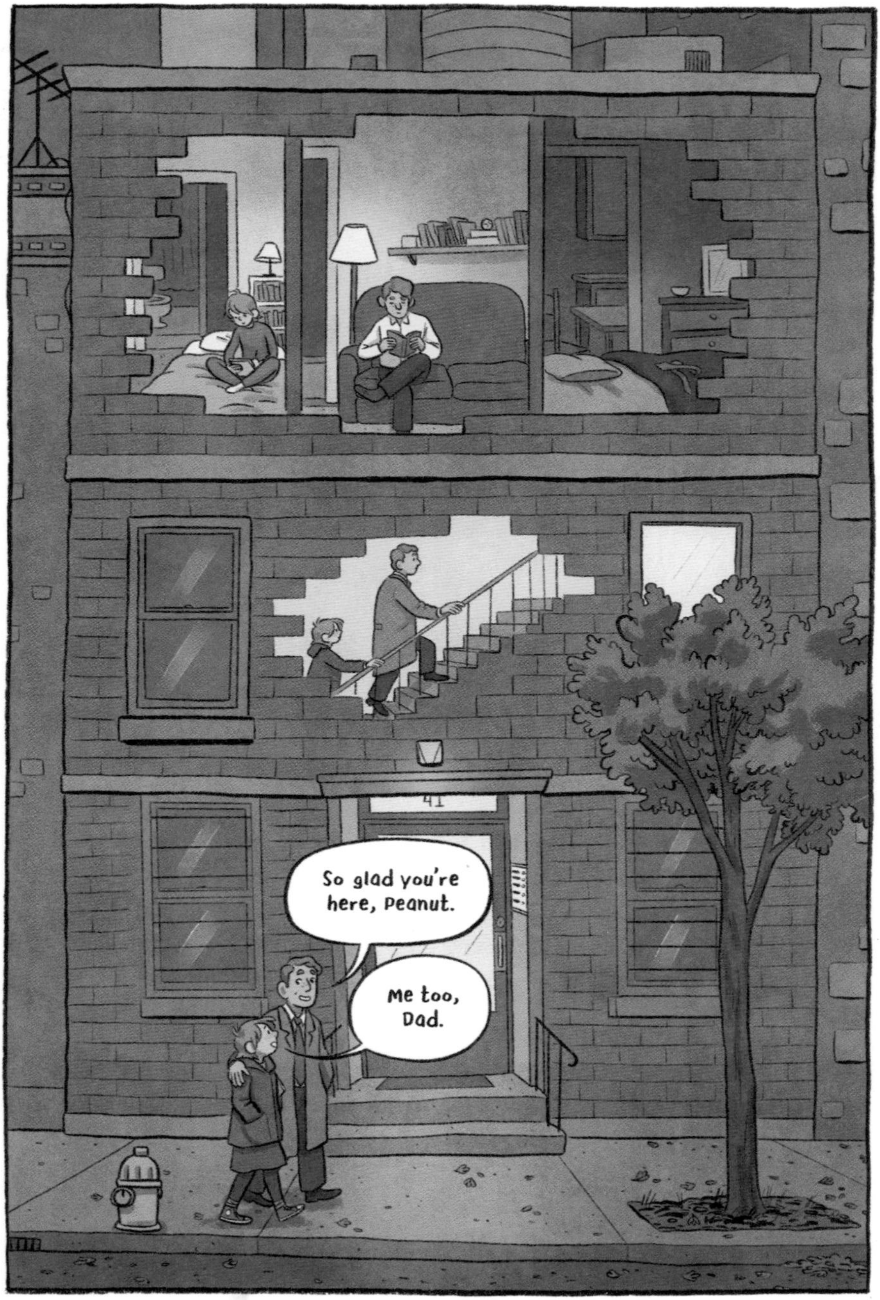
41
So glad you're here, Peanut.
Me too, Dad.

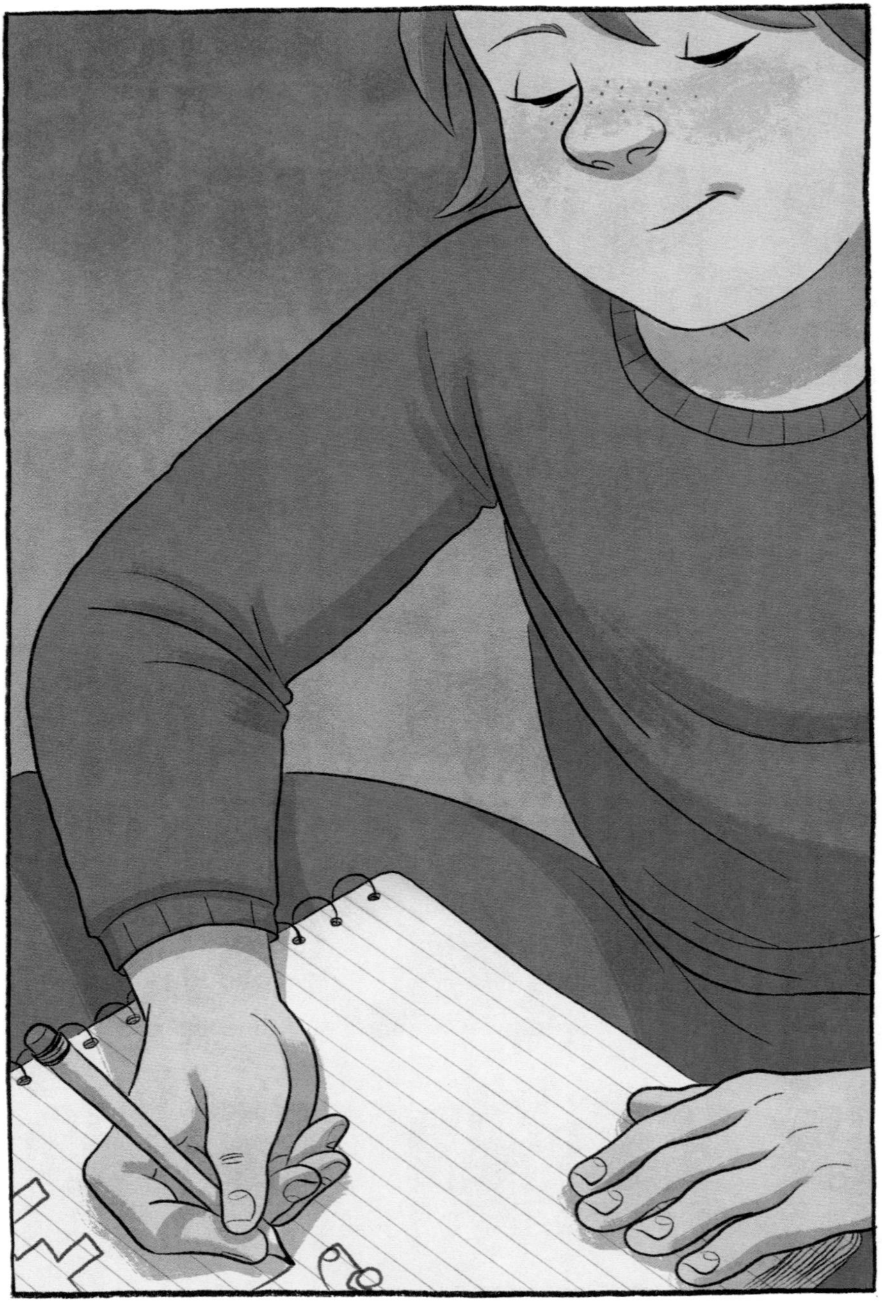

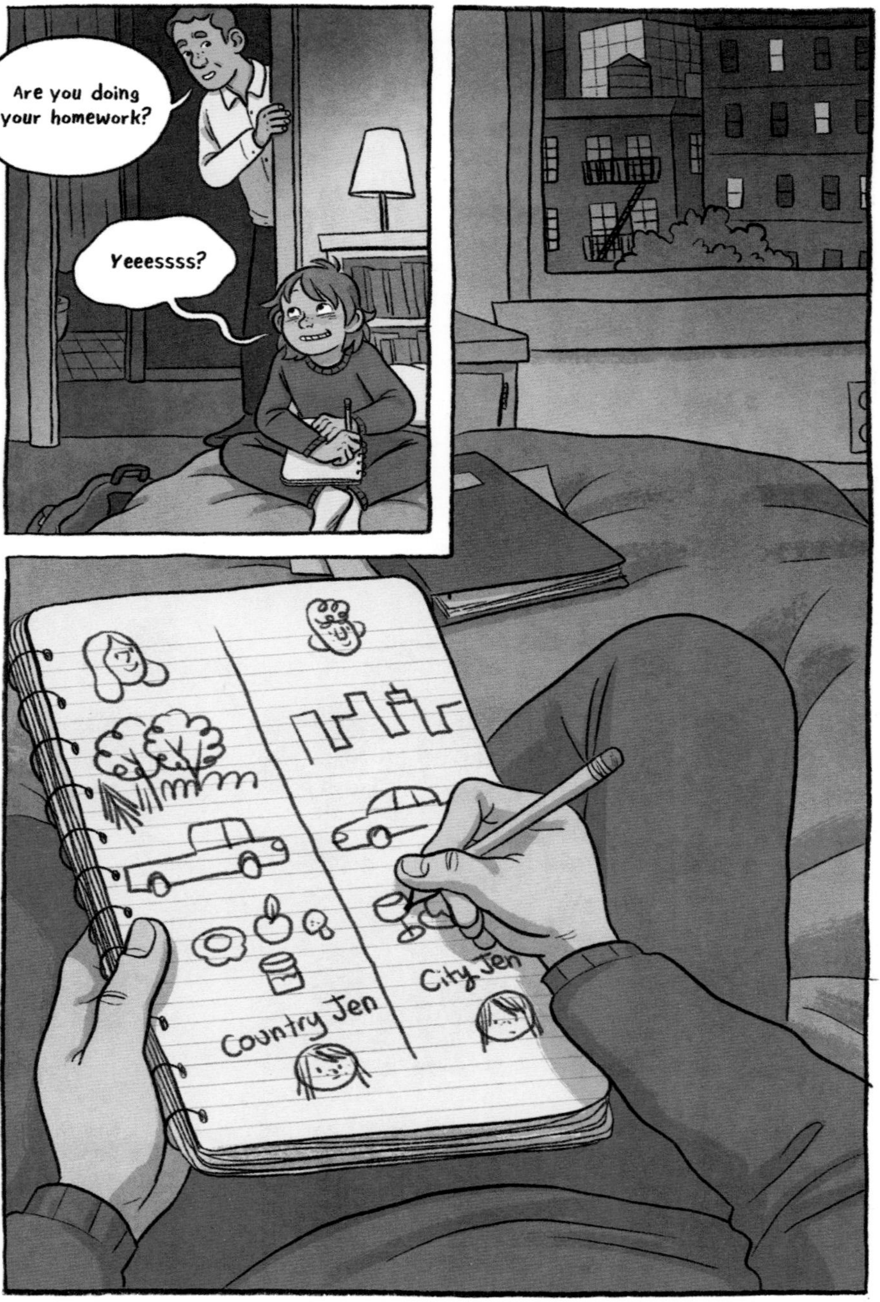
Are you doing your homework?
Yeeessss?
Country Jen
City Jen

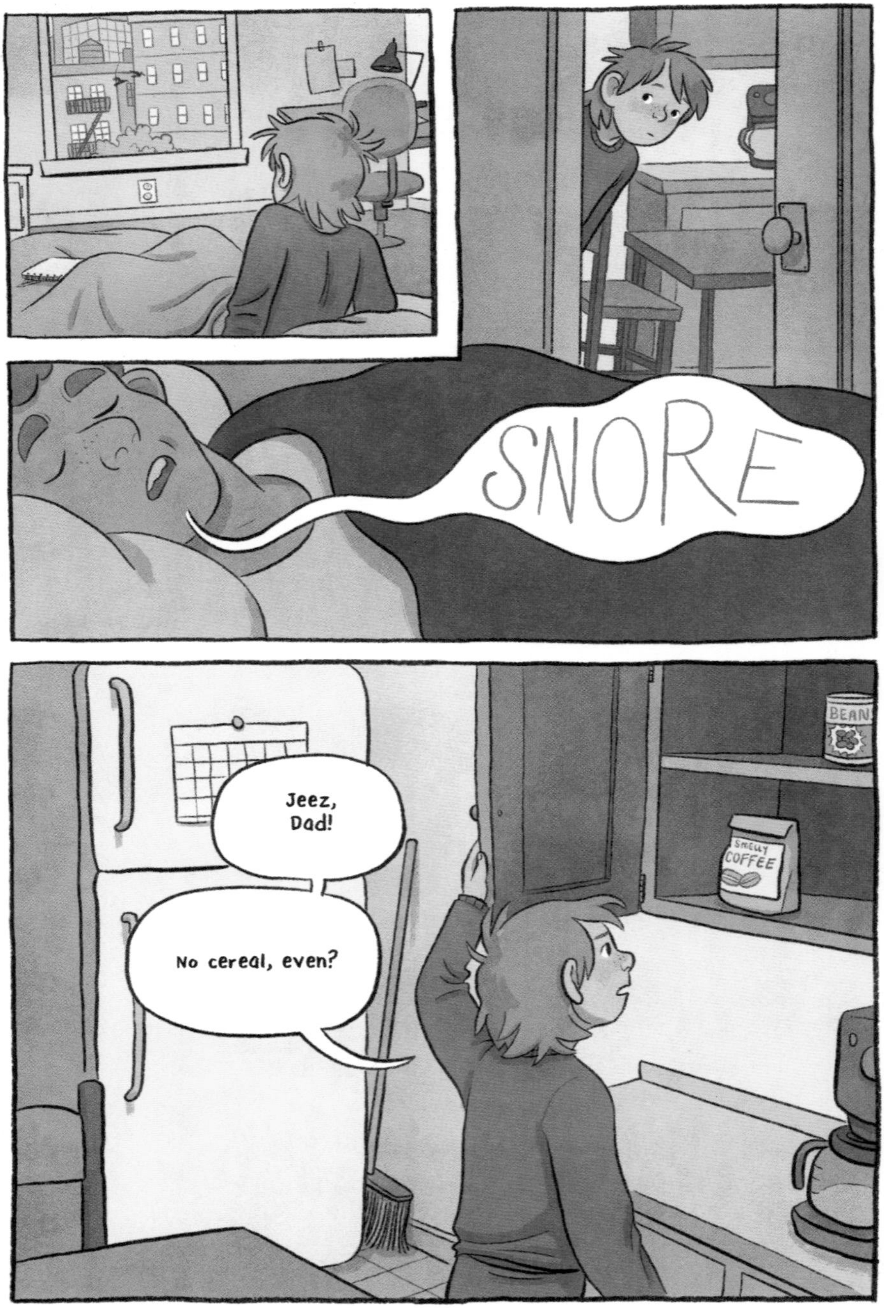
SNORE
Jeez, Dad!
No cereal, even?
BEANS
SMELLY COFFEE

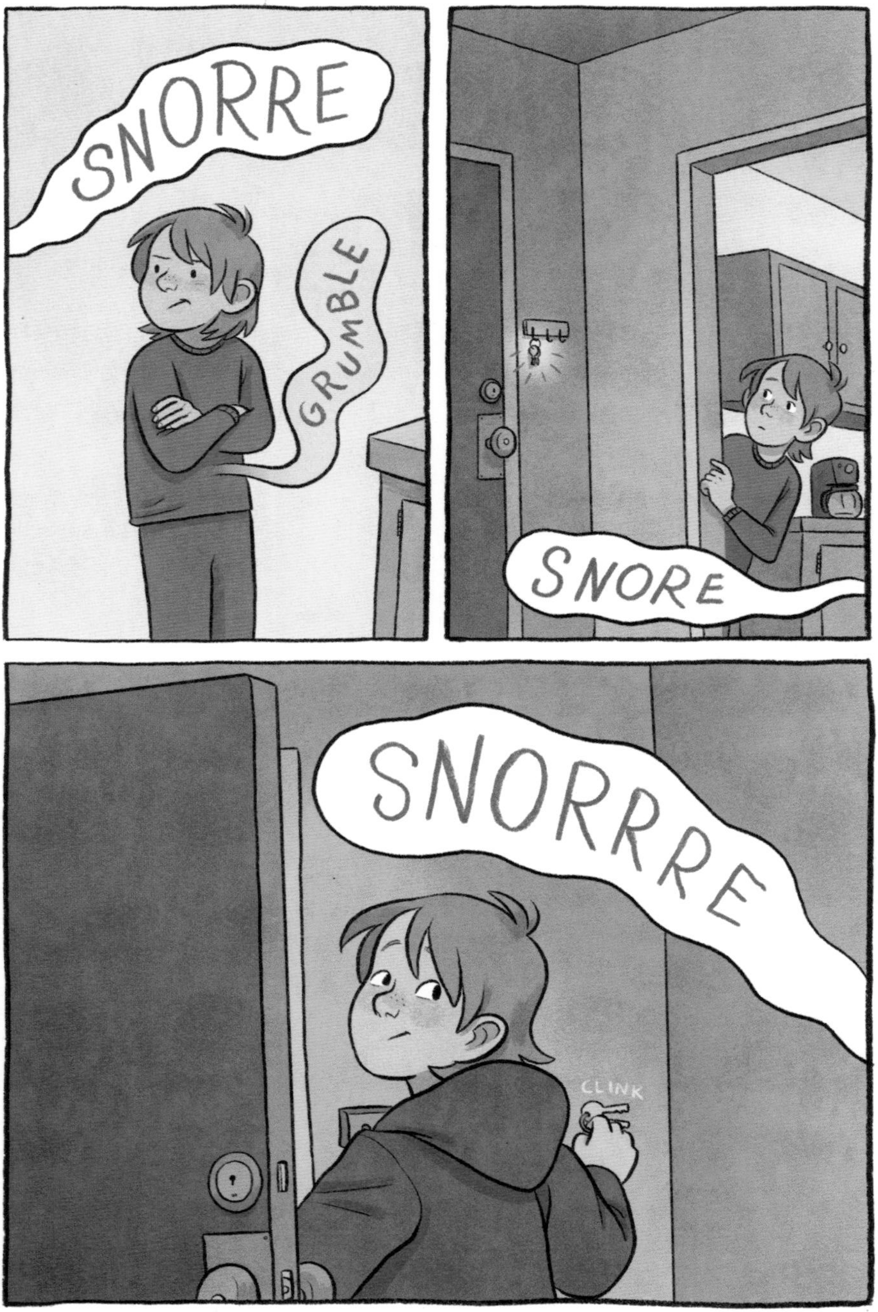
SNORRE
GRUMBLE
SNORE
SNORRRE
CLINK

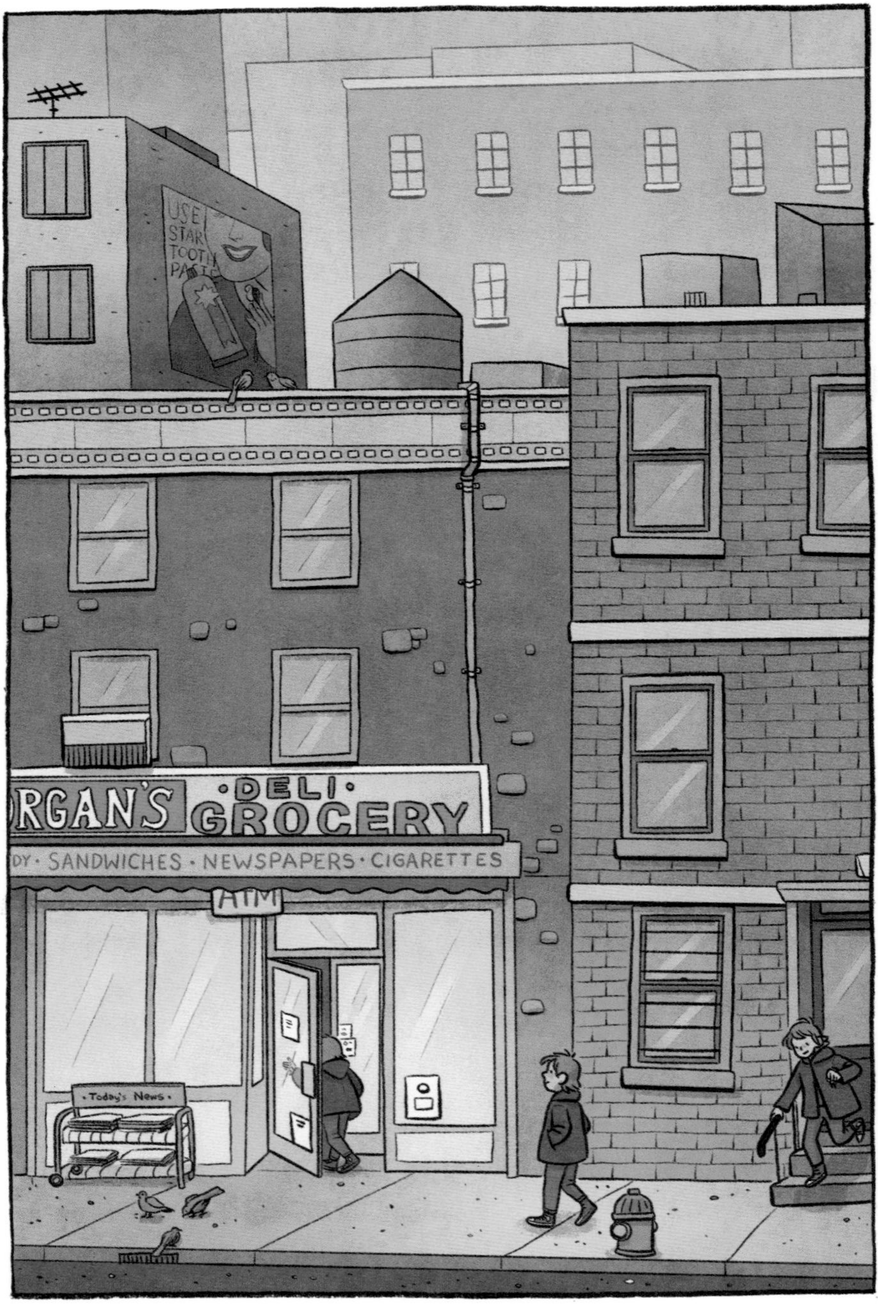
USE STAR TOOTH PASTE
RGAN'S
·DELI·
GROCERY
DY · SANDWICHES · NEWSPAPERS · CIGARETTES
ATM
Today's News

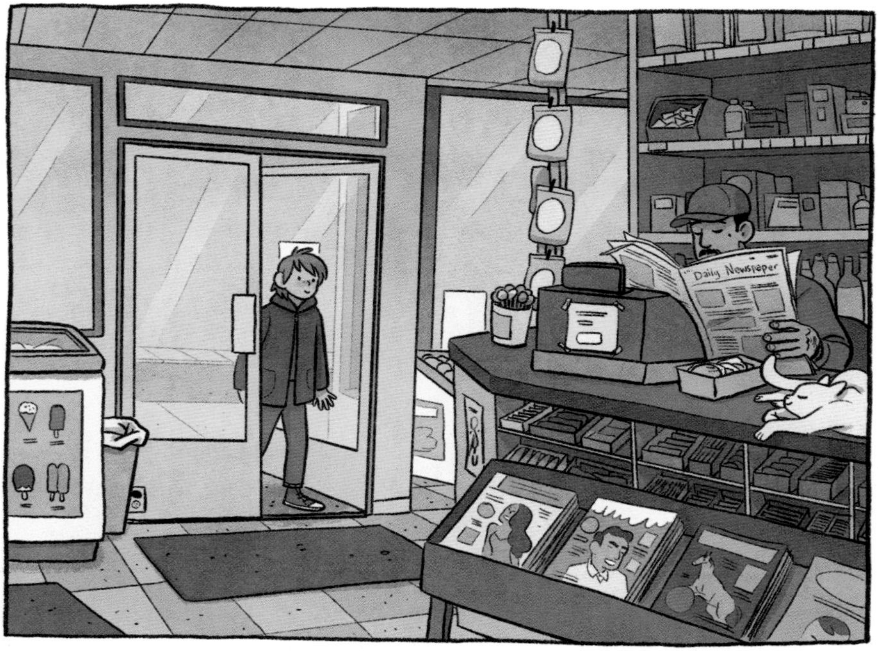
Daily Newspaper

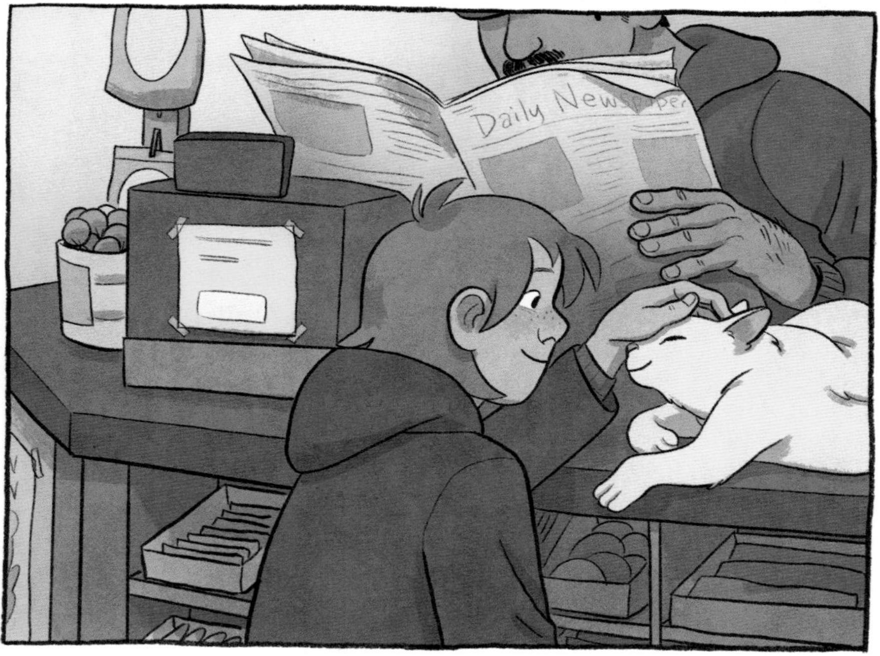
Daily Newspaper

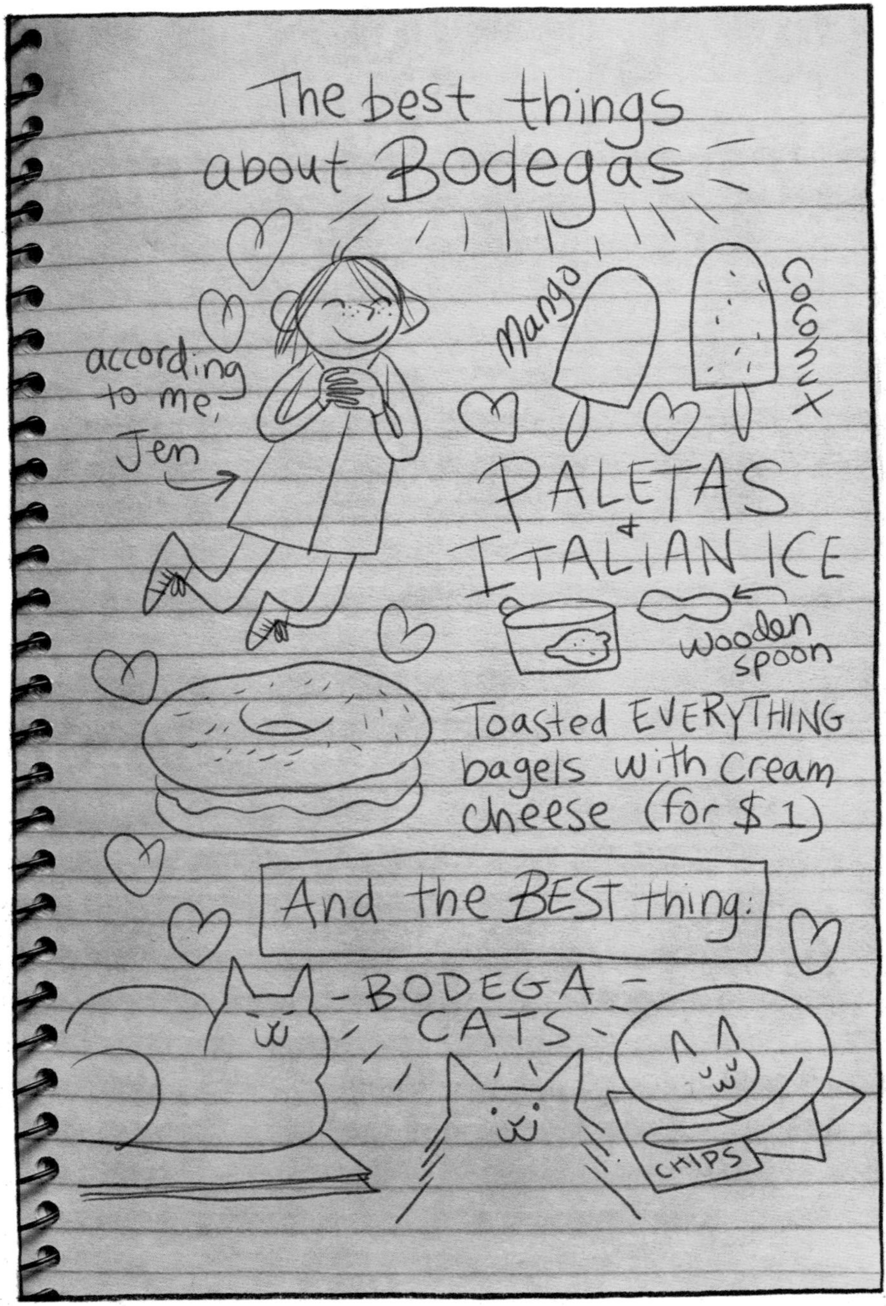
The best things about Bodegas
according to me, Jen
Mango
Coconut
PALETAS & ITALIAN ICE
wooden spoon
Toasted EVERYTHING bagels with cream cheese (for $ 1)
And the BEST thing:
-BODEGA-
CATS
CHIPS

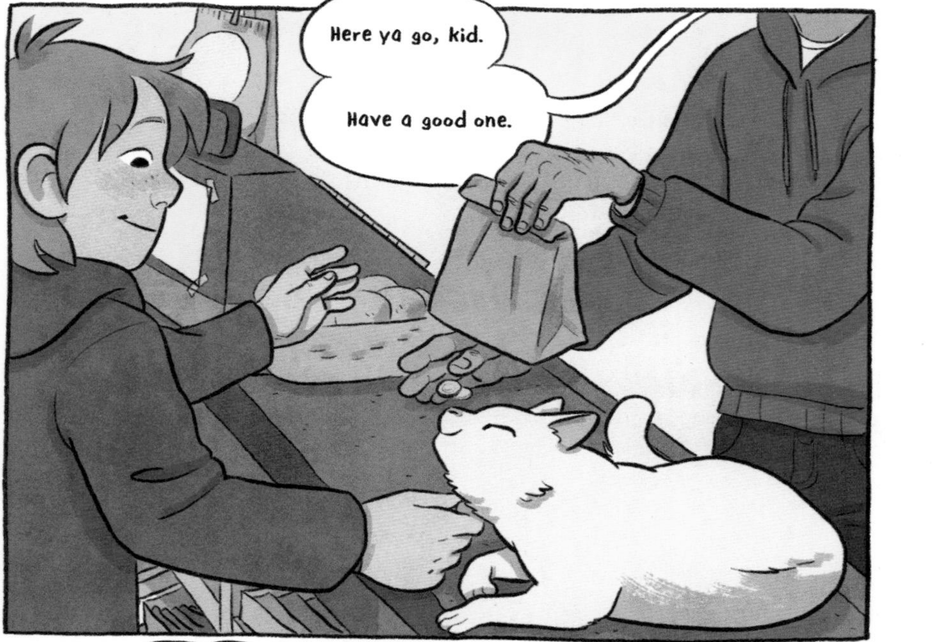
Here ya go, kid.
Have a good one.

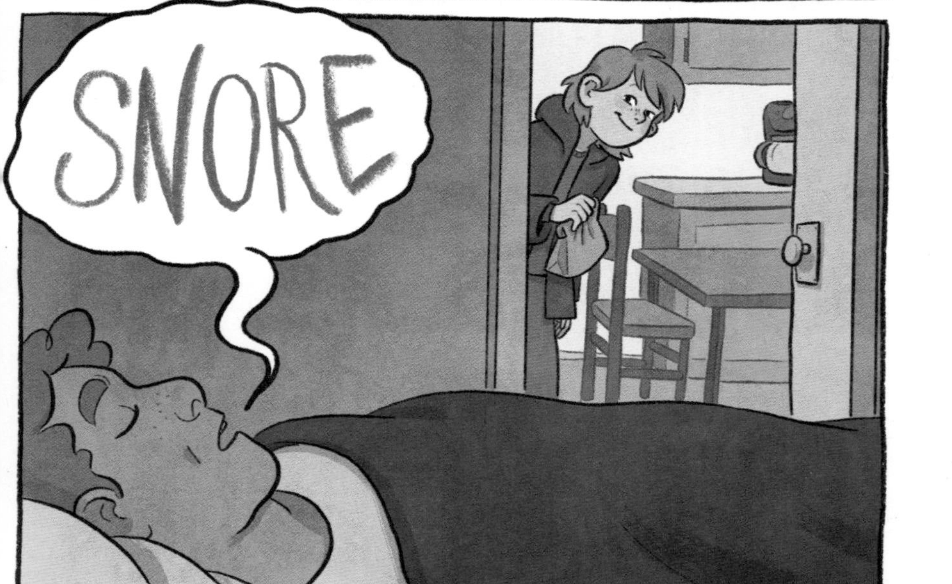
SNORE

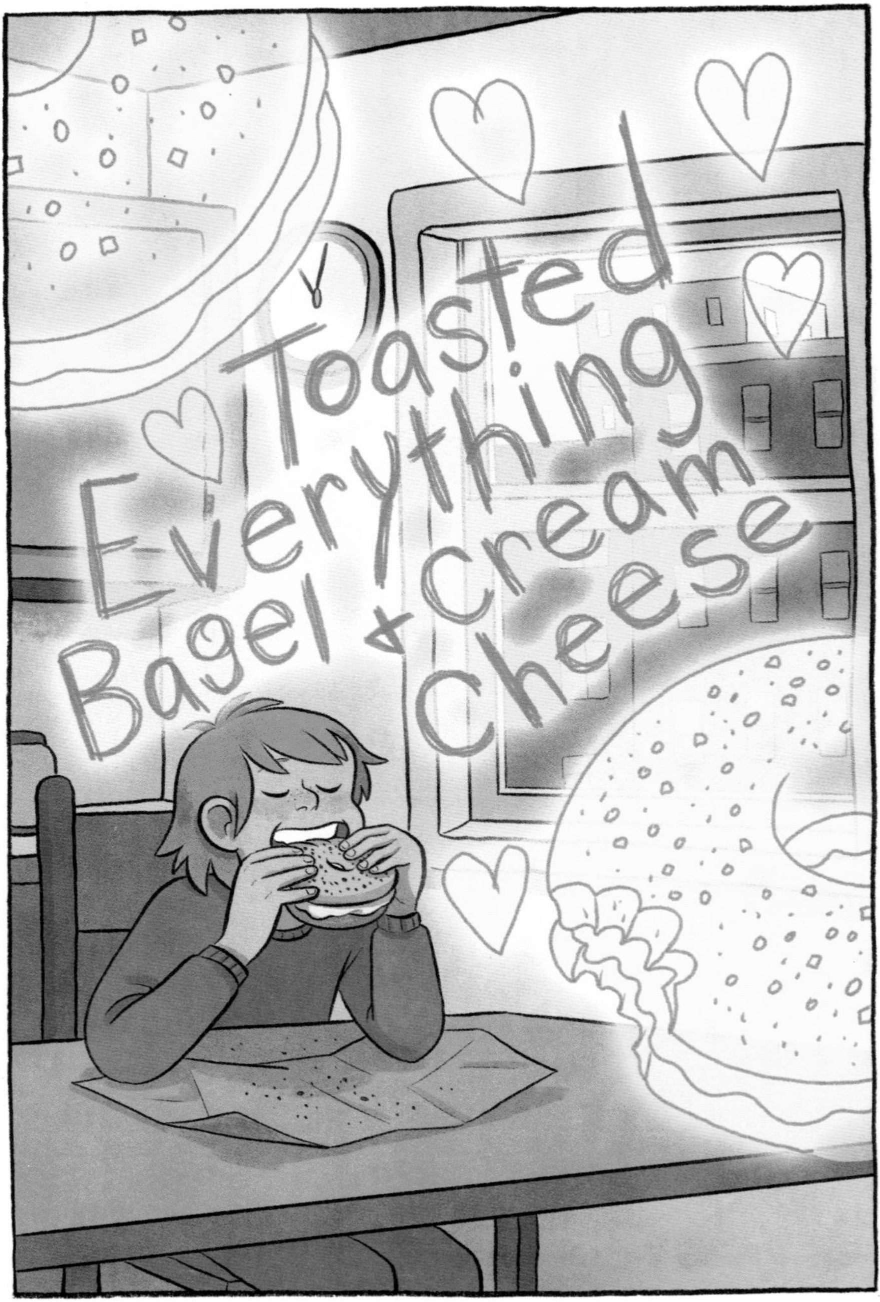
Toasted Everything Bagel & Cream Cheese

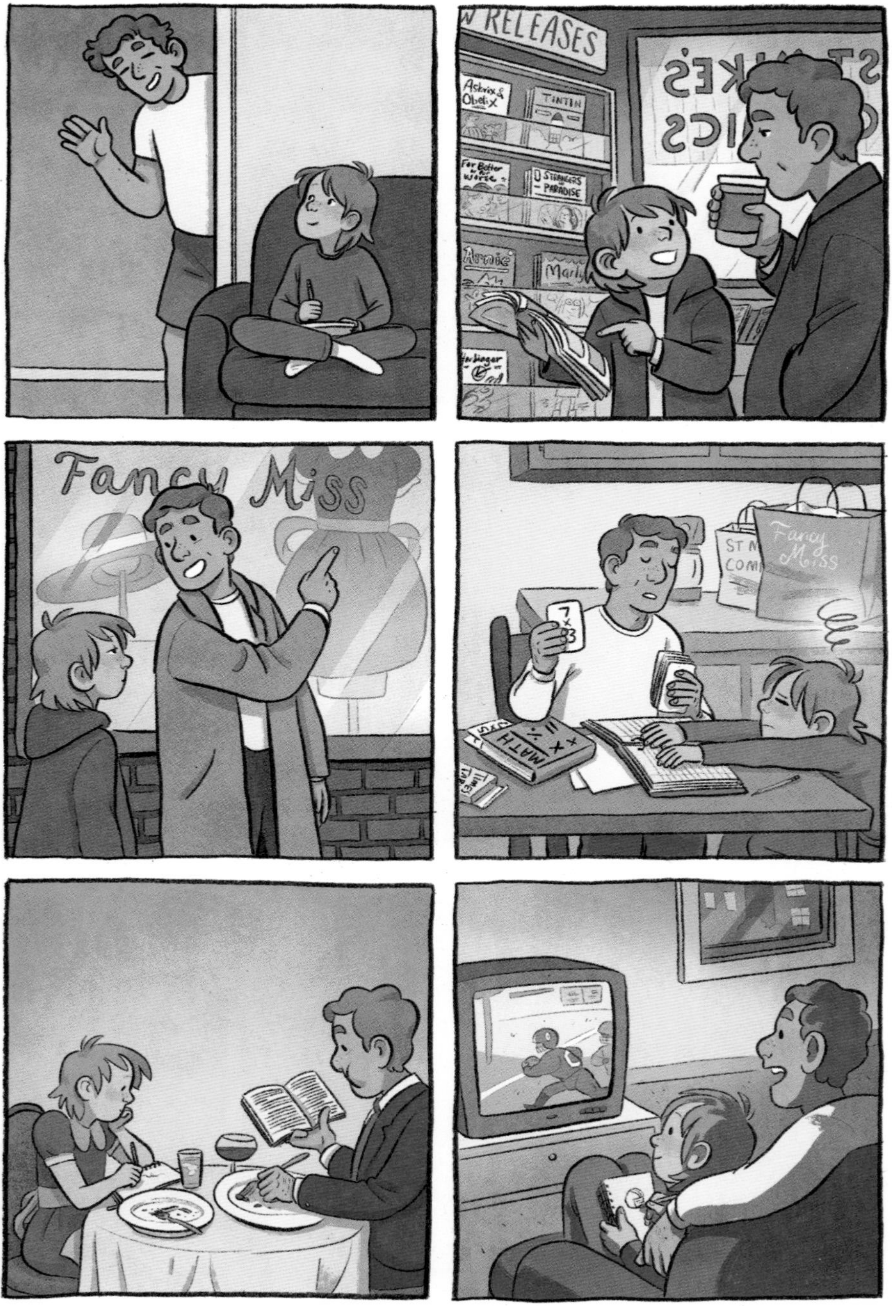
RELEASES
Asterix & Obelix
TINTIN
For Better or Worse
Fancy Miss
MATH
Fancy Miss

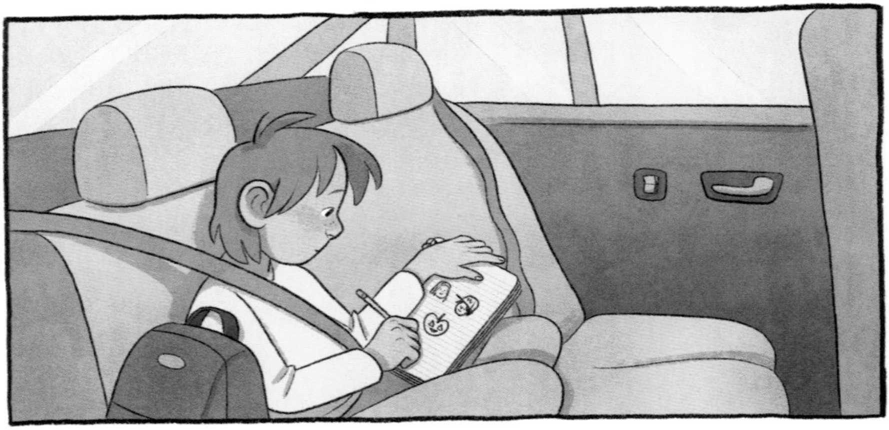

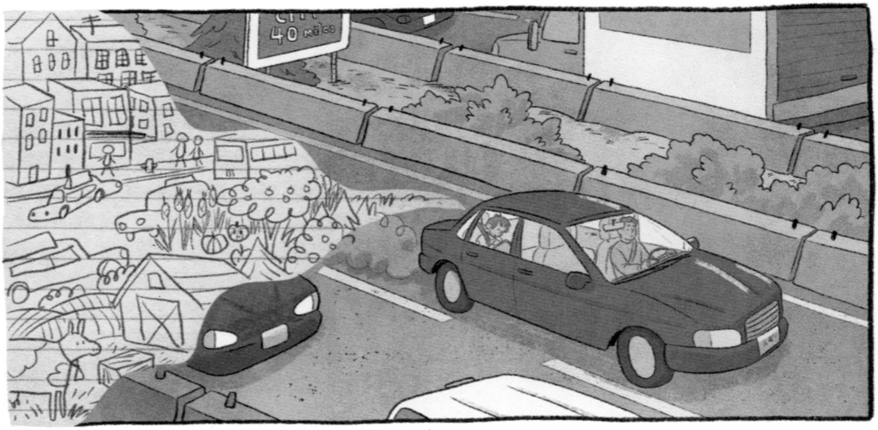
40 miles

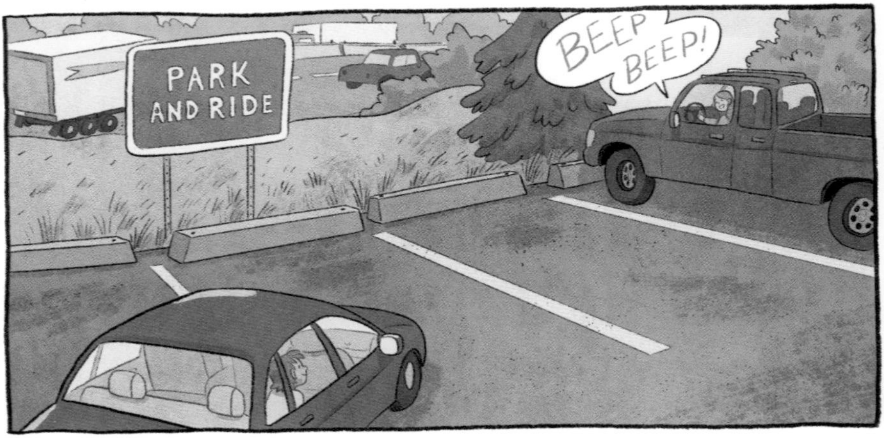
PARK AND RIDE
BEEP BEEP!

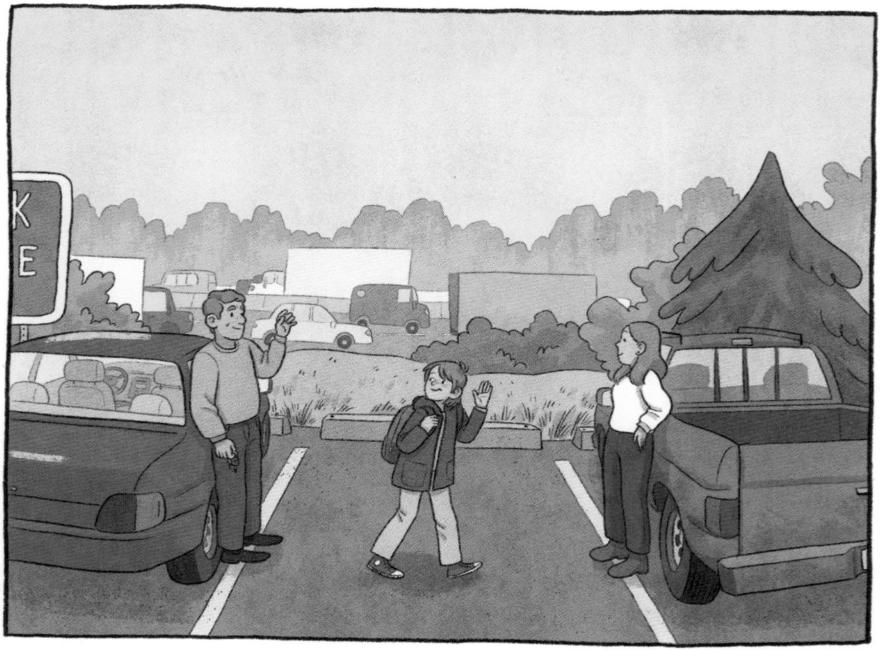
K
E

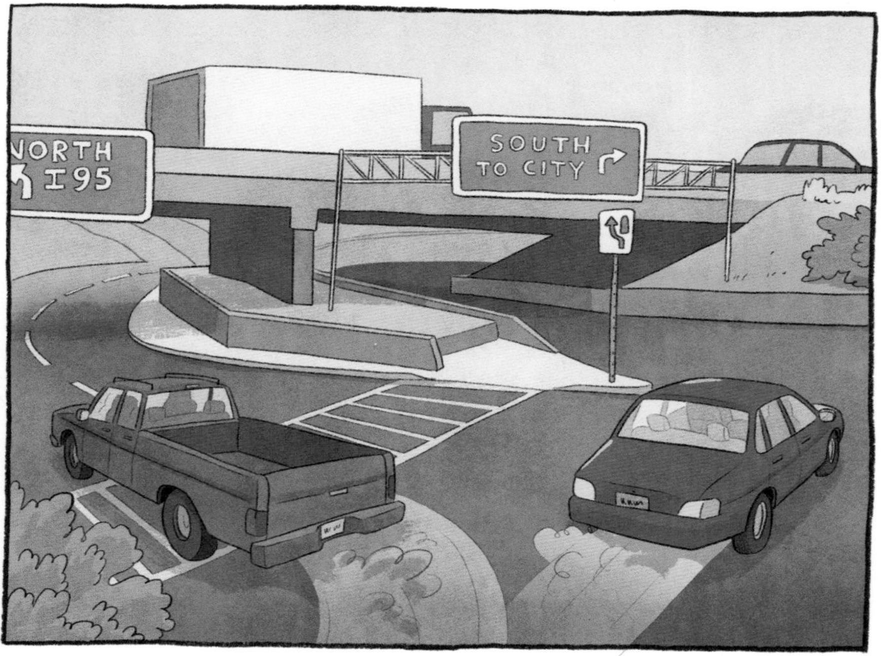
NORTH
I95
SOUTH
TO CITY

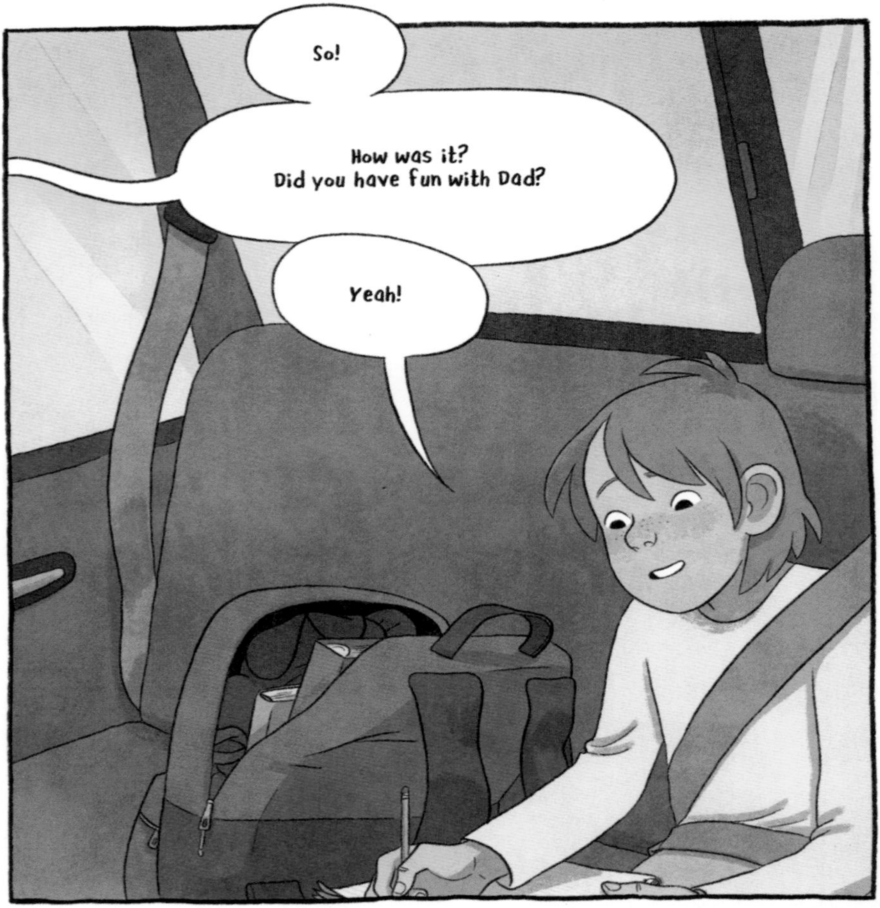
So!
How was it? Did you have fun with Dad?
Yeah!

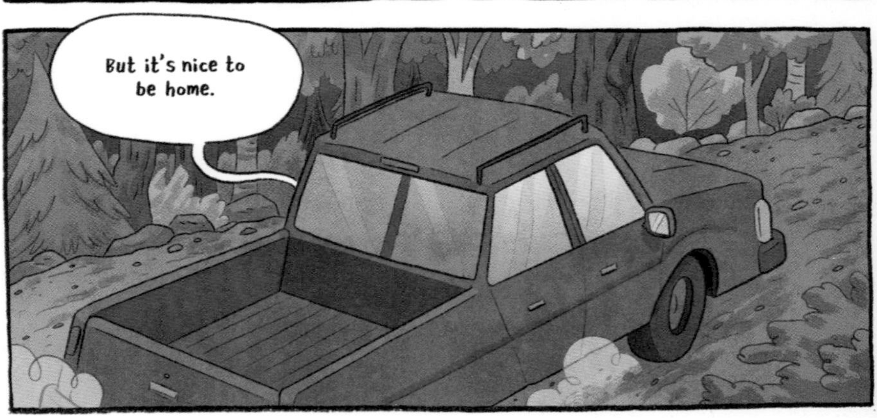
But it's nice to be home.

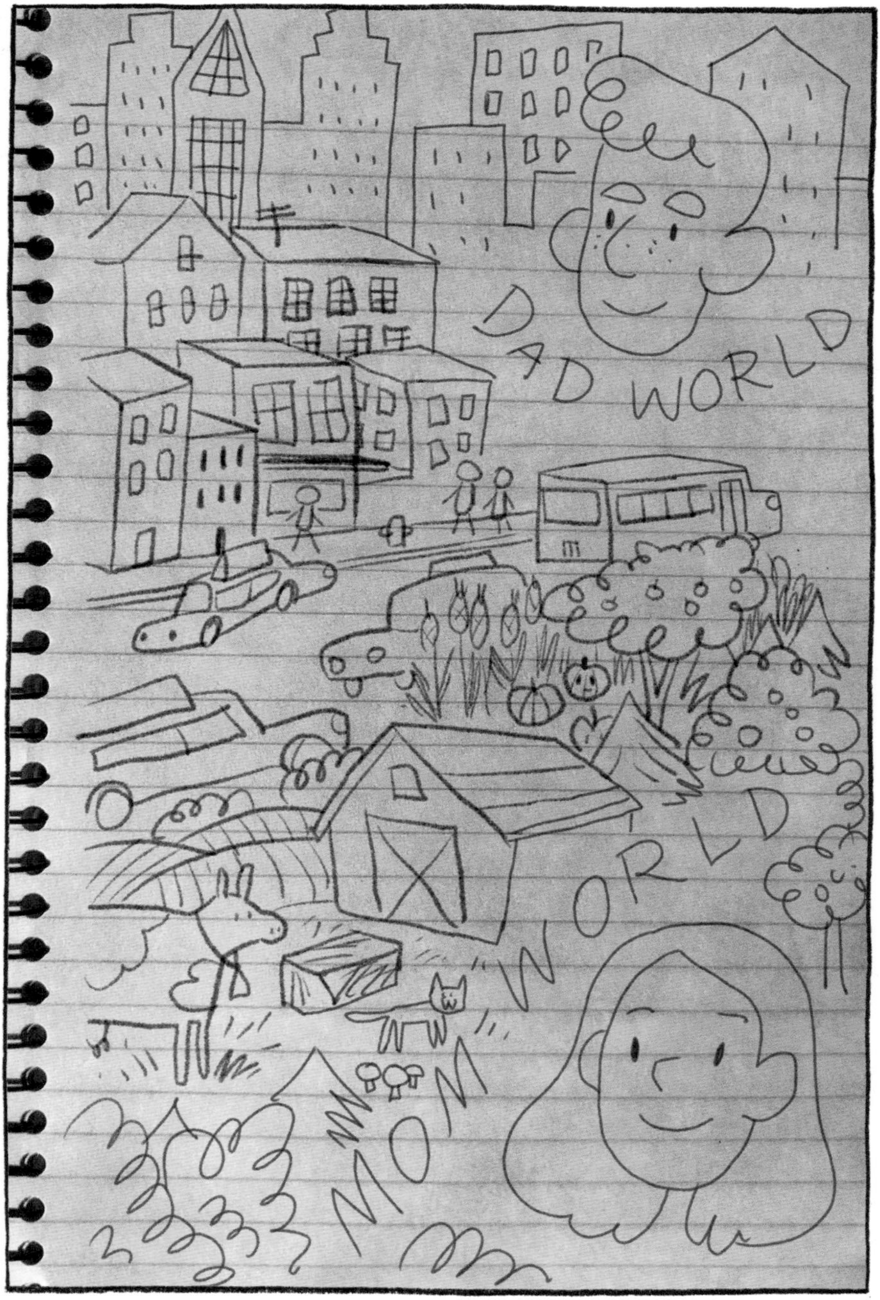
DAD WORLD
MOM WORLD

Chapter Five

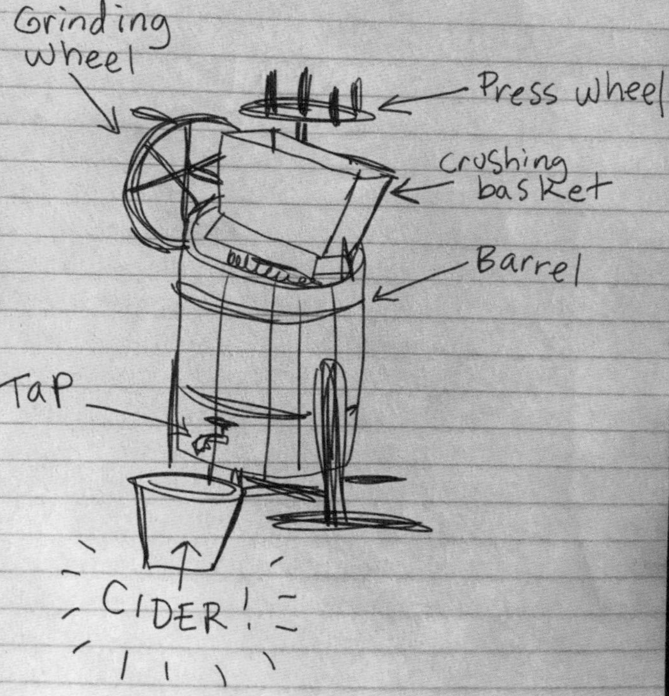
Grinding wheel
Press wheel
crushing basket
Barrel
Tap
CIDER!

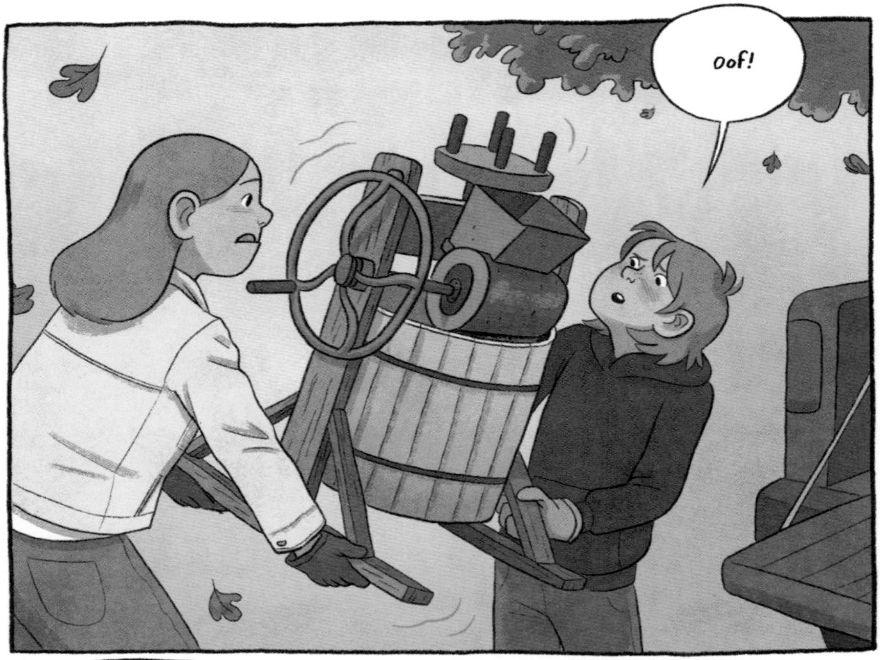
Oof!

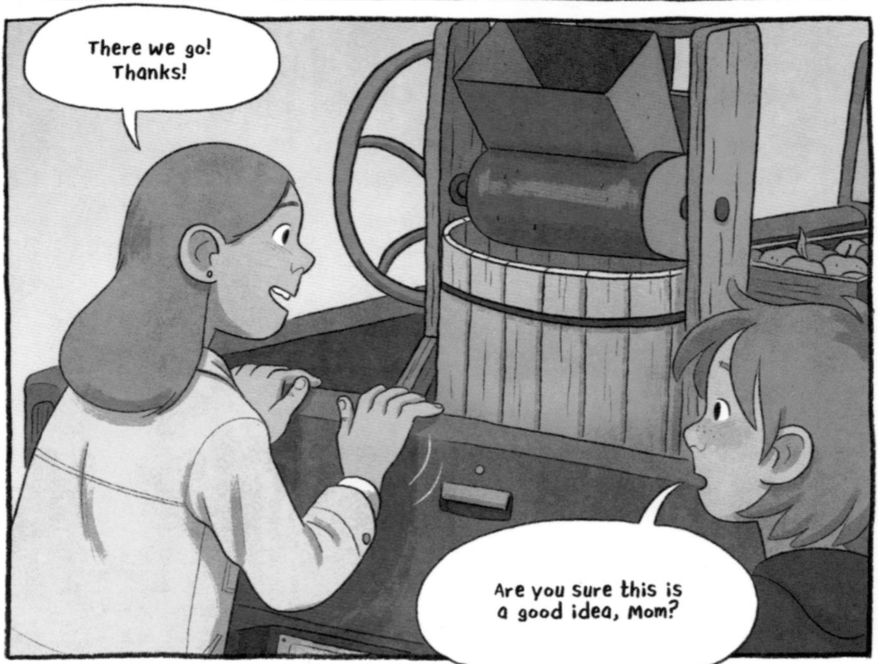
There we go!
Thanks!
Are you sure this is
a good idea, Mom?

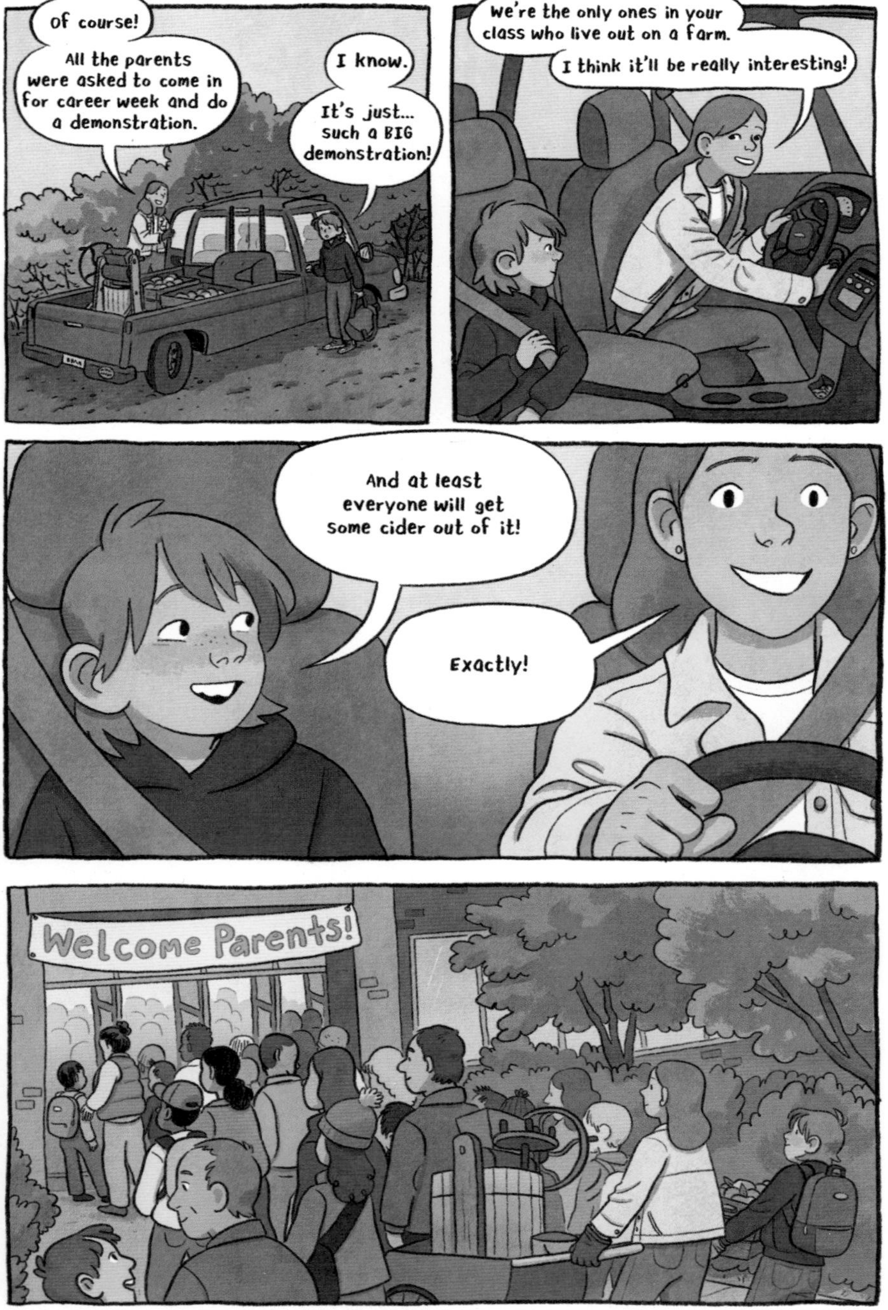
Of course!
All the parents were asked to come in for career week and do a demonstration.
I know.
It's just... such a BIG demonstration!
We're the only ones in your class who live out on a farm.
I think it'll be really interesting!
And at least everyone will get some cider out of it!
Exactly!
Welcome Parents!

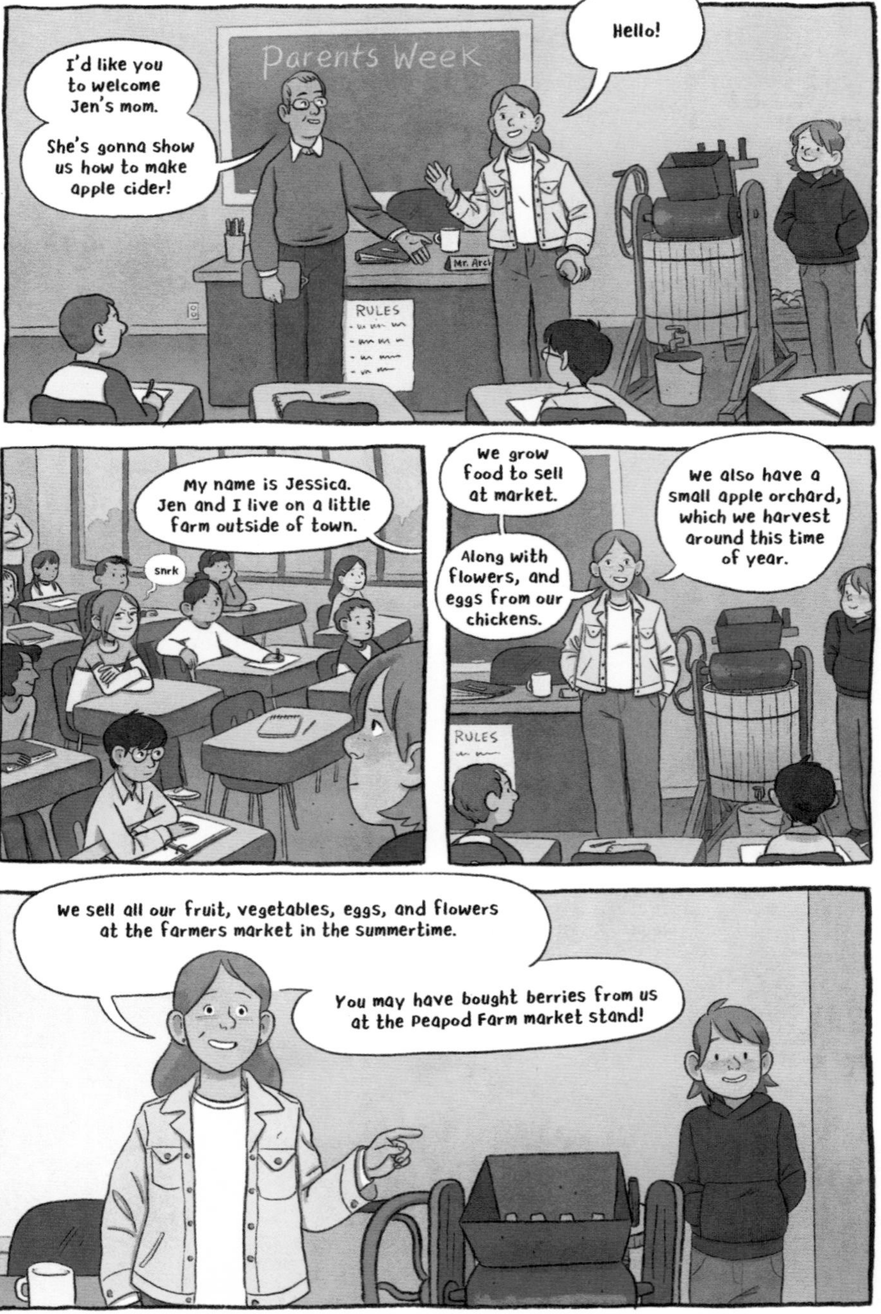
Parents Week
I'd like you to welcome Jen's mom.
She's gonna show us how to make apple cider!
Hello!
RULES
Mr. Arch
My name is Jessica. Jen and I live on a little farm outside of town.
snrk
We grow food to sell at market.
Along with flowers, and eggs from our chickens.
We also have a small apple orchard, which we harvest around this time of year.
RULES
We sell all our fruit, vegetables, eggs, and flowers at the farmers market in the summertime.
You may have bought berries from us at the Peapod Farm market stand!

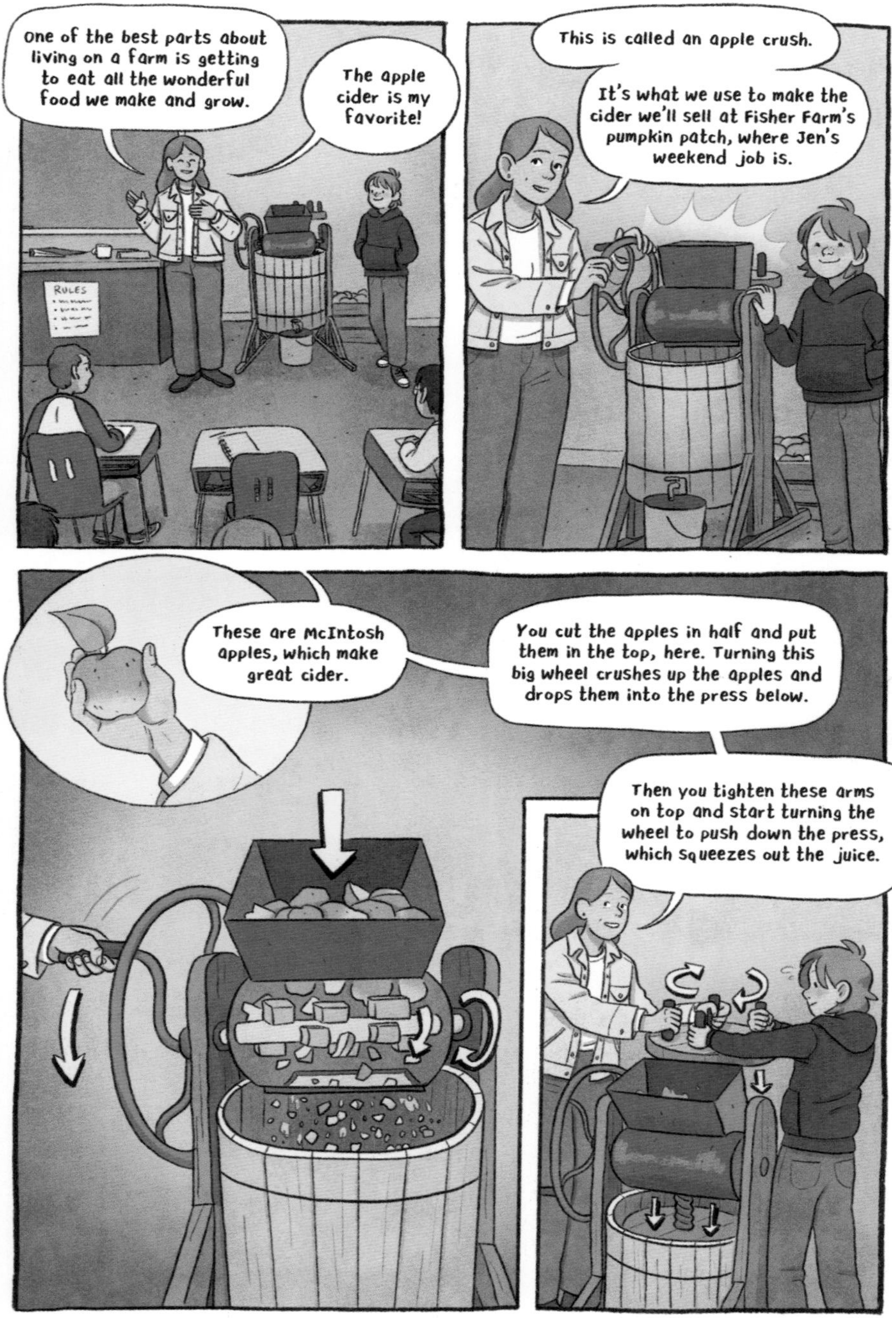
One of the best parts about living on a farm is getting to eat all the wonderful food we make and grow.
The apple cider is my favorite!
This is called an apple crush.
It's what we use to make the cider we'll sell at Fisher Farm's pumpkin patch, where Jen's weekend job is.
These are McIntosh apples, which make great cider.
You cut the apples in half and put them in the top, here. Turning this big wheel crushes up the apples and drops them into the press below.
Then you tighten these arms on top and start turning the wheel to push down the press, which squeezes out the juice.
RULES

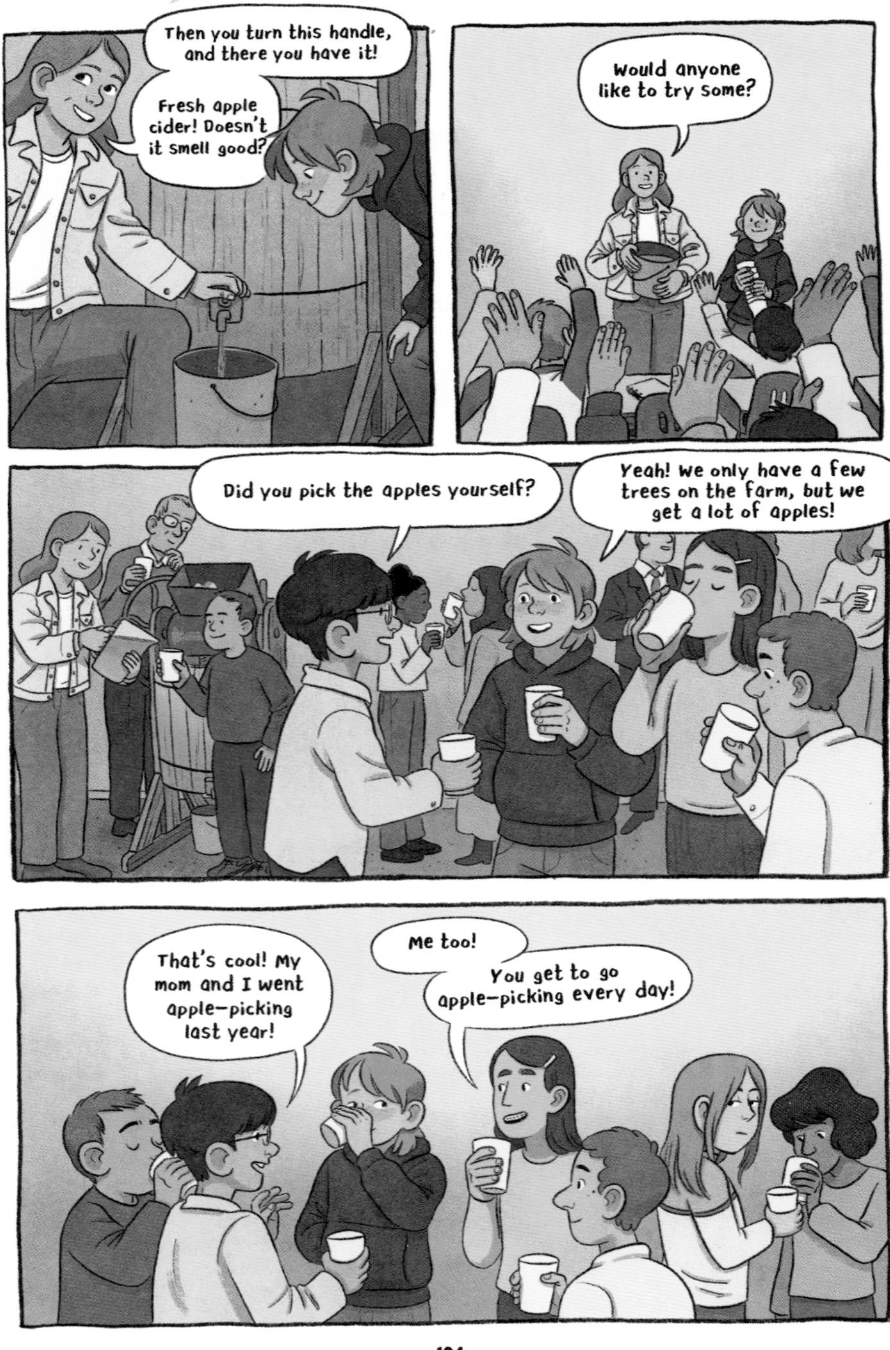

Then you turn this handle, and there you have it!
Fresh apple cider! Doesn't it smell good?
Would anyone like to try some?
Did you pick the apples yourself?
Yeah! We only have a few trees on the farm, but we get a lot of apples!
That's cool! My mom and I went apple-picking last year!
Me too!
You get to go apple-picking every day!

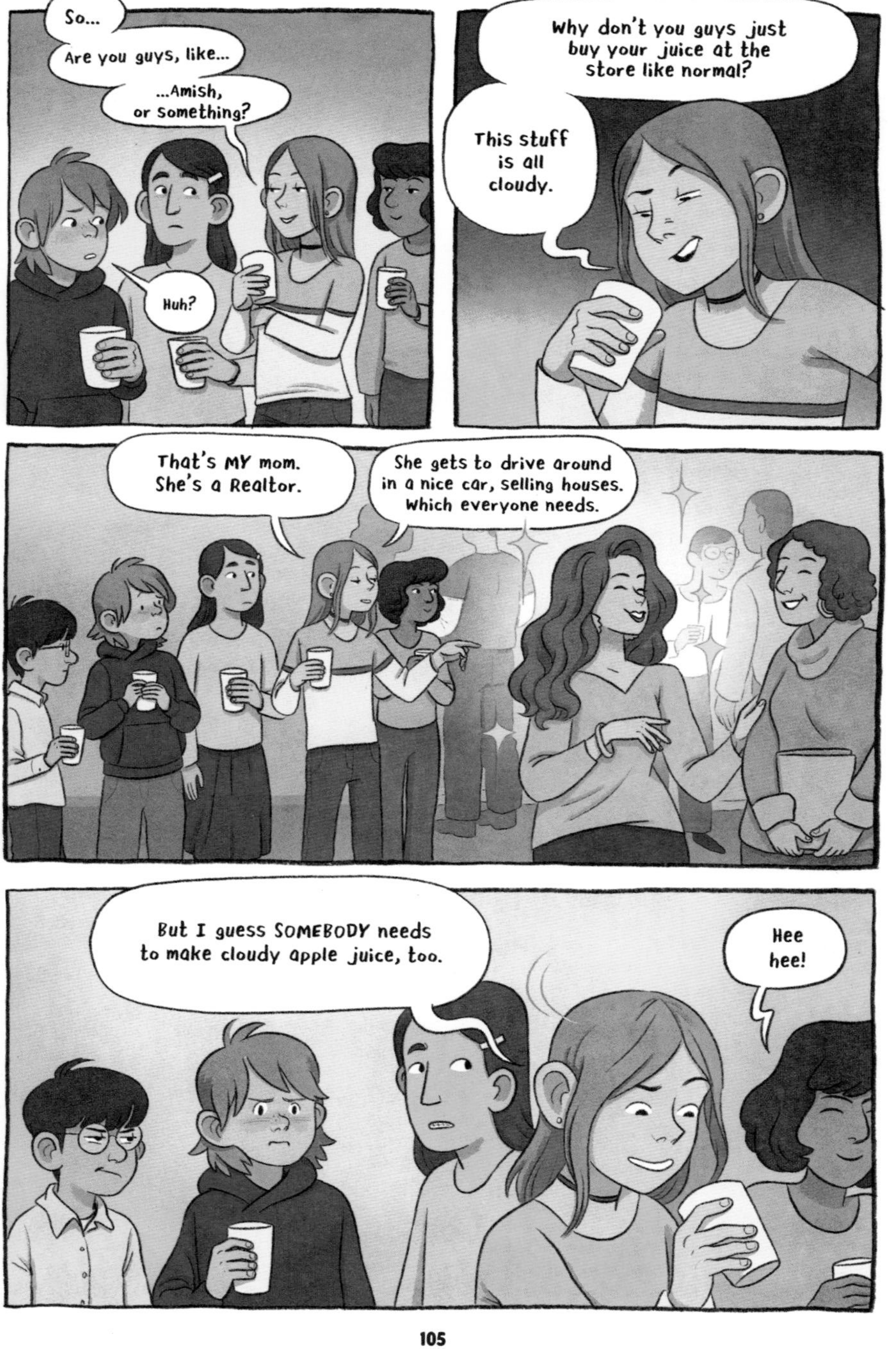
So...
Are you guys, like...
...Amish, or something?
Huh?
Why don't you guys just buy your juice at the store like normal?
This stuff is all cloudy.
That's MY mom. She's a Realtor.
She gets to drive around in a nice car, selling houses. Which everyone needs.
But I guess SOMEBODY needs to make cloudy apple juice, too.
Hee hee!

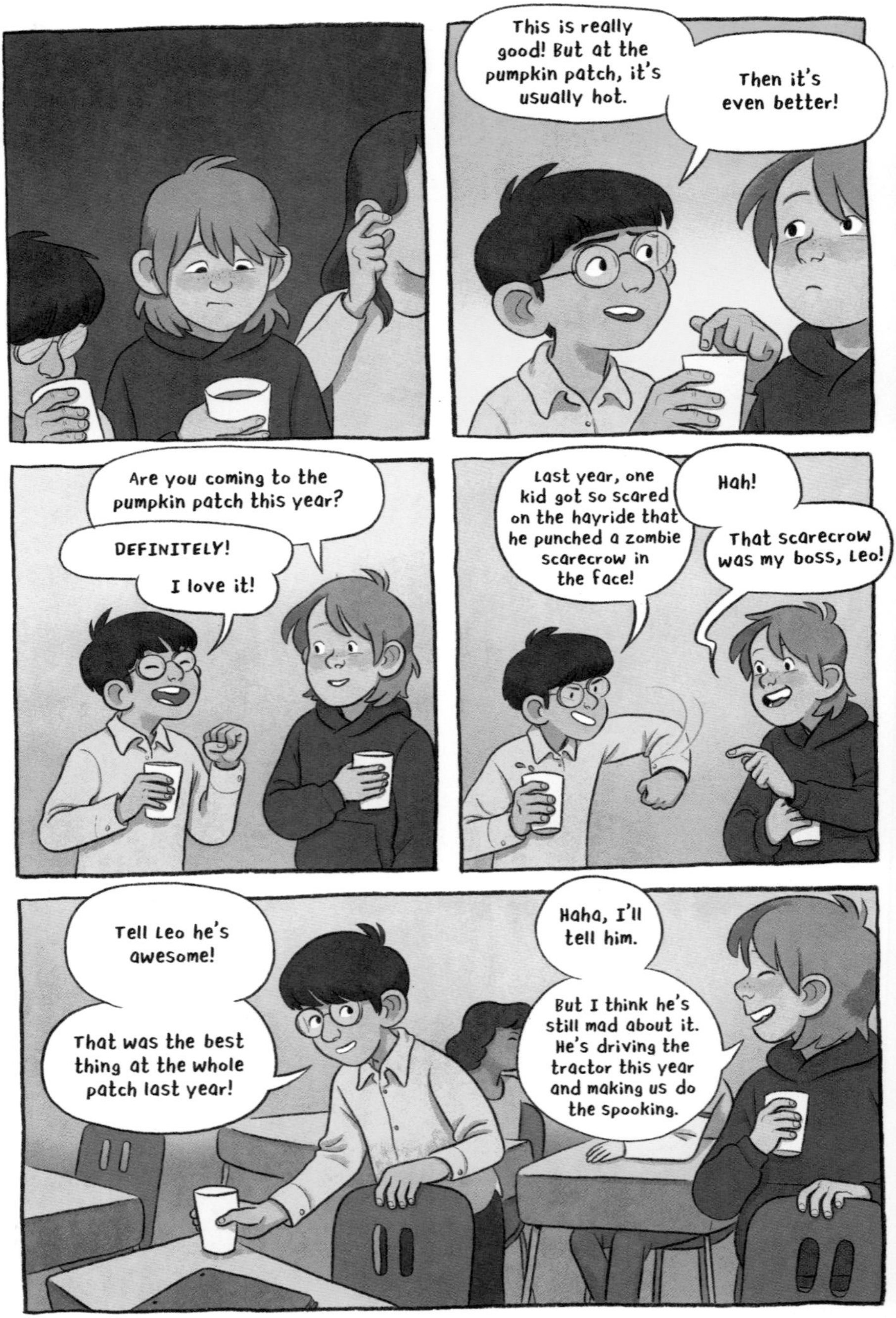
This is really good! But at the pumpkin patch, it's usually hot.
Then it's even better!
Are you coming to the pumpkin patch this year?
DEFINITELY!
I love it!
Last year, one kid got so scared on the hayride that he punched a zombie scarecrow in the face!
Hah!
That scarecrow was my boss, Leo!
Tell Leo he's awesome!
That was the best thing at the whole patch last year!
Haha, I'll tell him.
But I think he's still mad about it. He's driving the tractor this year and making us do the spooking.

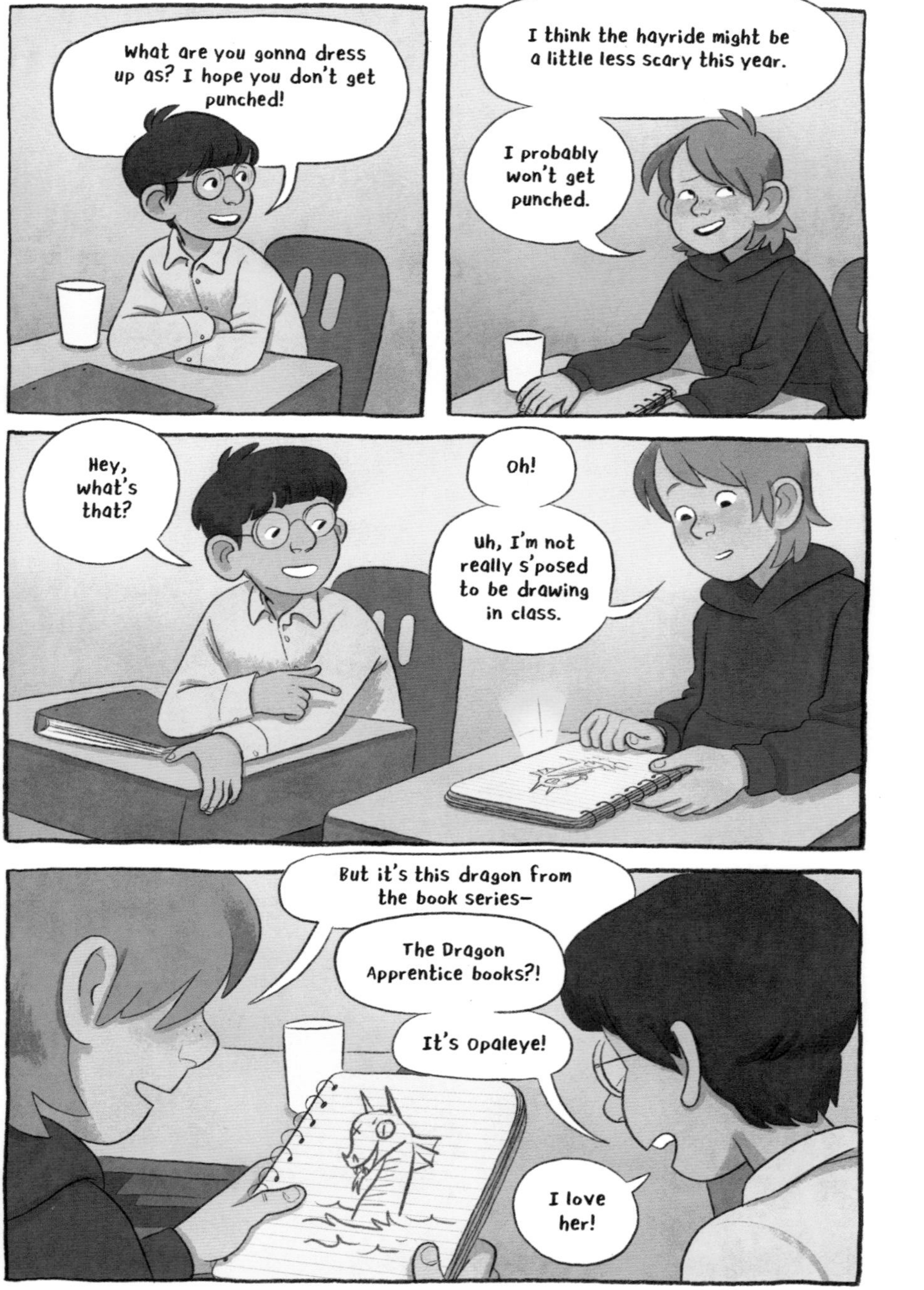
What are you gonna dress up as? I hope you don't get punched!
I think the hayride might be a little less scary this year.
I probably won't get punched.
Hey, what's that?
Oh!
Uh, I'm not really s'posed to be drawing in class.
But it's this dragon from the book series—
The Dragon Apprentice books?!
It's Opaleye!
I love her!

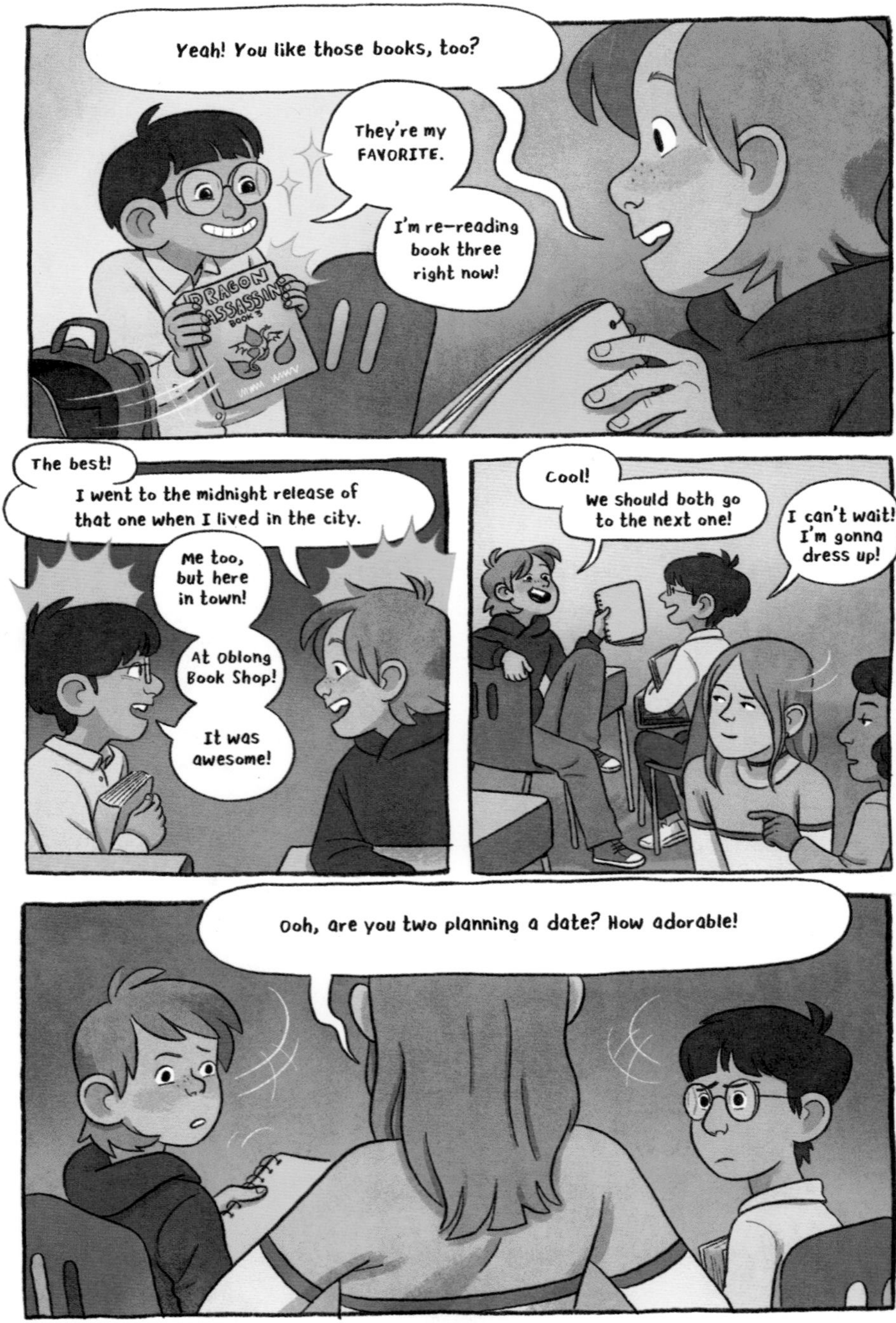
Yeah! You like those books, too?
They're my FAVORITE.
I'm re-reading book three right now!
DRAGON ASSASSIN BOOK 3
The best!
I went to the midnight release of that one when I lived in the city.
Me too, but here in town!
At Oblong Book Shop!
It was awesome!
Cool!
We should both go to the next one!
I can't wait! I'm gonna dress up!
Ooh, are you two planning a date? How adorable!

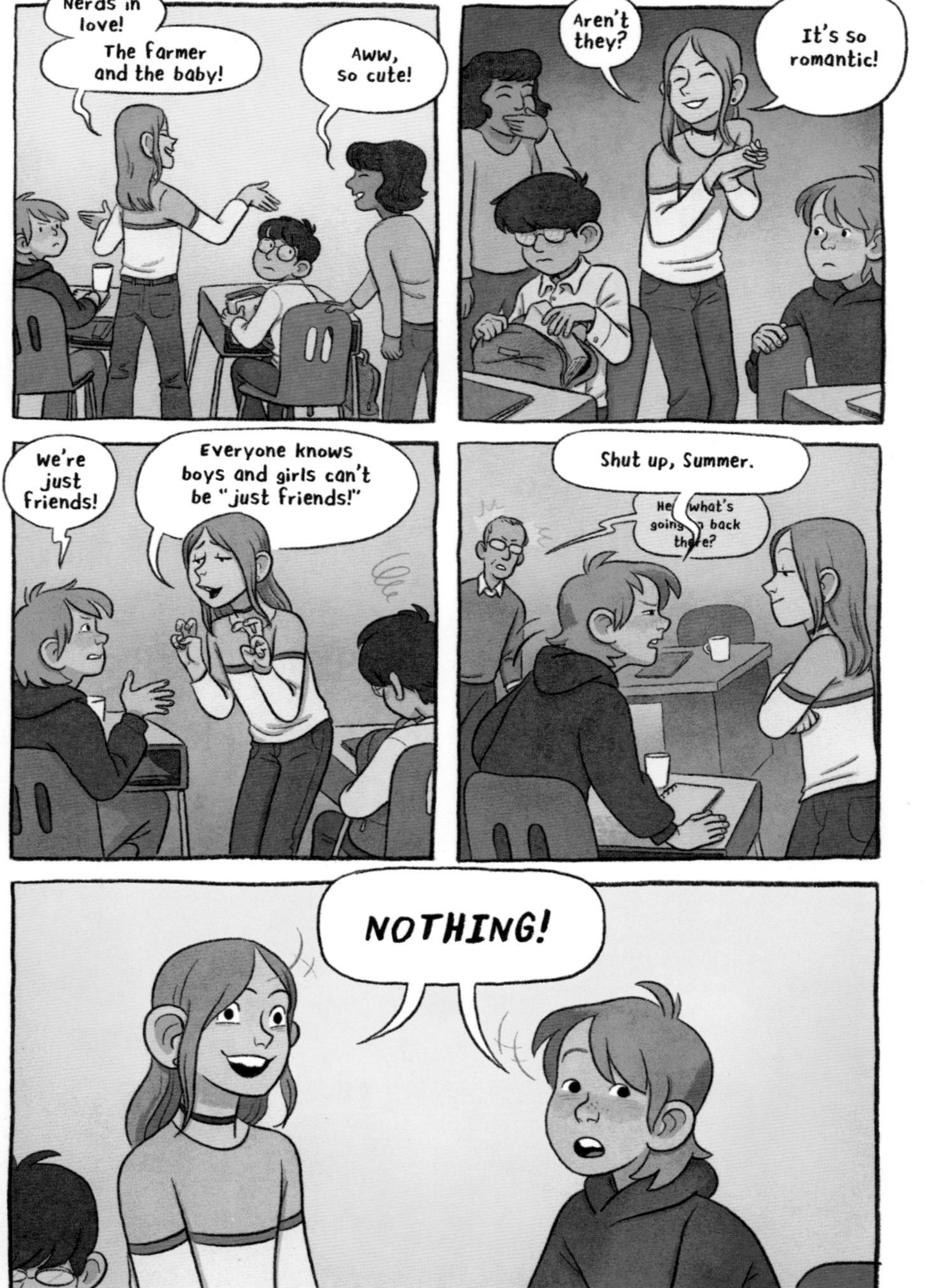

Nerds in love!
The farmer and the baby!
Aww, so cute!
Aren't they?
It's so romantic!
We're just friends!
Everyone knows boys and girls can't be "just friends!"
Shut up, Summer.
He what's going back there?
NOTHING!

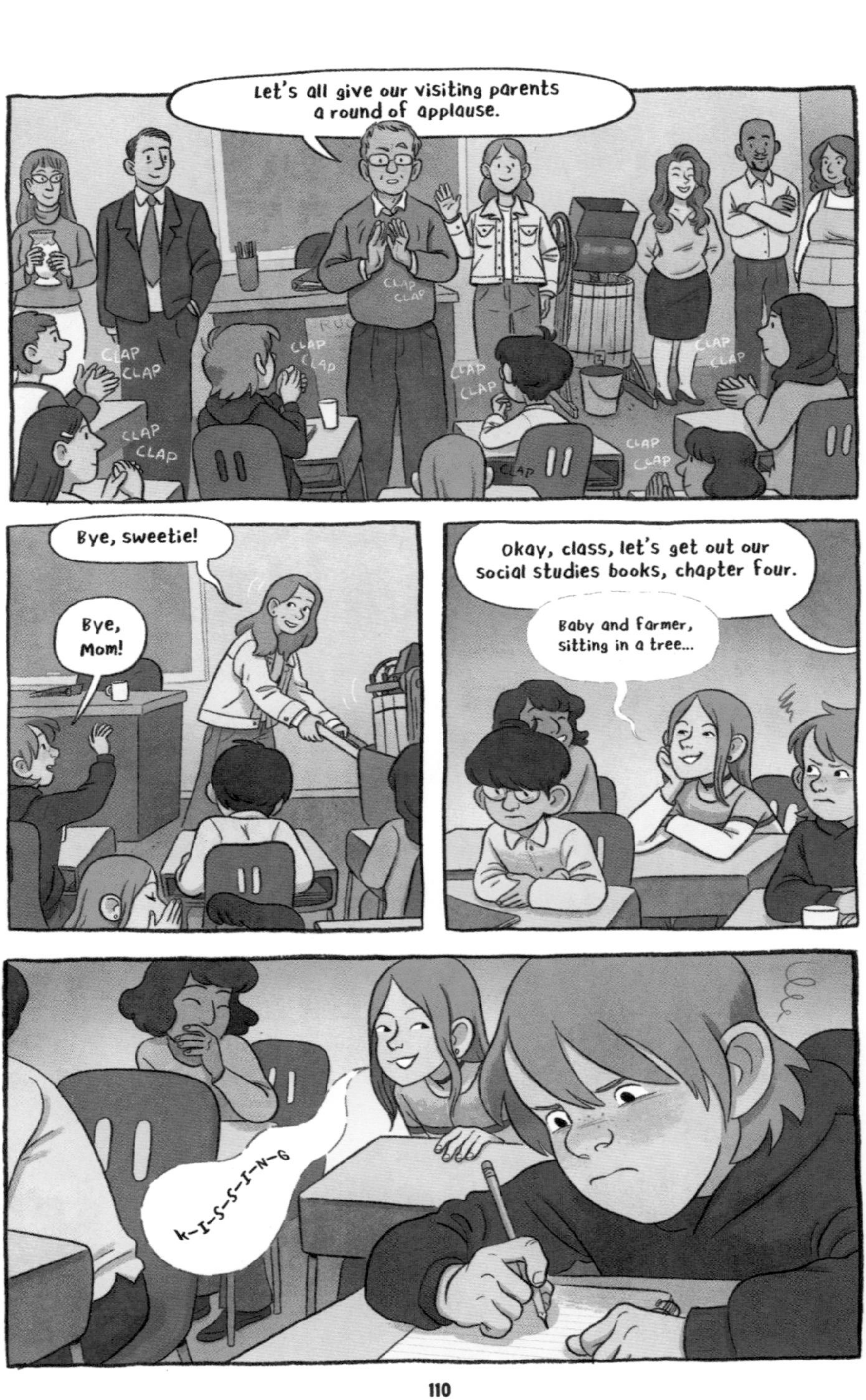
Let's all give our visiting parents a round of applause.
CLAP CLAP
CLAP CLAP
CLAP CLAP
CLAP CLAP
CLAP CLAP
CLAP CLAP
CLAP CLAP
CLAP
Bye, sweetie!
Bye, Mom!
Okay, class, let's get out our social studies books, chapter four.
Baby and farmer, sitting in a tree...
K-I-S-S-I-N-G

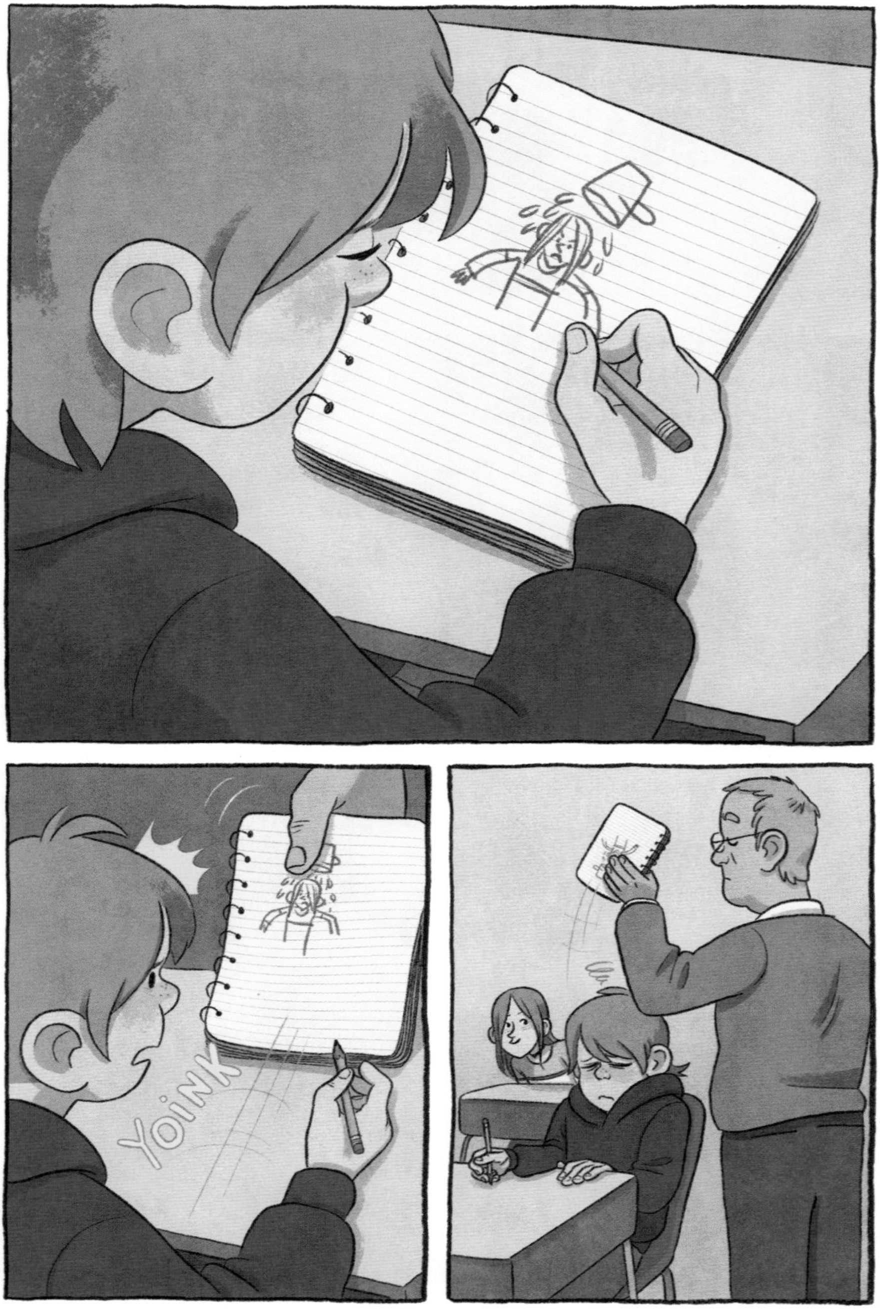
YOINK

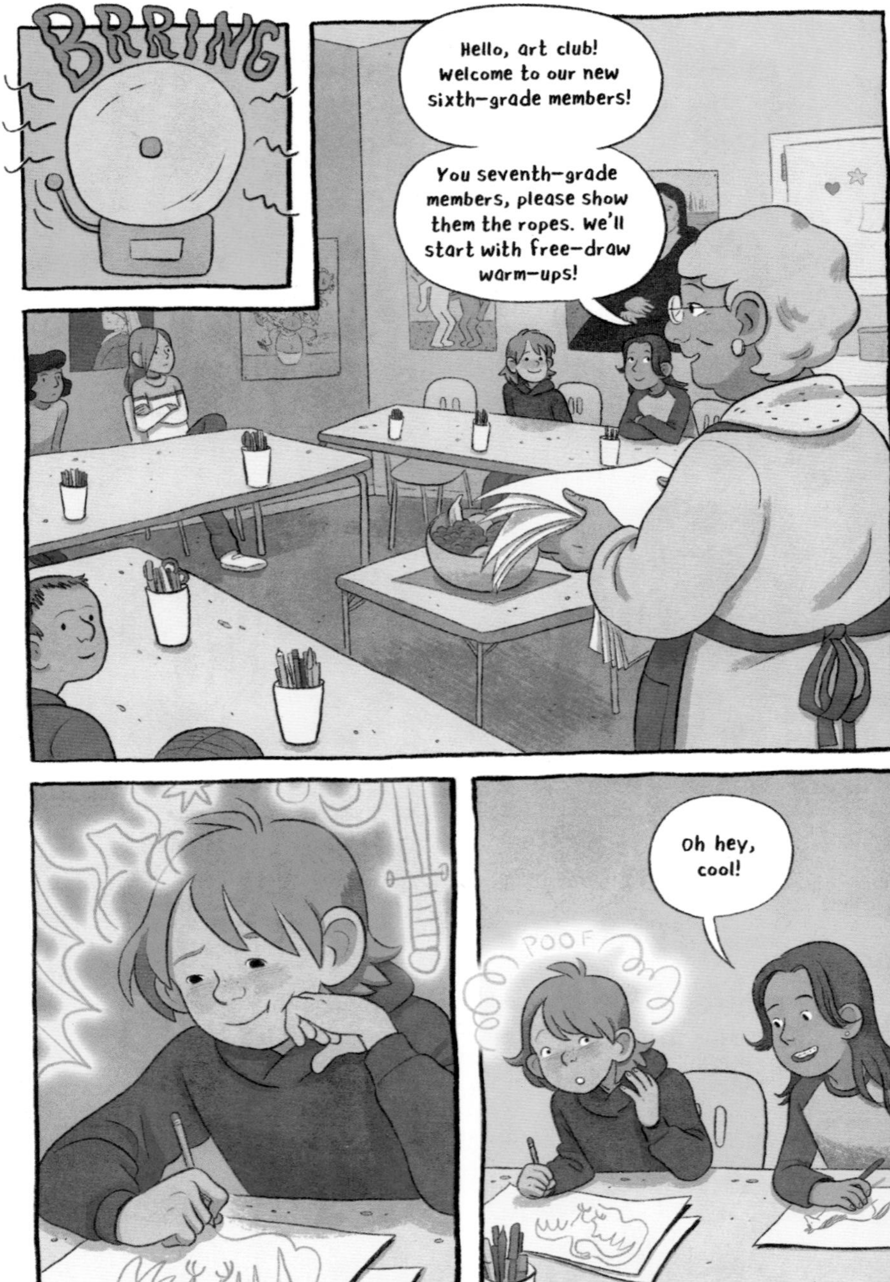
BRRING
Hello, art club! Welcome to our new sixth-grade members!
You seventh-grade members, please show them the ropes. We'll start with free-draw warm-ups!
POOF
Oh hey, cool!

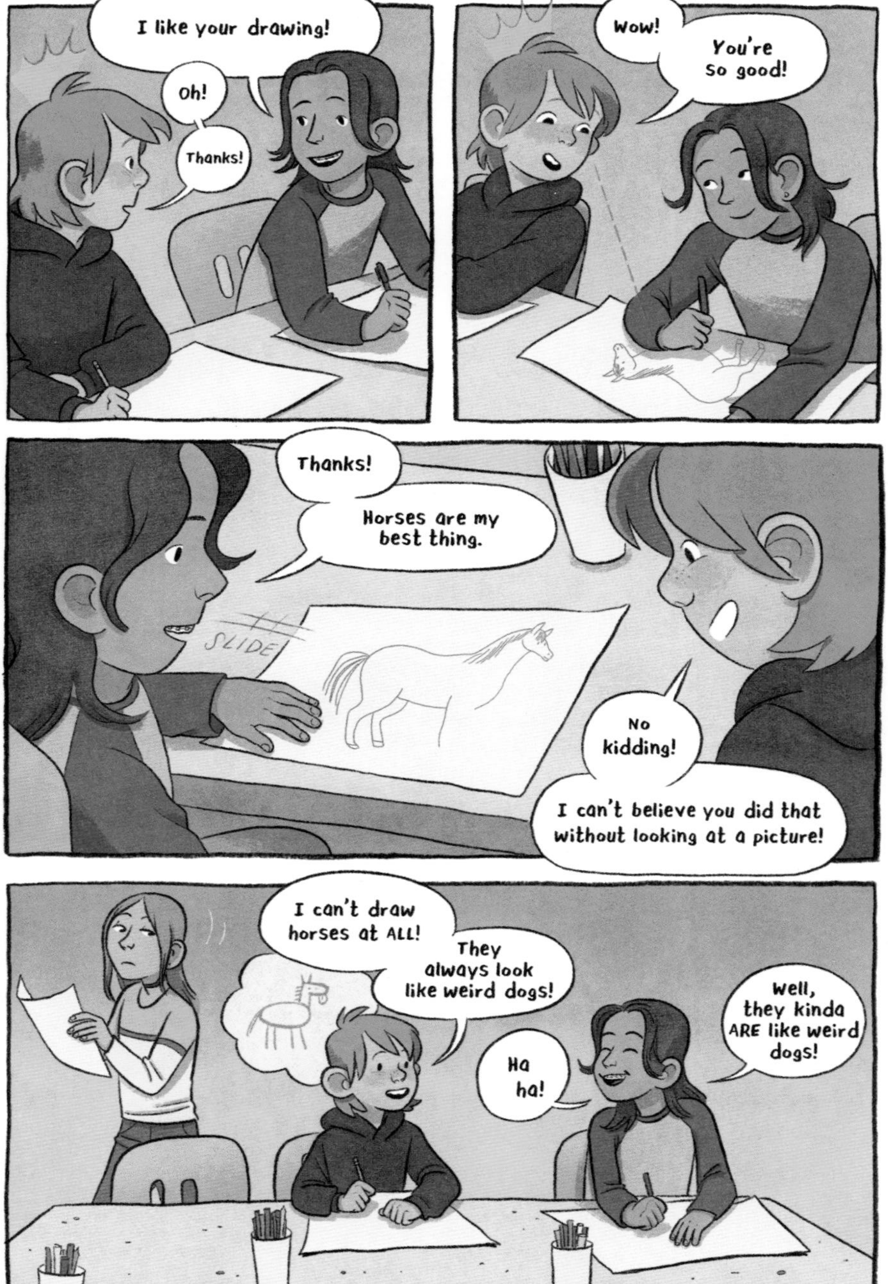
I like your drawing!
Oh!
Thanks!
Wow!
You're so good!
Thanks!
Horses are my best thing.
SLIDE
No kidding!
I can't believe you did that without looking at a picture!
I can't draw horses at ALL!
They always look like weird dogs!
Ha ha!
Well, they kinda ARE like weird dogs!

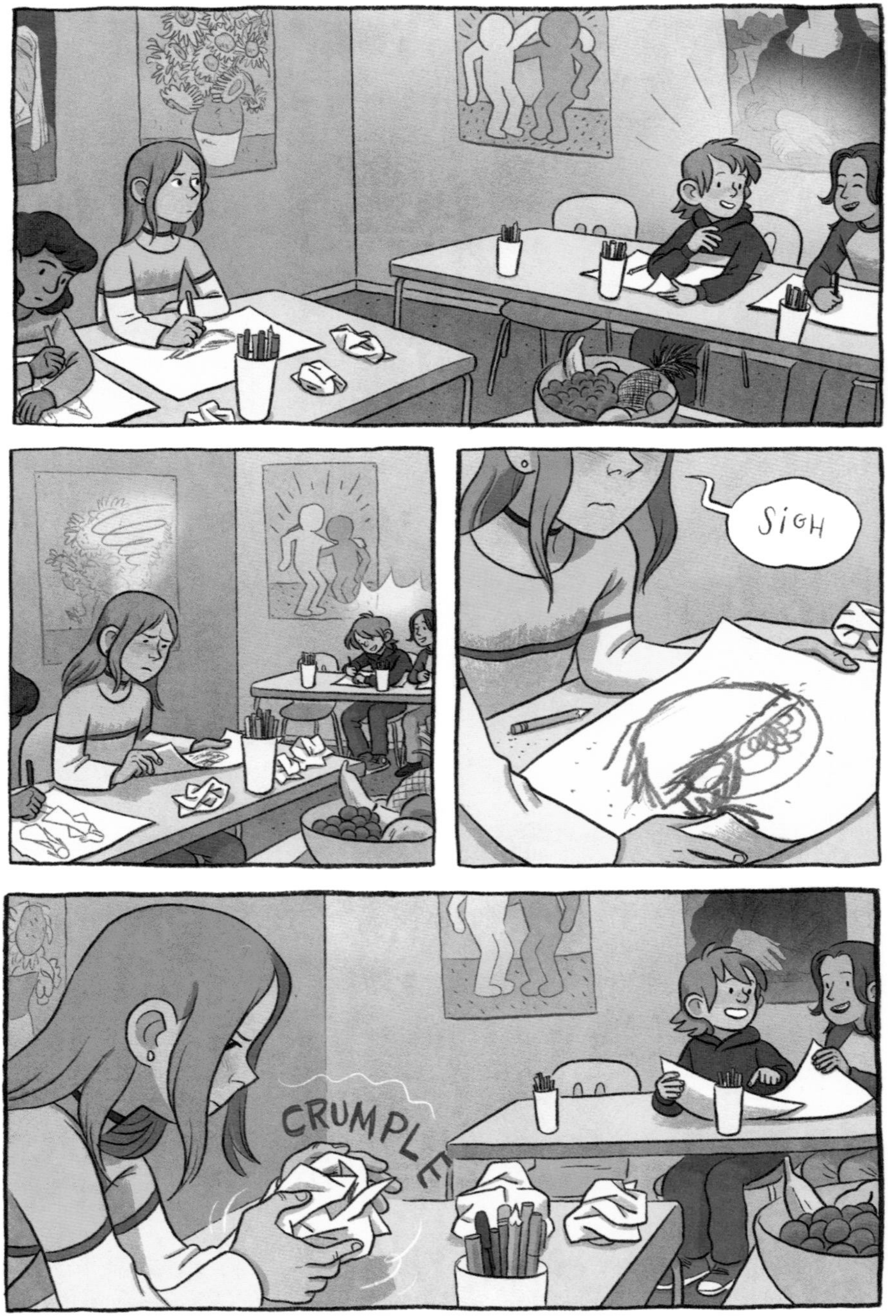
SIGH
CRUMPLE

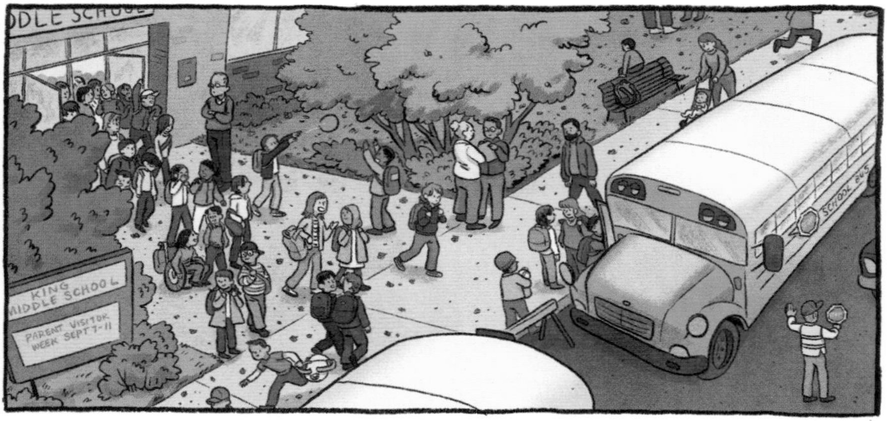
DDLE SCHOOL
KING
MIDDLE SCHOOL
PARENT VISITOR
WEEK SEPT 7-11
SCHOOL BUS

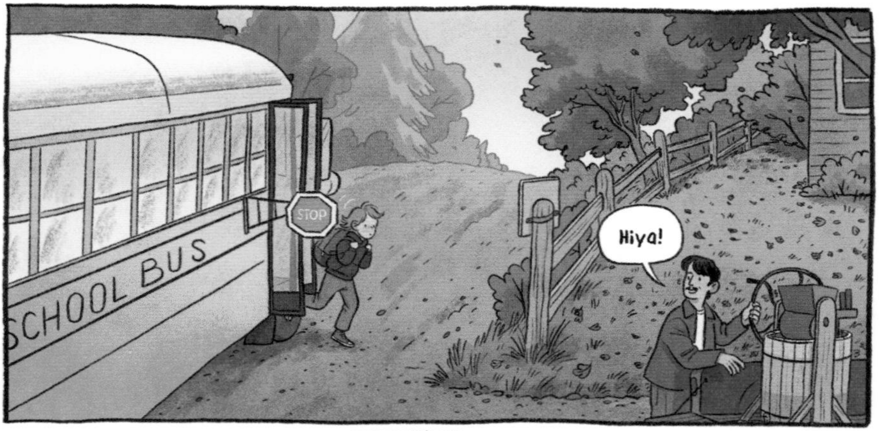
SCHOOL BUS
STOP
Hiya!

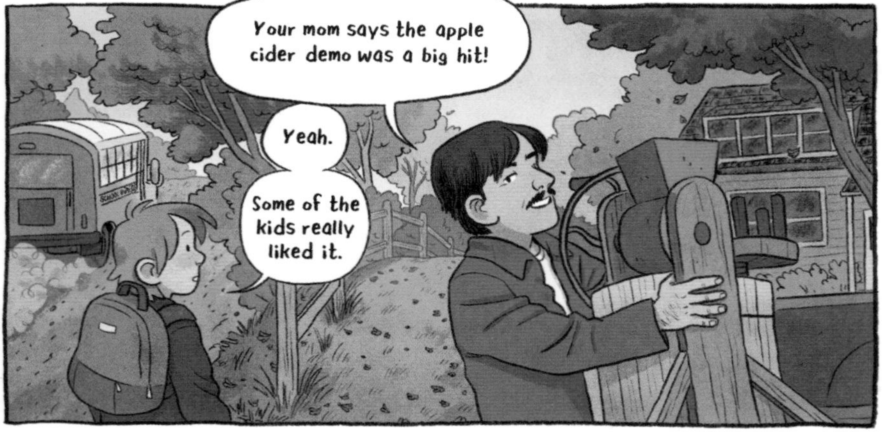
Your mom says the apple cider demo was a big hit!
Yeah.
Some of the kids really liked it.

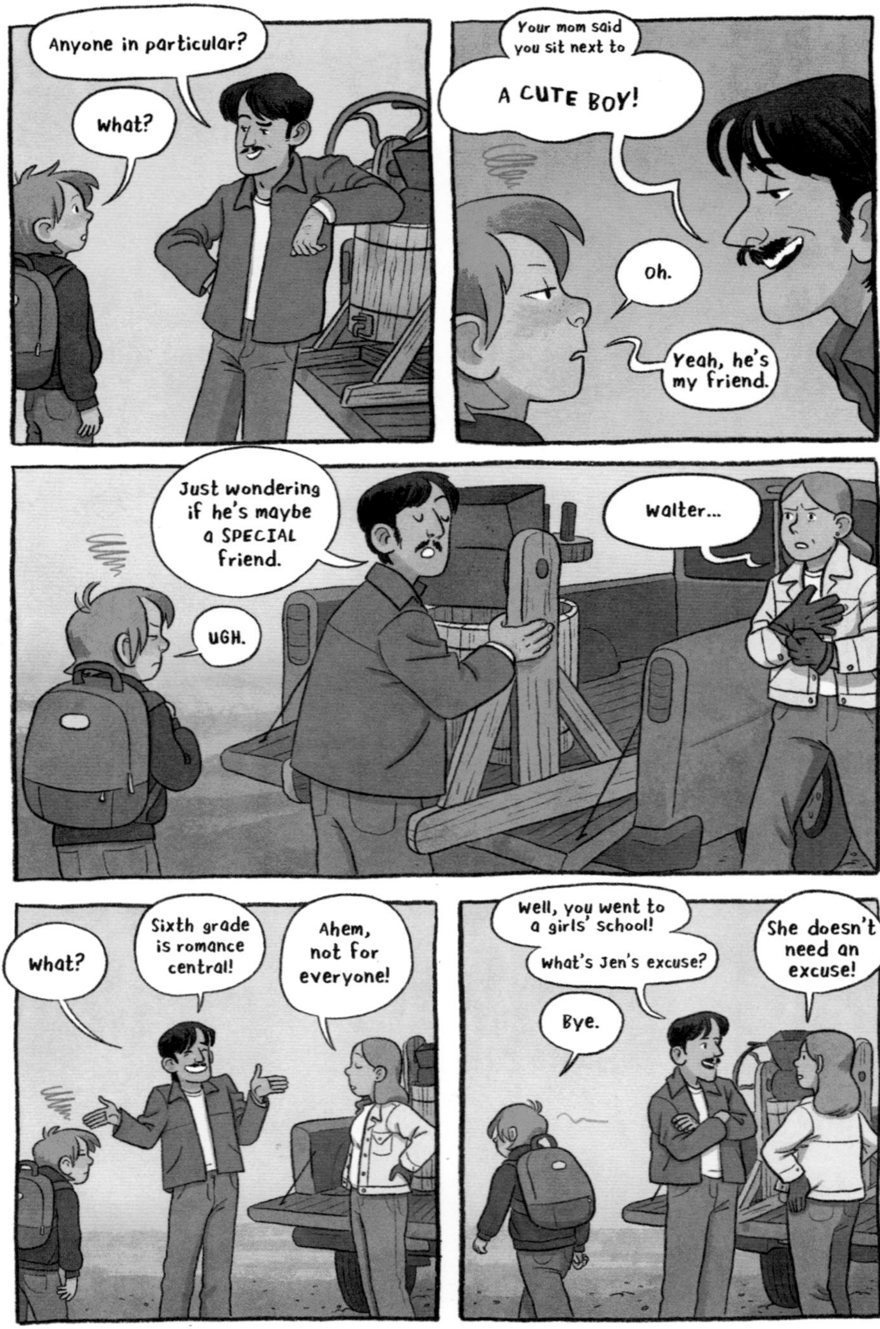

Anyone in particular?
What?
Your mom said you sit next to
A CUTE BOY!
Oh.
Yeah, he's my friend.
Just wondering if he's maybe a SPECIAL friend.
UGH.
Walter...
What?
Sixth grade is romance central!
Ahem, not for everyone!
Well, you went to a girls' school!
What's Jen's excuse?
She doesn't need an excuse!
Bye.

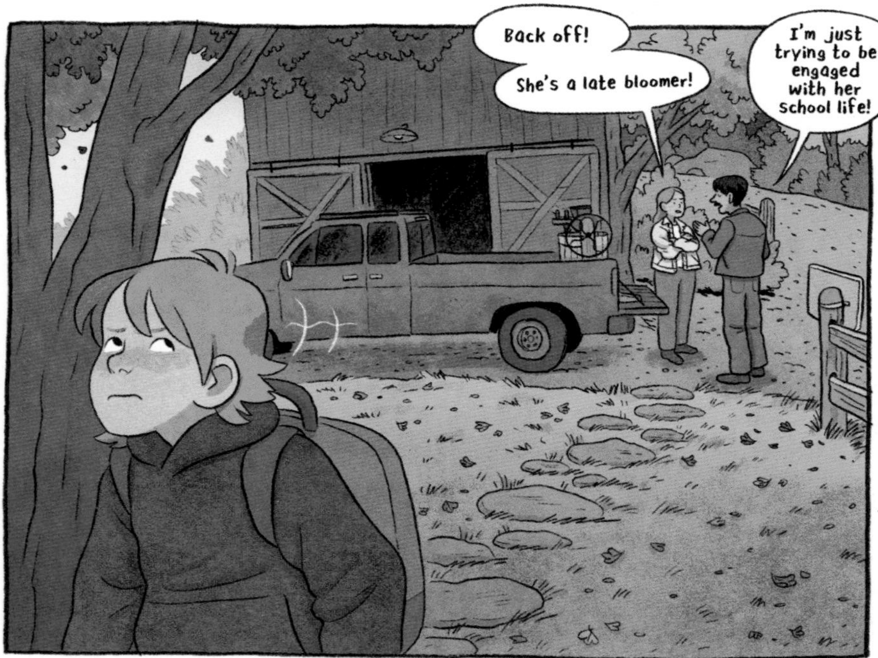
Back off!
She's a late bloomer!
I'm just trying to be engaged with her school life!

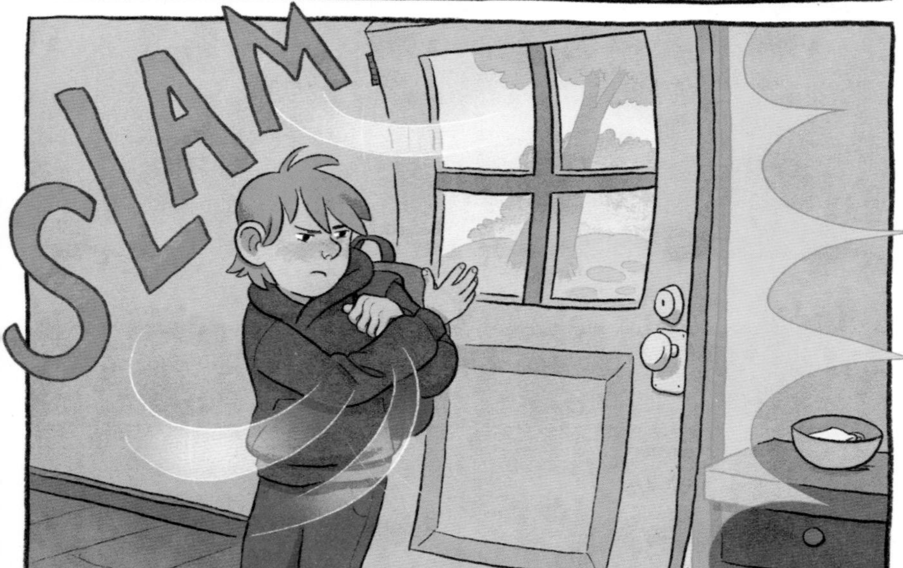
SLAM

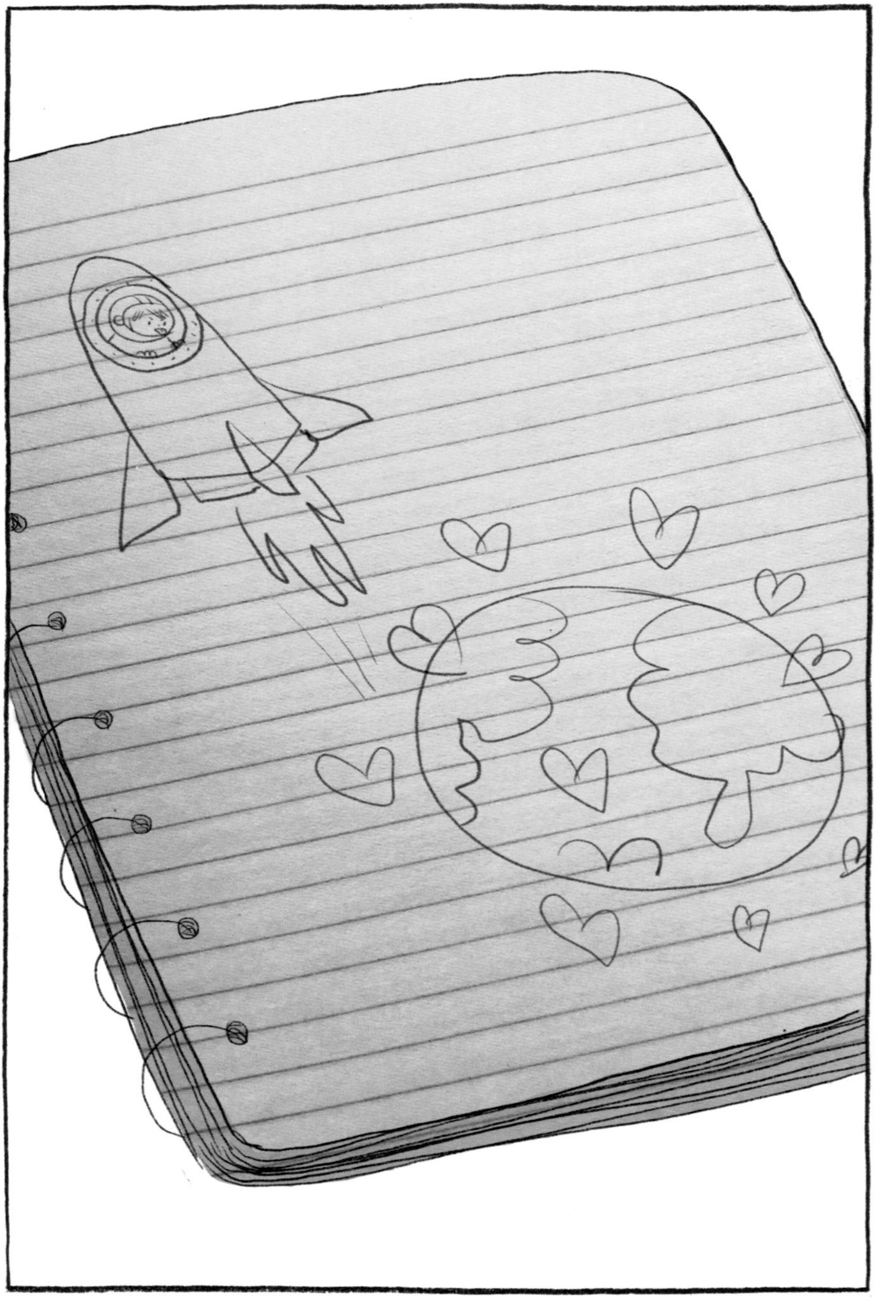

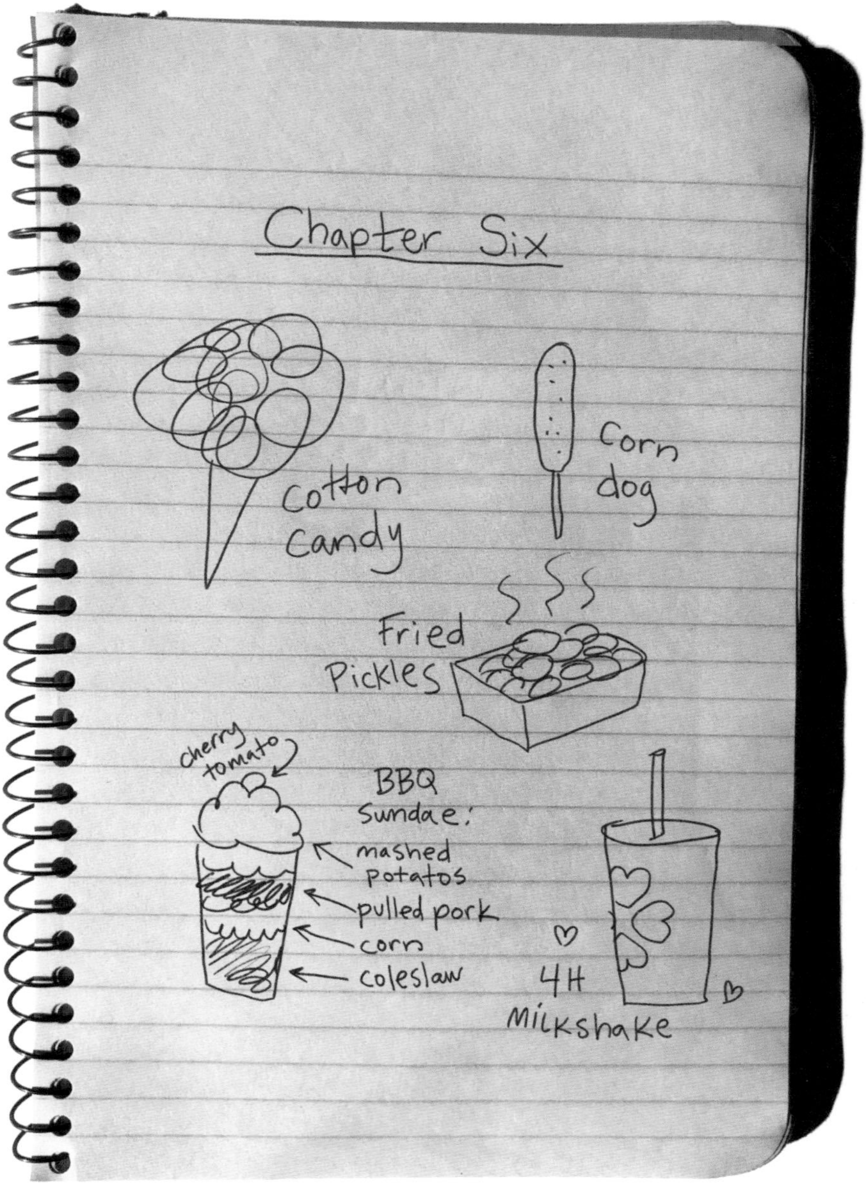
Chapter Six
cotton candy
corn dog
Fried Pickles
cherry tomato
BBQ Sundae:
mashed potatos
pulled pork
corn
coleslaw
4H Milkshake

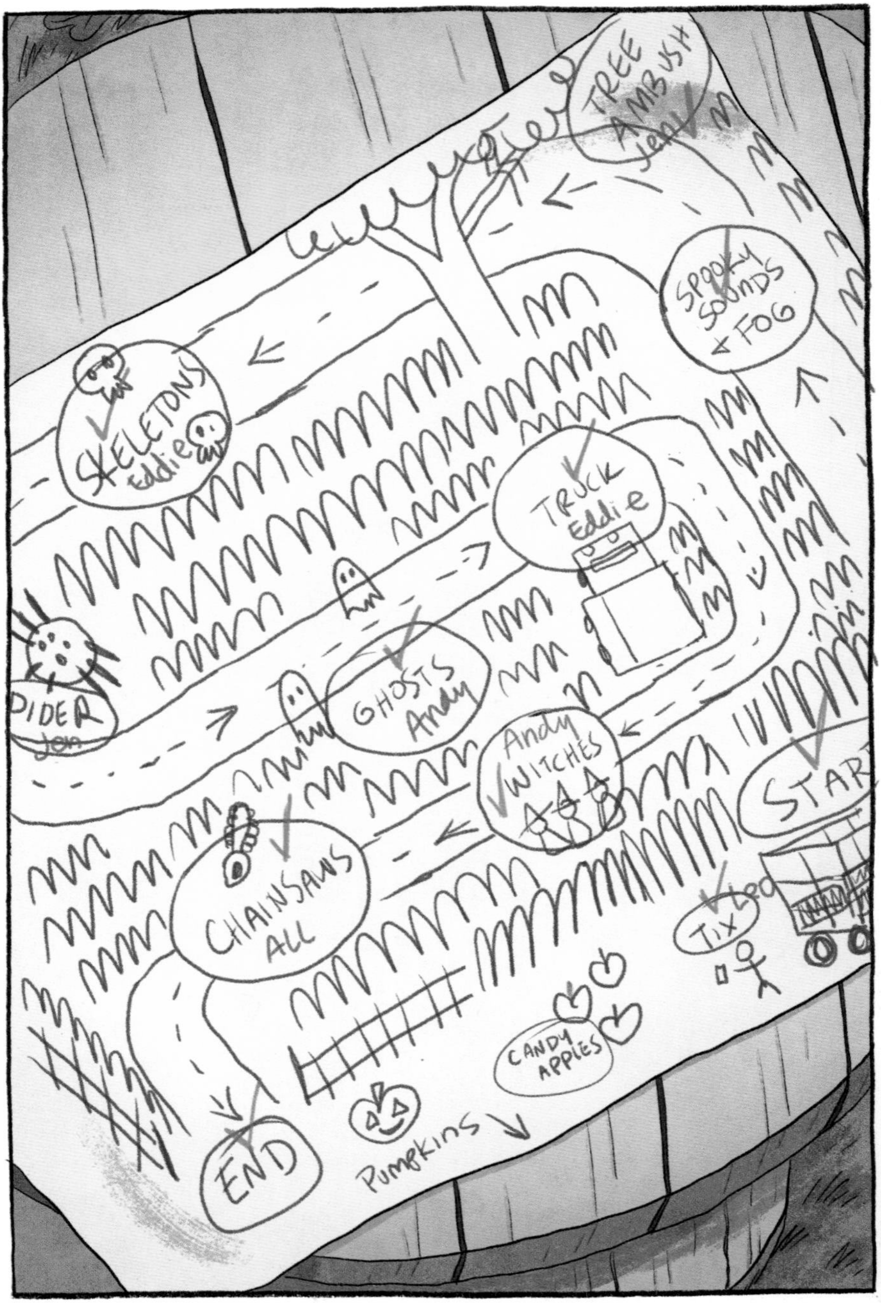
TREE AMBUSH Jen
SPOOKY SOUNDS + FOG
SKELETONS Eddie
TRUCK Eddie
GHOSTS Andy
PIDER Jen
Andy WITCHES
STAR
CHAINSAWS ALL
TIX LEO
CANDY APPLES
PUMPKINS
END

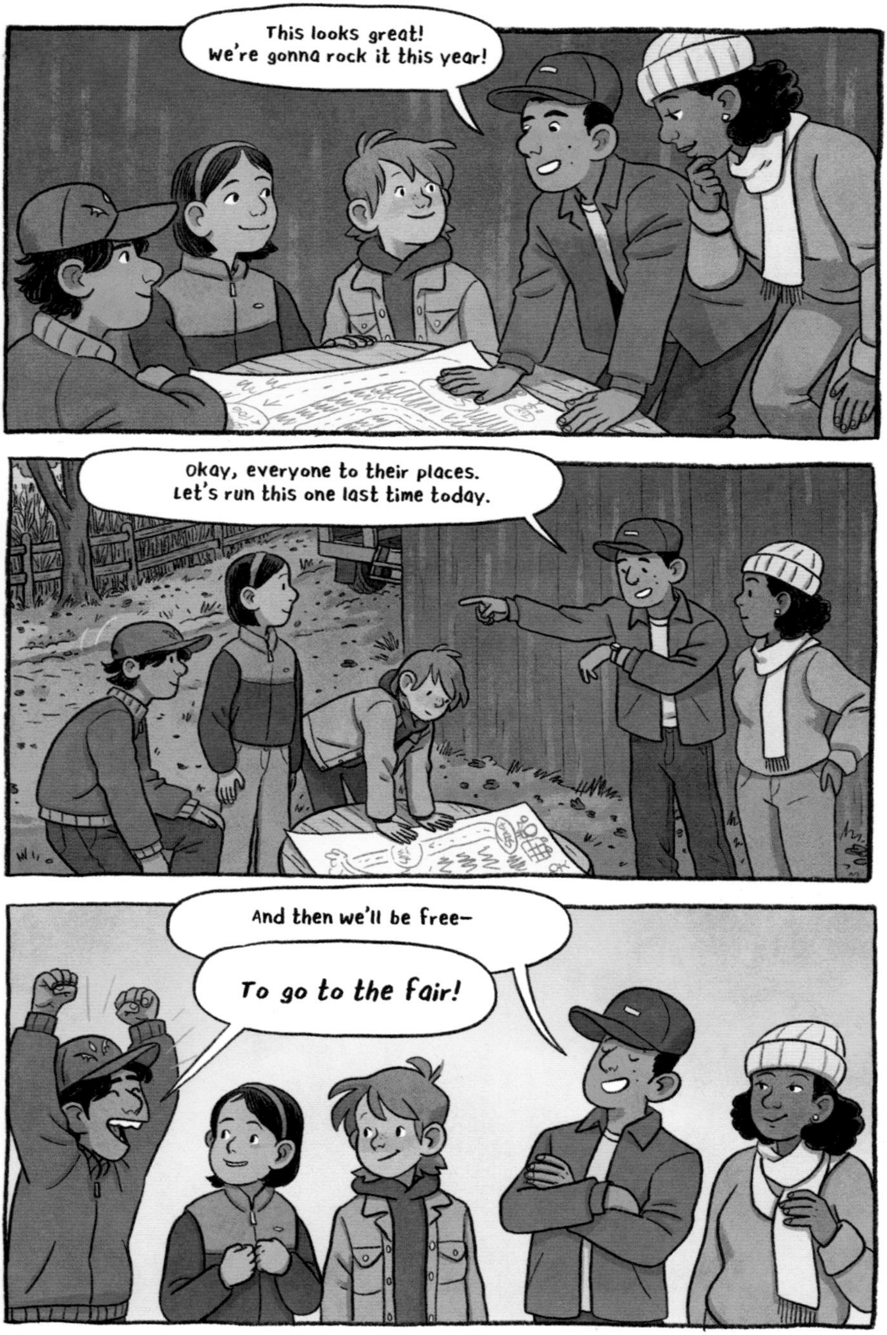
This looks great!
We're gonna rock it this year!
Okay, everyone to their places.
Let's run this one last time today.
And then we'll be free—
To go to the fair!

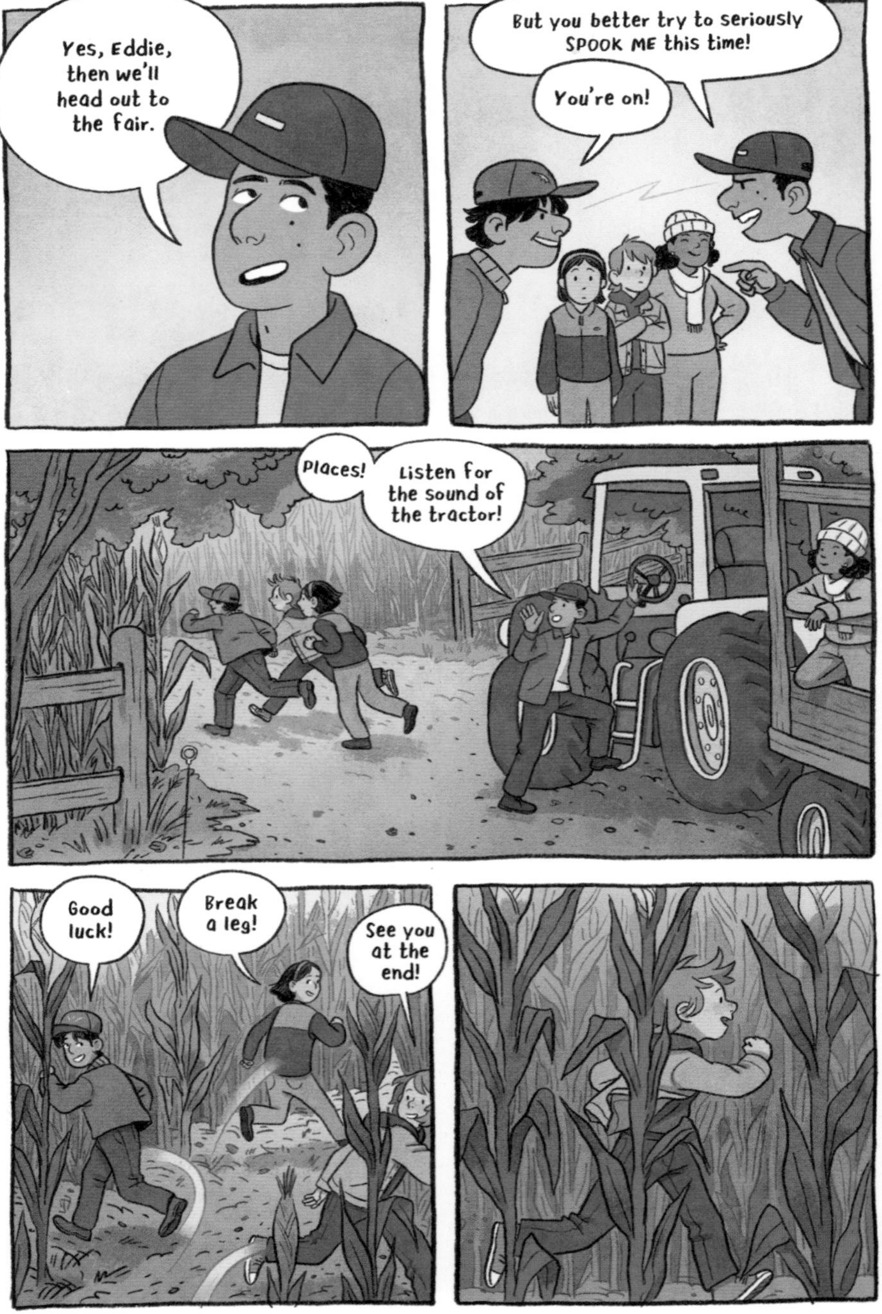

Yes, Eddie, then we'll head out to the fair.
But you better try to seriously SPOOK ME this time!
You're on!
Places!
Listen for the sound of the tractor!
Good luck!
Break a leg!
See you at the end!

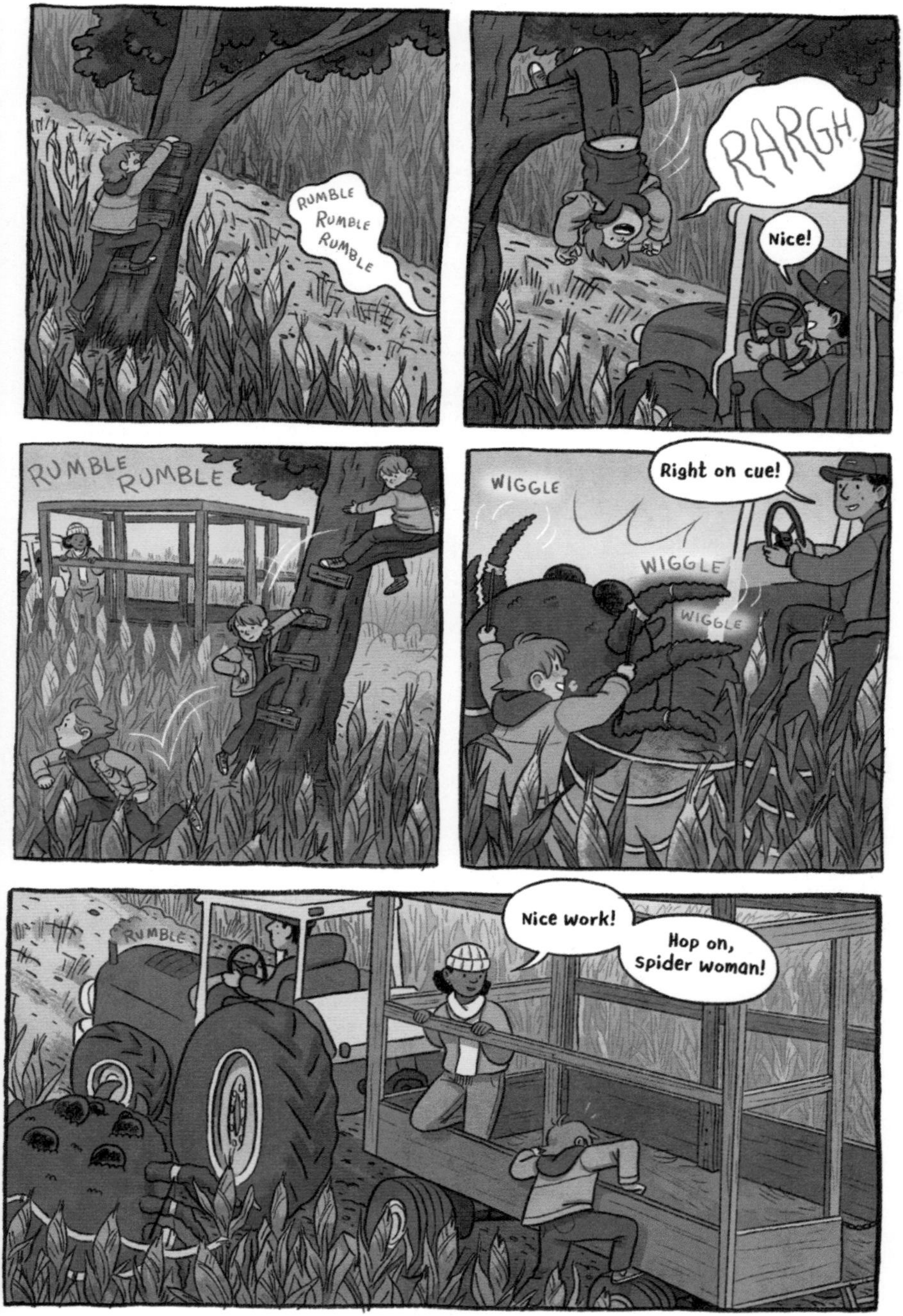
RUMBLE
RUMBLE
RUMBLE
RARGH
Nice!
RUMBLE
RUMBLE
WIGGLE
Right on cue!
WIGGLE
WIGGLE
RUMBLE
Nice work!
Hop on,
spider woman!

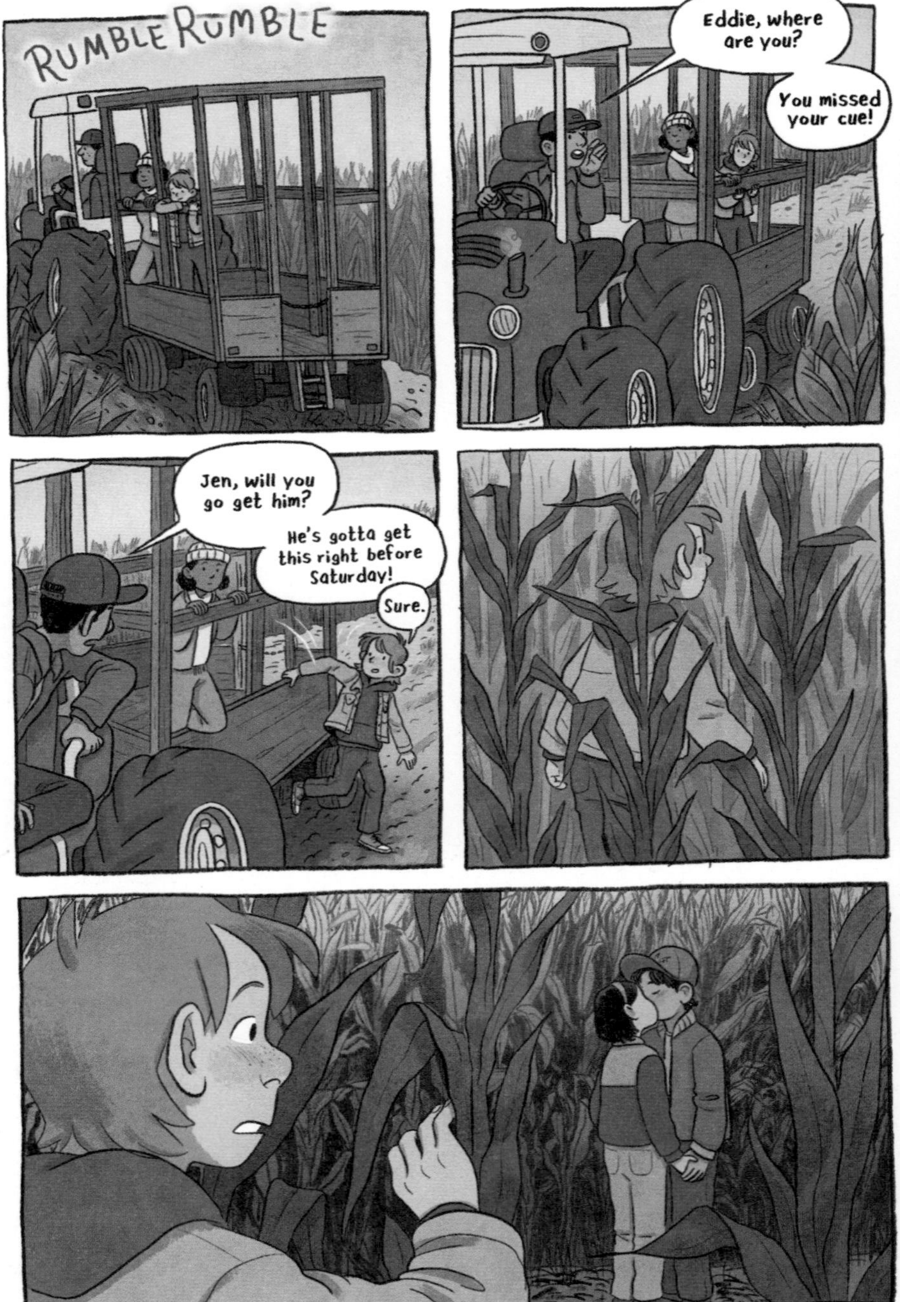
RUMBLE RUMBLE
Eddie, where are you?
You missed your cue!
Jen, will you go get him?
He's gotta get this right before Saturday!
Sure.

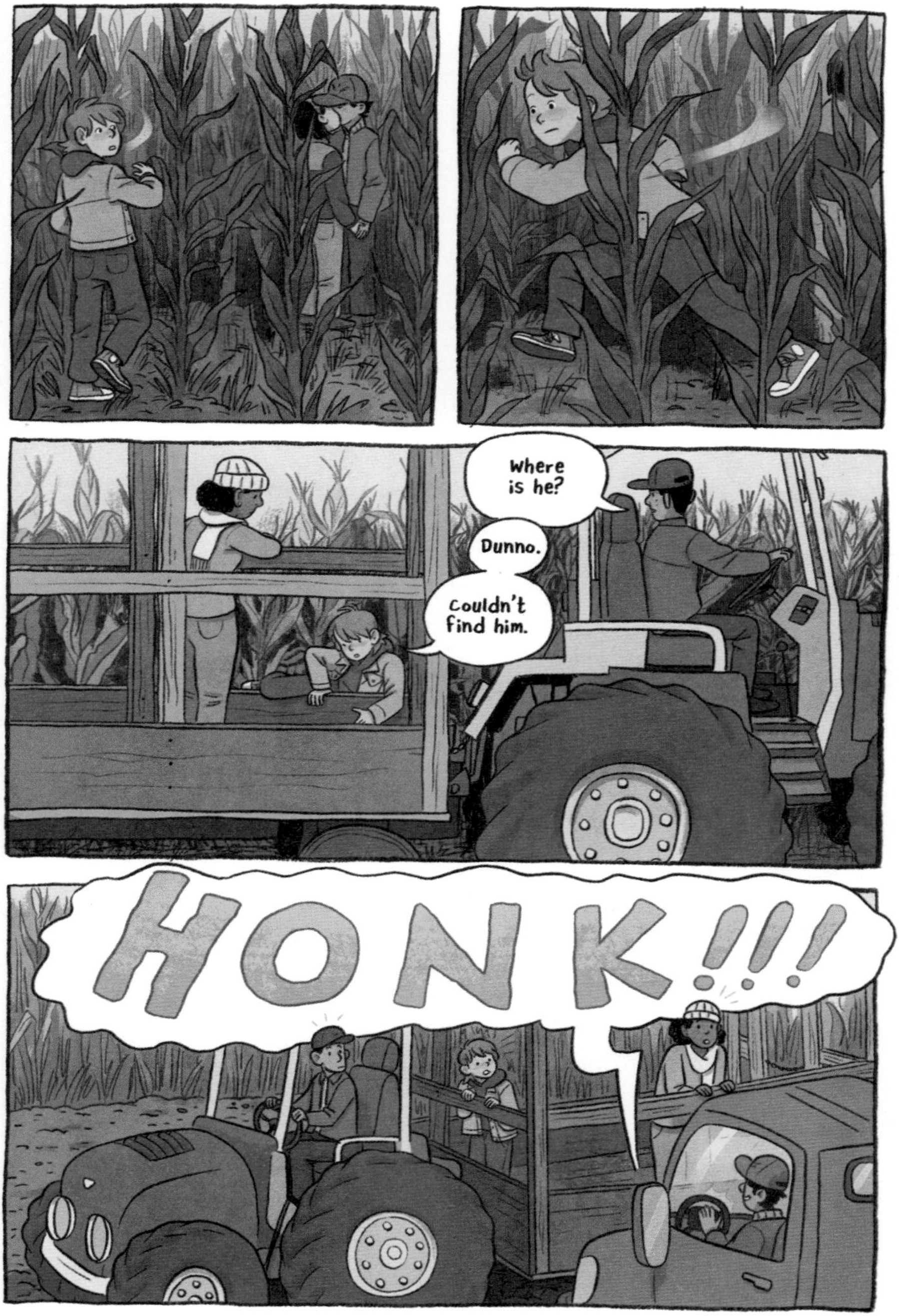
Where is he?
Dunno.
Couldn't find him.
HONK!!!

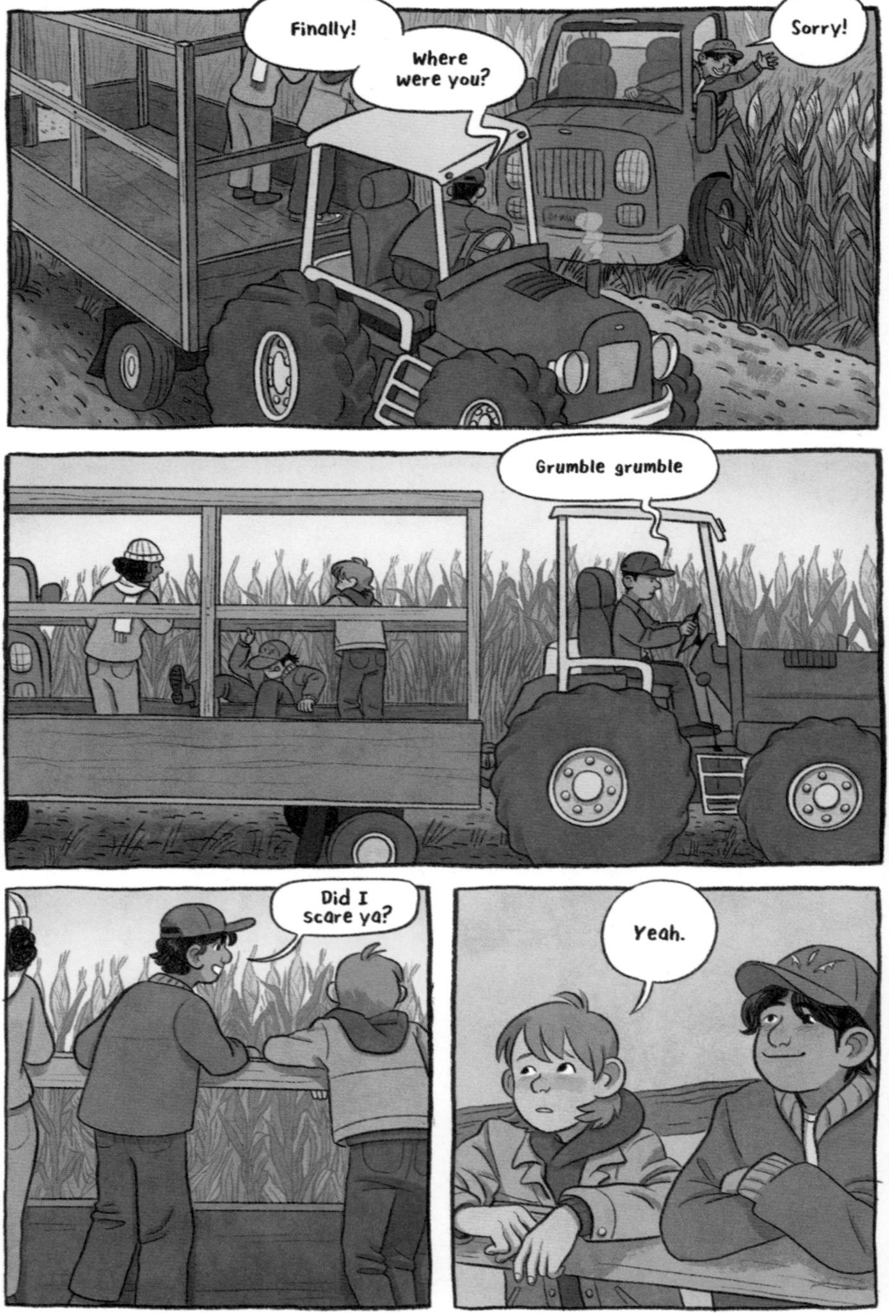
Finally!
Where were you?
Sorry!
Grumble grumble
Did I scare ya?
Yeah.

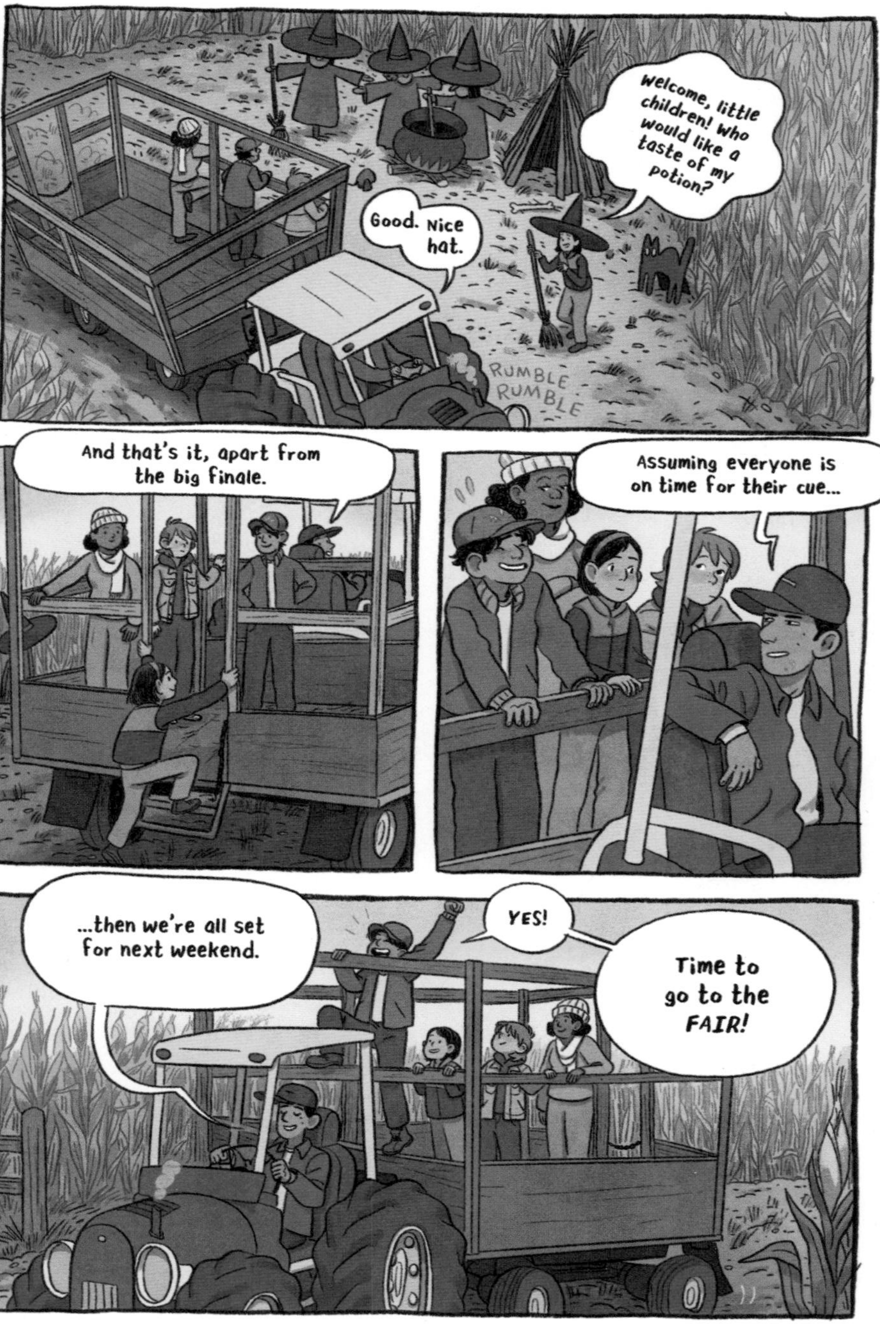
Welcome, little children! Who would like a taste of my potion?
Good. Nice hat.
RUMBLE RUMBLE
And that's it, apart from the big finale.
Assuming everyone is on time for their cue...
...then we're all set for next weekend.
YES!
Time to go to the FAIR!

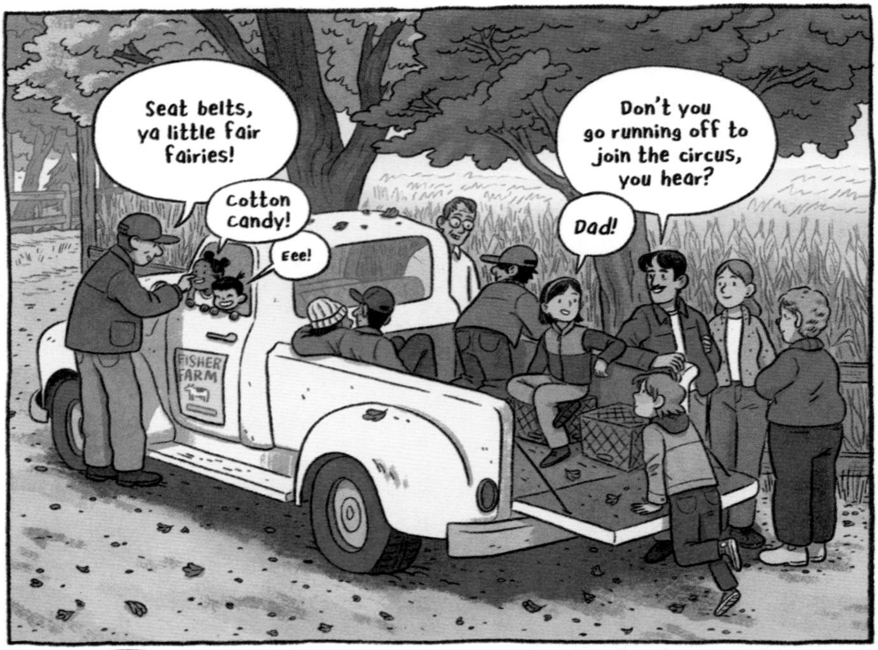
Seat belts, ya little fair fairies!
Cotton candy!
Eee!
Don't you go running off to join the circus, you hear?
Dad!
FISHER FARM

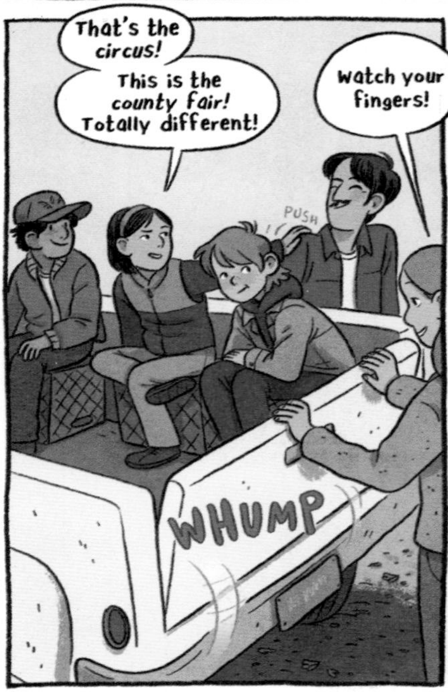
That's the *circus!*
This is the *county fair!* Totally different!
Watch your fingers!
PUSH
WHUMP

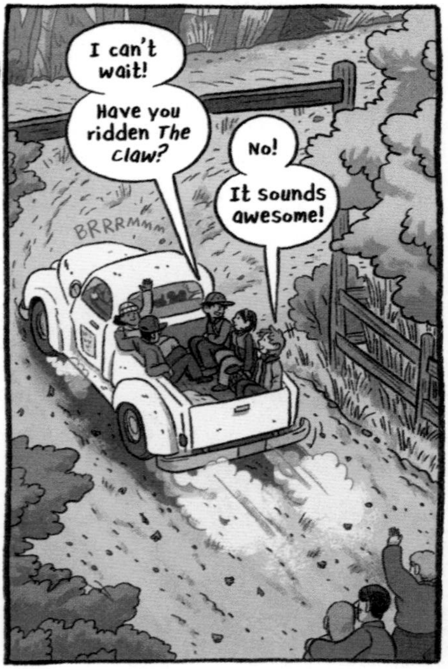
I can't wait!
Have you ridden *The Claw?*
No!
It sounds awesome!
BRRRMMM

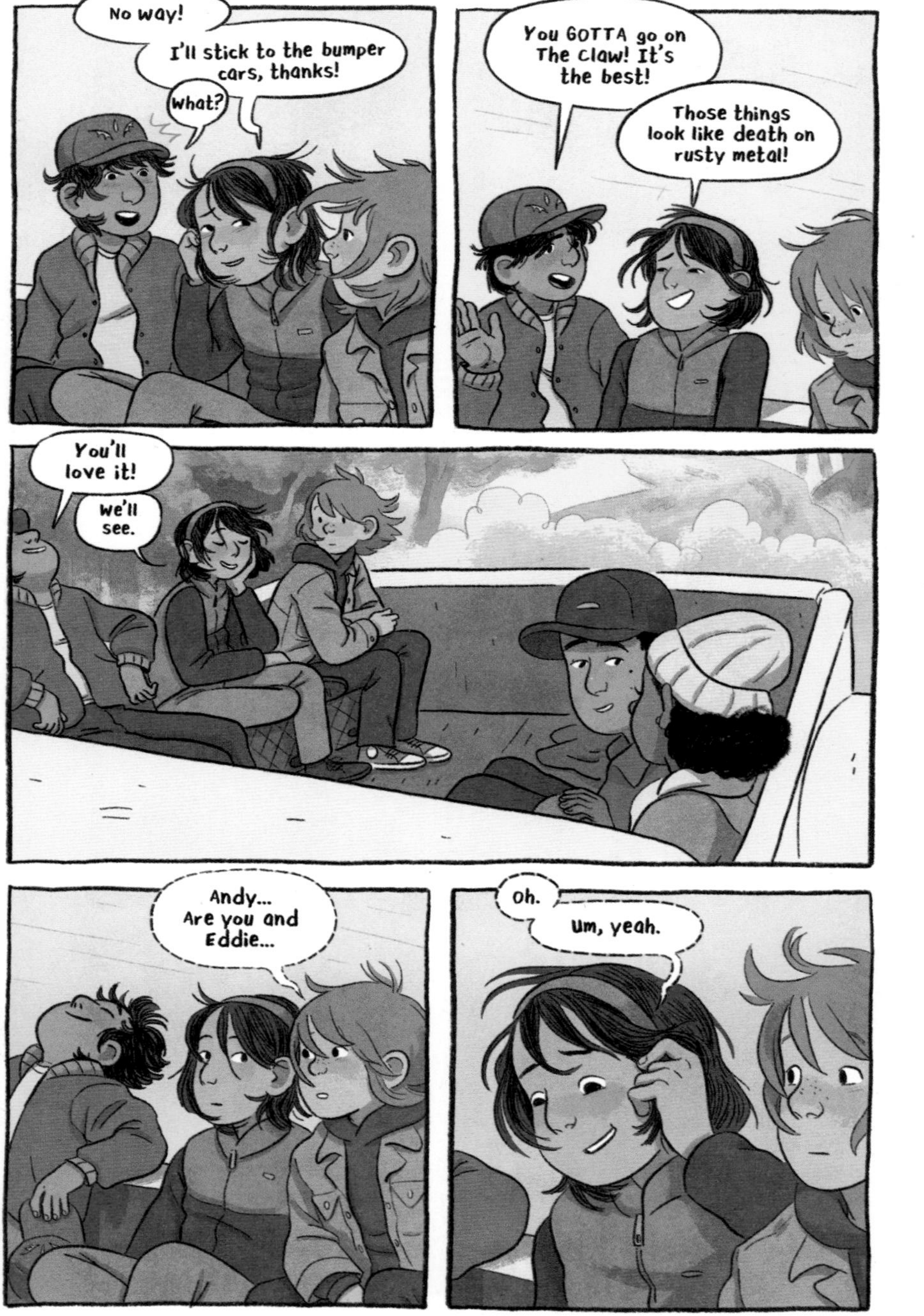
No way!
I'll stick to the bumper cars, thanks!
What?
You GOTTA go on The Claw! It's the best!
Those things look like death on rusty metal!
You'll love it!
We'll see.
Andy... Are you and Eddie...
Oh.
Um, yeah.

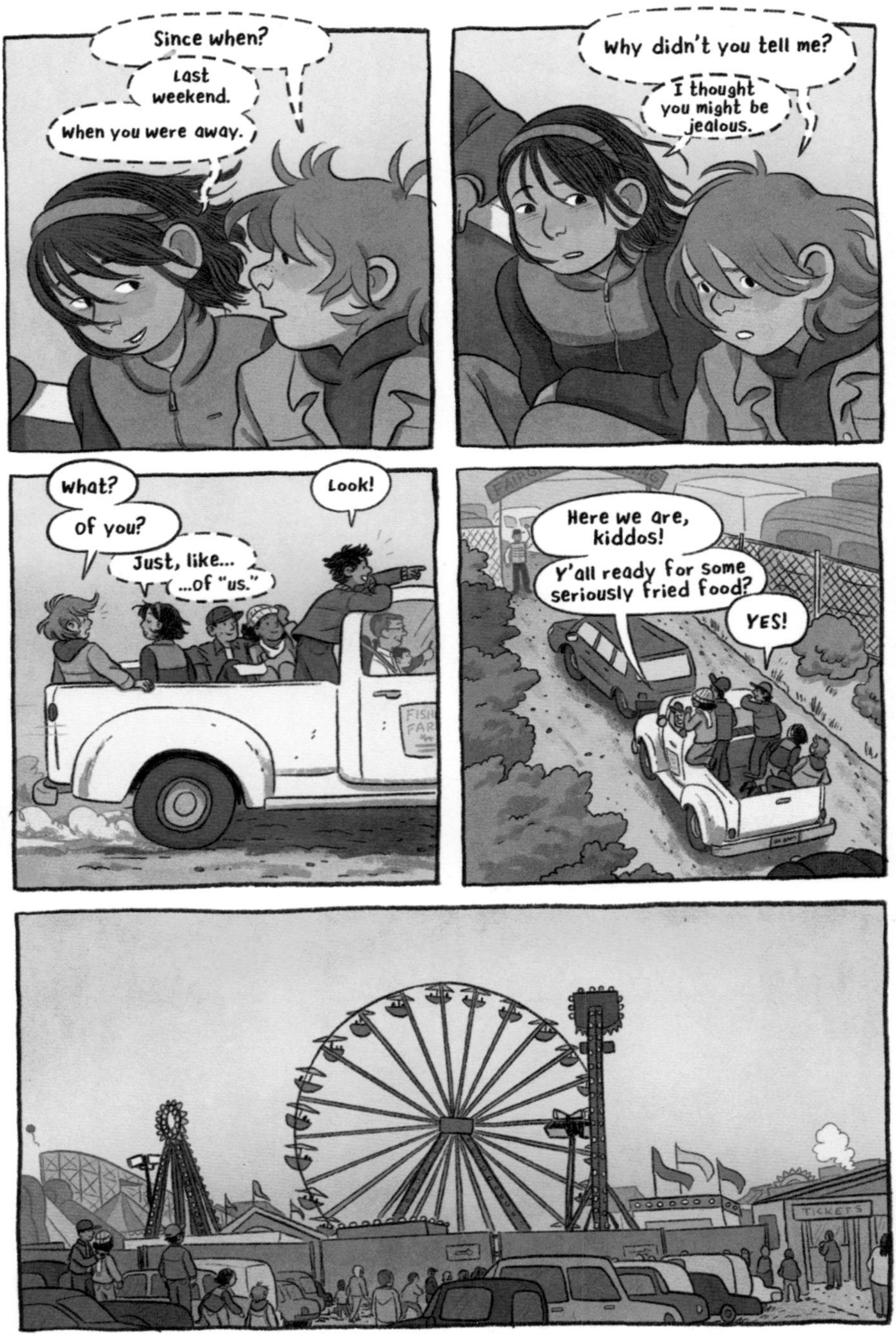
Since when?
Last weekend.
When you were away.
Why didn't you tell me?
I thought you might be jealous.
What?
Of you?
Just, like...
...of "us."
Look!
Here we are, kiddos!
Y'all ready for some seriously fried food?
YES!
TICKETS

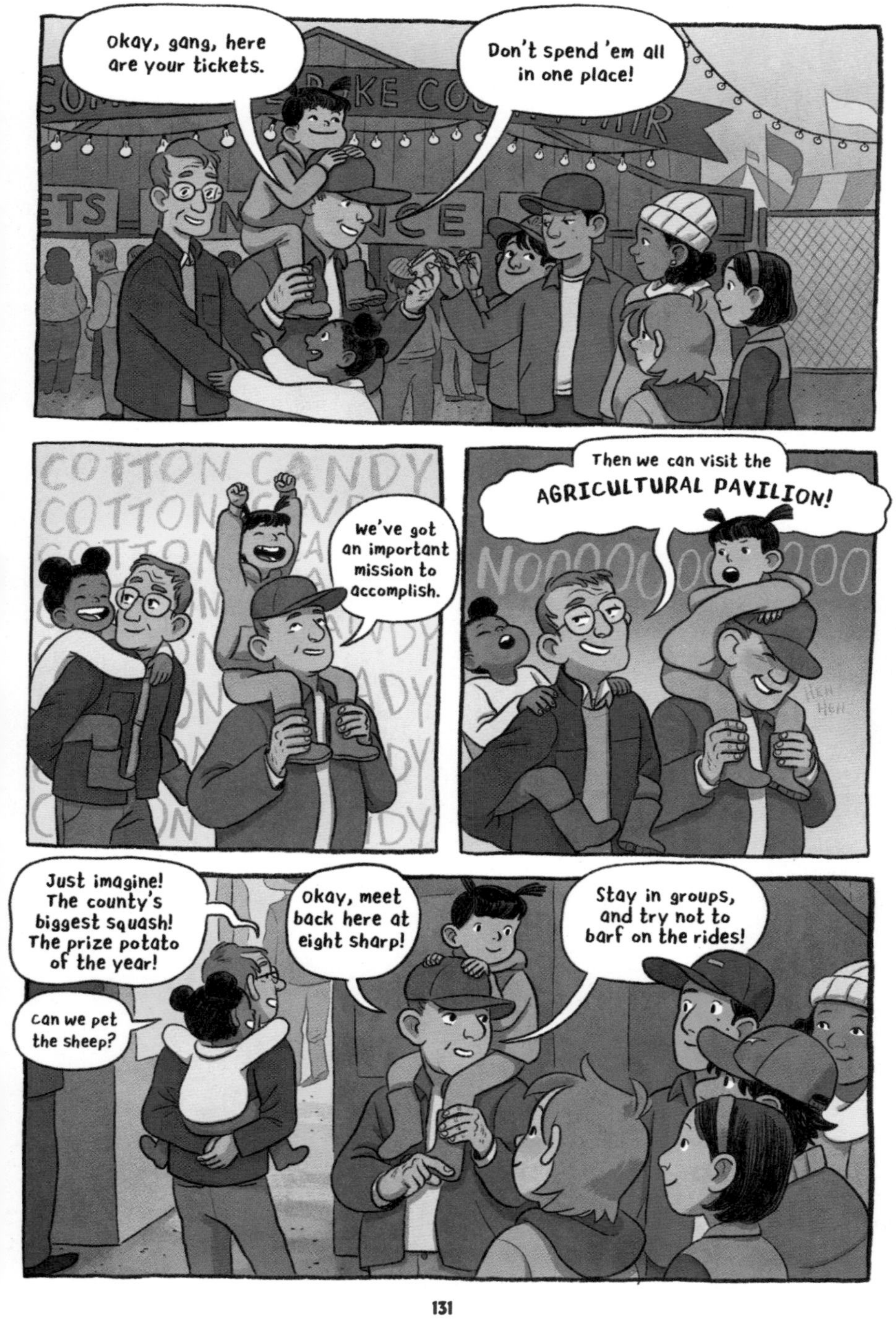
Okay, gang, here are your tickets.
Don't spend 'em all in one place!
COTTON CANDY
We've got an important mission to accomplish.
Then we can visit the AGRICULTURAL PAVILION!
HEH HEH
Just imagine! The county's biggest squash! The prize potato of the year!
Can we pet the sheep?
Okay, meet back here at eight sharp!
Stay in groups, and try not to barf on the rides!

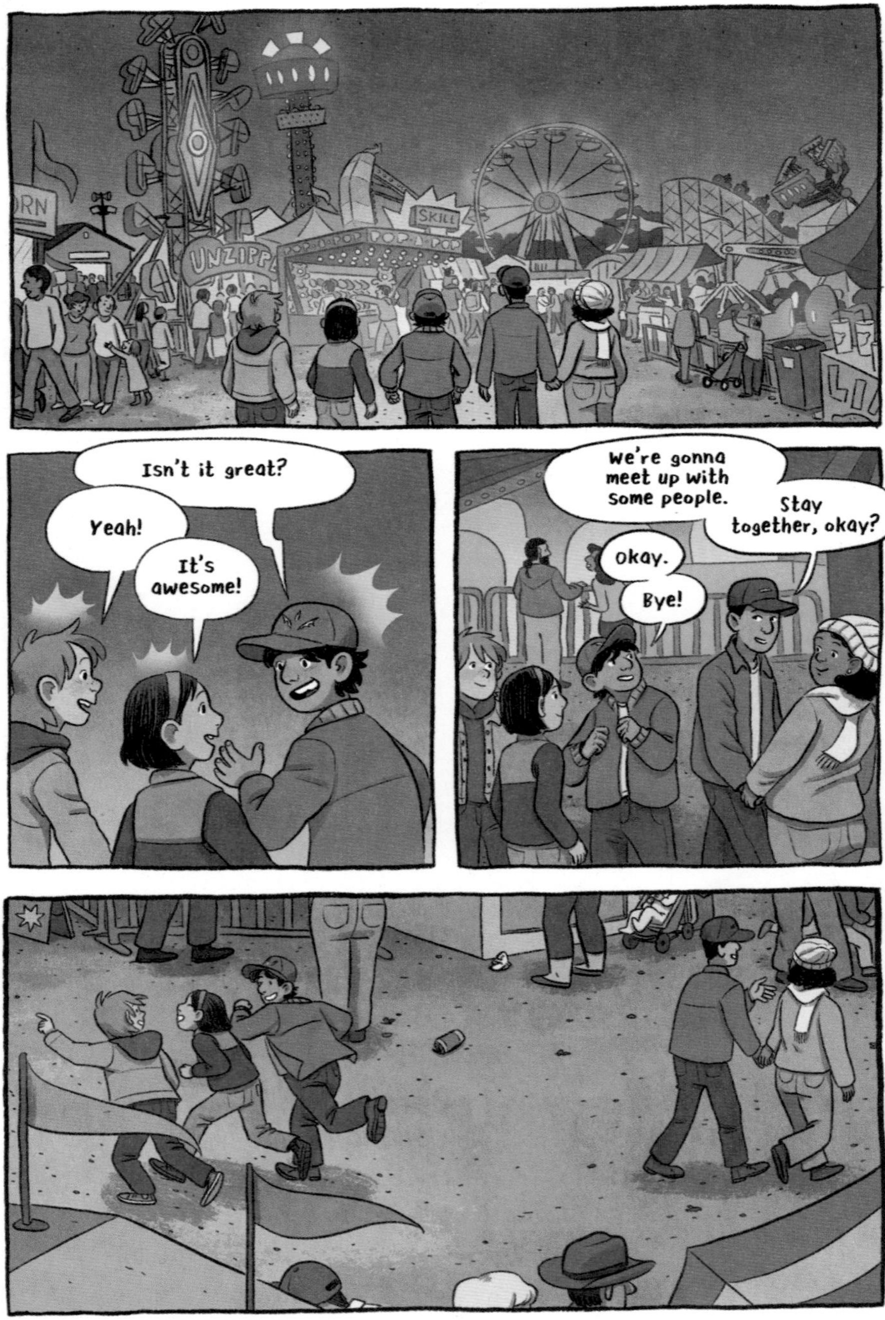
POP-A-POP
SKILL
Isn't it great?
Yeah!
It's awesome!
We're gonna meet up with some people.
Stay together, okay?
Okay.
Bye!

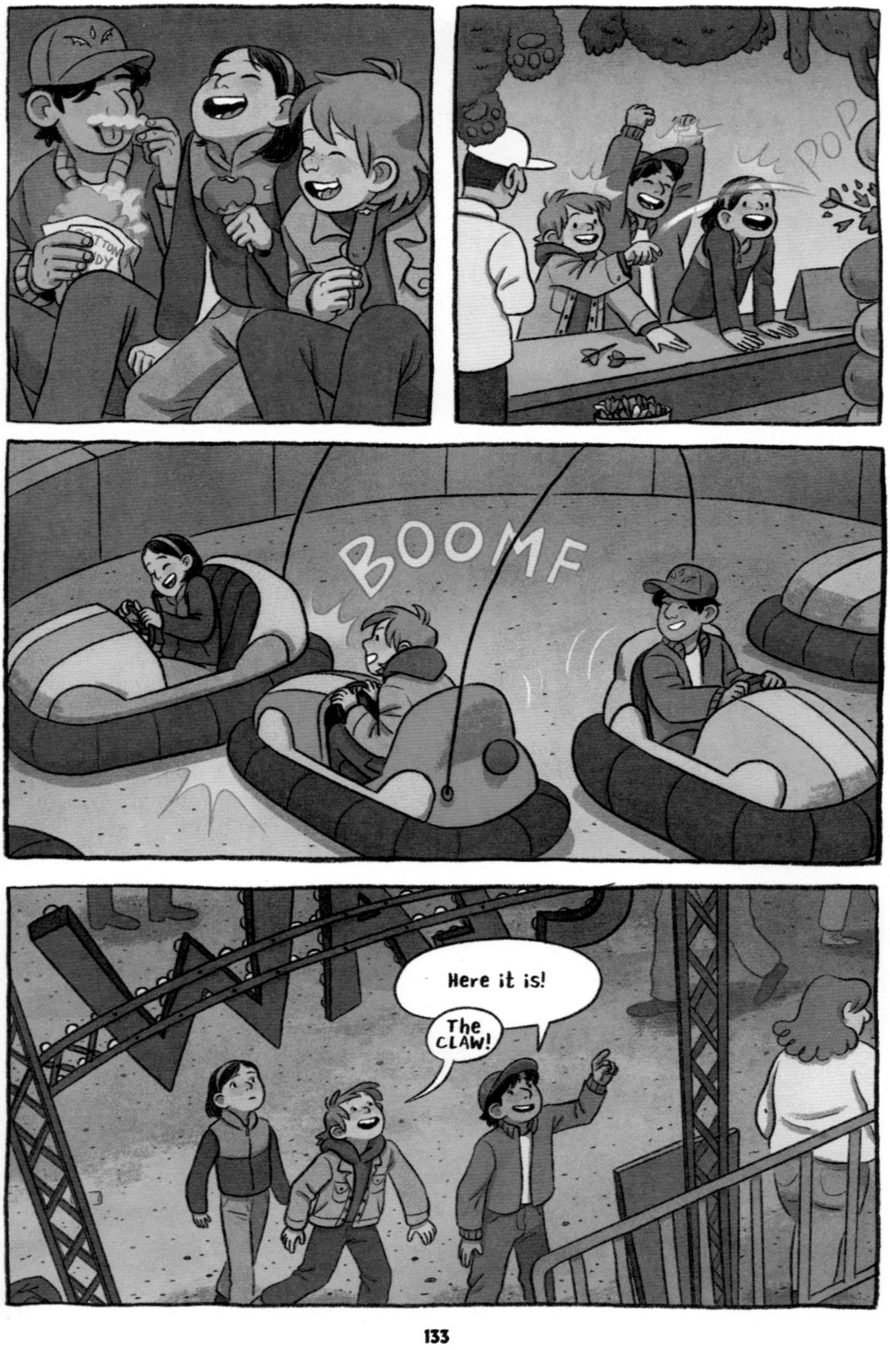
POP
BOOMF
Here it is!
The CLAW!

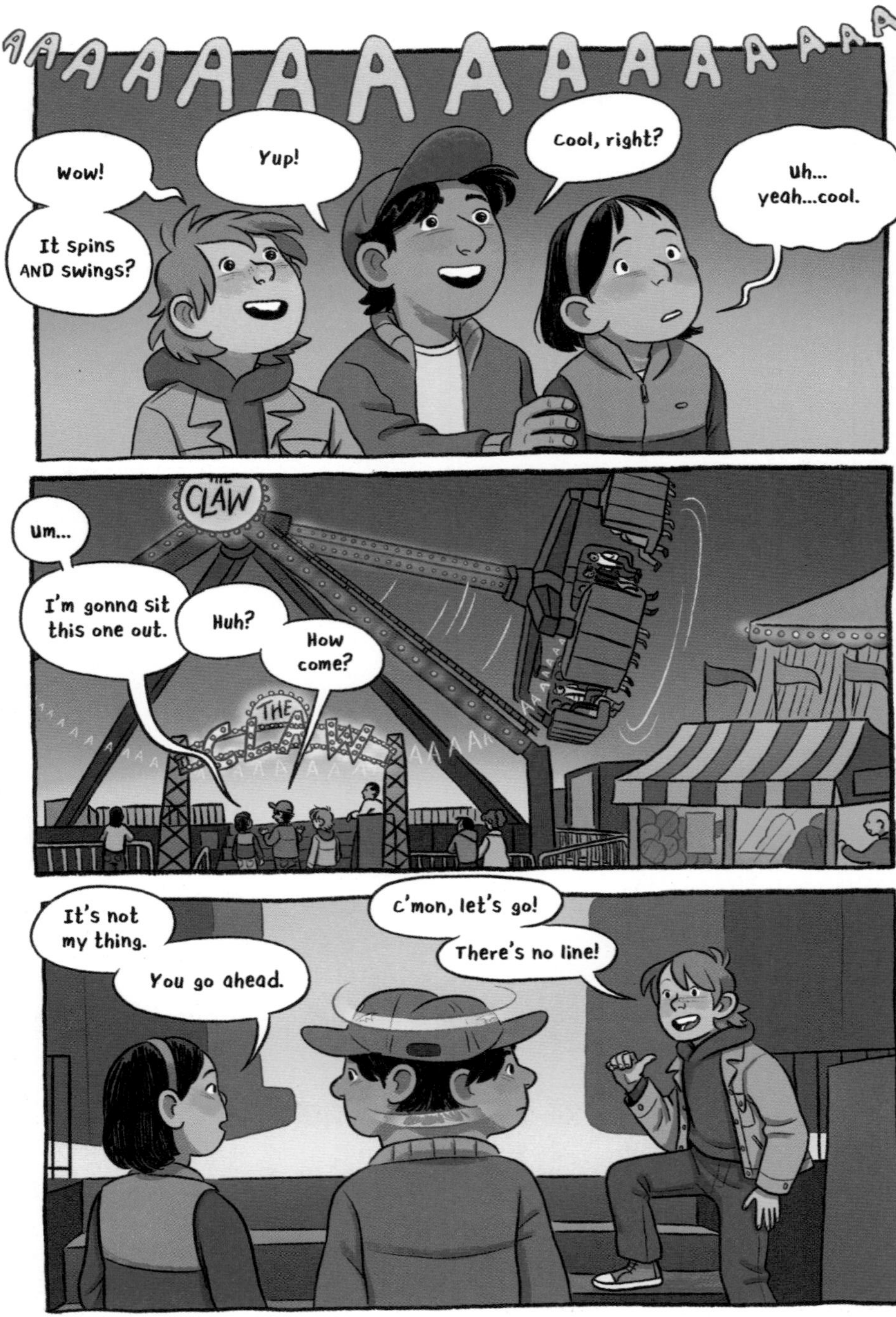
AAAAAAAAAAAAAAAA
Wow!
It spins AND swings?
Yup!
Cool, right?
Uh... yeah...cool.
THE CLAW
Um...
I'm gonna sit this one out.
Huh?
How come?
THE CLAW
It's not my thing.
You go ahead.
C'mon, let's go!
There's no line!

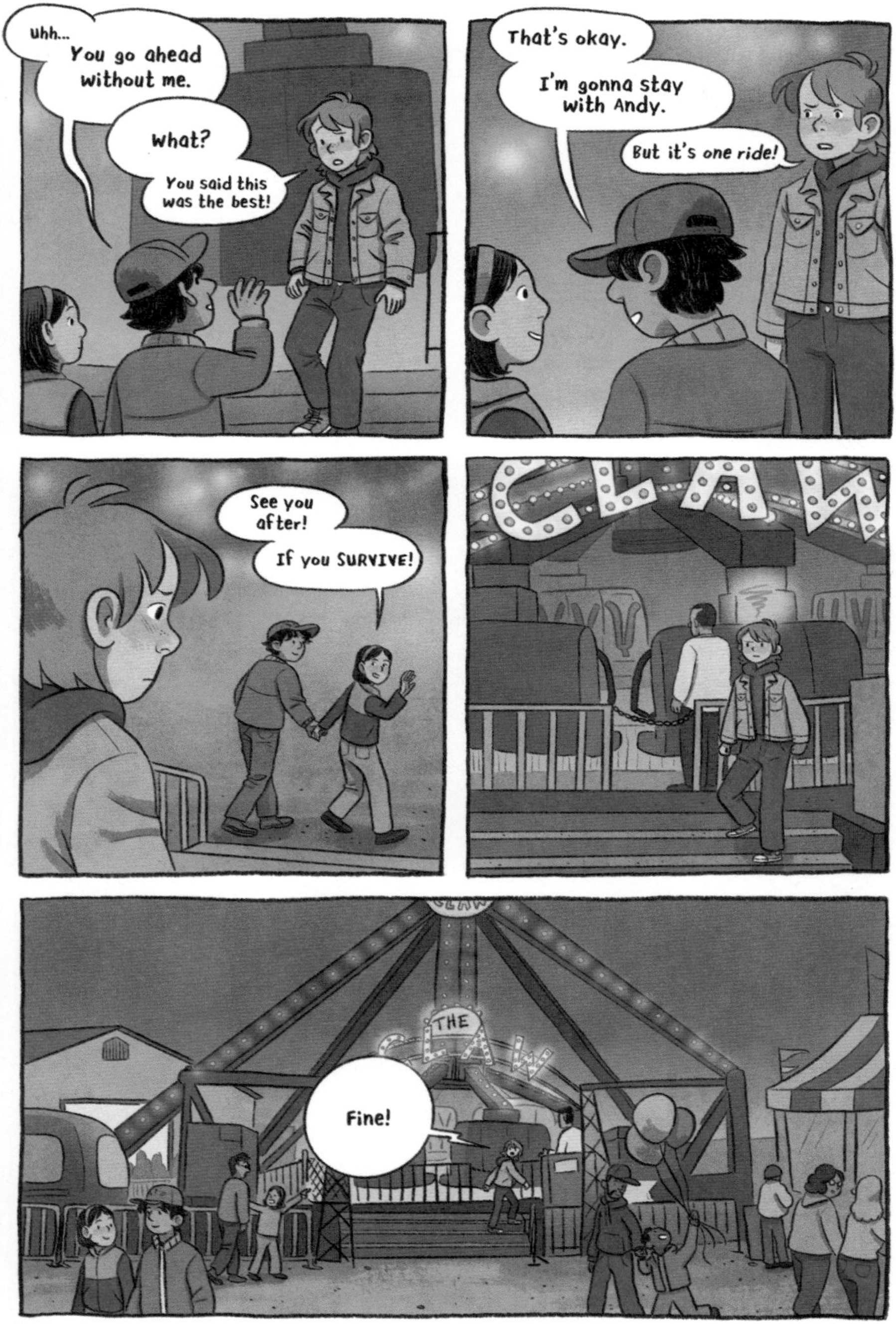
uhh... You go ahead without me.
What?
You said this was the best!
That's okay.
I'm gonna stay with Andy.
But it's one ride!
See you after!
If you SURVIVE!
CLAW
THE CLAW
Fine!

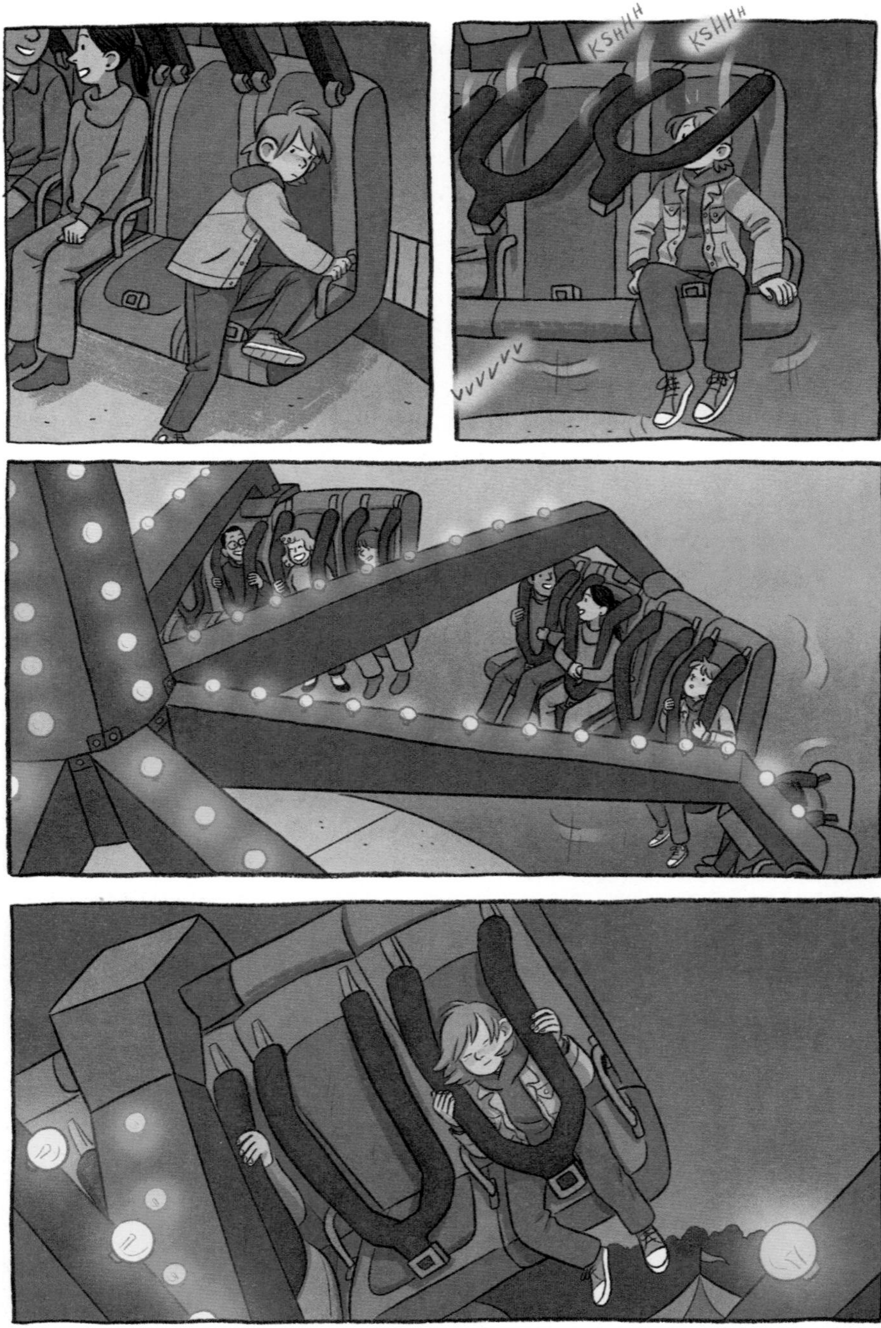
KSHHH
KSHHH
VVVVVV

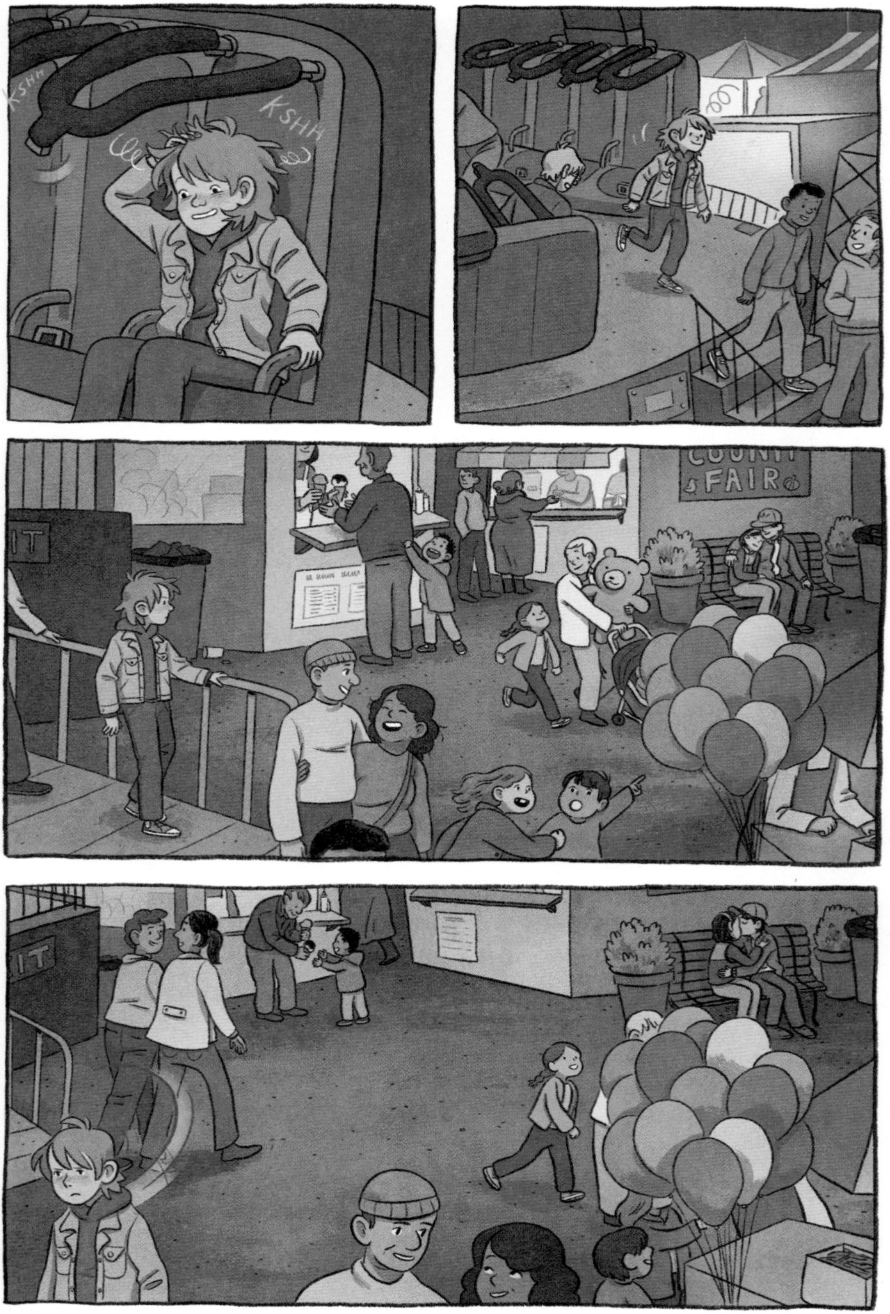
KSHH
KSHH
FAIR

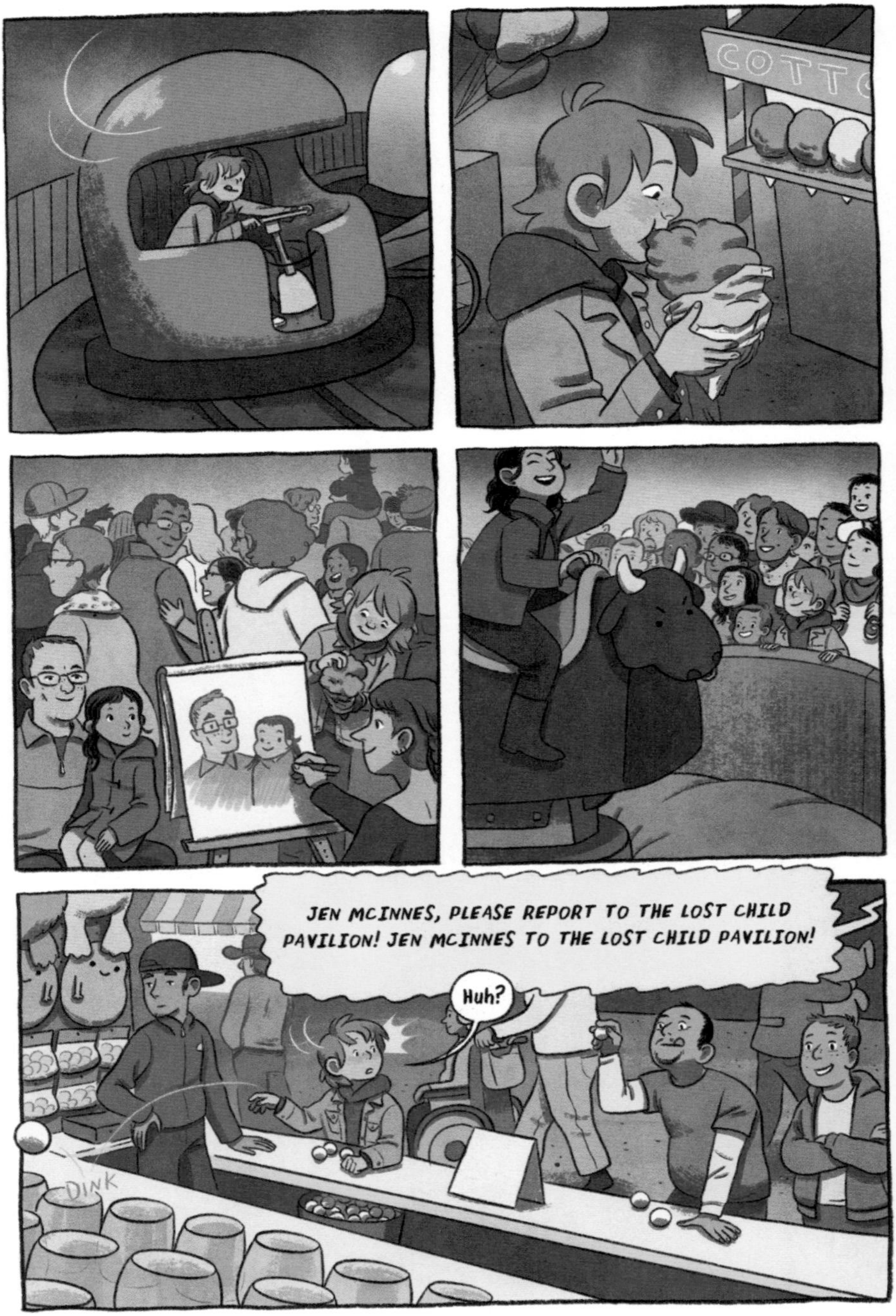
COTTO
JEN MCINNES, PLEASE REPORT TO THE LOST CHILD PAVILION! JEN MCINNES TO THE LOST CHILD PAVILION!
Huh?
DINK

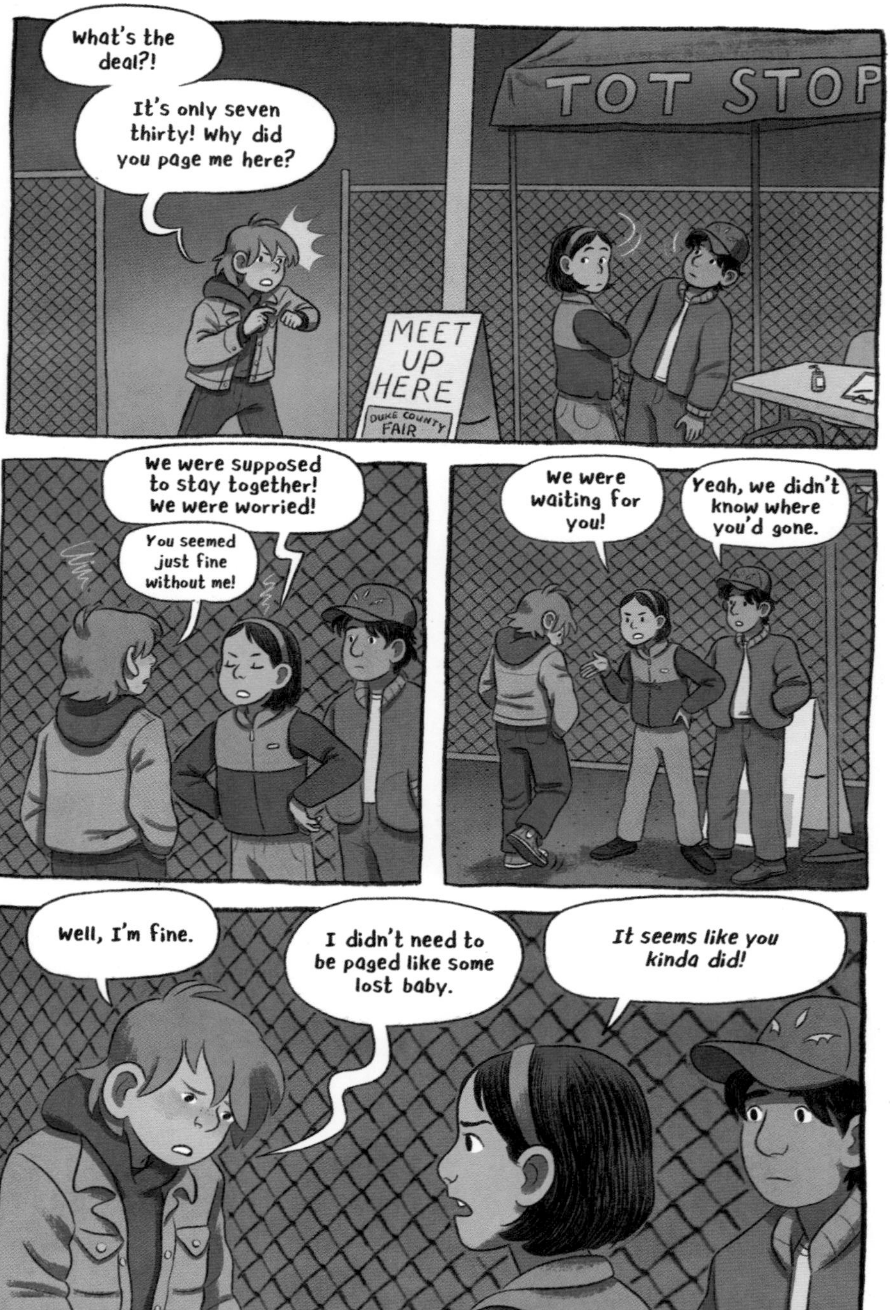
What's the deal?!
It's only seven thirty! Why did you page me here?
TOT STOP
MEET UP HERE
DUKE COUNTY FAIR
We were supposed to stay together! We were worried!
You seemed just fine without me!
We were waiting for you!
Yeah, we didn't know where you'd gone.
Well, I'm fine.
I didn't need to be paged like some lost baby.
It seems like you kinda did!

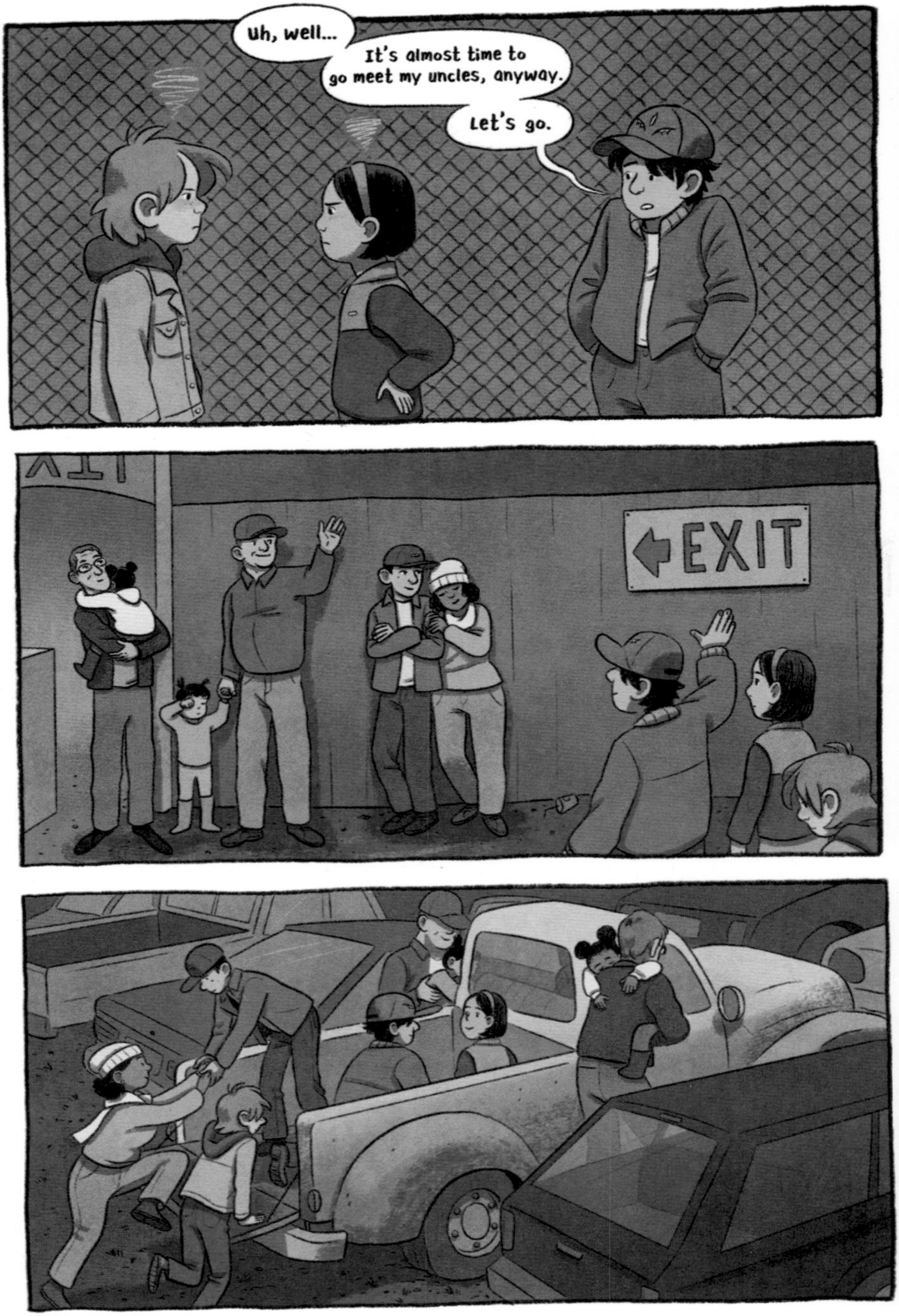

Uh, well...
It's almost time to go meet my uncles, anyway.
Let's go.
EXIT

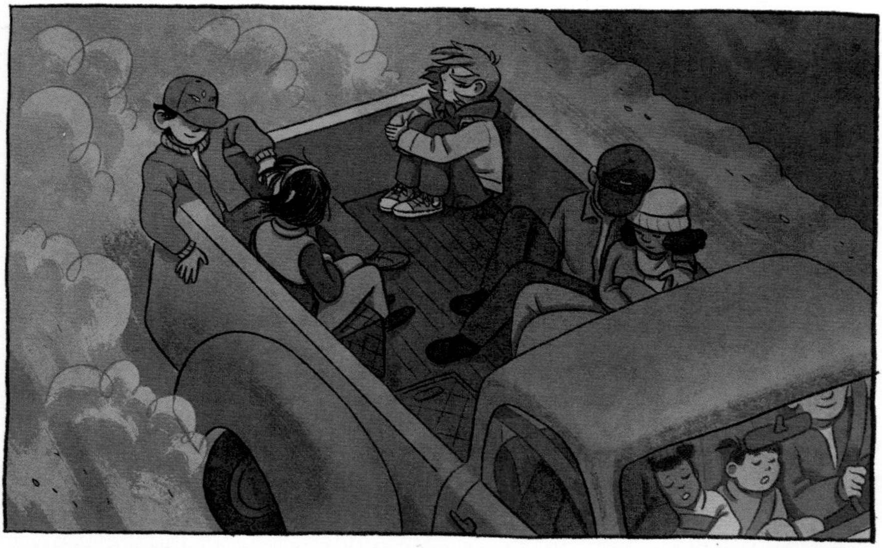

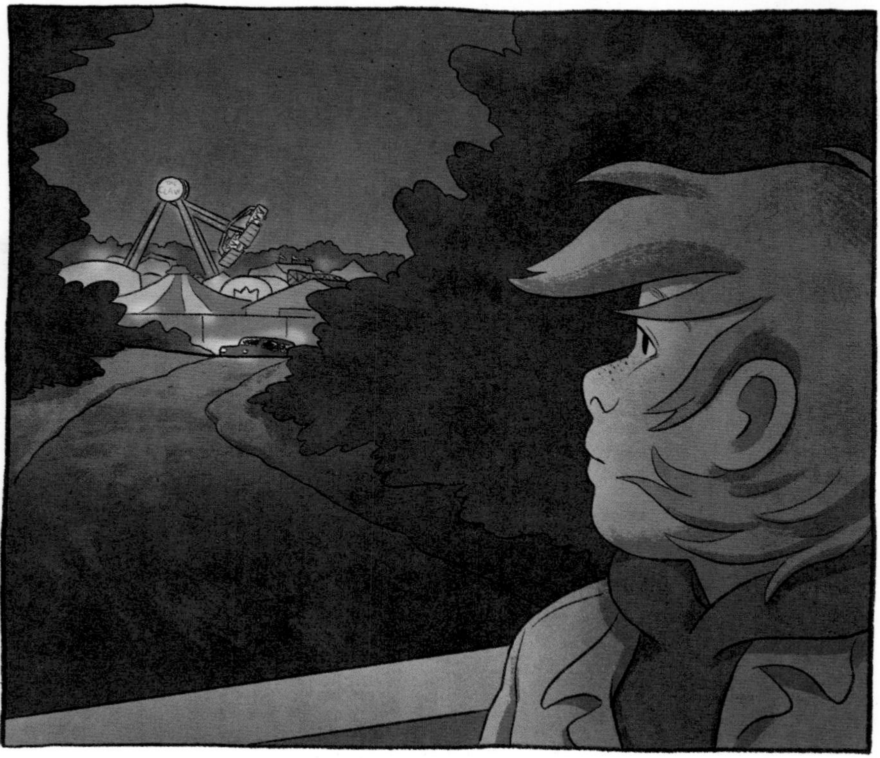
THE CLAW

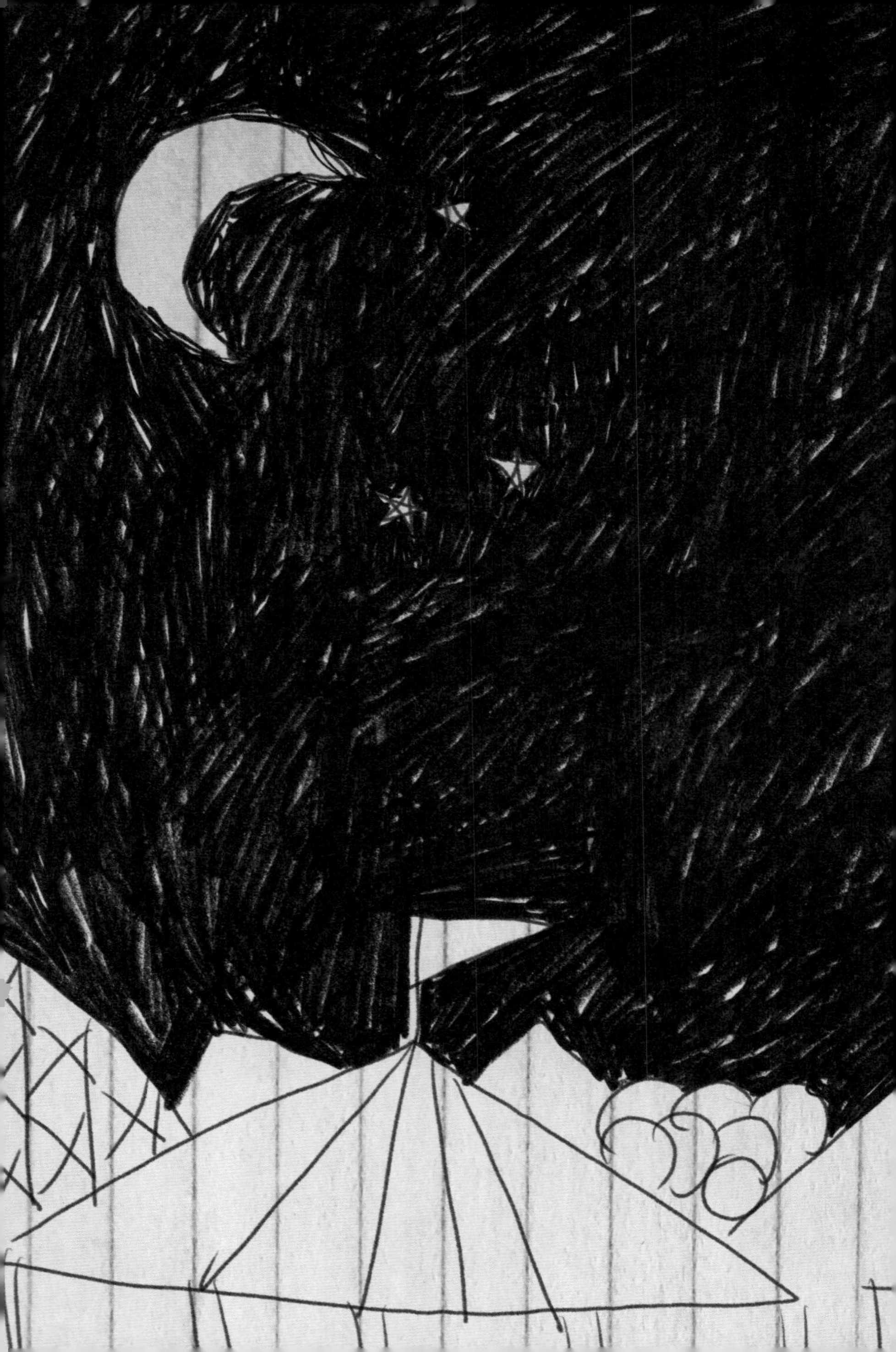

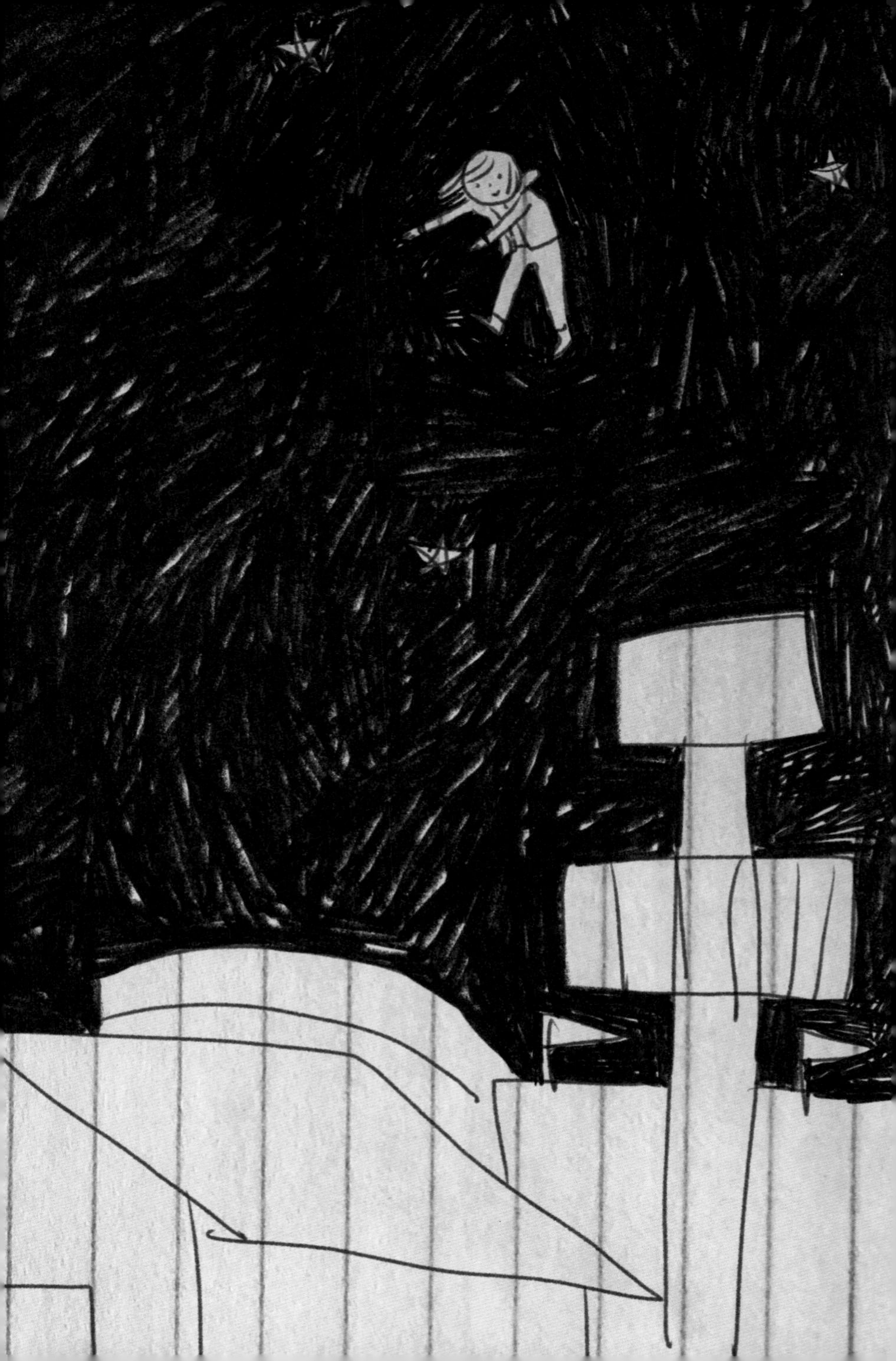

Chapter Seven

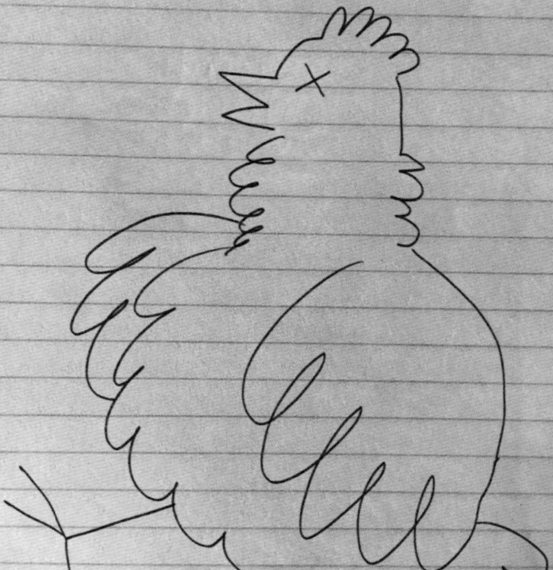

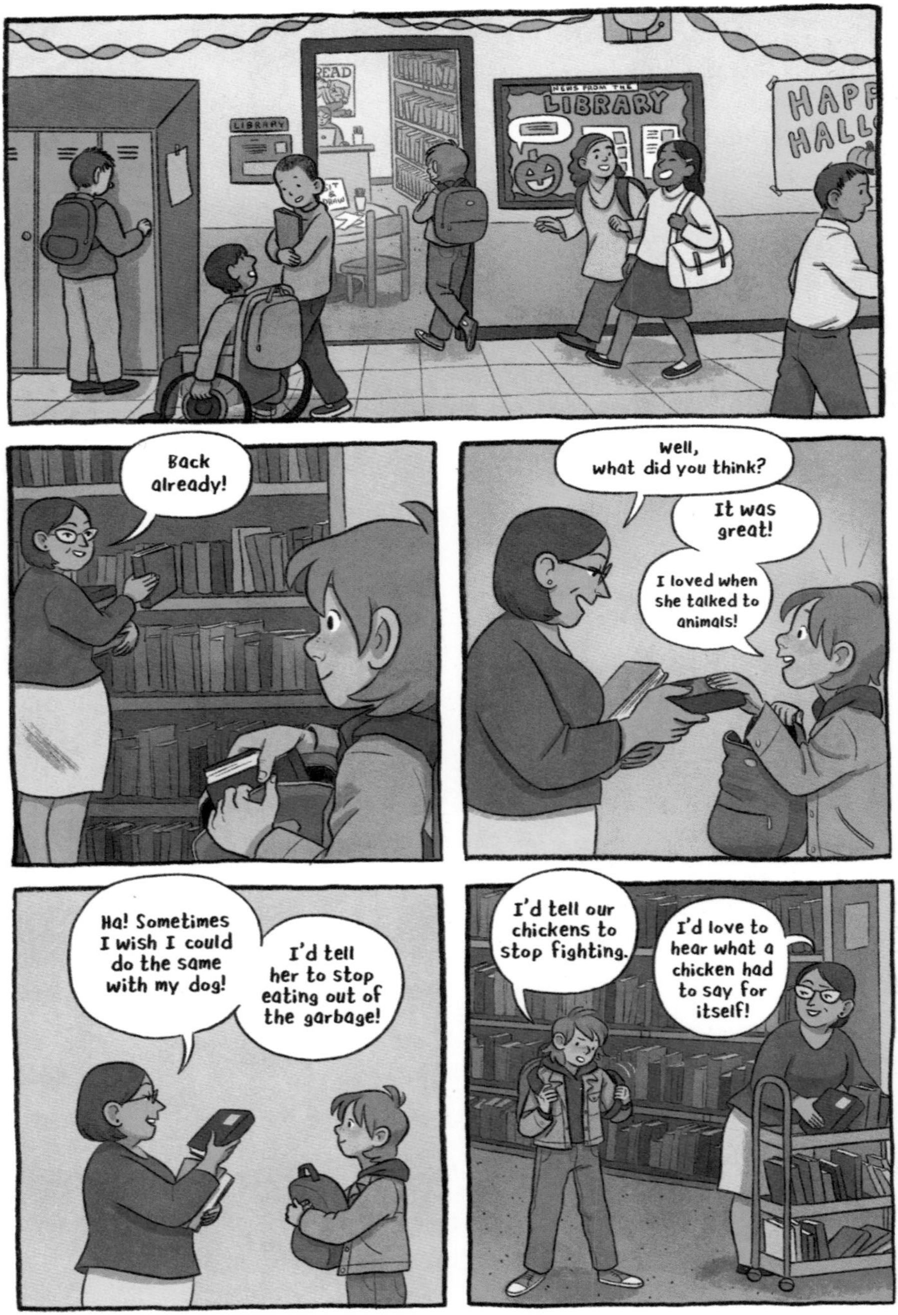

LIBRARY
NEWS FROM THE LIBRARY
HAPP HALL
Back already!
Well, what did you think?
It was great!
I loved when she talked to animals!
Ha! Sometimes I wish I could do the same with my dog!
I'd tell her to stop eating out of the garbage!
I'd tell our chickens to stop fighting.
I'd love to hear what a chicken had to say for itself!

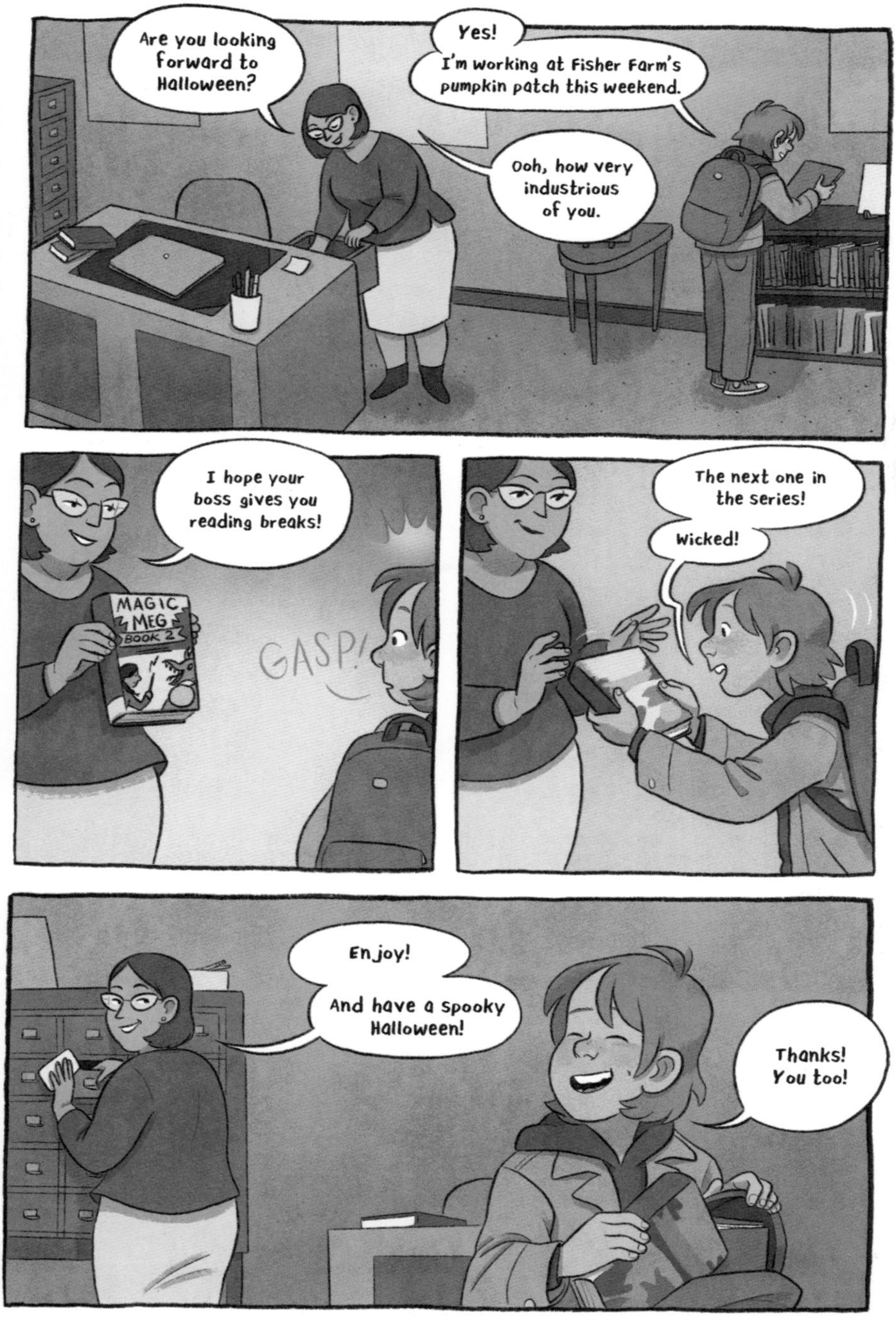

Are you looking forward to Halloween?
Yes!
I'm working at Fisher Farm's pumpkin patch this weekend.
Ooh, how very industrious of you.
I hope your boss gives you reading breaks!
MAGIC MEG BOOK 2
GASP!
The next one in the series!
Wicked!
Enjoy!
And have a spooky Halloween!
Thanks! You too!

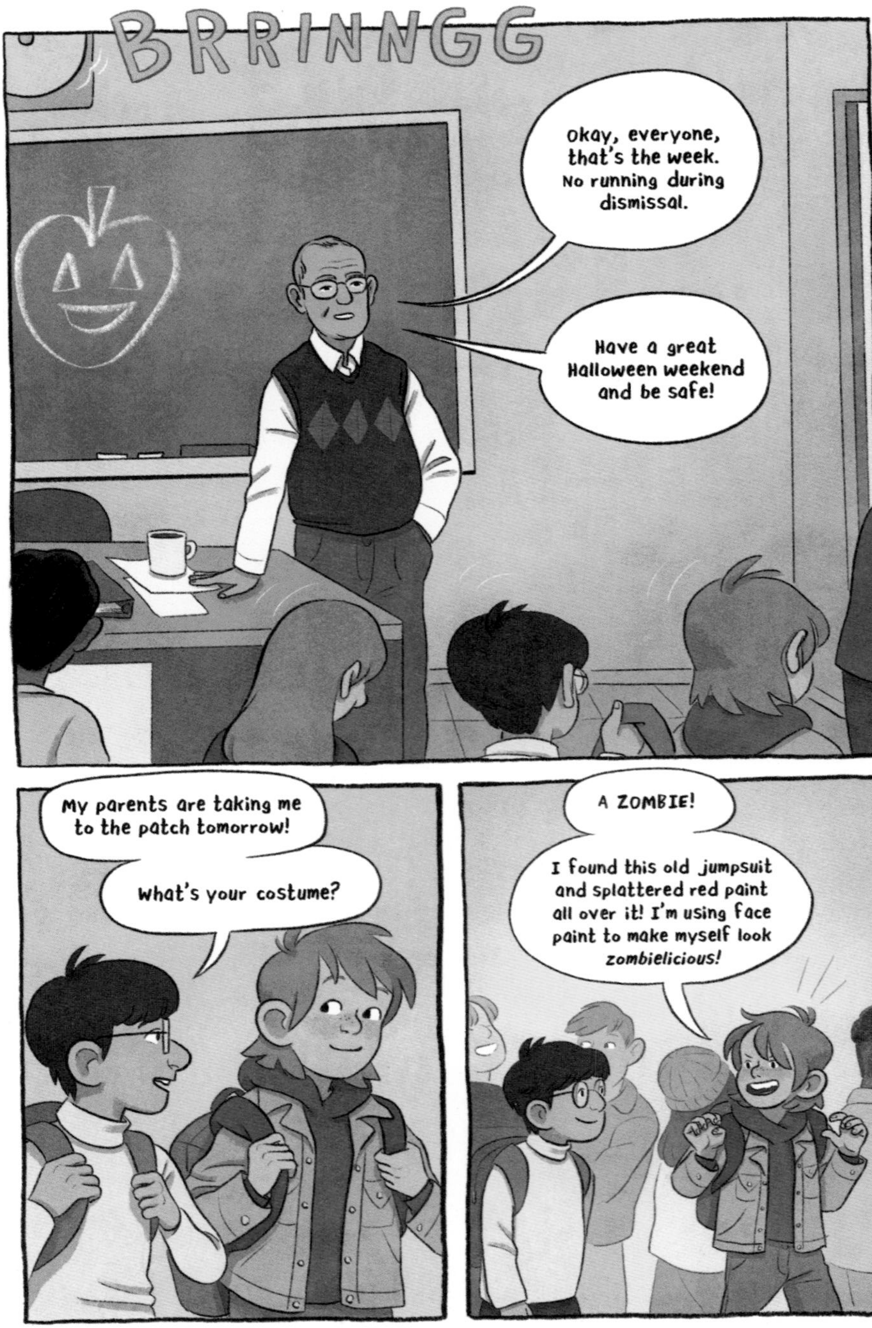
BRRINNGG
Okay, everyone, that's the week. No running during dismissal.
Have a great Halloween weekend and be safe!
My parents are taking me to the patch tomorrow!
What's your costume?
A ZOMBIE!
I found this old jumpsuit and splattered red paint all over it! I'm using face paint to make myself look *zombielicious!*

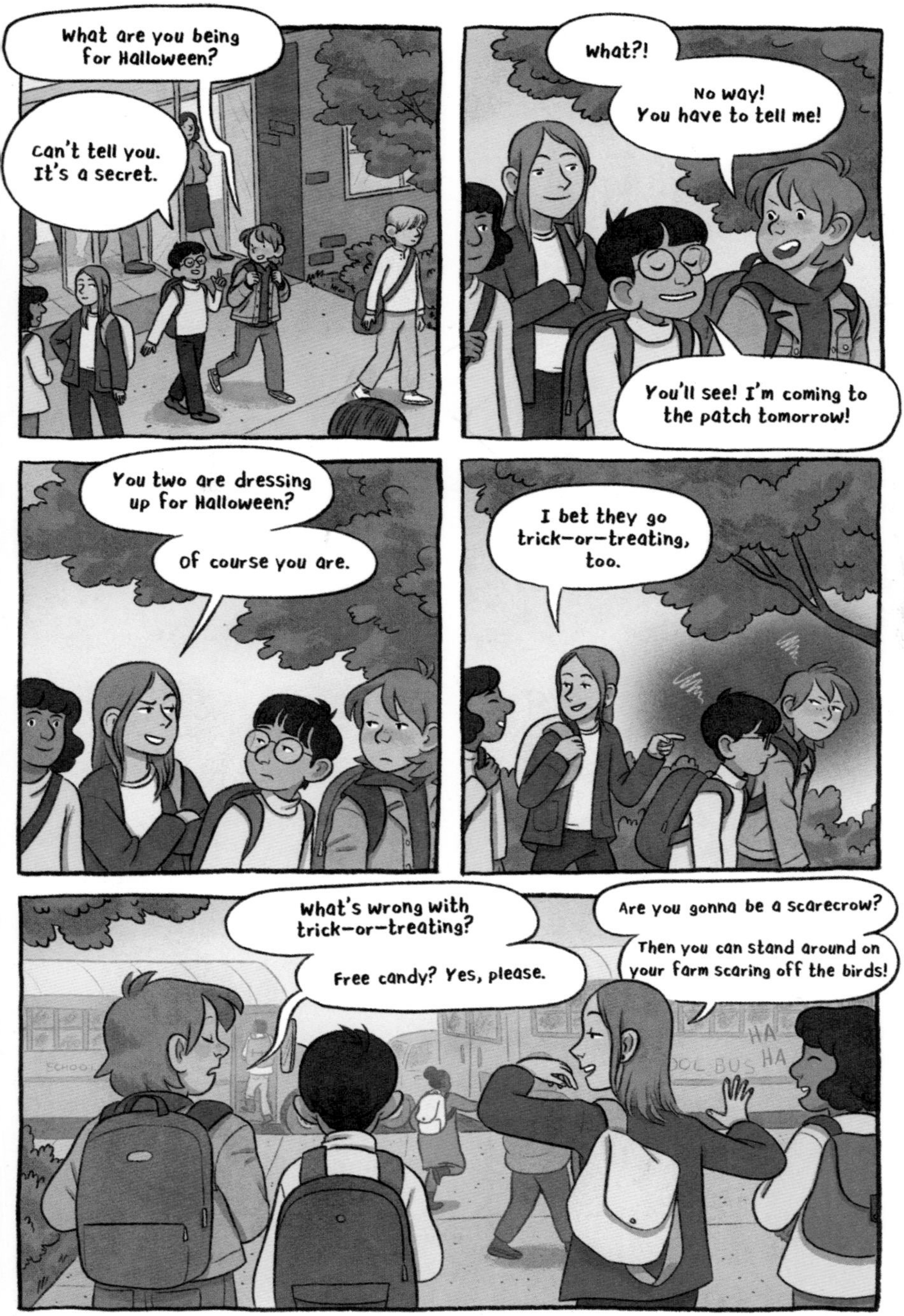
What are you being for Halloween?
Can't tell you. It's a secret.
What?!
No way! You have to tell me!
You'll see! I'm coming to the patch tomorrow!
You two are dressing up for Halloween?
Of course you are.
I bet they go trick-or-treating, too.
What's wrong with trick-or-treating?
Free candy? Yes, please.
Are you gonna be a scarecrow?
Then you can stand around on your farm scaring off the birds!
HA HA

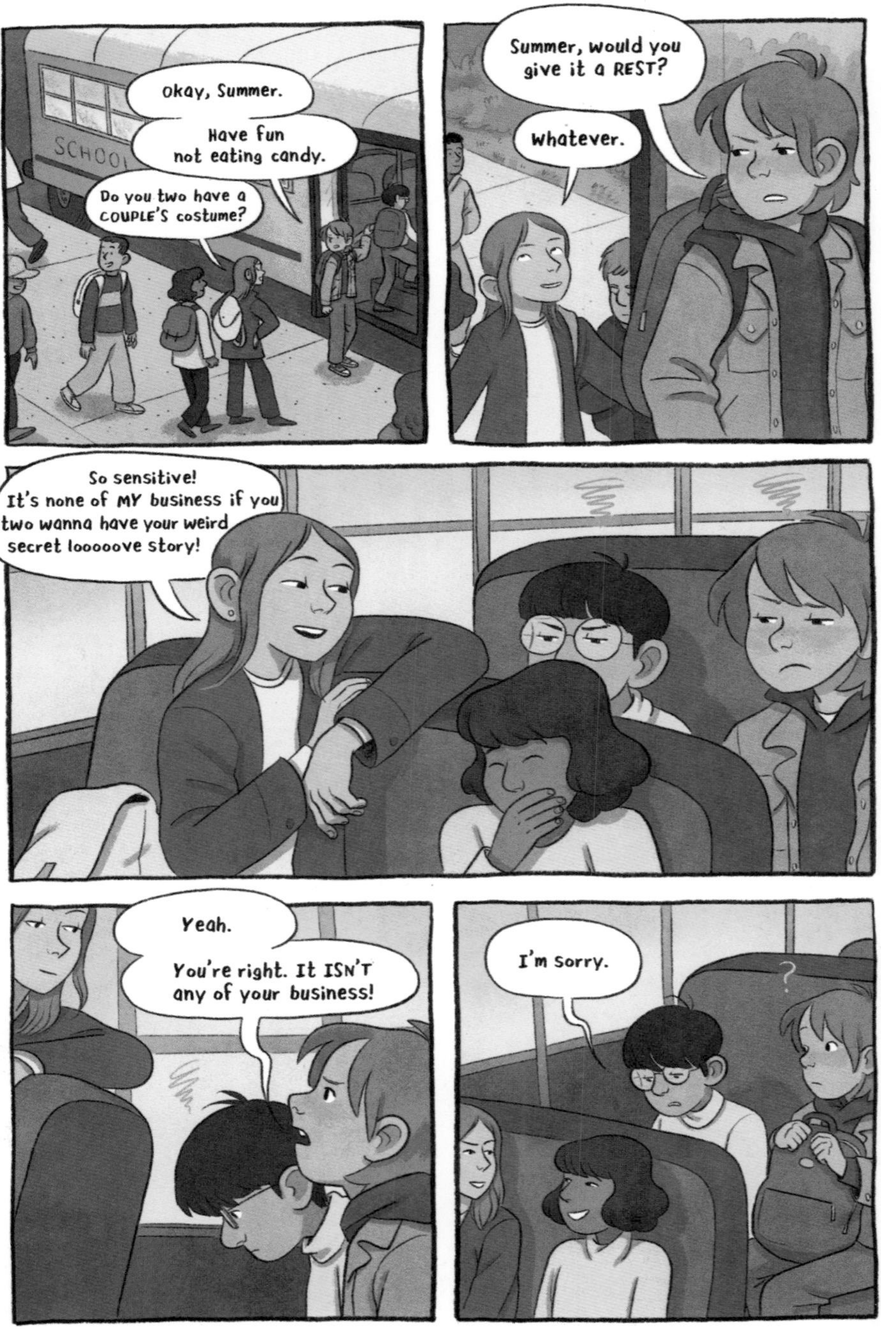
Okay, Summer.
Have fun not eating candy.
Do you two have a COUPLE'S costume?
SCHOOL
Summer, would you give it a REST?
Whatever.
So sensitive! It's none of MY business if you two wanna have your weird secret looooove story!
Yeah.
You're right. It ISN'T any of your business!
I'm sorry.
?

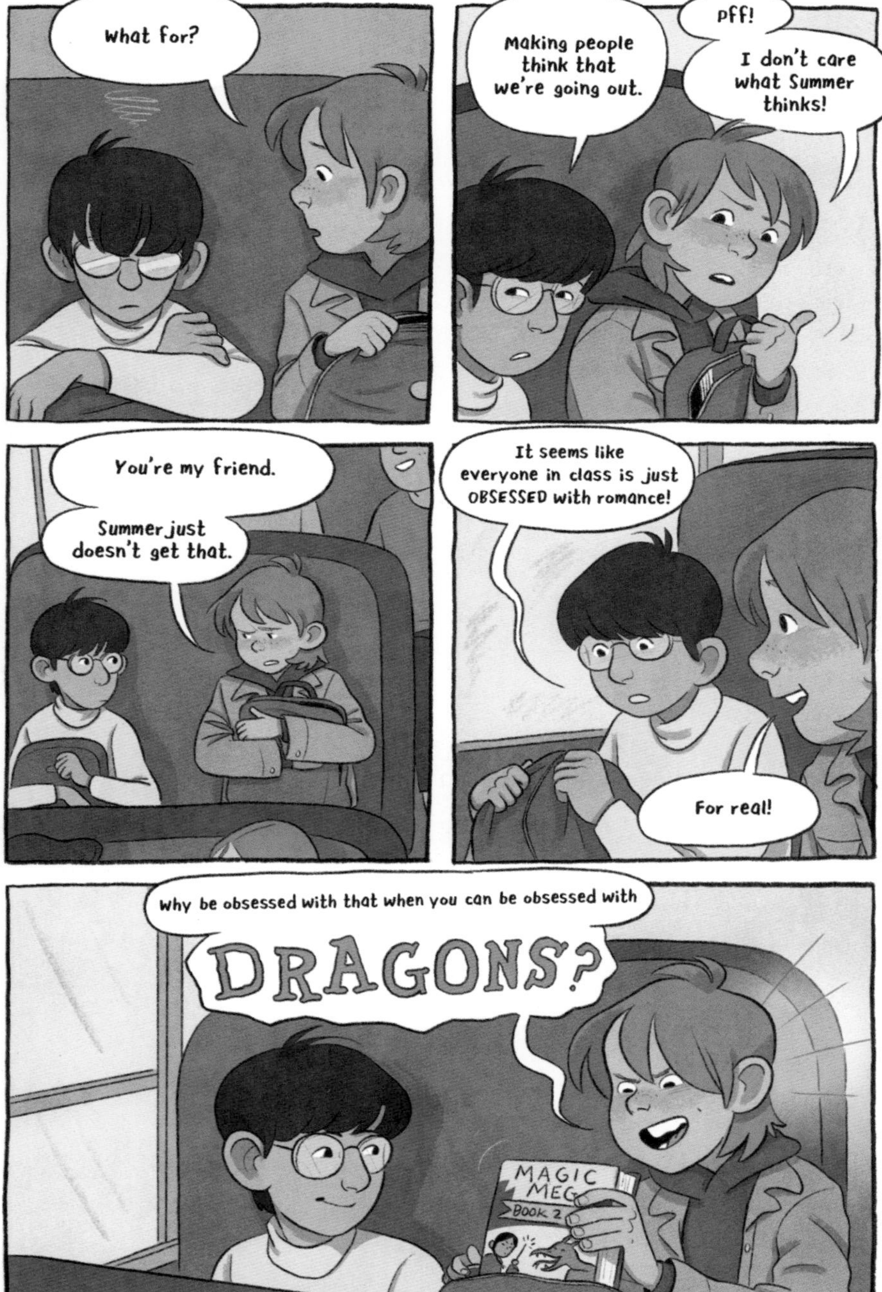
What for?
Making people think that we're going out.
pff!
I don't care what Summer thinks!
You're my friend.
Summer just doesn't get that.
It seems like everyone in class is just OBSESSED with romance!
For real!
Why be obsessed with that when you can be obsessed with
DRAGONS?
MAGIC MEG BOOK 2

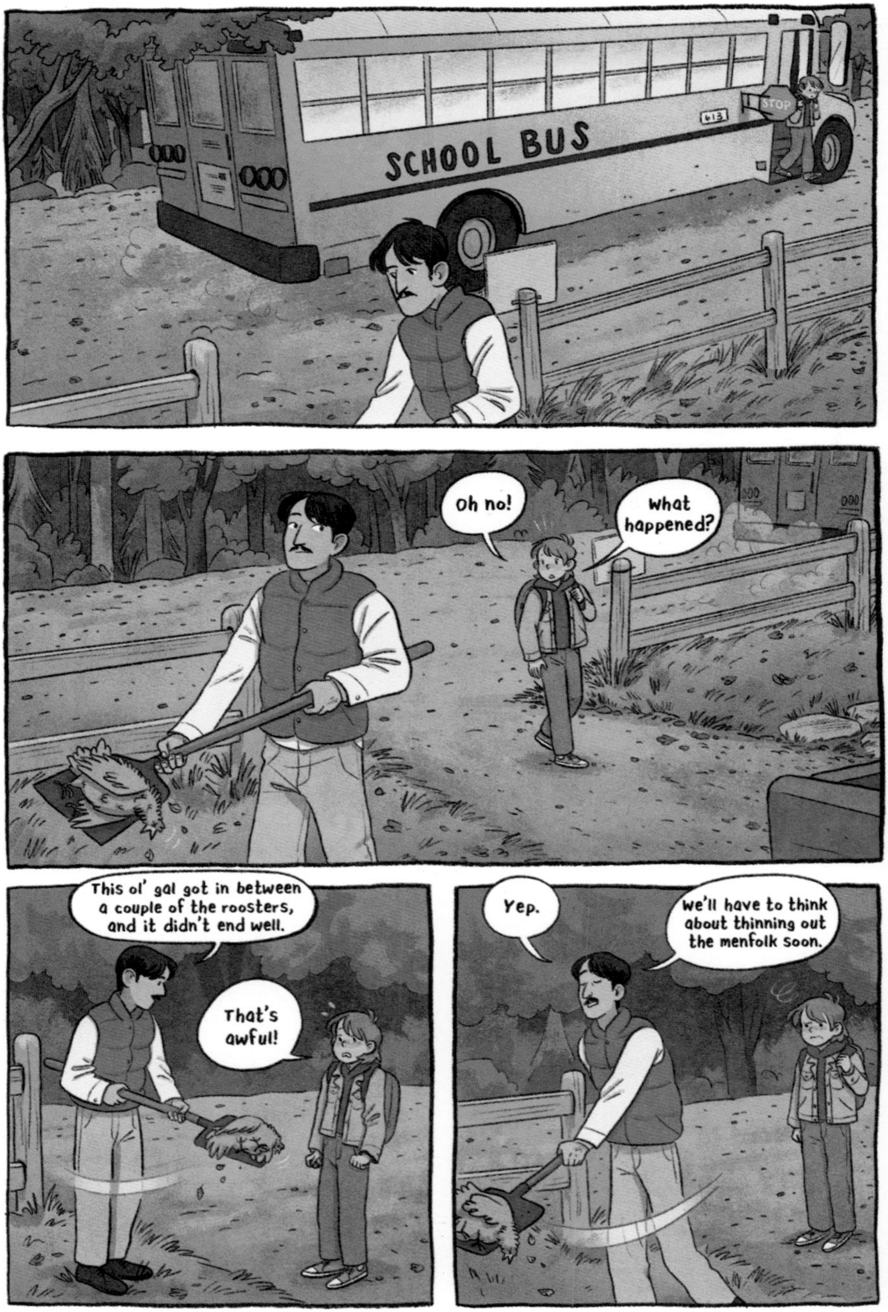
SCHOOL BUS
STOP
613
Oh no!
What happened?
This ol' gal got in between a couple of the roosters, and it didn't end well.
That's awful!
Yep.
We'll have to think about thinning out the menfolk soon.

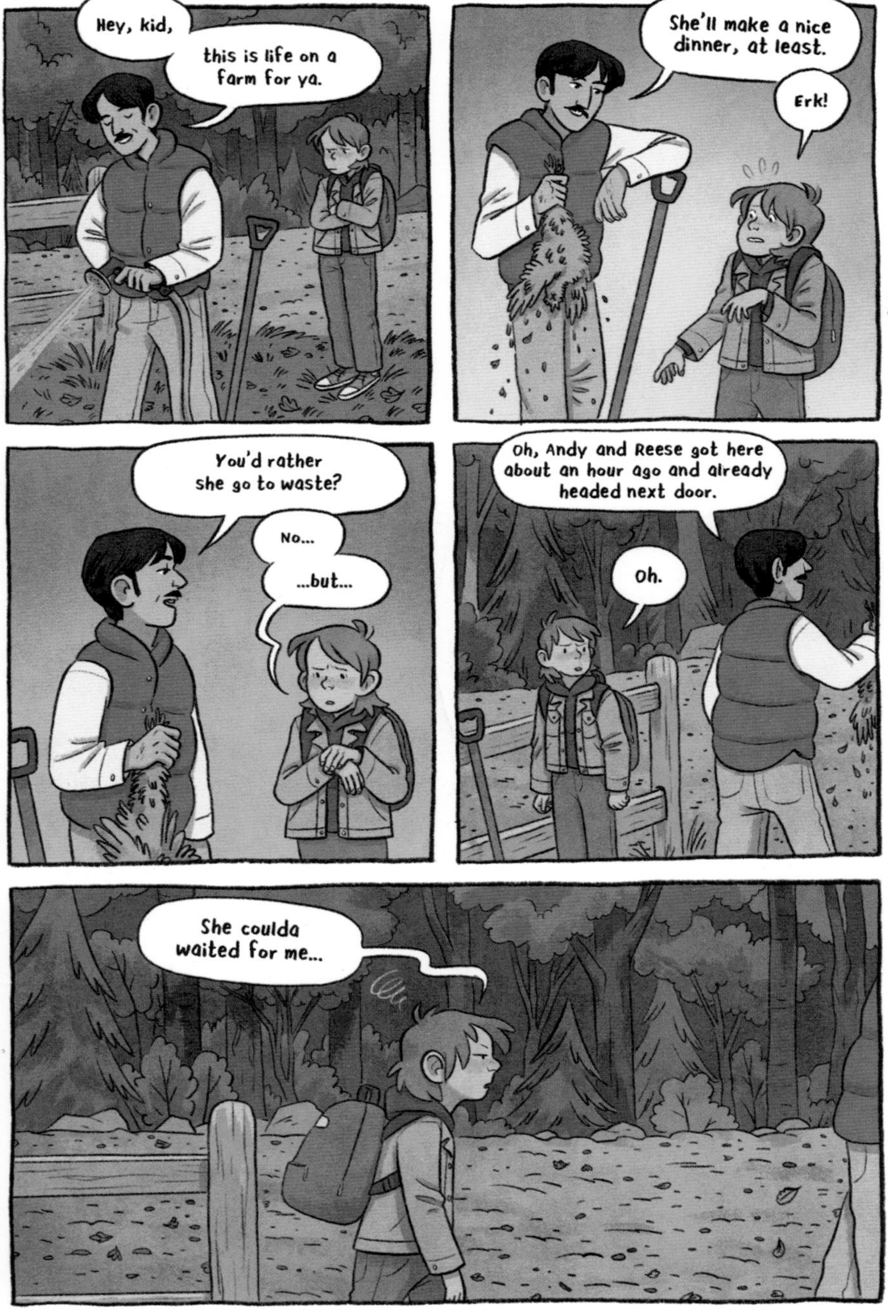
Hey, kid,
this is life on a farm for ya.
She'll make a nice dinner, at least.
Erk!
You'd rather she go to waste?
No...
...but...
Oh, Andy and Reese got here about an hour ago and already headed next door.
Oh.
She coulda waited for me...

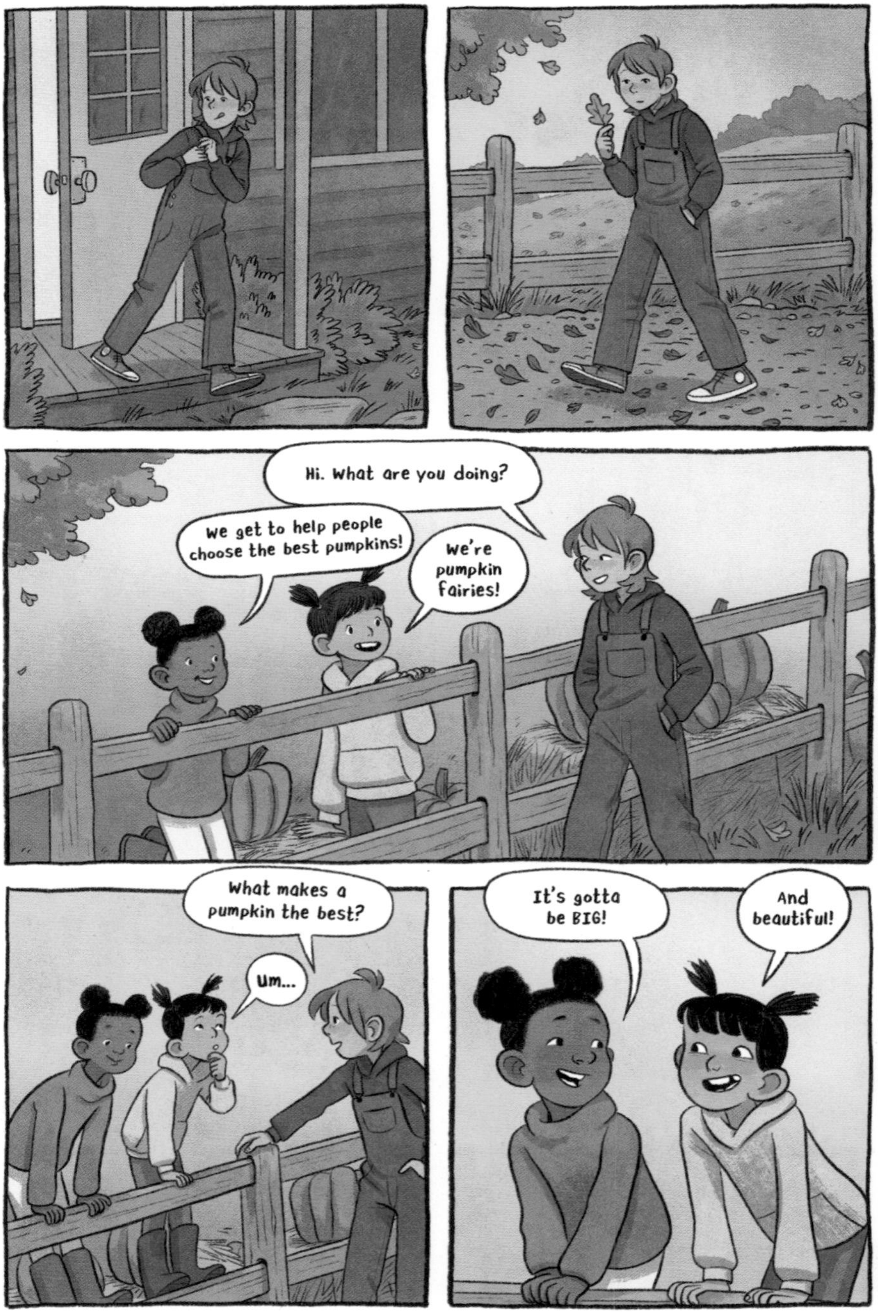
Hi. What are you doing?
We get to help people choose the best pumpkins!
We're pumpkin fairies!
What makes a pumpkin the best?
Um...
It's gotta be BIG!
And beautiful!

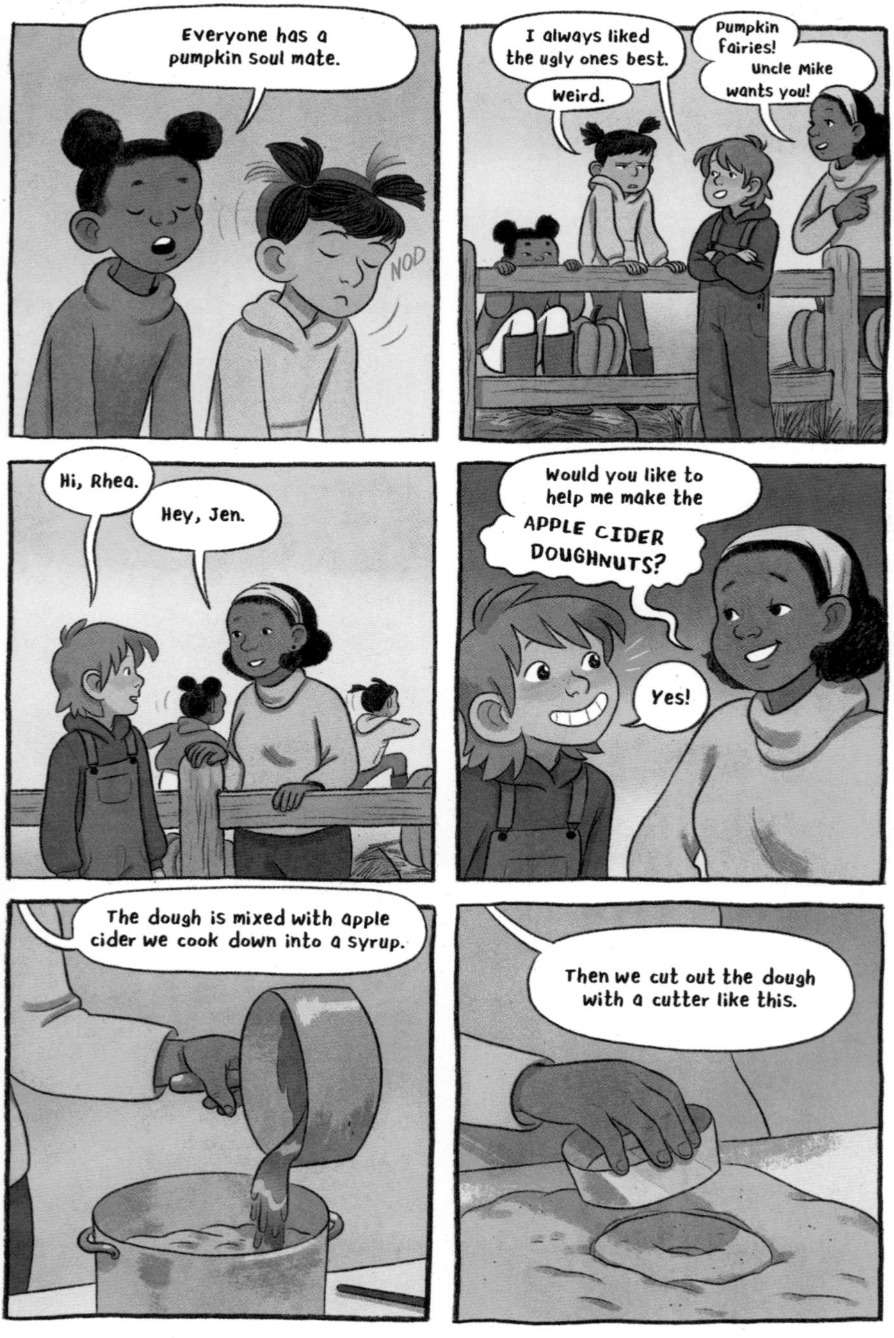
Everyone has a pumpkin soul mate.
NOD
I always liked the ugly ones best.
Weird.
Pumpkin fairies!
Uncle Mike wants you!
Hi, Rhea.
Hey, Jen.
Would you like to help me make the APPLE CIDER DOUGHNUTS?
Yes!
The dough is mixed with apple cider we cook down into a syrup.
Then we cut out the dough with a cutter like this.

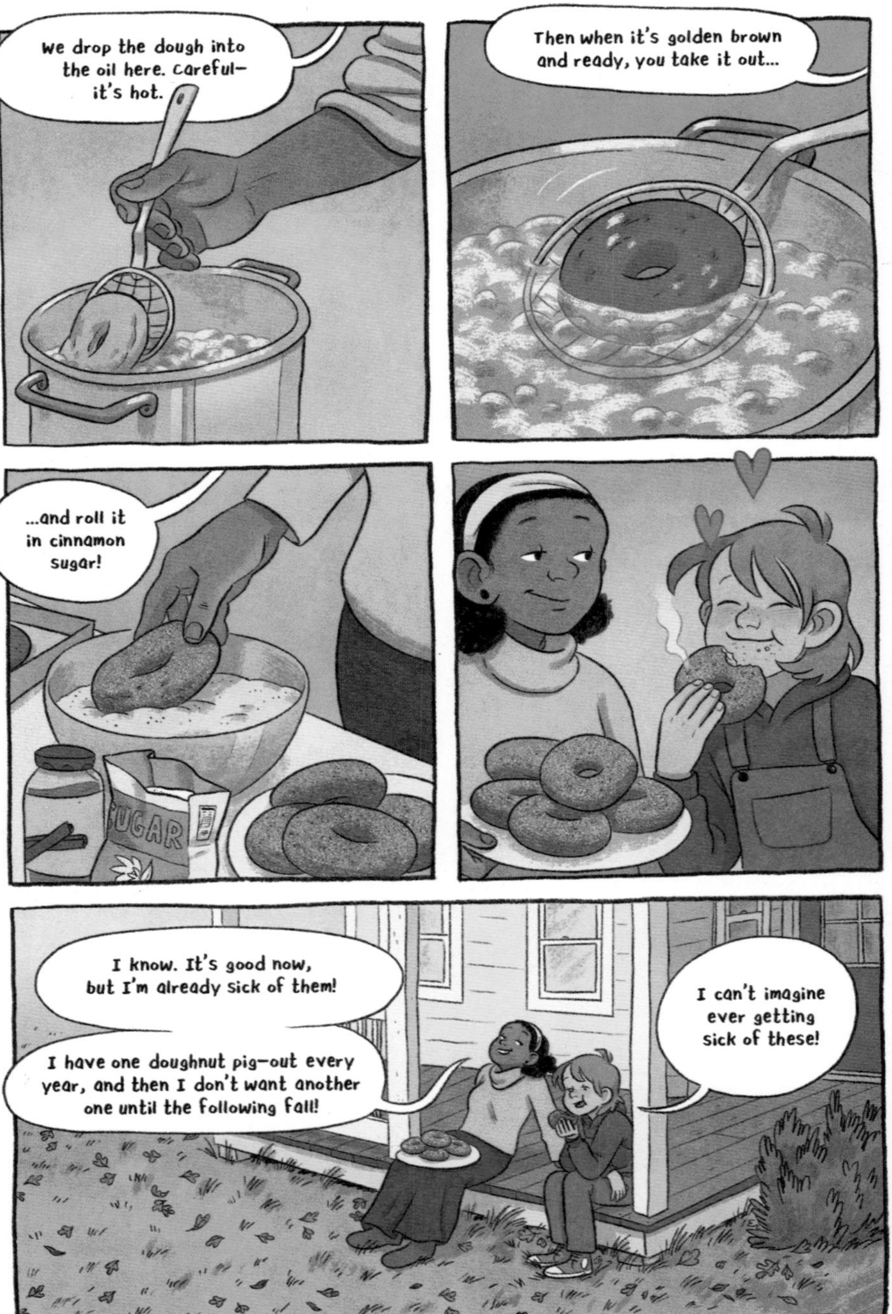

We drop the dough into the oil here. Careful—it's hot.
Then when it's golden brown and ready, you take it out...
...and roll it in cinnamon sugar!
SUGAR
I know. It's good now, but I'm already sick of them!
I have one doughnut pig-out every year, and then I don't want another one until the following fall!
I can't imagine ever getting sick of these!

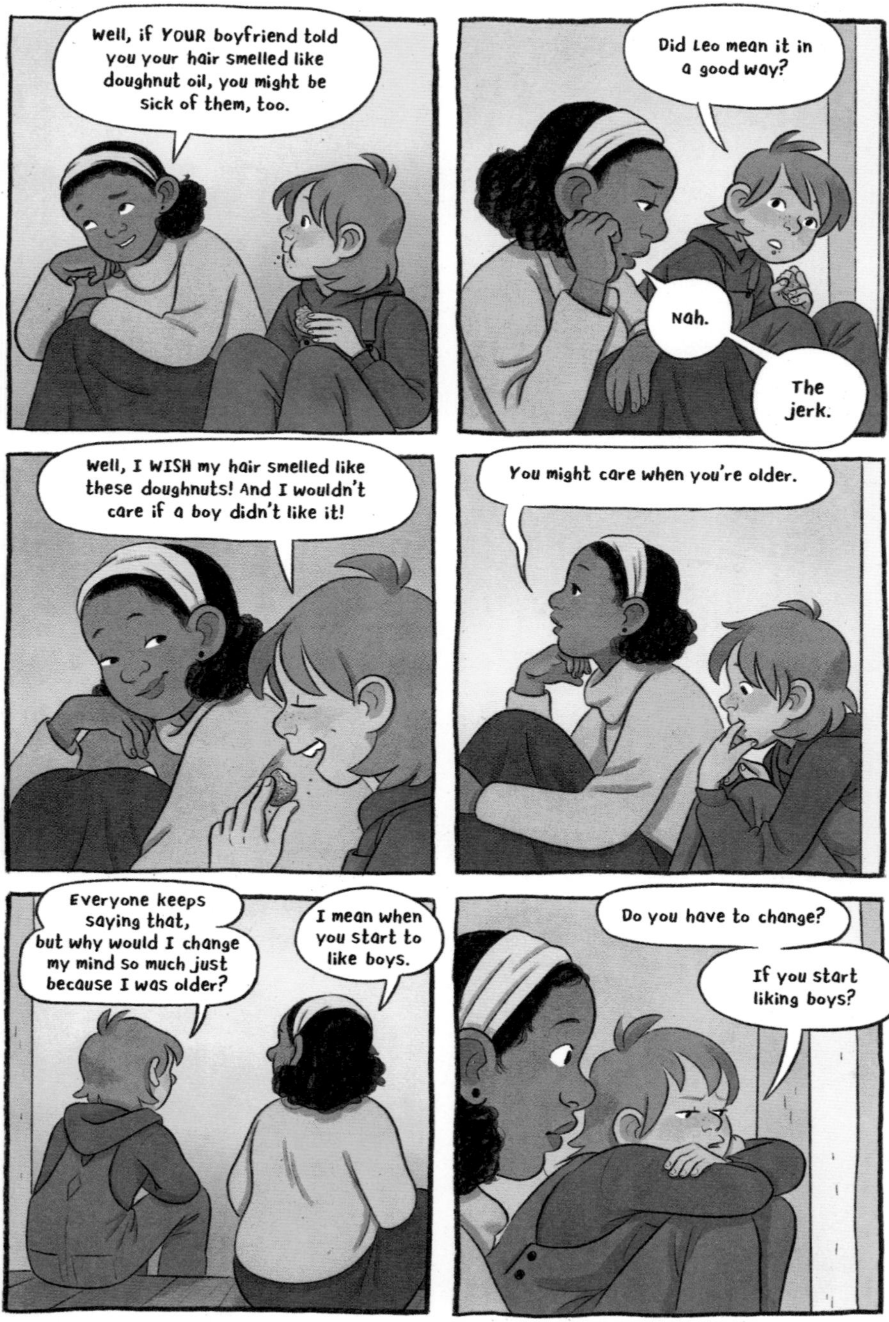
Well, if YOUR boyfriend told you your hair smelled like doughnut oil, you might be sick of them, too.
Did Leo mean it in a good way?
Nah.
The jerk.
Well, I WISH my hair smelled like these doughnuts! And I wouldn't care if a boy didn't like it!
You might care when you're older.
Everyone keeps saying that, but why would I change my mind so much just because I was older?
I mean when you start to like boys.
Do you have to change?
If you start liking boys?

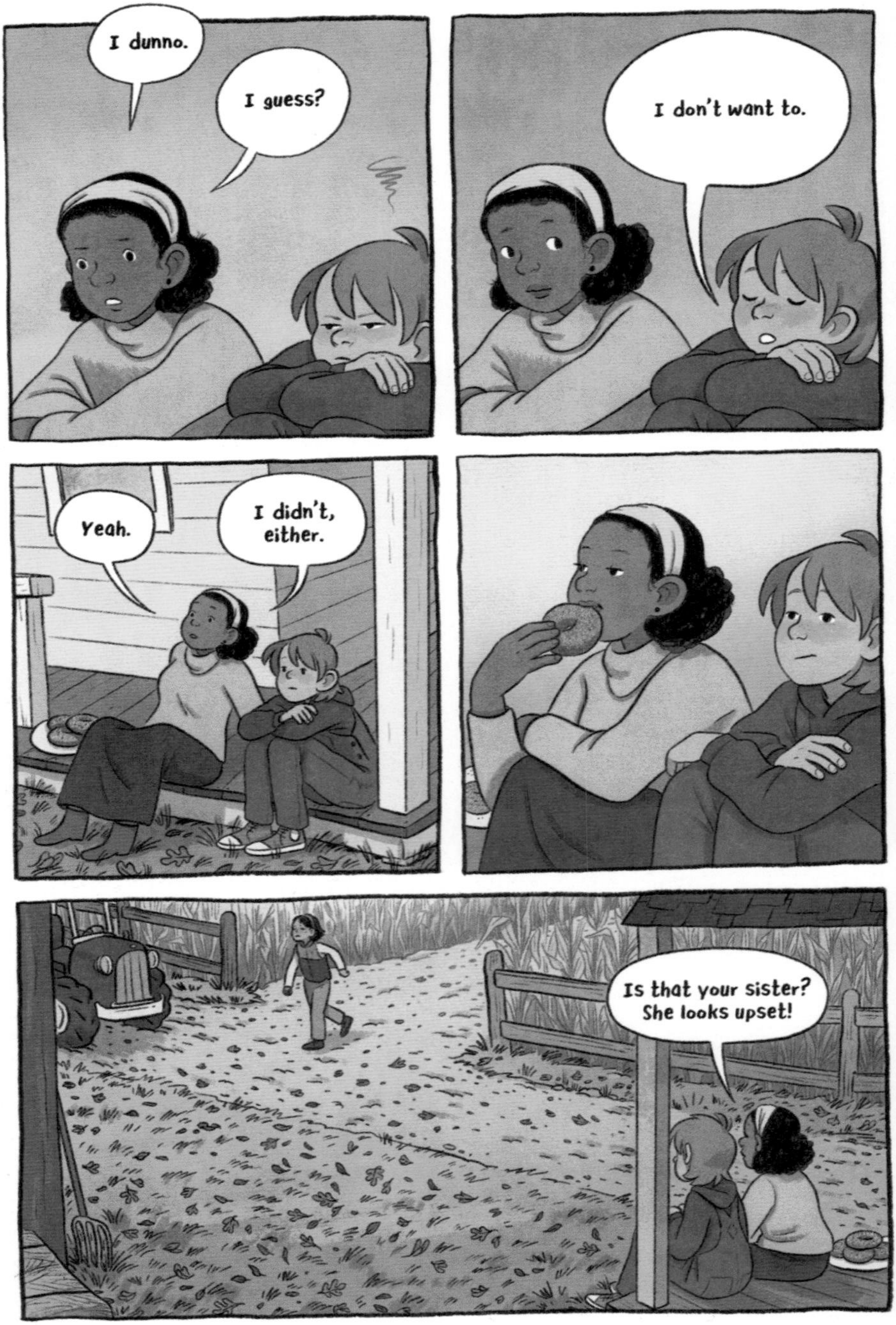
I dunno.
I guess?
I don't want to.
Yeah.
I didn't, either.
Is that your sister? She looks upset!

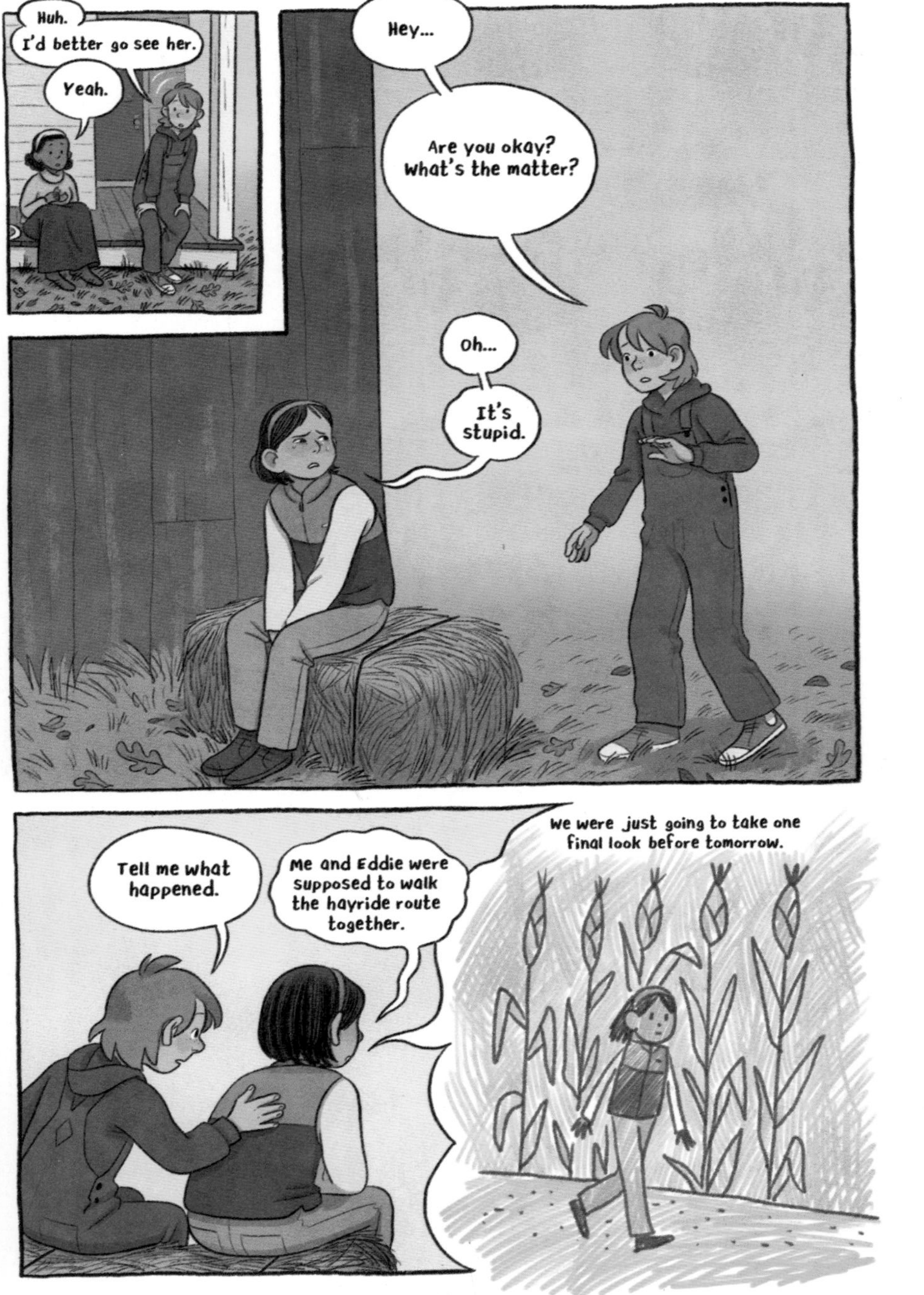
Huh.
I'd better go see her.
Yeah.
Hey...
Are you okay? What's the matter?
Oh...
It's stupid.
Tell me what happened.
Me and Eddie were supposed to walk the hayride route together.
We were just going to take one final look before tomorrow.

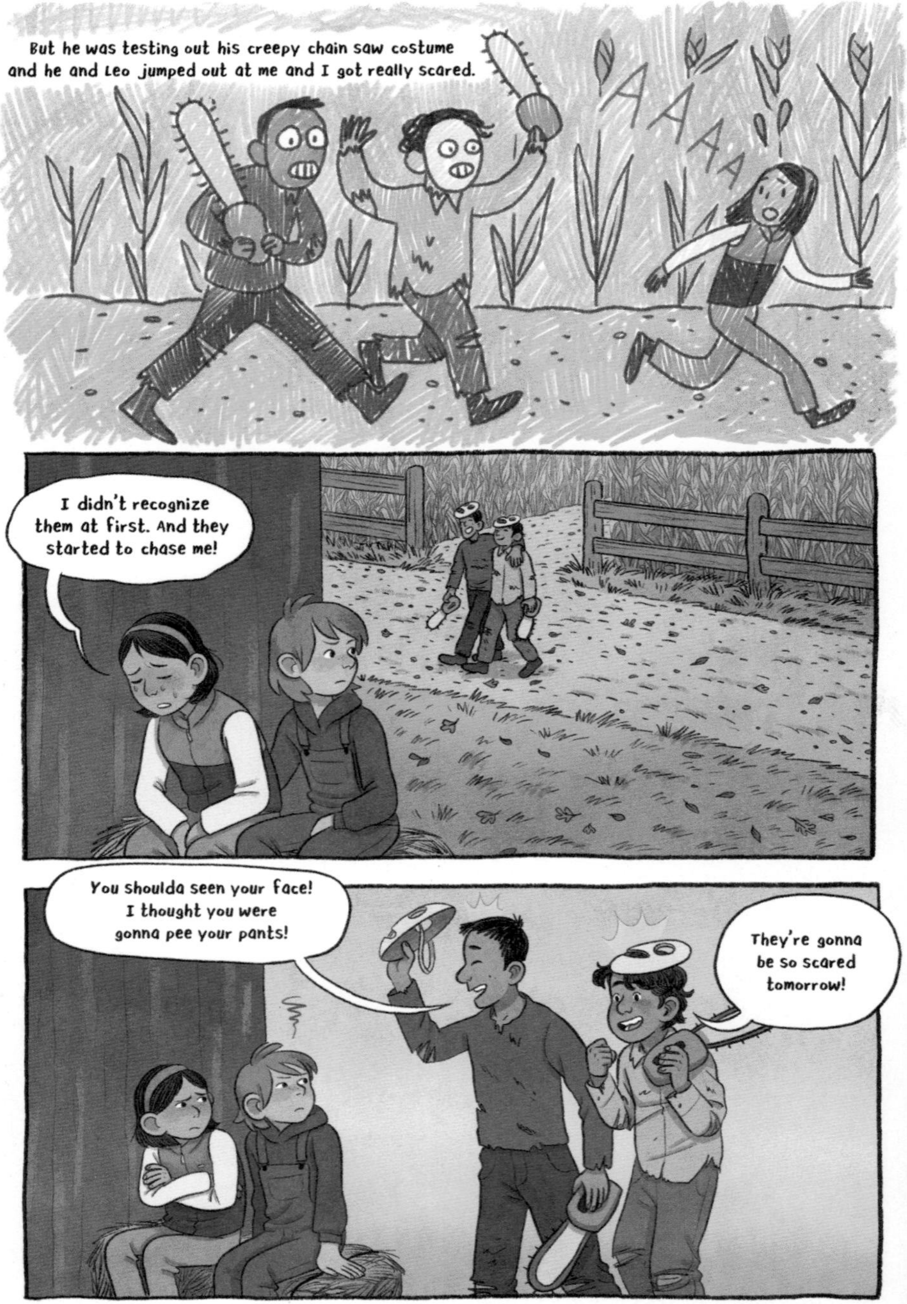
But he was testing out his creepy chain saw costume and he and Leo jumped out at me and I got really scared.
AAAA
I didn't recognize them at first. And they started to chase me!
You shoulda seen your face! I thought you were gonna pee your pants!
They're gonna be so scared tomorrow!

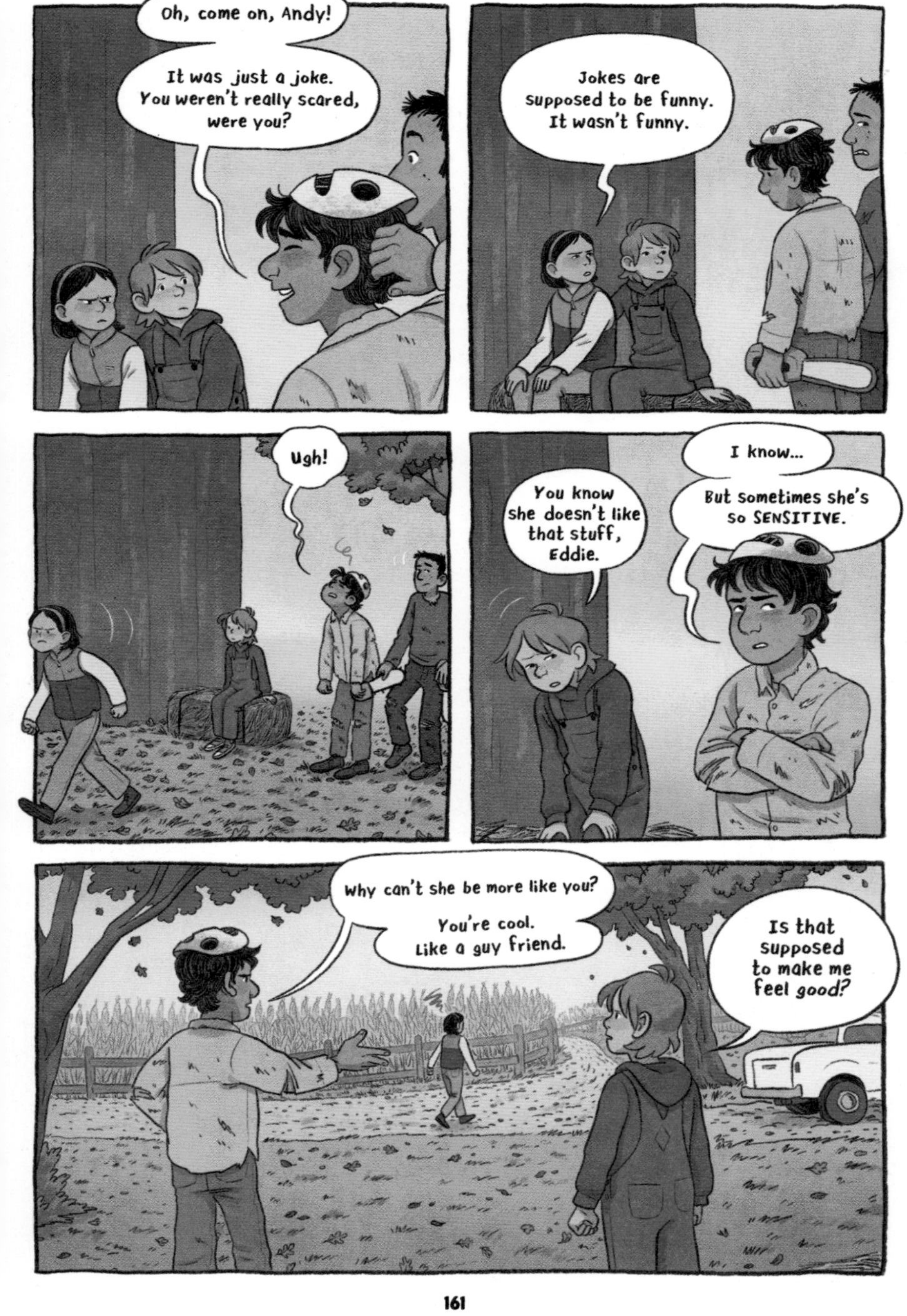
Oh, come on, Andy!
It was just a joke. You weren't really scared, were you?
Jokes are supposed to be funny. It wasn't funny.
Ugh!
You know she doesn't like that stuff, Eddie.
I know...
But sometimes she's so SENSITIVE.
Why can't she be more like you?
You're cool. Like a guy friend.
Is that supposed to make me feel *good?*

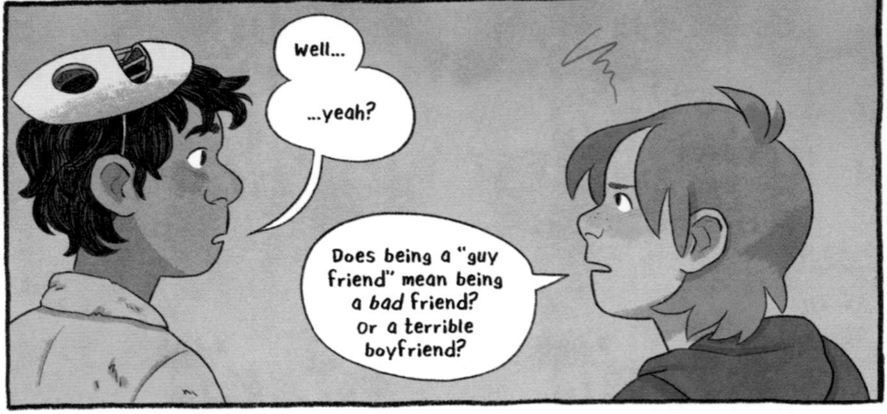
Well...
...yeah?
Does being a "guy friend" mean being a *bad* friend? Or a terrible boyfriend?

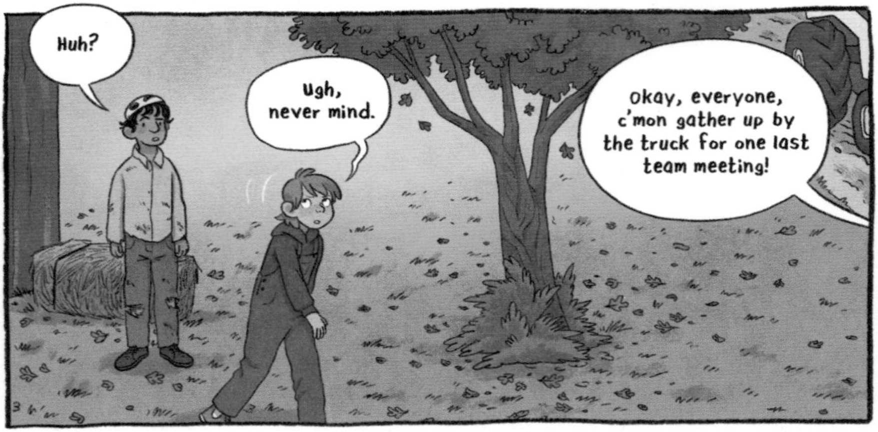
Huh?
Ugh, never mind.
Okay, everyone, c'mon gather up by the truck for one last team meeting!

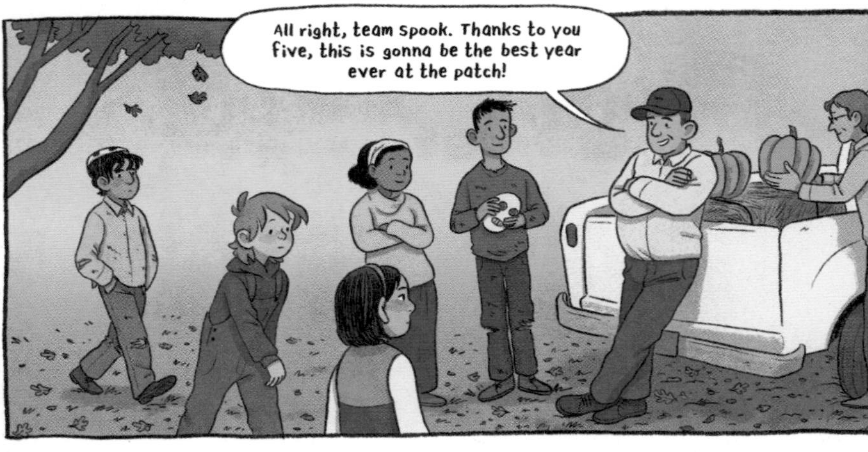
All right, team Spook. Thanks to you five, this is gonna be the best year ever at the patch!

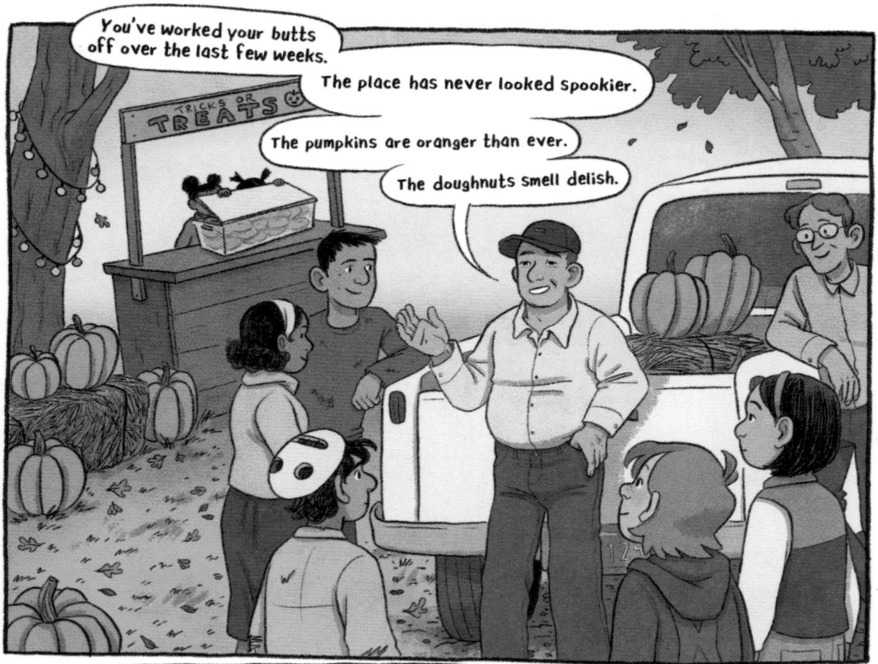
You've worked your butts off over the last few weeks.
The place has never looked spookier.
The pumpkins are oranger than ever.
The doughnuts smell delish.
TRICKS OR TREATS

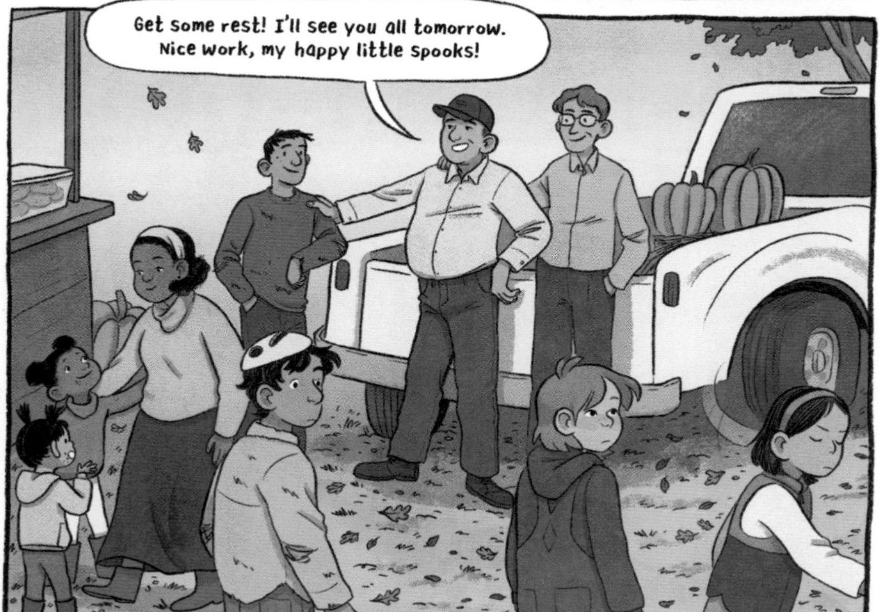
Get some rest! I'll see you all tomorrow. Nice work, my happy little spooks!

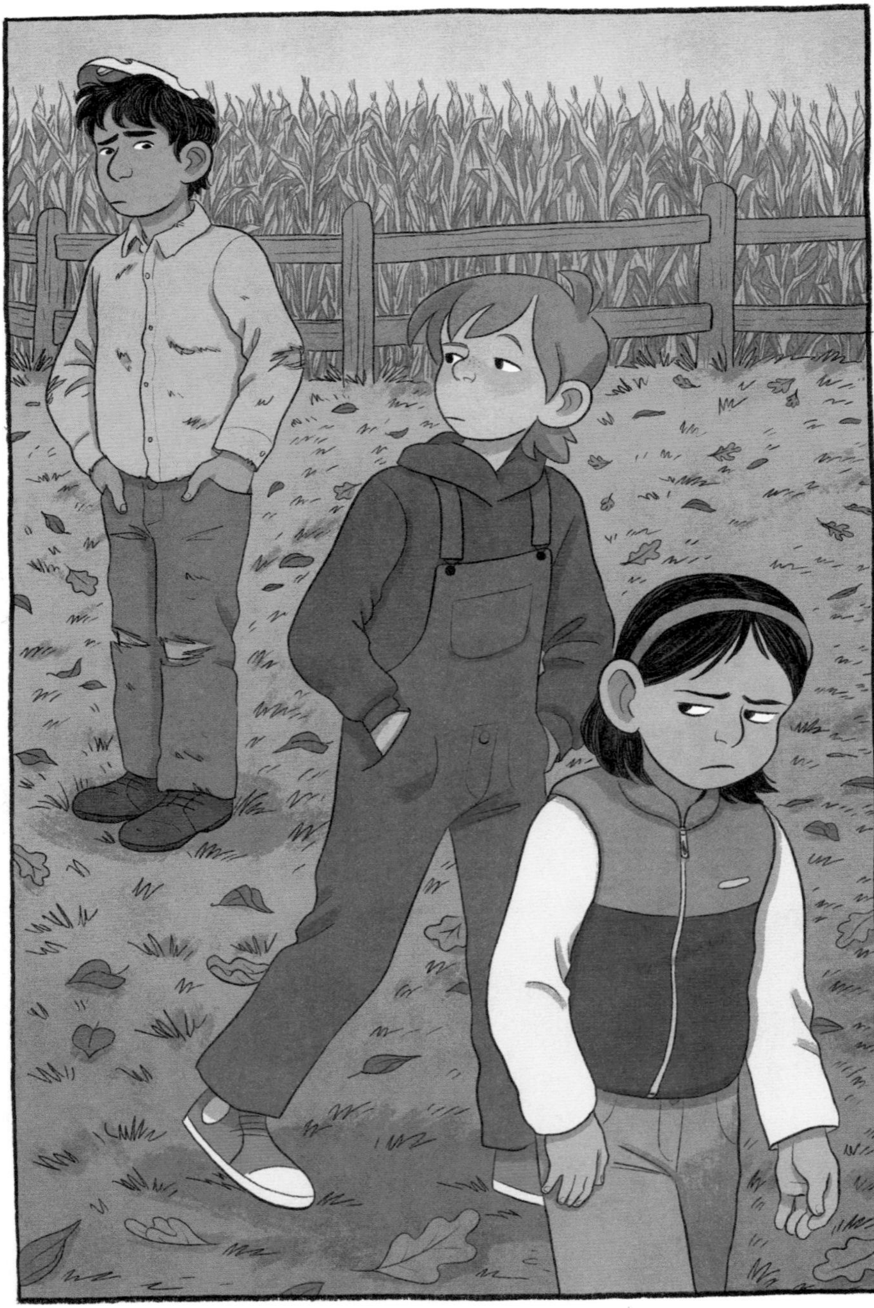

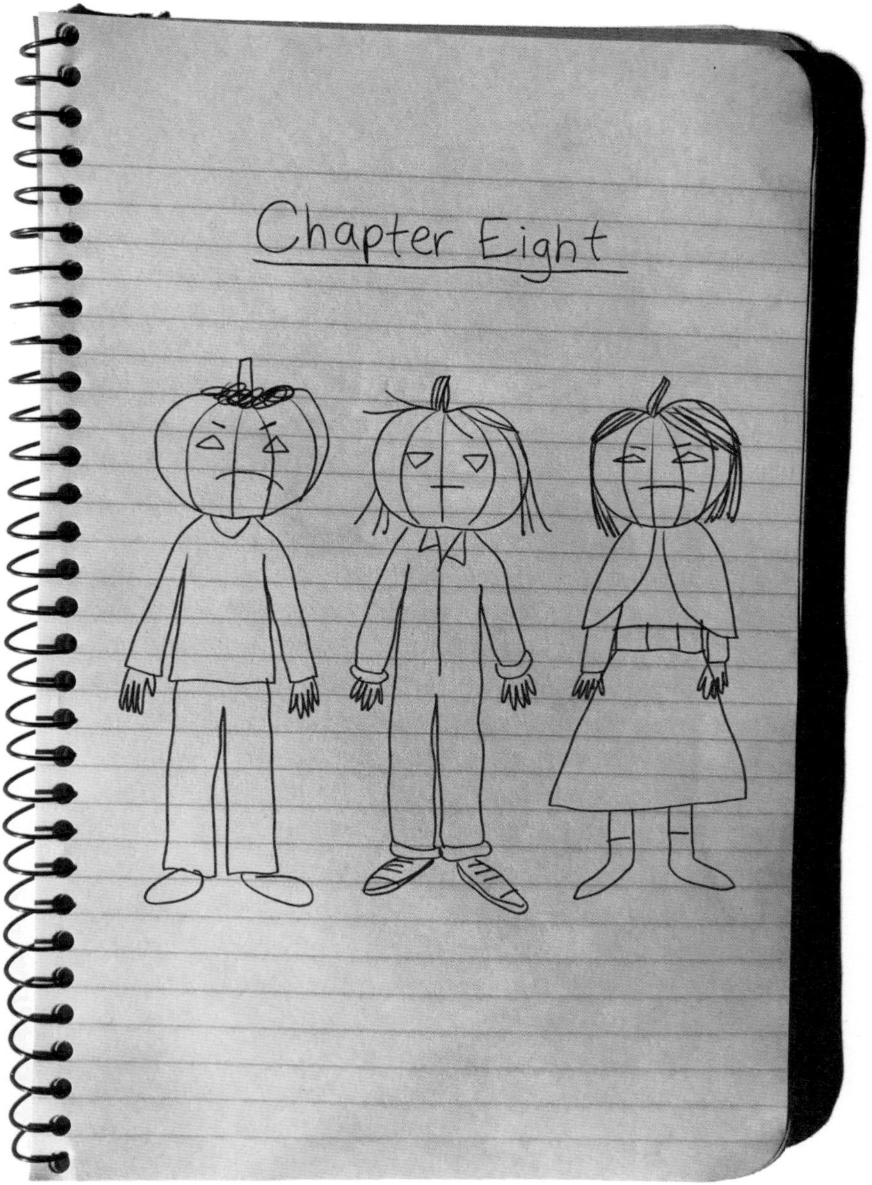
Chapter Eight

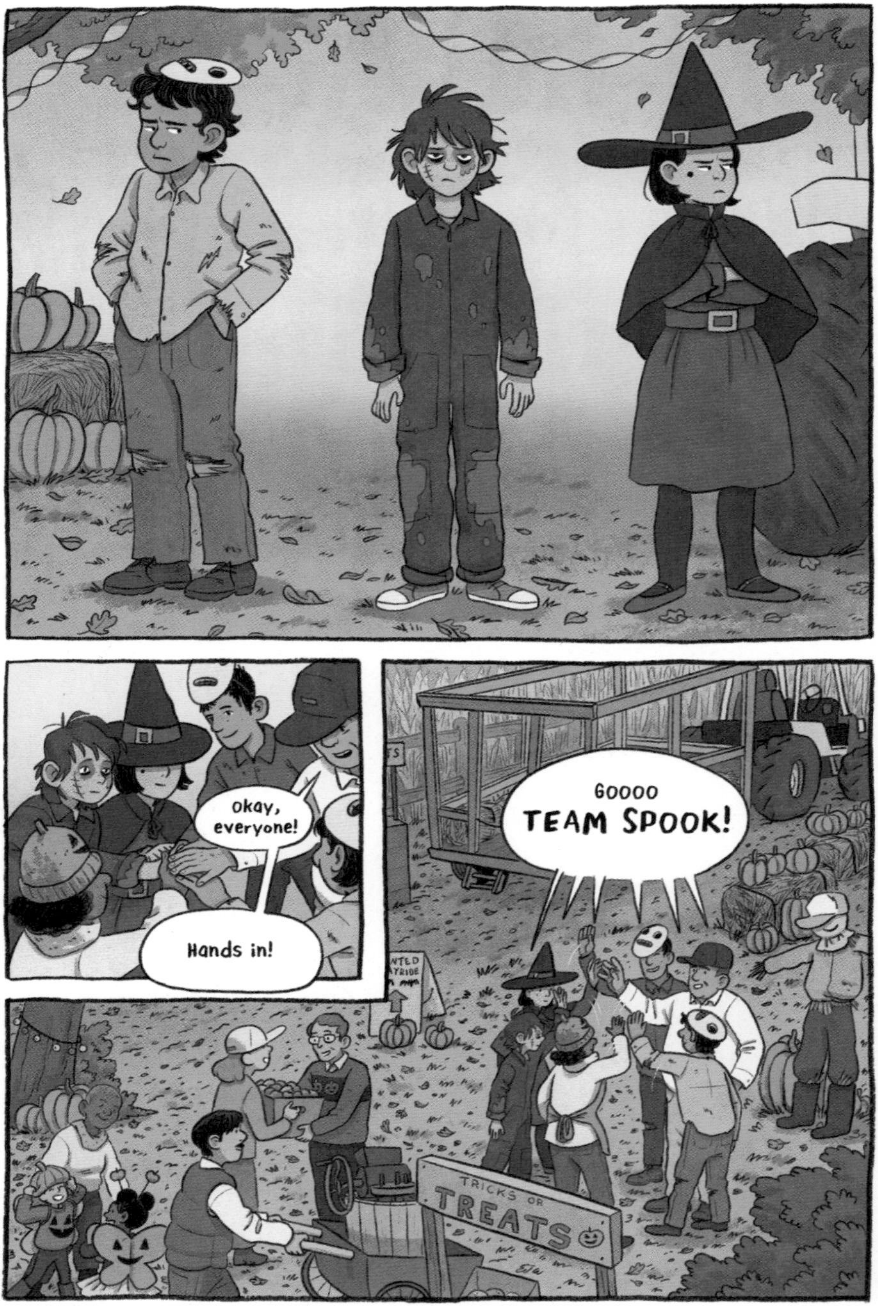
Okay, everyone!
Hands in!
Goooo TEAM SPOOK!
TRICKS OR TREATS

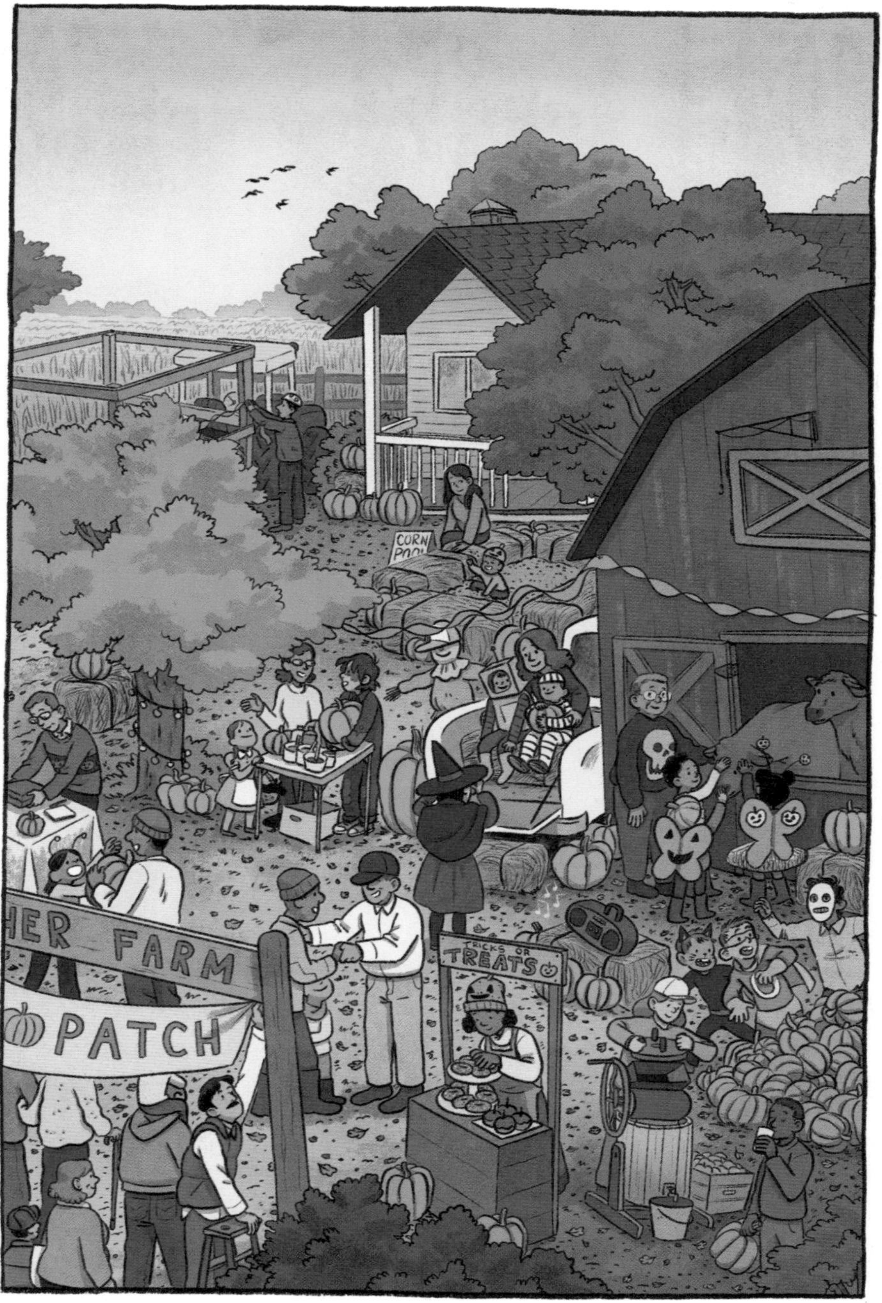
CORN
HER FARM
PATCH
TRICKS OR
TREATS

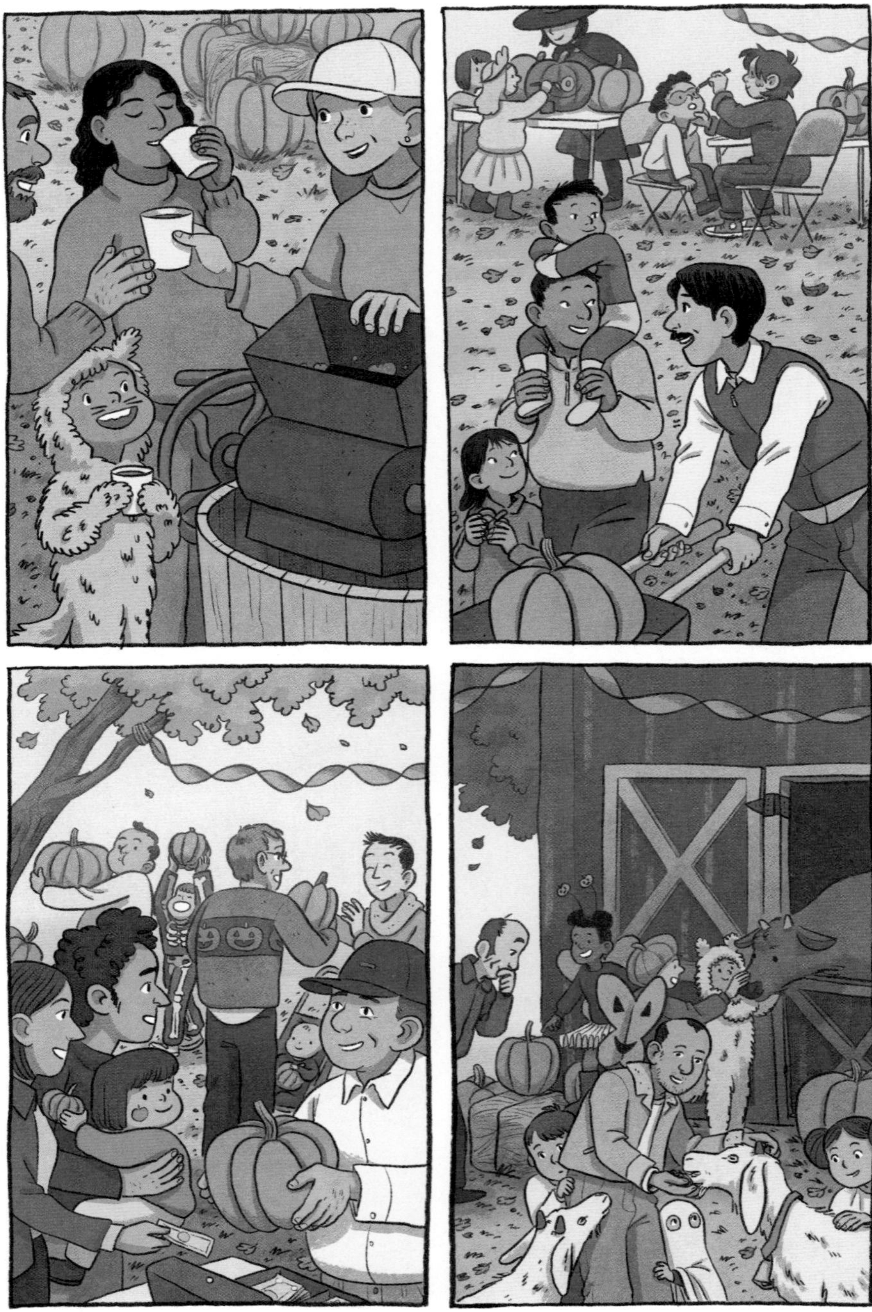

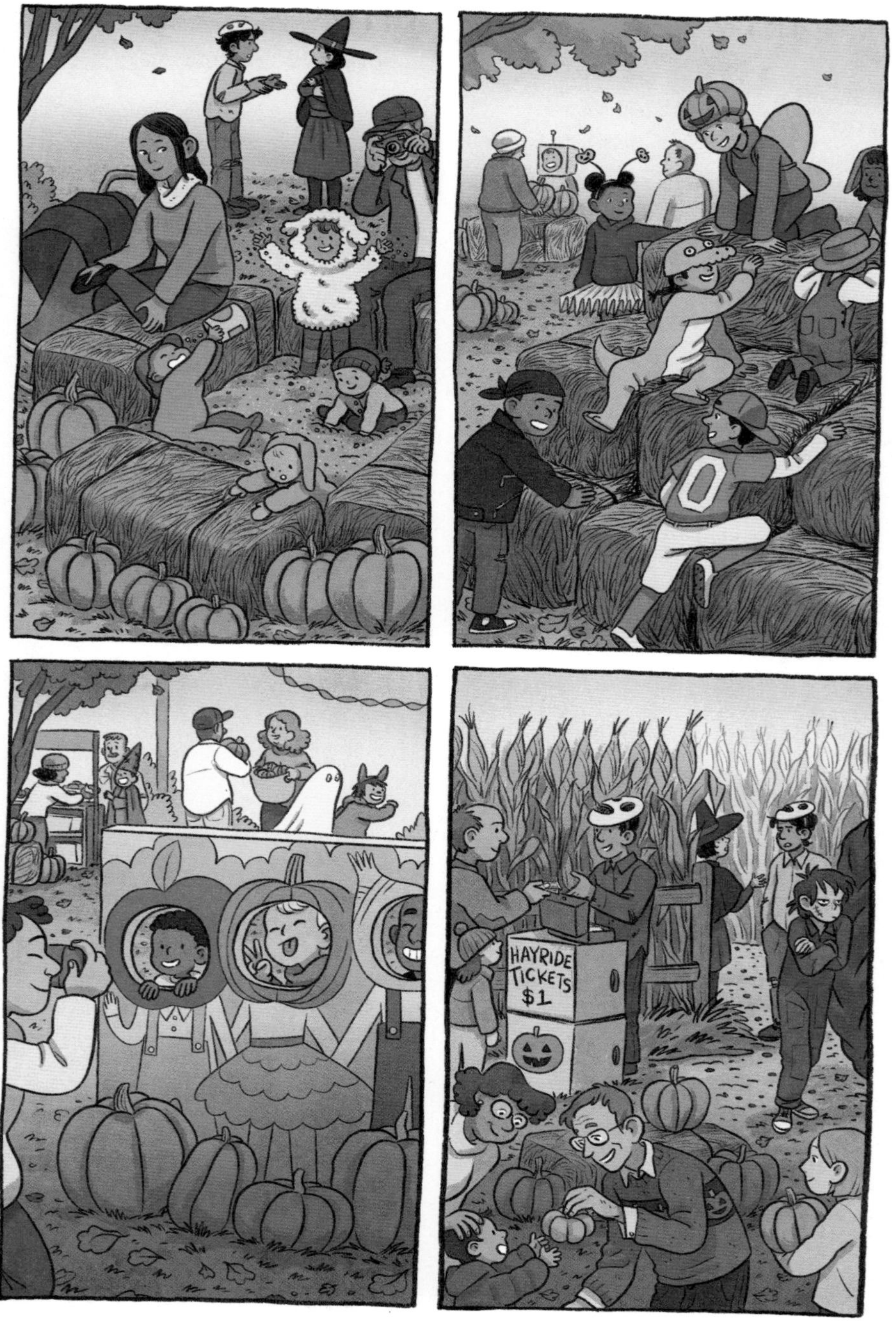
HAYRIDE TICKETS $1

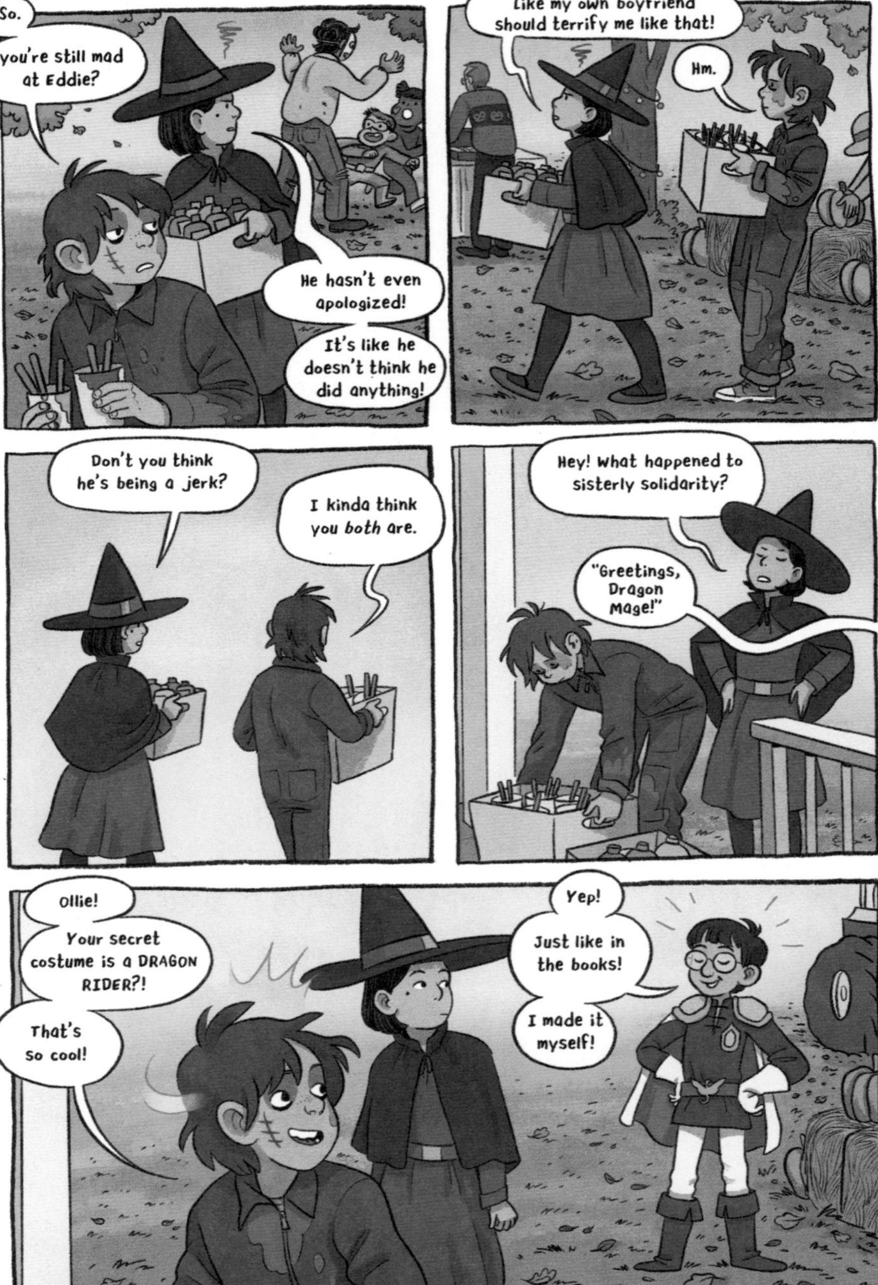
So.
you're still mad at Eddie?
He hasn't even apologized!
It's like he doesn't think he did anything!
Like my own boyfriend should terrify me like that!
Hm.
Don't you think he's being a jerk?
I kinda think you *both* are.
Hey! What happened to sisterly solidarity?
"Greetings, Dragon Mage!"
Ollie!
Your secret costume is a DRAGON RIDER?!
That's so cool!
Yep!
Just like in the books!
I made it myself!

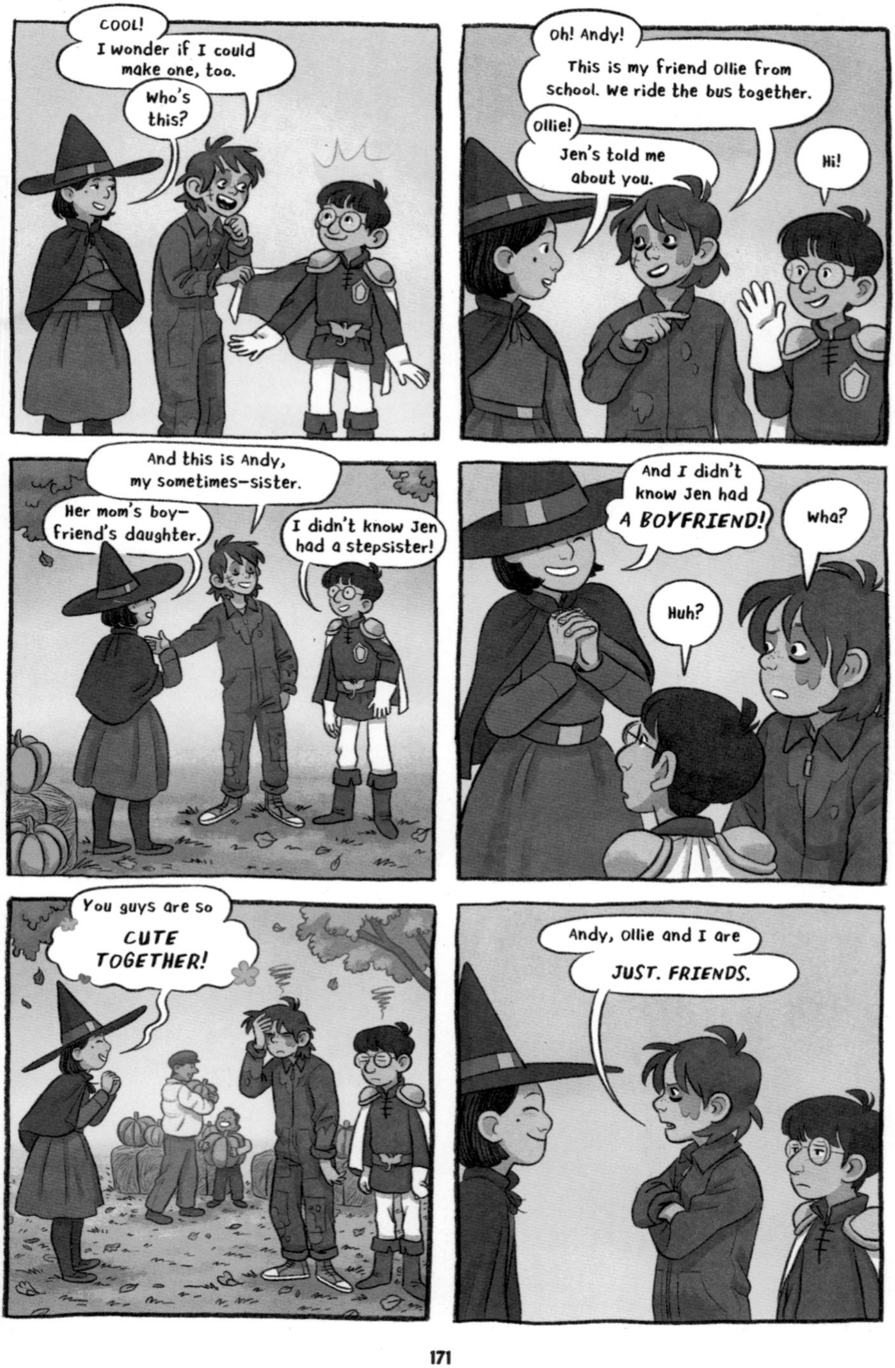
COOL!
I wonder if I could make one, too.
Who's this?
Oh! Andy!
This is my friend Ollie from school. We ride the bus together.
Ollie!
Jen's told me about you.
Hi!
And this is Andy, my sometimes-sister.
Her mom's boy-friend's daughter.
I didn't know Jen had a stepsister!
And I didn't know Jen had A BOYFRIEND!
Wha?
Huh?
You guys are so CUTE TOGETHER!
Andy, Ollie and I are JUST. FRIENDS.

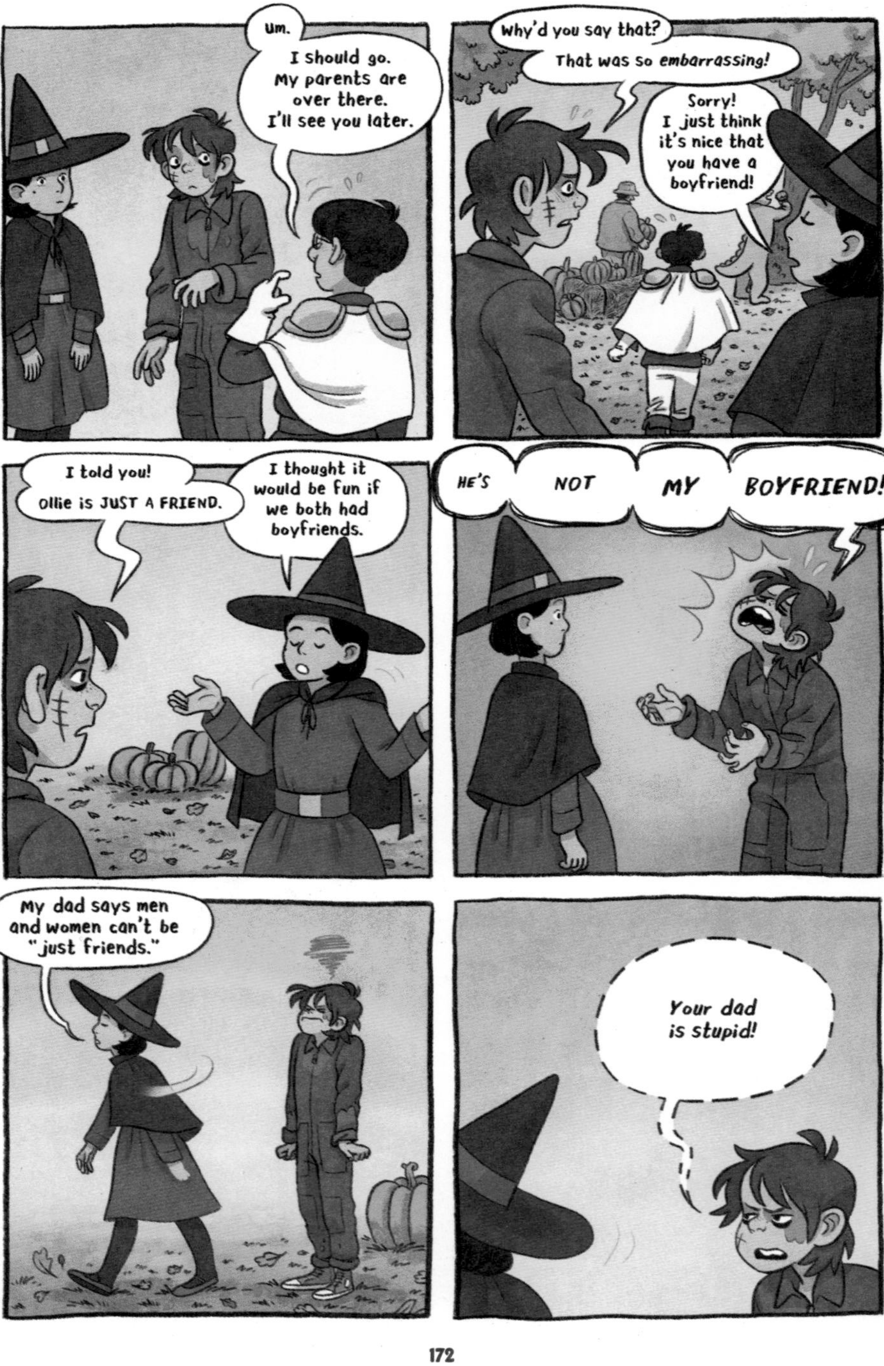
Um.
I should go. My parents are over there. I'll see you later.
Why'd you say that?
That was so embarrassing!
Sorry! I just think it's nice that you have a boyfriend!
I told you!
Ollie is JUST A FRIEND.
I thought it would be fun if we both had boyfriends.
HE'S NOT MY BOYFRIEND!
My dad says men and women can't be "just friends."
Your dad is stupid!

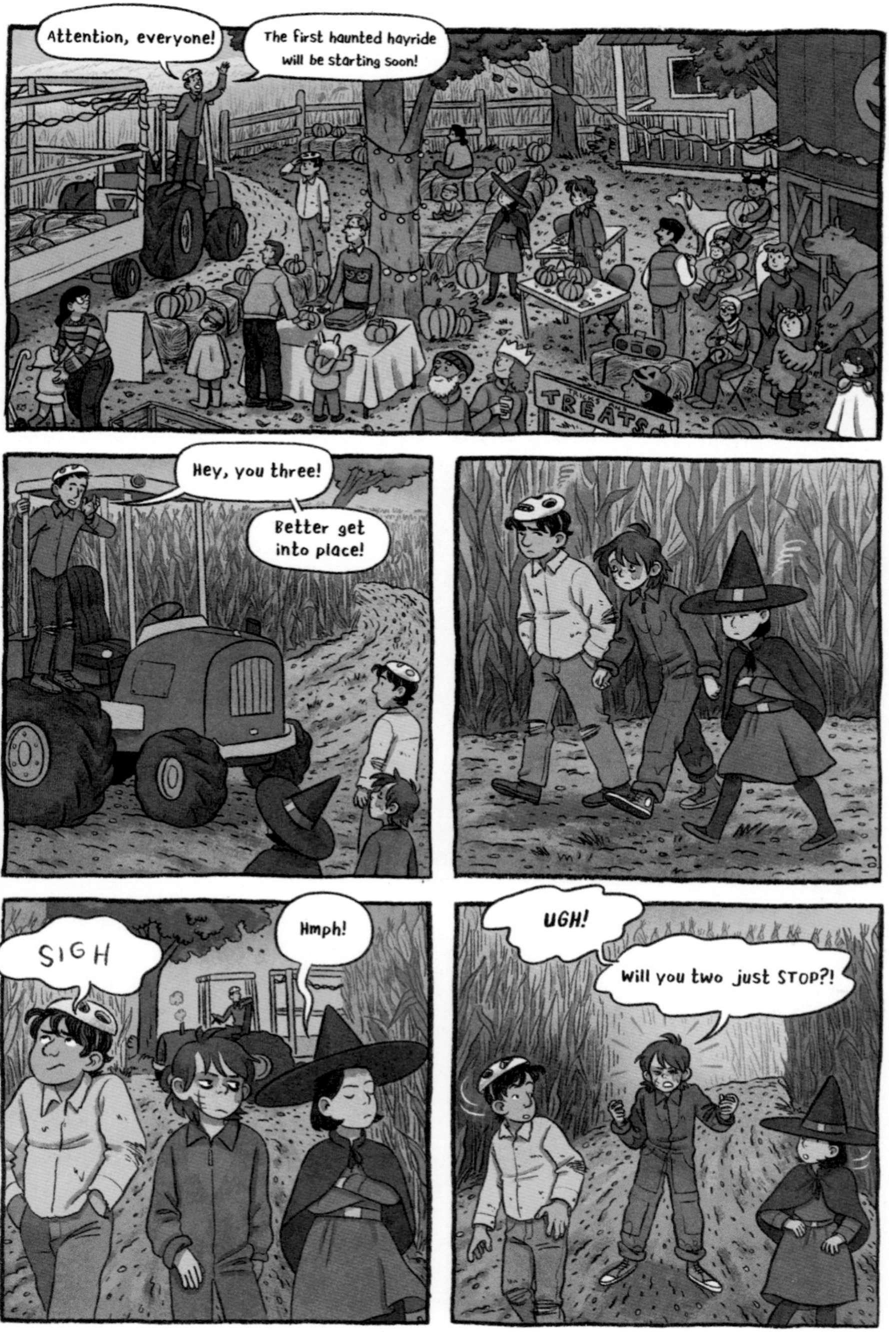
Attention, everyone!
The first haunted hayride will be starting soon!
TREATS
Hey, you three!
Better get into place!
SIGH
Hmph!
UGH!
Will you two just STOP?!

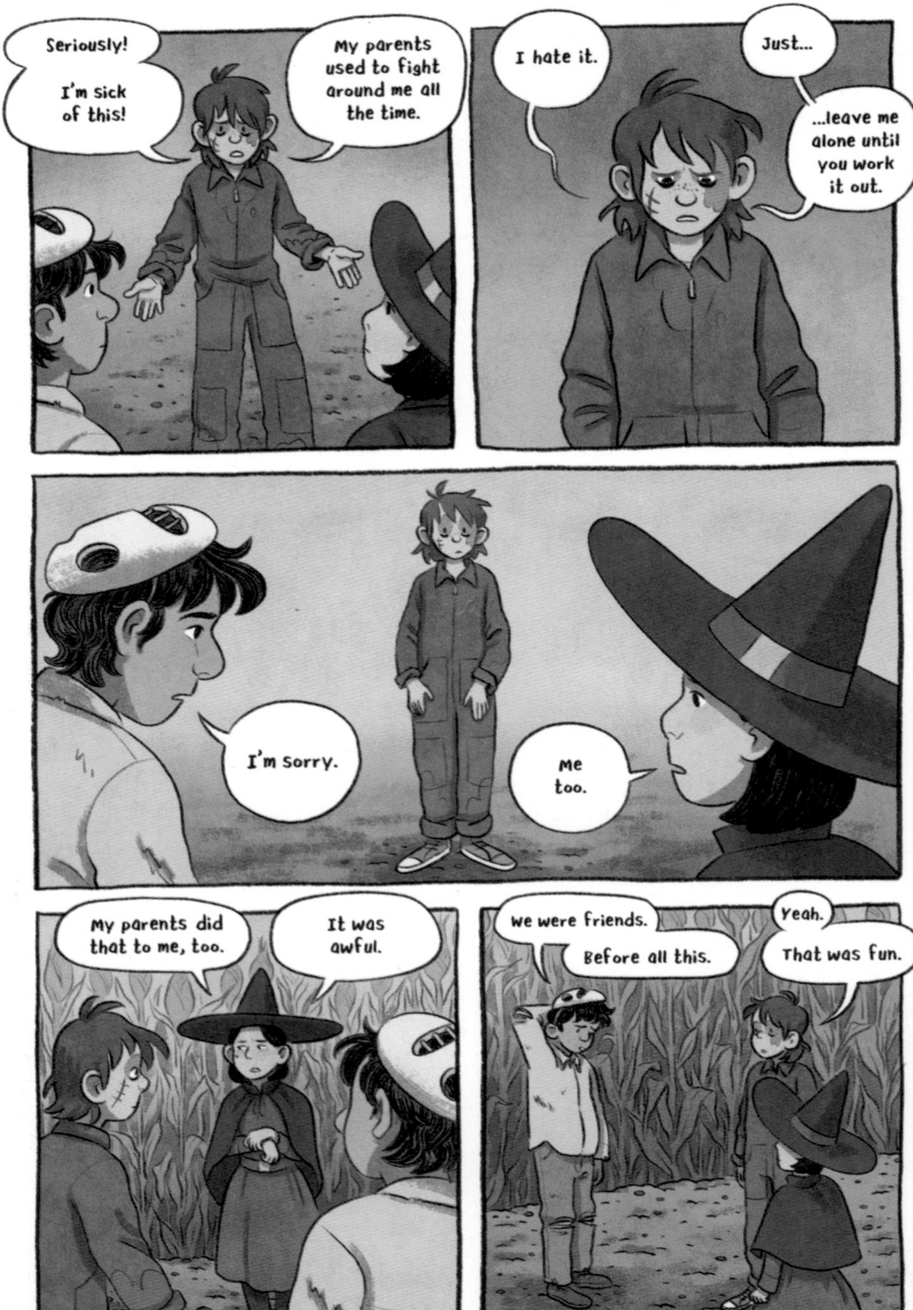
Seriously!
I'm sick of this!
My parents used to fight around me all the time.
I hate it.
Just...
...leave me alone until you work it out.
I'm sorry.
Me too.
My parents did that to me, too.
It was awful.
We were friends.
Before all this.
Yeah.
That was fun.

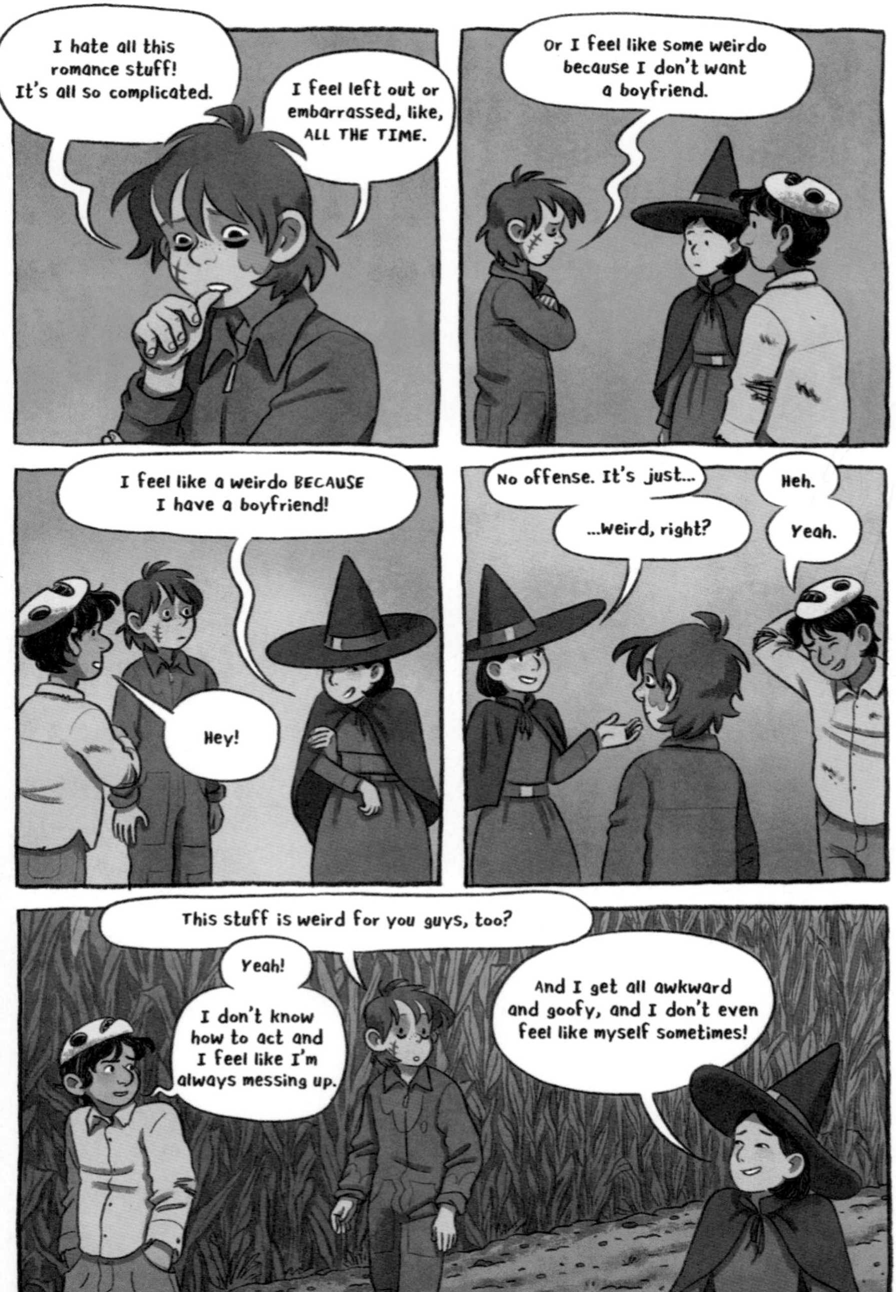
I hate all this romance stuff! It's all so complicated.
I feel left out or embarrassed, like, ALL THE TIME.
Or I feel like some weirdo because I don't want a boyfriend.
I feel like a weirdo BECAUSE I have a boyfriend!
Hey!
No offense. It's just...
...weird, right?
Heh.
Yeah.
This stuff is weird for you guys, too?
Yeah!
I don't know how to act and I feel like I'm always messing up.
And I get all awkward and goofy, and I don't even feel like myself sometimes!

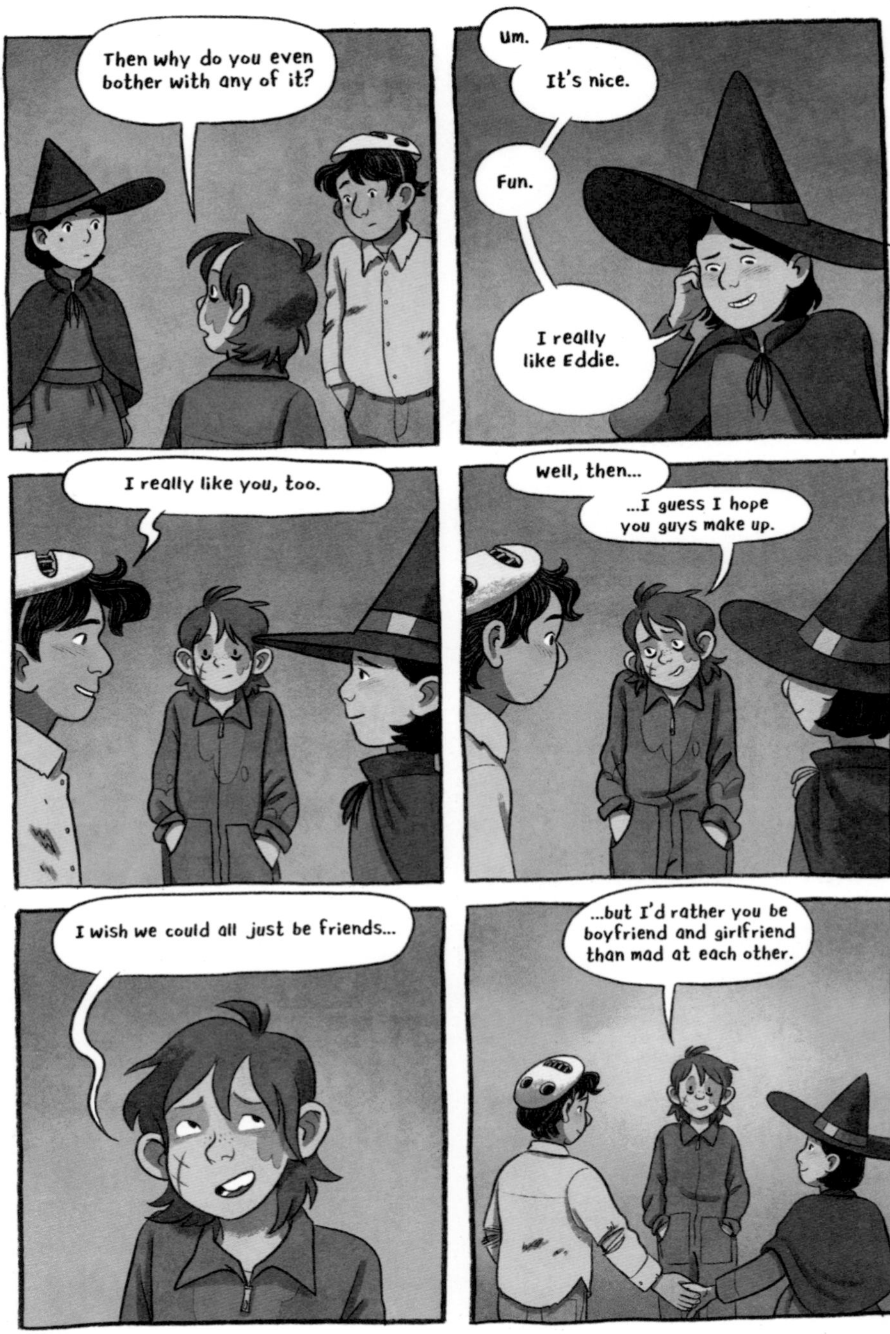
Then why do you even bother with any of it?
Um.
It's nice.
Fun.
I really like Eddie.
I really like you, too.
Well, then...
...I guess I hope you guys make up.
I wish we could all just be friends...
...but I'd rather you be boyfriend and girlfriend than mad at each other.

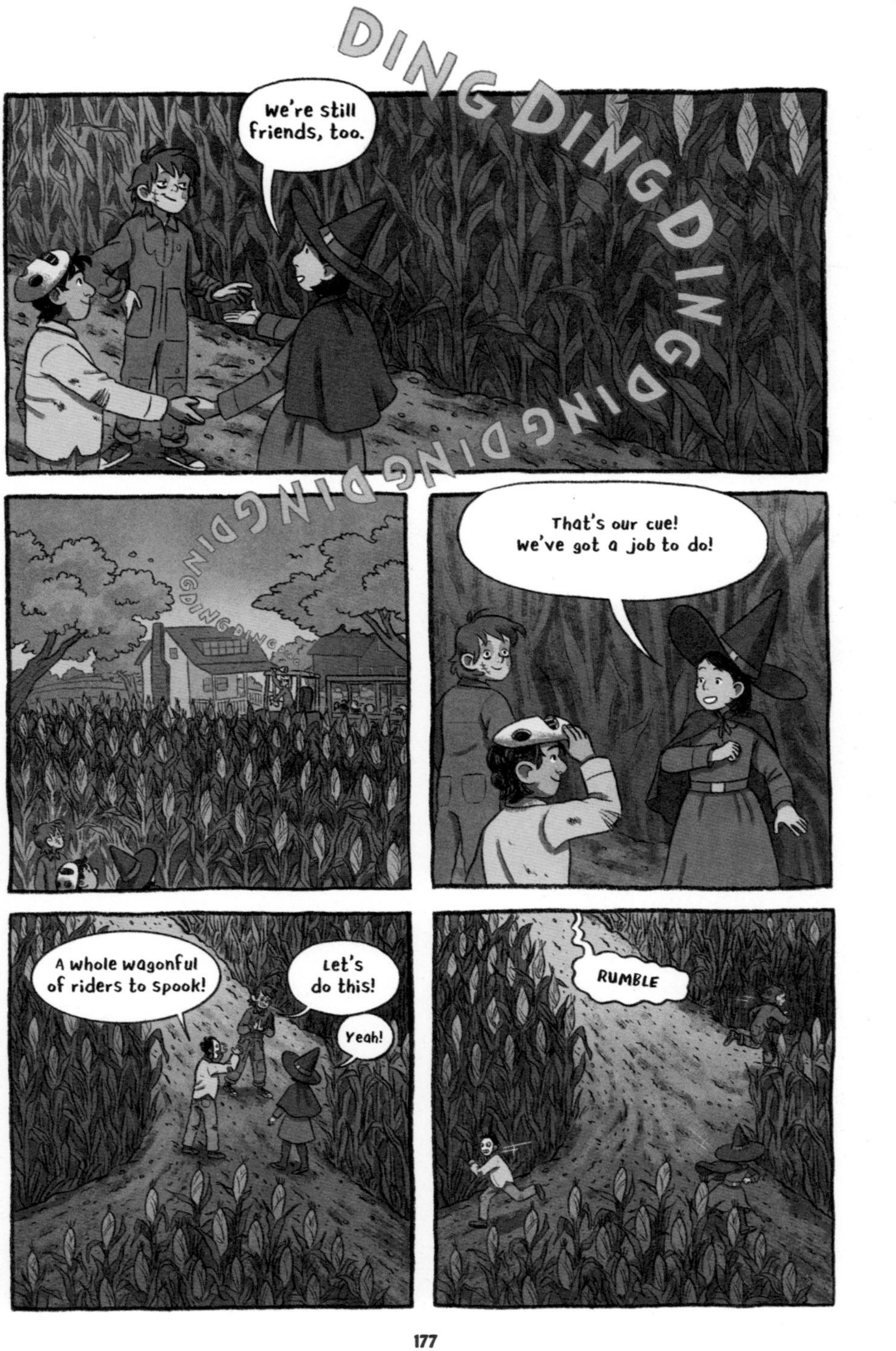
DING DING DING DING DING
We're still friends, too.
DING DING DING
That's our cue! We've got a job to do!
A whole wagonful of riders to spook!
Let's do this!
Yeah!
RUMBLE

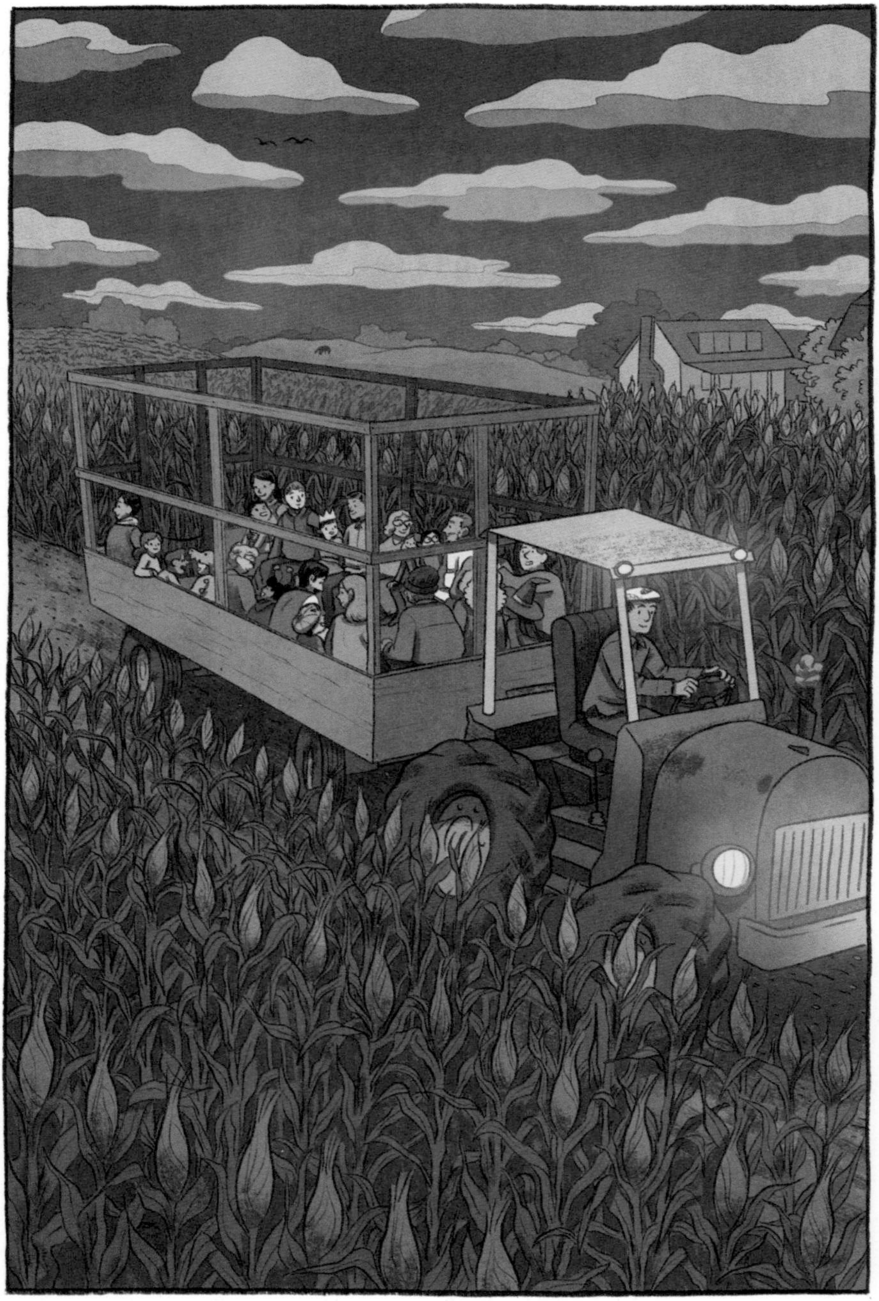

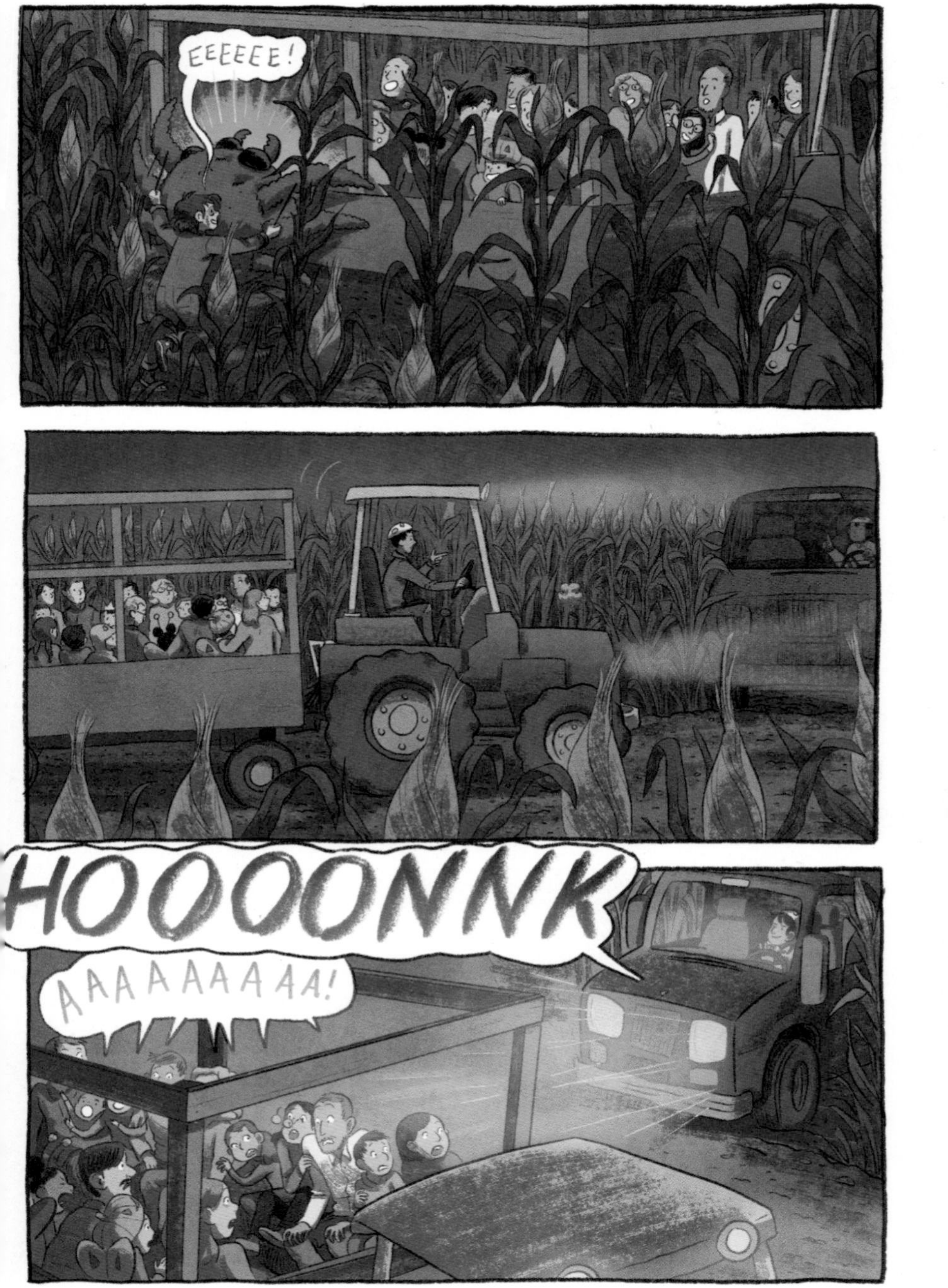
EEEEEE!
HOOOONNK
AAAAAAAA!

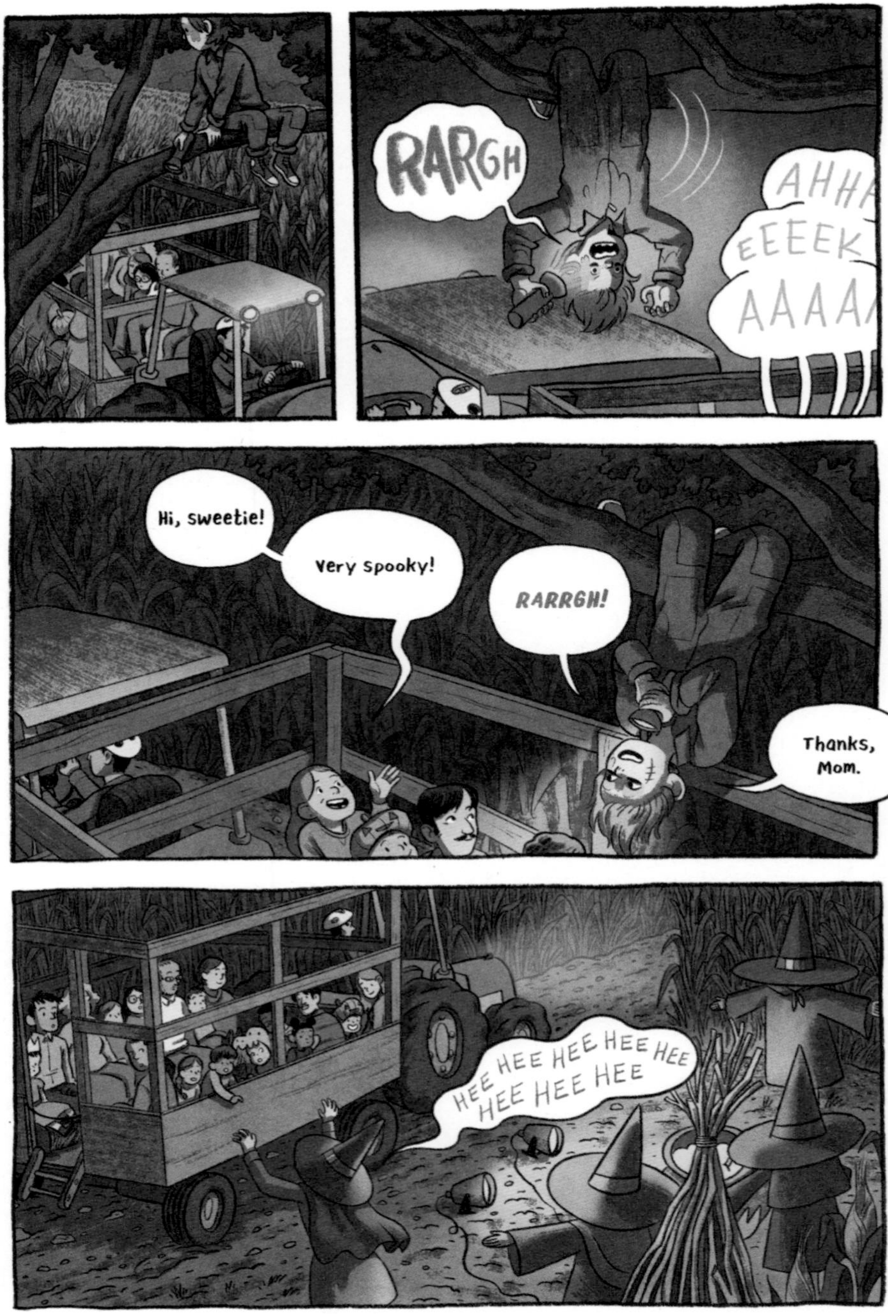
RARGH
AHH
EEEEK
AAAA
Hi, sweetie!
Very spooky!
RARRGH!
Thanks, Mom.
HEE HEE HEE HEE HEE
HEE HEE HEE

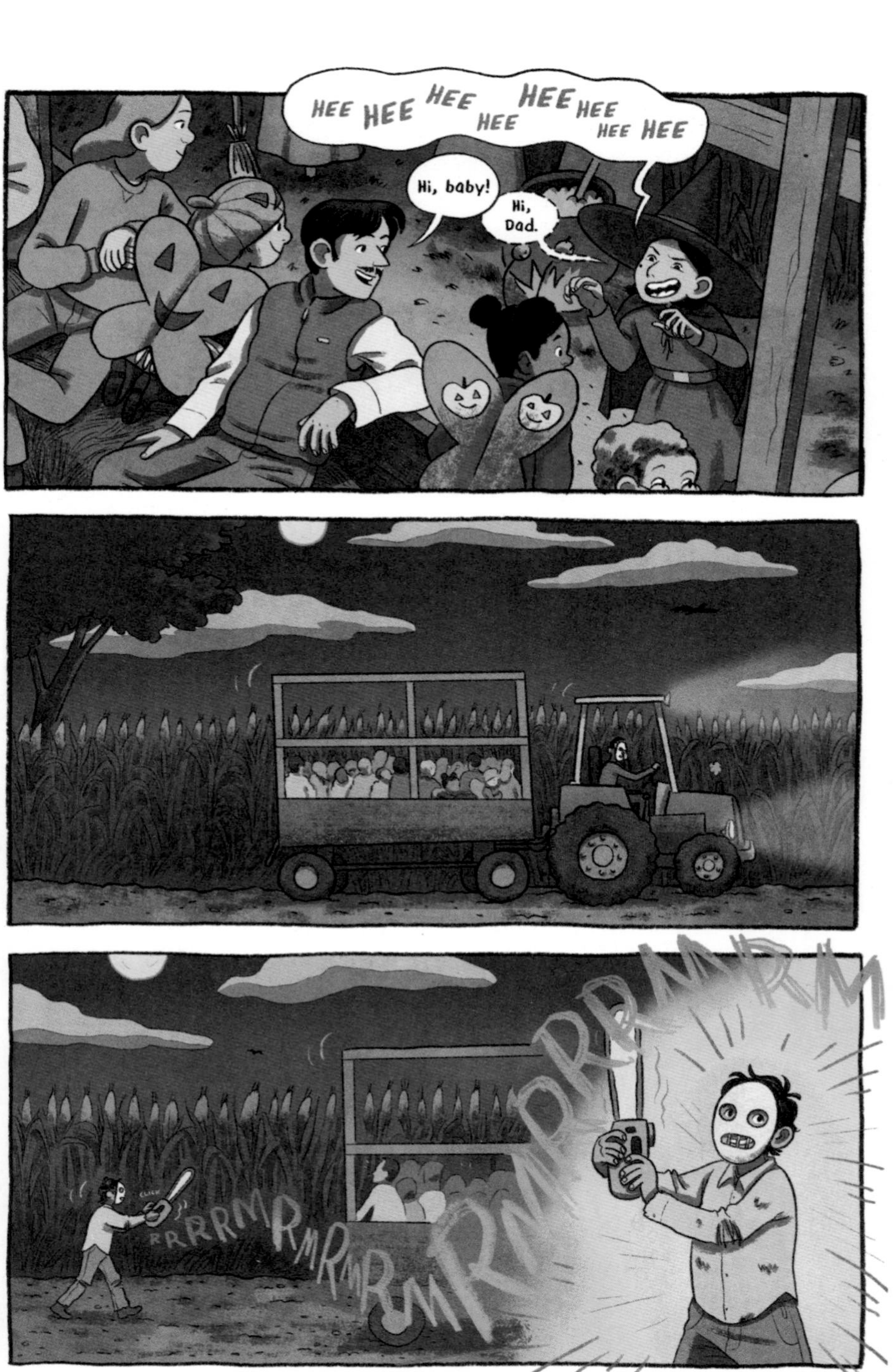
HEE HEE HEE HEE HEE HEE HEE HEE
Hi, baby!
Hi, Dad.
CLICK
RRRRRMRMRMRMRMRRRRRMRM

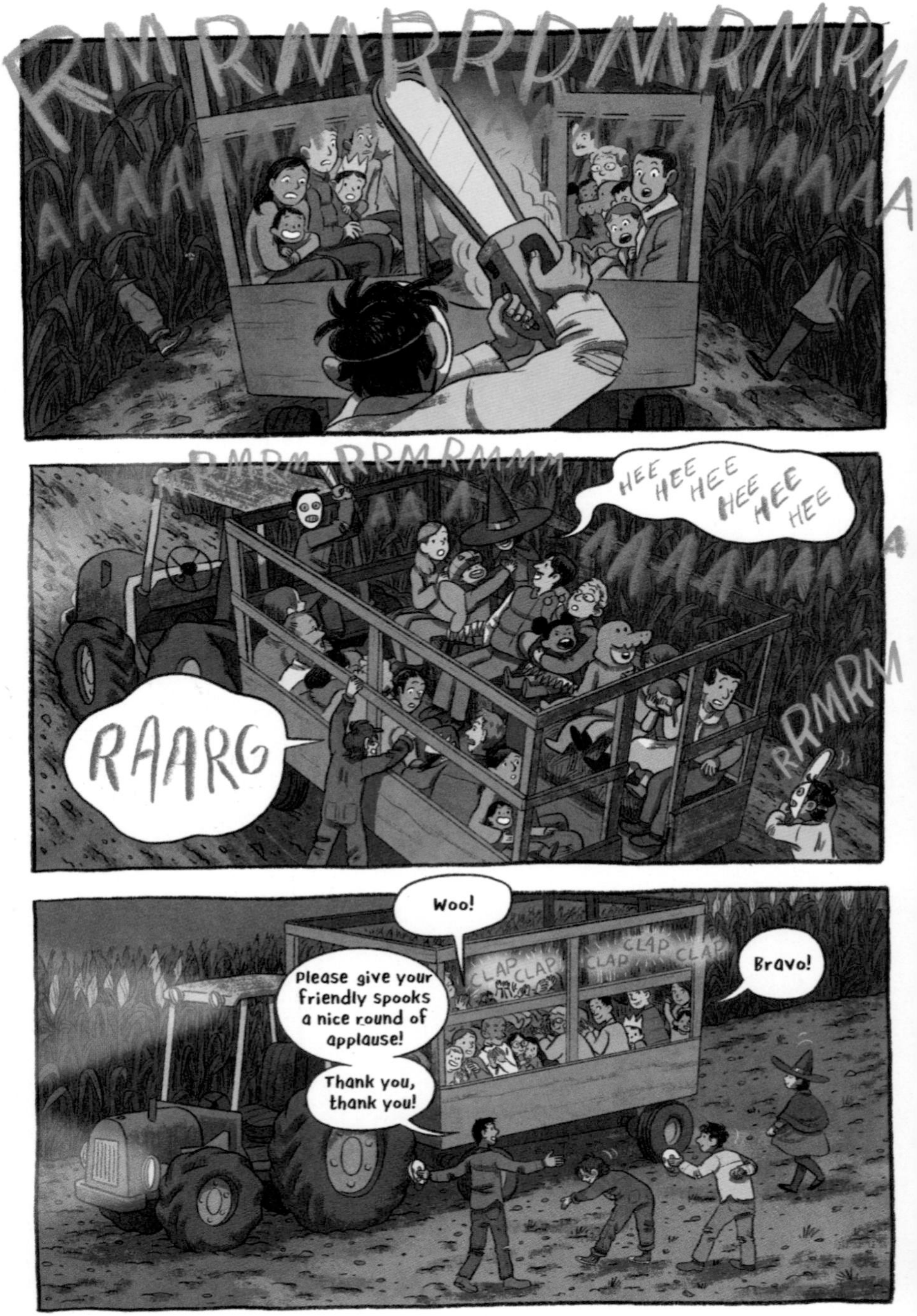
RMRMRRRMRMRM
AAAA
AAAAAA
RMRM RRMRMMM
HEE HEE HEE HEE HEE HEE
RAARG
RMRM
Woo!
Please give your friendly spooks a nice round of applause!
Thank you, thank you!
CLAP CLAP CLAP CLAP CLAP
Bravo!

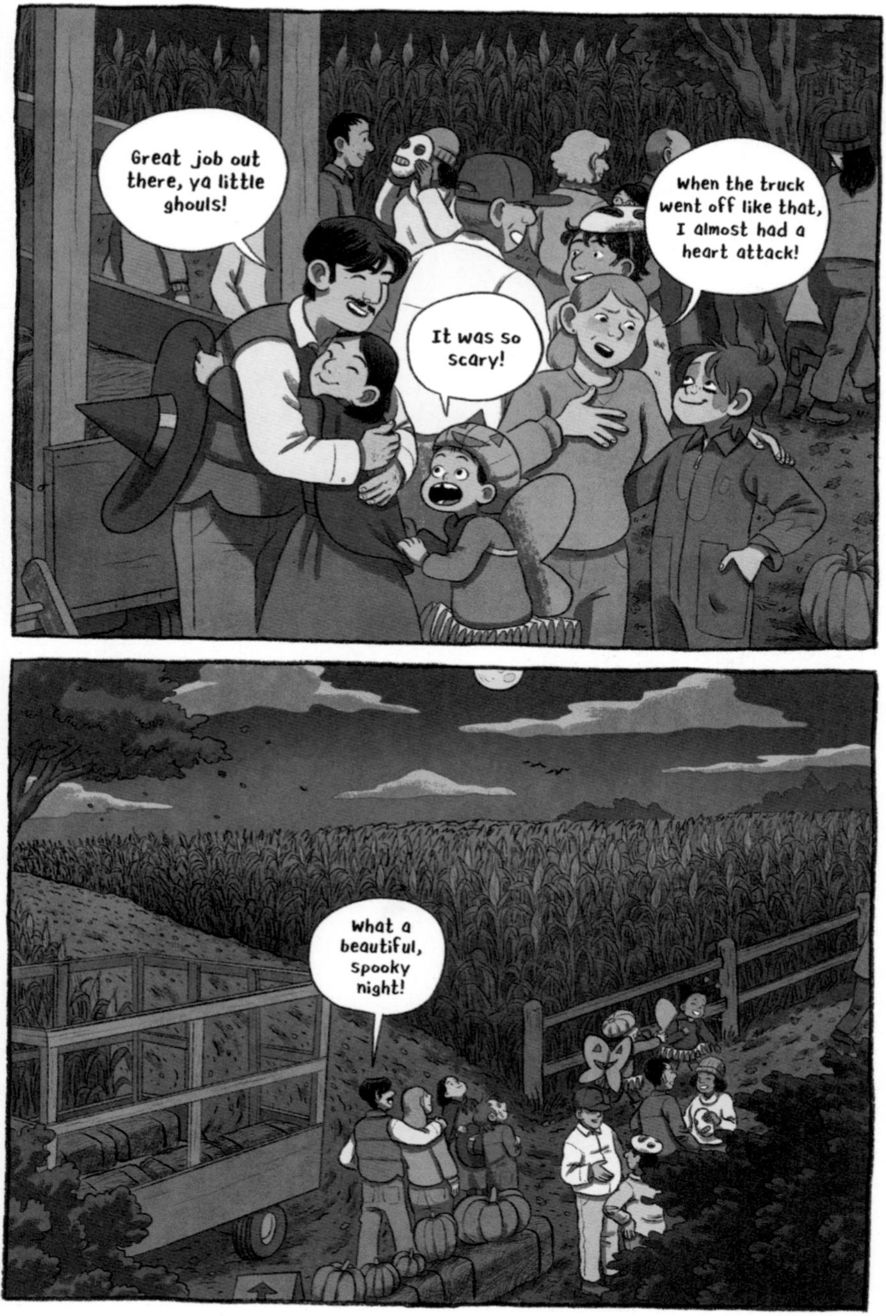
Great job out there, ya little ghouls!
It was so scary!
When the truck went off like that, I almost had a heart attack!
What a beautiful, spooky night!

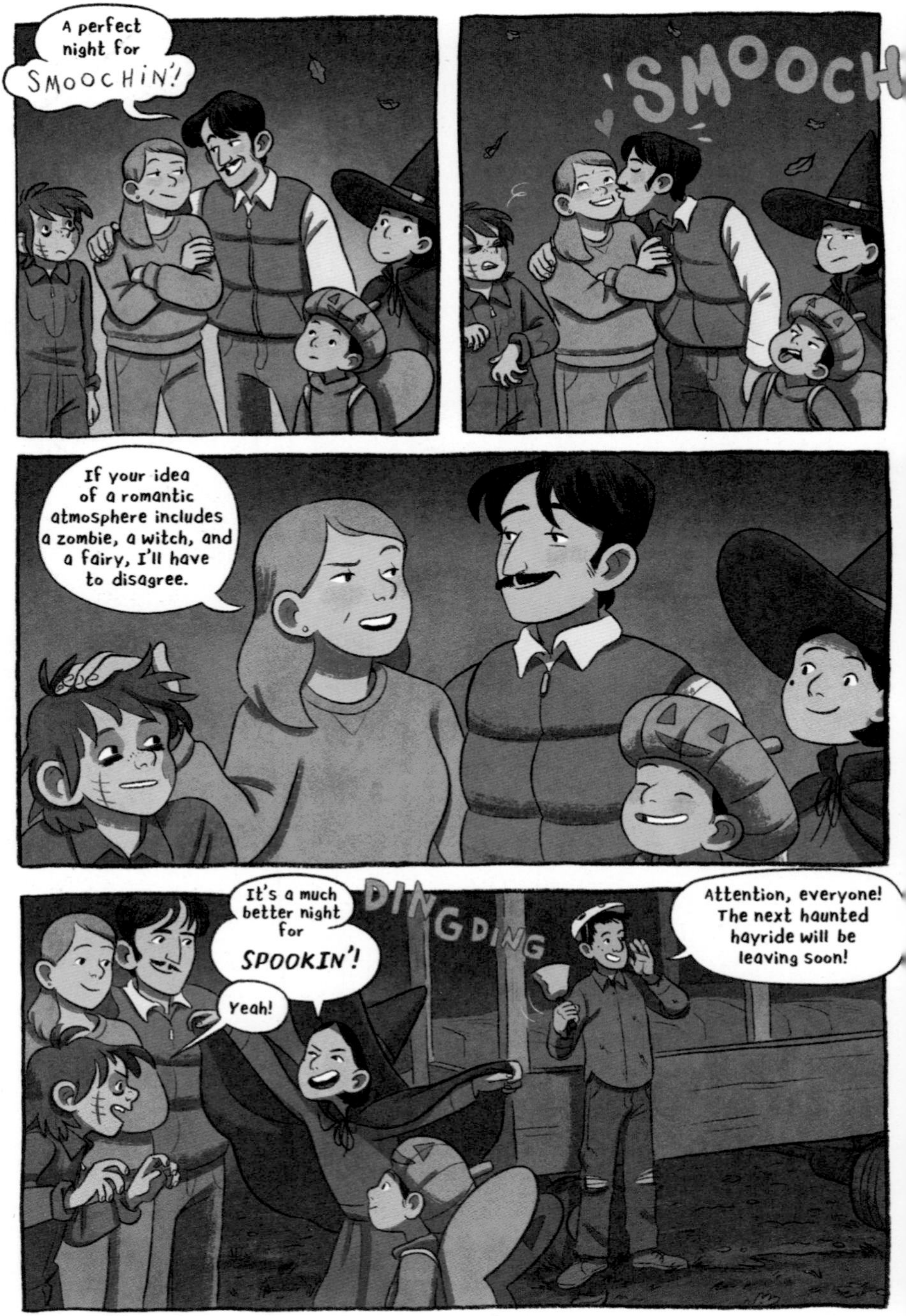
A perfect night for SMOOCHIN'!
SMOOCH
If your idea of a romantic atmosphere includes a zombie, a witch, and a fairy, I'll have to disagree.
It's a much better night for SPOOKIN'!
Yeah!
DING DING
Attention, everyone! The next haunted hayride will be leaving soon!

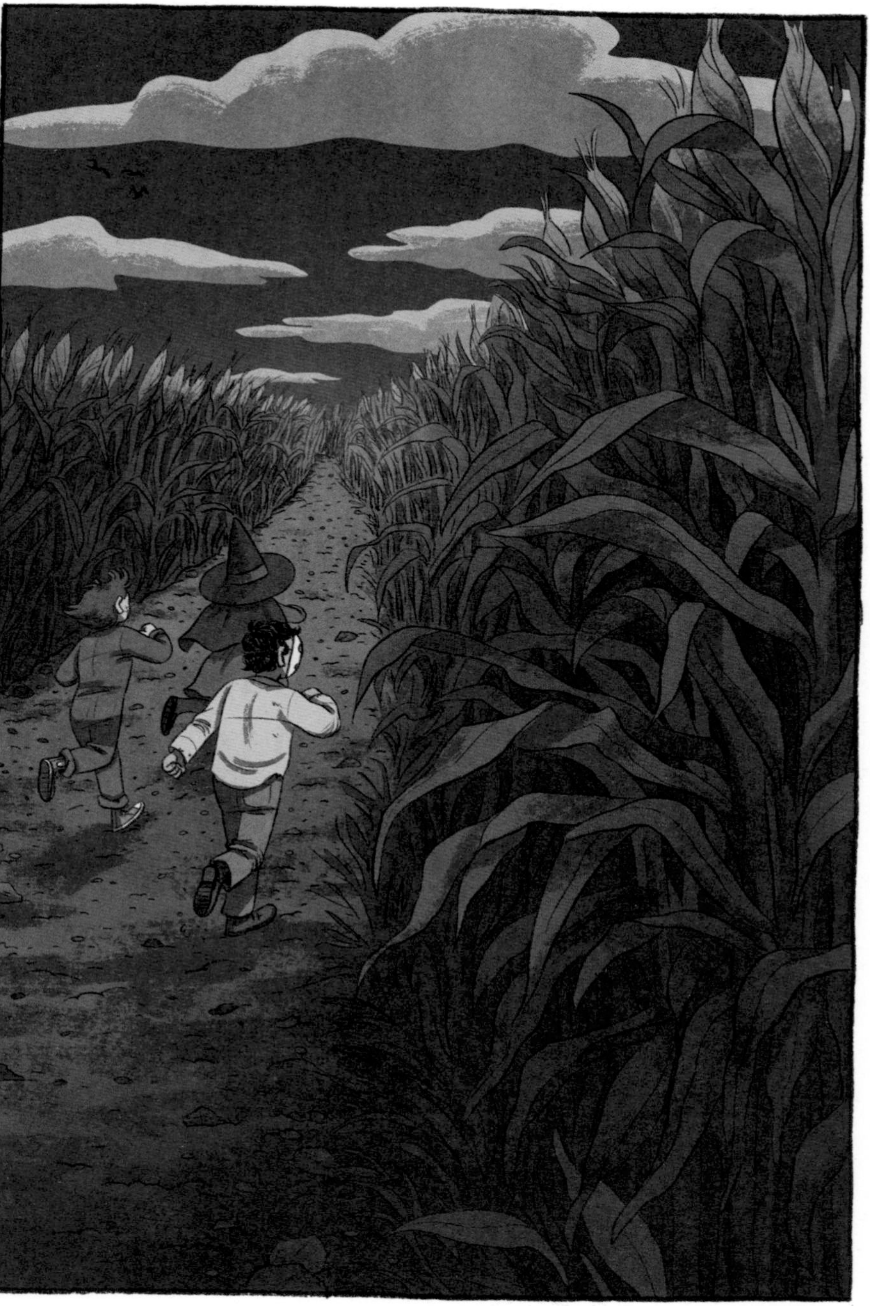

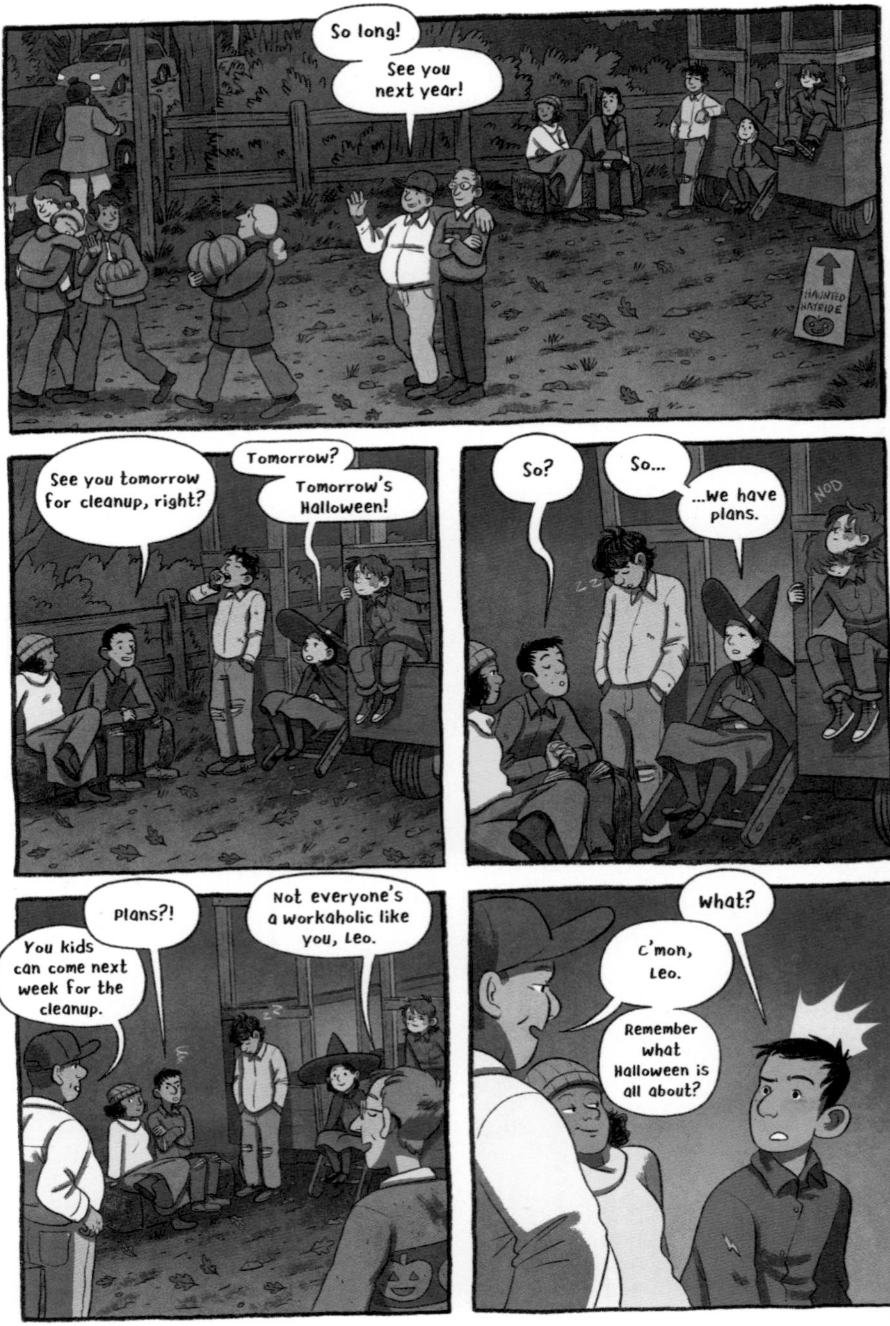
So long!
See you next year!
HAUNTED HAYRIDE
See you tomorrow for cleanup, right?
Tomorrow?
Tomorrow's Halloween!
So?
So...
...We have plans.
NOD
Plans?!
You kids can come next week for the cleanup.
Not everyone's a workaholic like you, Leo.
What?
C'mon, Leo.
Remember what Halloween is all about?

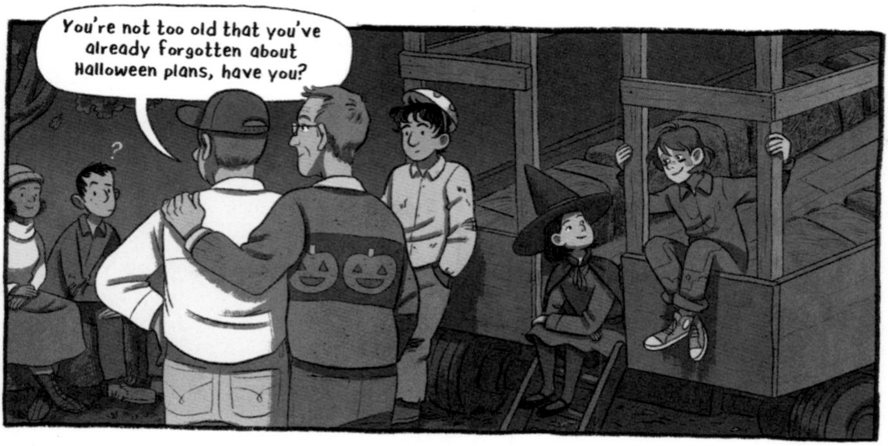
You're not too old that you've already forgotten about Halloween plans, have you?
?

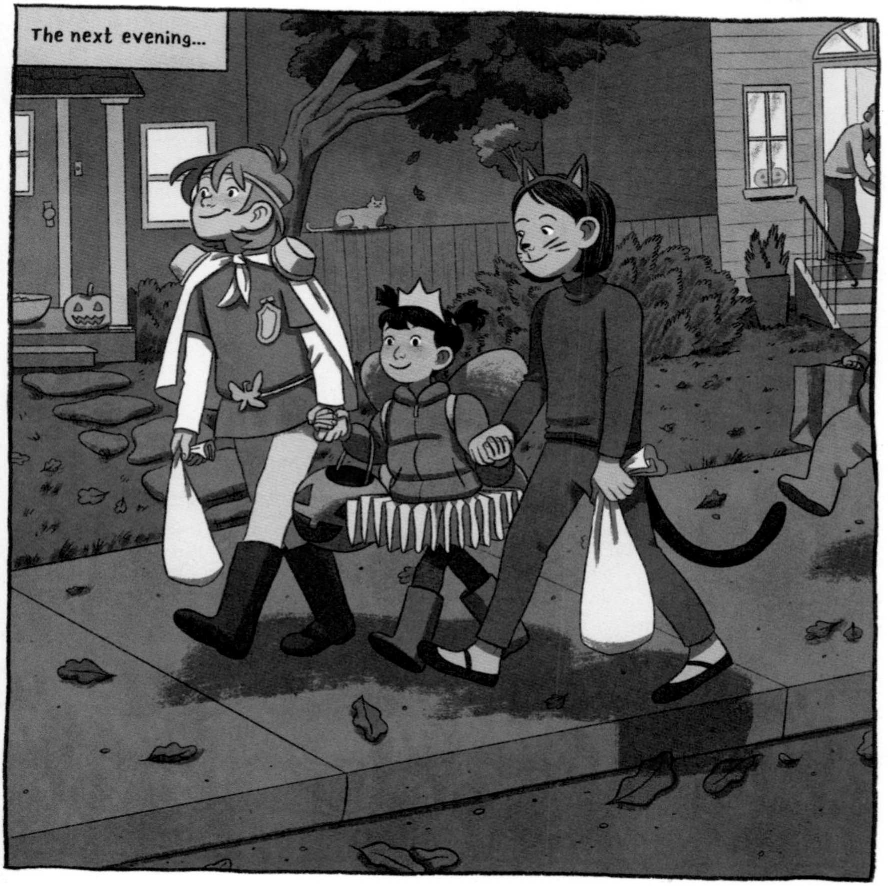
The next evening...

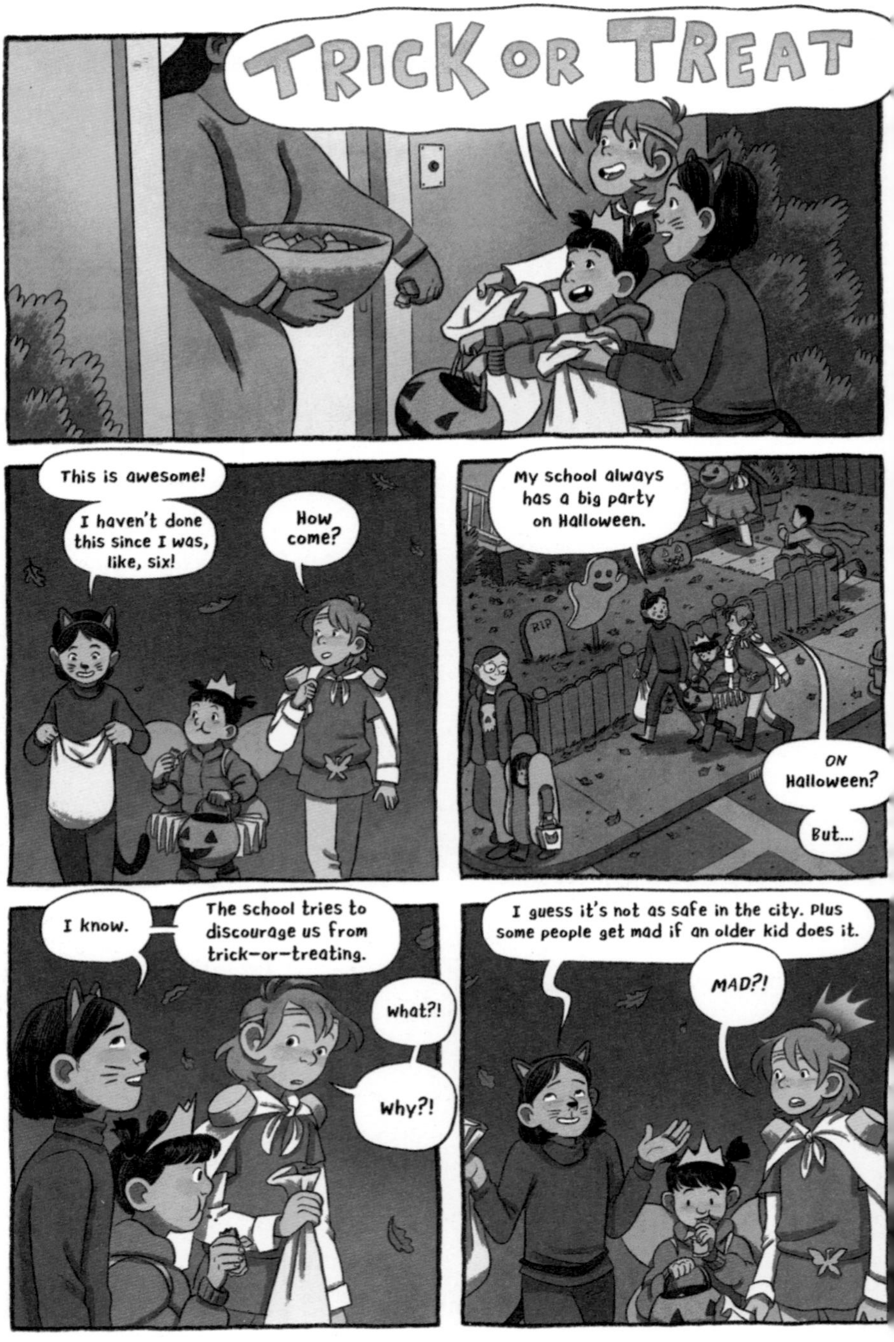
TRICK OR TREAT
This is awesome!
I haven't done this since I was, like, six!
How come?
My school always has a big party on Halloween.
RIP
ON Halloween?
But...
I know.
The school tries to discourage us from trick-or-treating.
What?!
Why?!
I guess it's not as safe in the city. Plus some people get mad if an older kid does it.
MAD?!

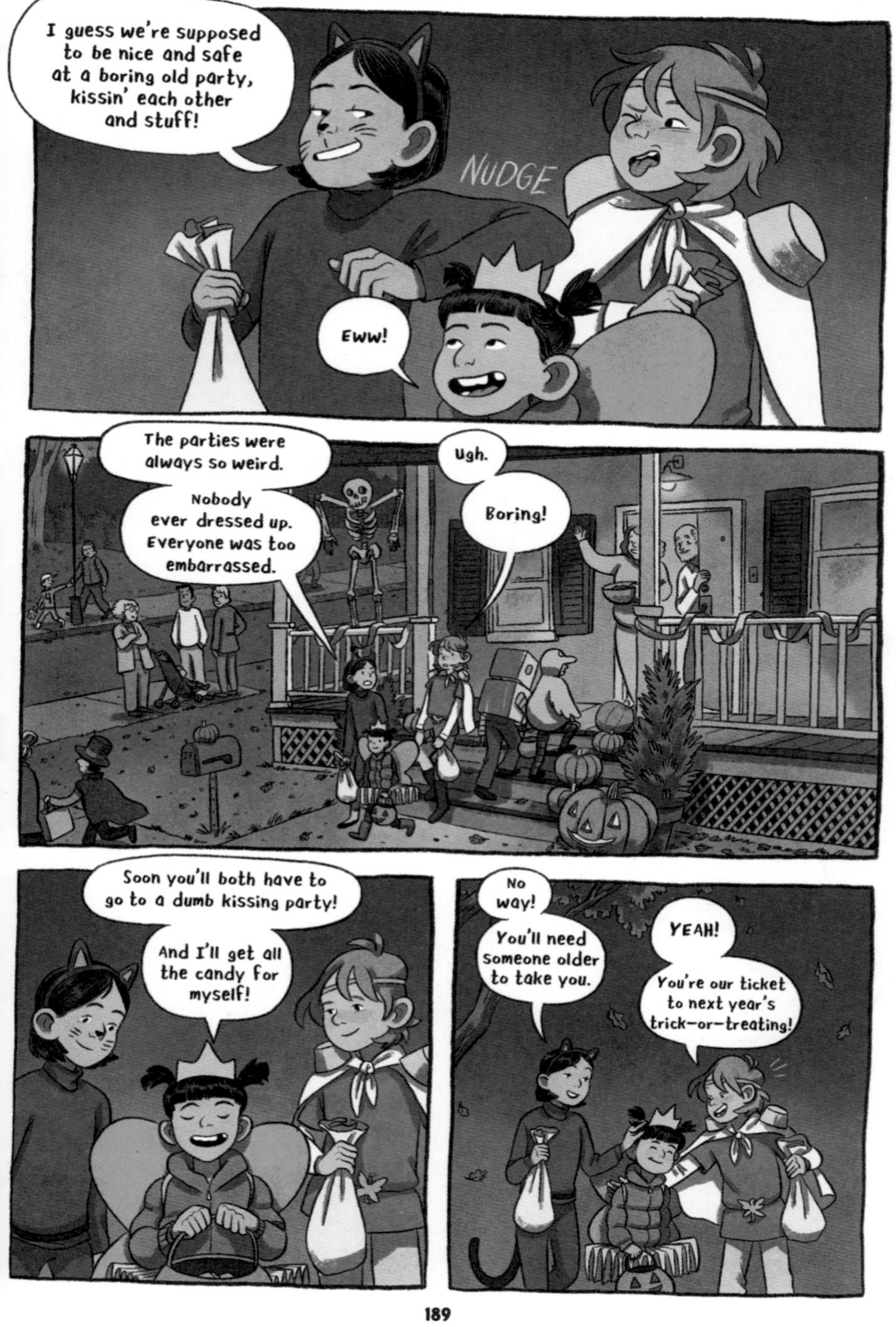
I guess we're supposed to be nice and safe at a boring old party, kissin' each other and stuff!
NUDGE
EWW!
The parties were always so weird.
Nobody ever dressed up. Everyone was too embarrassed.
Ugh.
Boring!
Soon you'll both have to go to a dumb kissing party!
And I'll get all the candy for myself!
No way!
You'll need someone older to take you.
YEAH!
You're our ticket to next year's trick-or-treating!

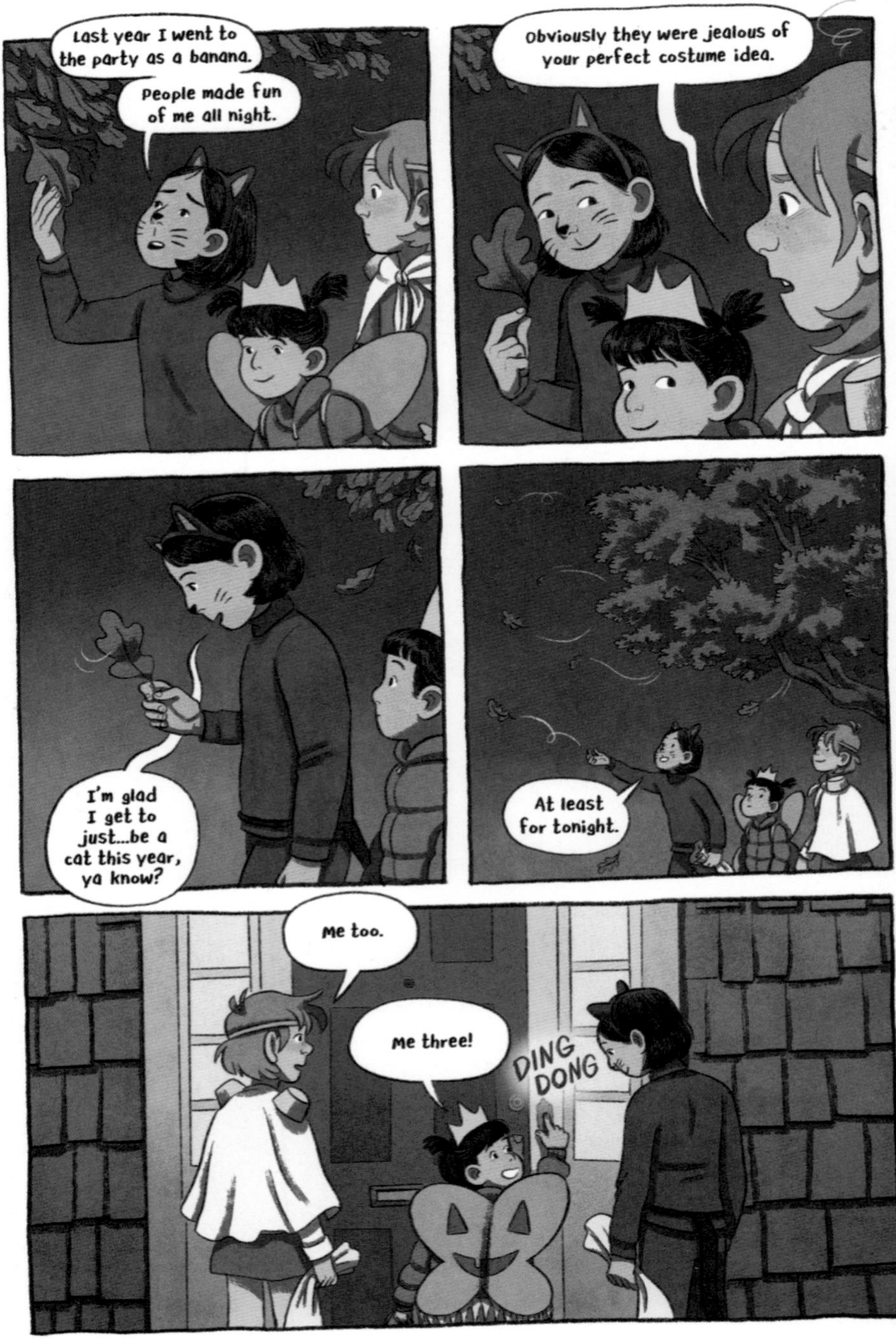
Last year I went to the party as a banana.
People made fun of me all night.
Obviously they were jealous of your perfect costume idea.
I'm glad I get to just...be a cat this year, ya know?
At least for tonight.
Me too.
Me three!
DING DONG

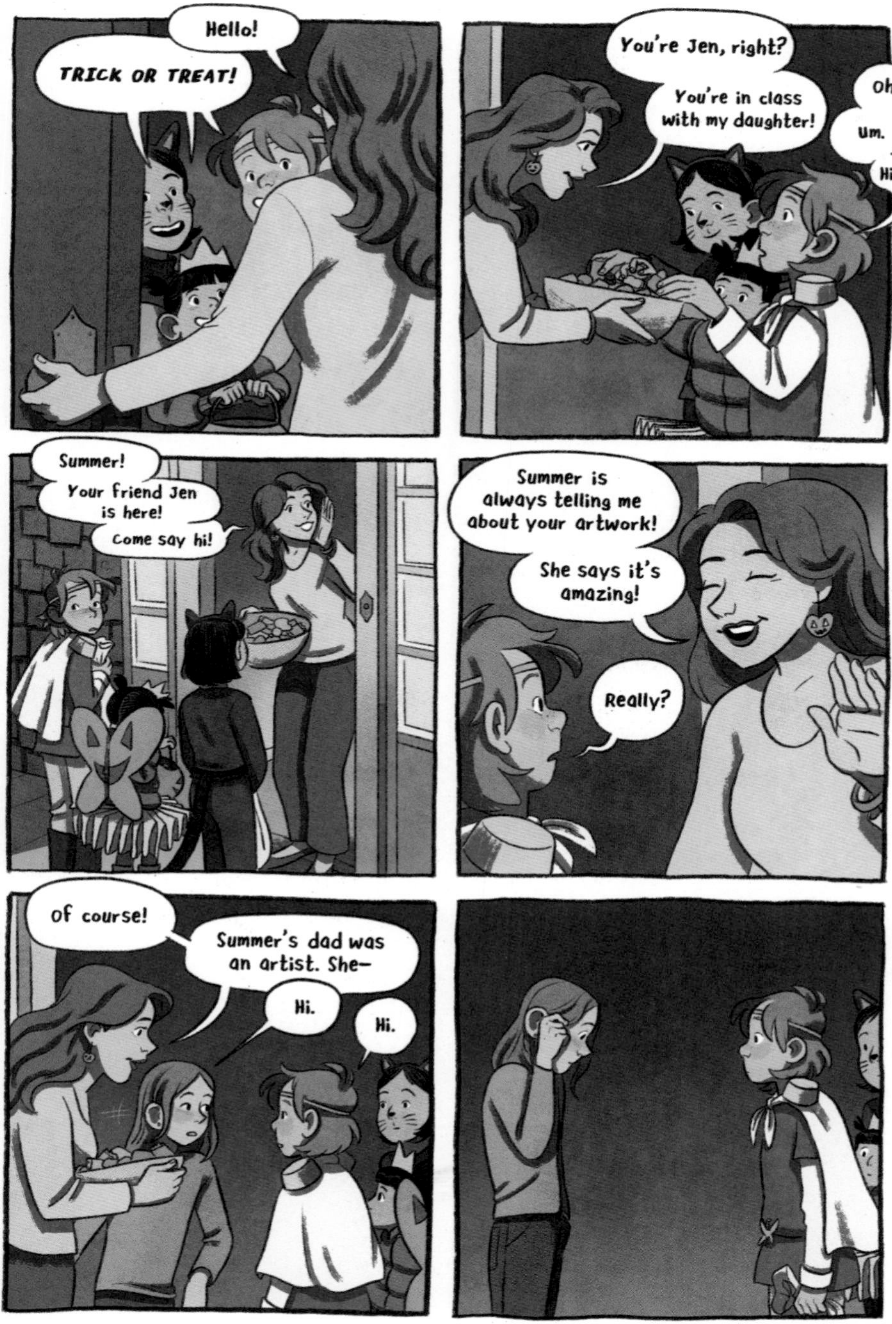
Hello!
TRICK OR TREAT!
You're Jen, right?
You're in class with my daughter!
Oh.
Um.
Hi.
Summer!
Your friend Jen is here!
Come say hi!
Summer is always telling me about your artwork!
She says it's amazing!
Really?
Of course!
Summer's dad was an artist. She—
Hi.
Hi.

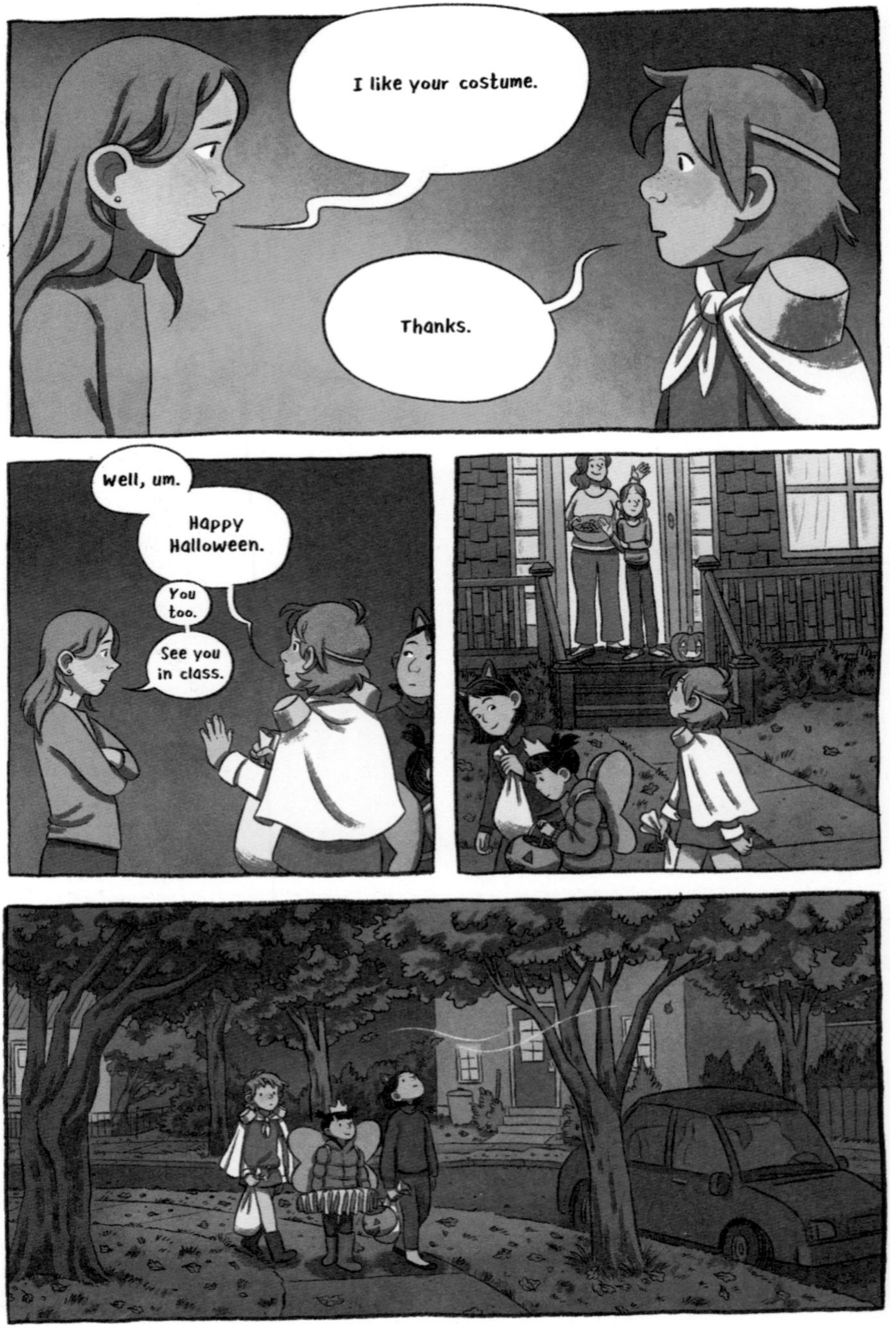
I like your costume.
Thanks.
Well, um.
Happy Halloween.
You too.
See you in class.

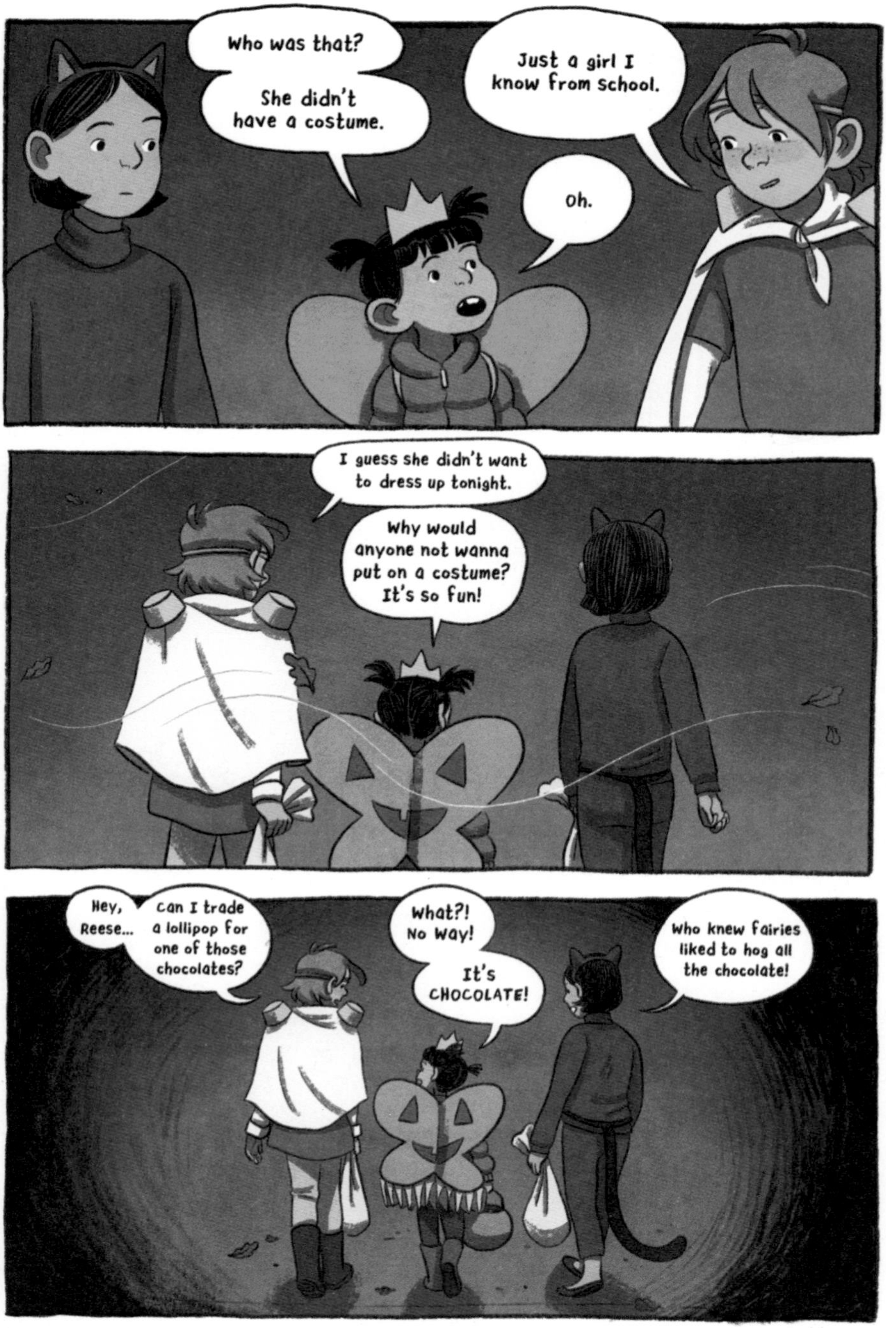
Who was that?
She didn't have a costume.
Just a girl I know from school.
Oh.
I guess she didn't want to dress up tonight.
Why would anyone not wanna put on a costume? It's so fun!
Hey, Reese...
Can I trade a lollipop for one of those chocolates?
What?! No way!
It's CHOCOLATE!
Who knew fairies liked to hog all the chocolate!

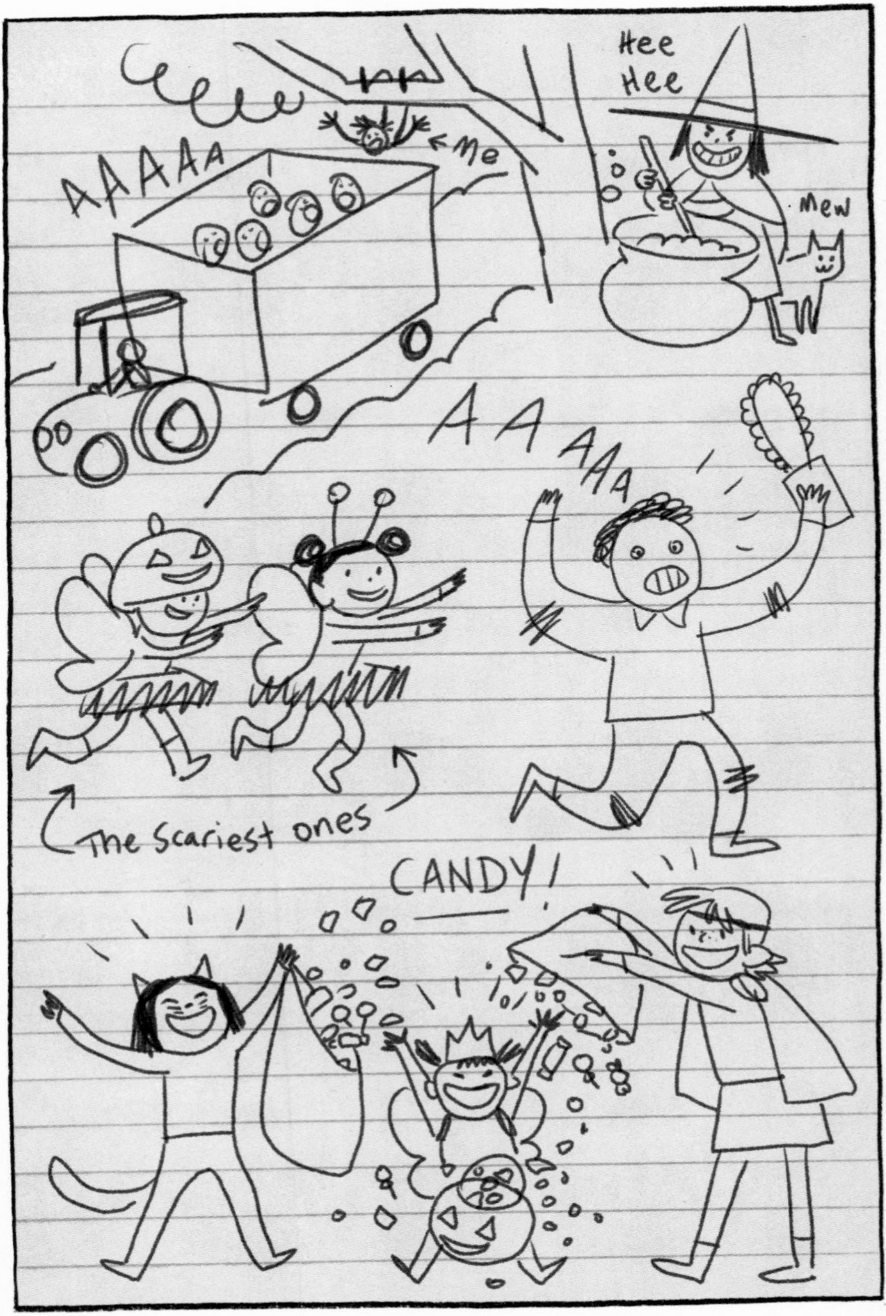

AAAAA
← me
Hee Hee
Mew
AAAAAA
The Scariest ones
CANDY!

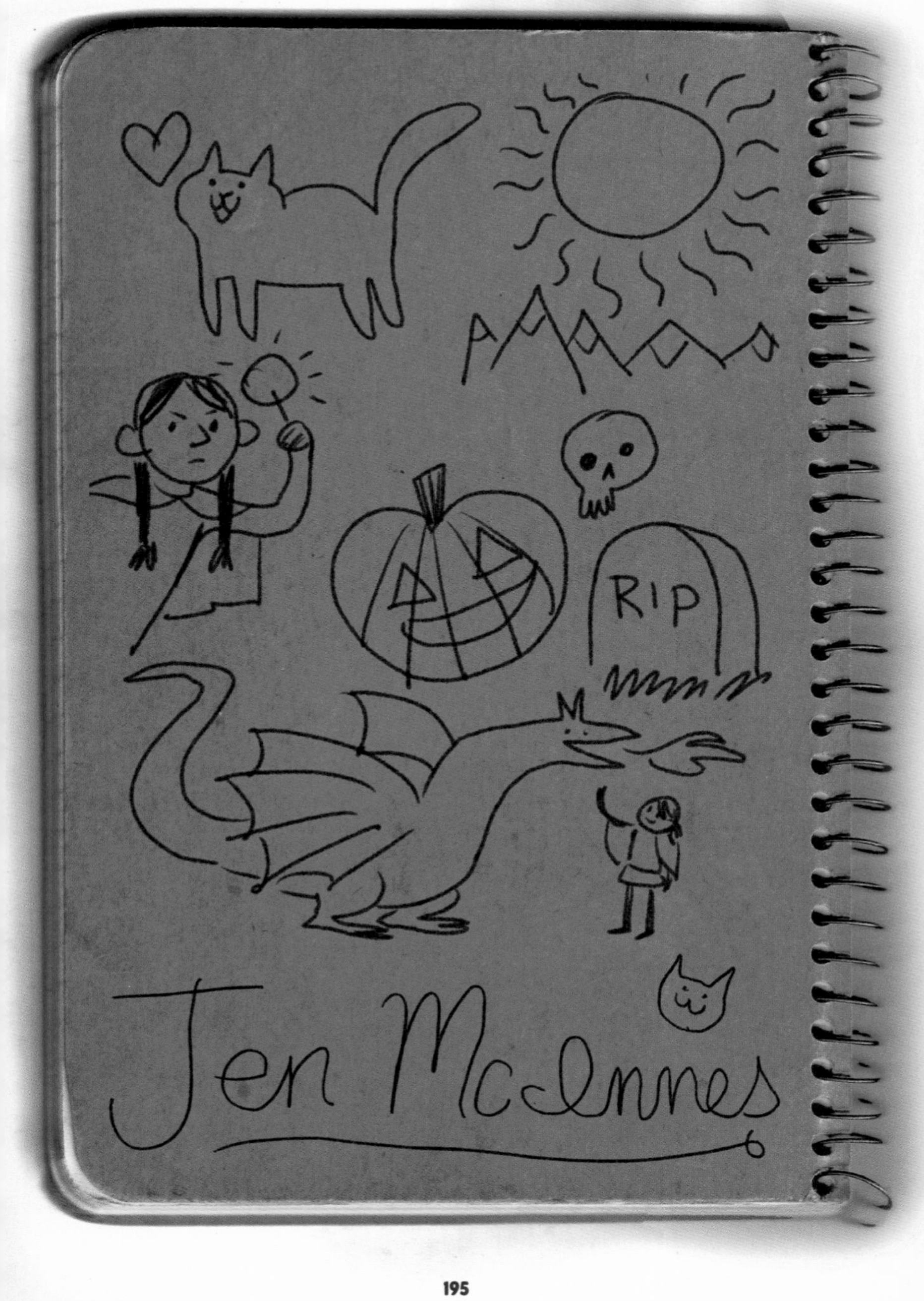
RIP
Jen McInnes

A note from the author/artist:

me

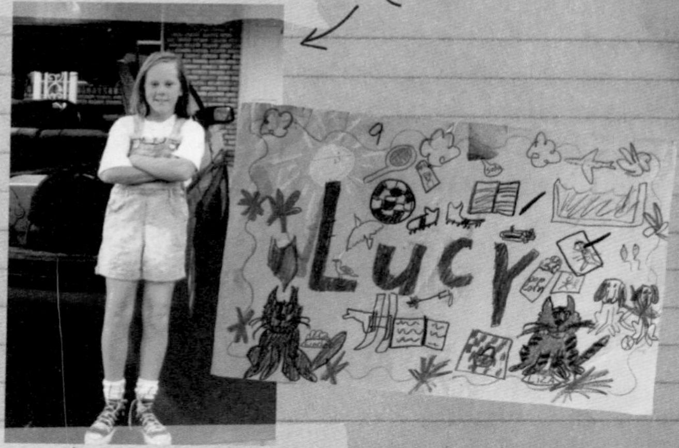
Lucy

overalls
4 EVER

"How much are you like Jen?"

Well, I was a freckled tomboy
with a math-based learning disability
who moved from the city to the country
when my parents divorced.
I liked to draw, loved cats,
and had two stepsisters.
I lived on a farm, liked books with dragons,
and got pretty frustrated when all my friends
suddenly got obsessed with ROMANCE, so...
....a lot like Jen.

"What do you or Jen have against romance?"

Not a thing! But it bugged me when my friendships suddenly became more complicated because of it. It took me a while to figure out, but, like everything, I learned that everyone has their own way of experiencing love and dating and that it shouldn't get in the way of friendships.

"Are haunted hayrides a real thing?"

Yes! If you've never had the pleasure of having your pants scared off on a slow-moving wagon of hay, I recommend it. Check out some farms near you in the fall, and be sure to eat a cider doughnut!

our neighbor's hayride ↘ (not haunted in photo)

"YAY, SCHOOL."
FACE
← Cool Socks

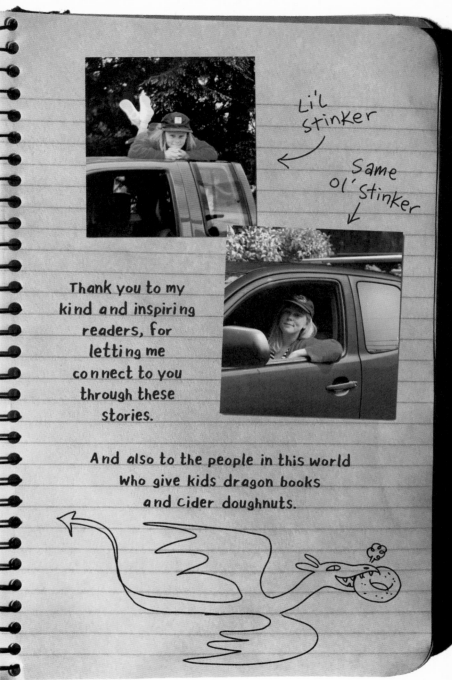

Li'l Stinker

Same Ol' Stinker

Thank you to my kind and inspiring readers, for letting me connect to you through these stories.

And also to the people in this world who give kids dragon books and cider doughnuts.

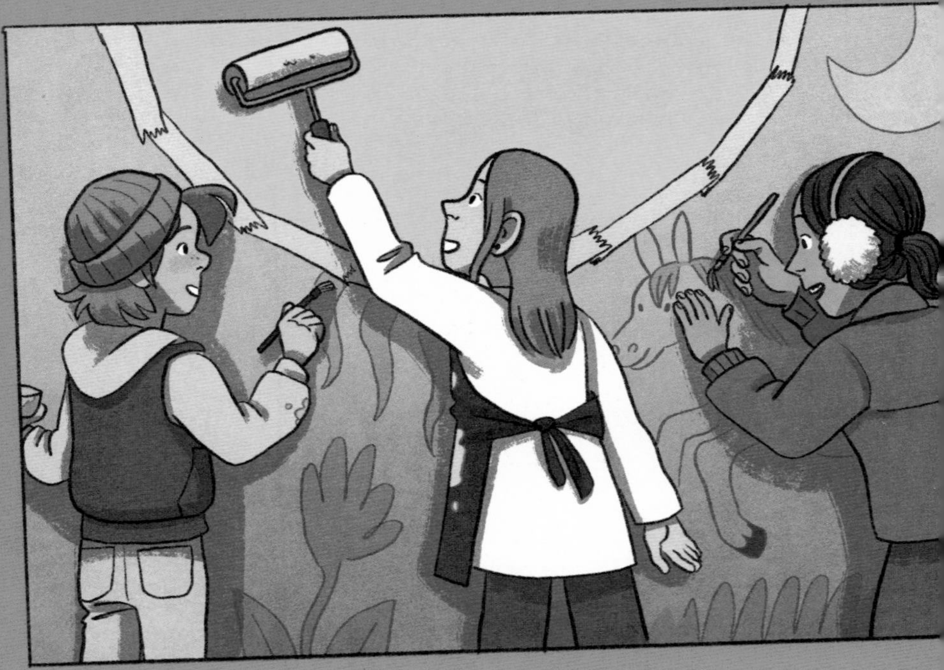

Family isn't the only thing growing on Peapod Farm!

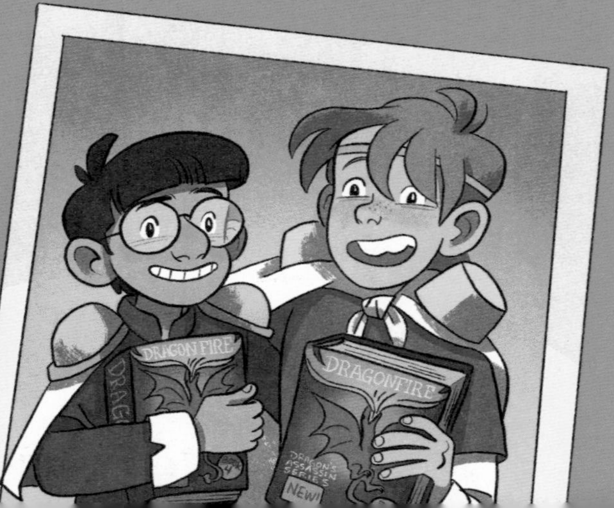
DRAGONFIRE
DRAGONFIRE
DRAGON'S ASSASSIN SERIES
NEW!

Jen's adventures will continue,

with all-new friends and the same old stepsisters!

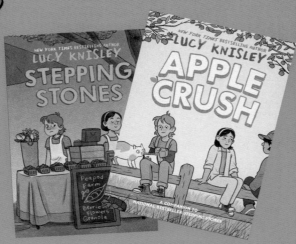

MAY 2022

FIND YOUR VOICE

WITH ONE OF THESE EXCITING GRAPHIC NOVELS

CHAD SELL
CREATOR OF THE CARDBOARD KINGDOM
DOODLEVILLE
"A masterpiece."
THE CARDBOARD KINGDOM
CHAD SELL
JADE ARMSTRONG
SCOUT IS NOT A BAND KID
NEW YORK TIMES BESTSELLING AUTHOR
LUCY KNISLEY
STEPPING STONES
JUST ROLL WITH IT
VERONICA AGARWALL & LEE DURFEY-LAVOIE
Séance Tea Party
Reimena Yee
KATIE THE CATSITTER
Colleen AF Venable
Illustrated by Stephanie Yue

PRESENTED BY RH GRAPHIC

@RHKIDSGRAPHIC

A GRAPHIC NOVEL ON EVERY BOOKSHELF

1447b